Nri
Warriors
of Peace

Chikodi Añunobi

10 9 8 7 6 5 4 3 2 1

Zp Zenith Publishers, LLC
PO Box 50386
Bellevue, WA 98015 USA
ZenithPublishers.com

Añunobi, Chikodi.

Nri warriors of peace / Chikodi Añunobi. -- 1st ed. -- Bellevue, WA : Zenith Publishers, 2006.

p. ; cm.

ISBN-13: 978-0-9767303-0-9
ISBN-10: 0-9767303-0-8

1. Igbo (African people)--Fiction. 2. Igbo (African people)--Social life and customs--Fiction. 3. Peaceful societies--Nigeria--Fiction. 4. Nigeria--Civilization--Fiction. 5. Nigeria--History--Fiction. 6. Historical fiction. I. Title.

PS3601.N866 N75 2006
813.6--dc22   0601

Book production managed by Jennifer McCord Associates LLC
Edited by Gloria Campbell
Cover/Back Artwork by Paul Blumenthal
Art Assistant Sarah DeMoney
Cover/Back Layout by Tami Taylor
Book Interior Design by Tami Taylor
Maps by Guirong Zhou

DEDICATION

I dedicate this book to all Nri warriors: all Eze Nri (Eze Umu-Nri), Ozo and Nze priests who lived and served according to the standard expected of their positions, and to their wives who supported them.

I also dedicate this book to the memories of my late father, Nze Samuel Ozoemene Añunobi, and my late mother, Mrs. Augustina Egonekwu Añunobi.

LIST OF CHARACTERS

Okoye:

Son of a peasant who became a King of Nri-Eze Nri.

Erike:

An Igbo immigrant who was banished from his village. He became a priest and Okoye's best friend at Nri.

Ezu:

The second most powerful man in Nri. He was also the leader of Oganiru, a subsect of the Ozo priesthood.

Igwe Nwadike:

The King of Nri-Eze Nri.

Ichie Idika:

A maverick and childhood friend of the King.

Oduh:

The head of the entire Ozo priestly sect. The highest administrative post in Nri. The supreme judge.

Ugocha Nwoye:

An inseparable friend of Ezu.

Chief Priest:

The palace chief priest (Adama Priest) and the spiritual counselor of the King.

Ijego:

An Igbo woman who was ostracized in her own village and migrated to Nri and became very rich and powerful.

Mgbafor:

Okoye's first wife.

Enenebe:

Okoye's junior wife and his soulmate.

Ozo Ikezuo:

Okoye's uncle and an Ozo priest.

Ozo Okolo:

Erike's adopted father and an Ozo priest.

Akalaka:

The head of Ozo Mkputu, a subsect within the Ozo priesthood.

Ike, the dwarf:

One of Akalaka's pupils and associates.

Umu-Uwa (Uwa Men):

Highway robbers. They were Igbo men but were called "Non-Igbo people." The term Uwa men means non-Igbo men.

Osondu: An Igbo merchant, a victim of Uwa men.

Ikenna: Okoye's personal assistant for life.

Nwama: A drifter who was cured of his long-term sore.

Isiaku: One of the two outcasts that Okoye adopted just before he became King.

Akalogheli: A trickster who encourages conflict and violence.

Eri: The father of Nri, the founder of Nri clan.

Nri or Uyanna: The founder of Nri clan.

Obuekie: Leader of the Adama Council (spiritual leaders and high priests)

Eze Nwanya: The King's first wife.

Okoyeocha: The first name of Igwe Nwadike.

Okoye rope: Okoye's nickname that he does not like.

Nri Menri: The council of ascended Nri Kings.

Oganiru: The Progressives. They were the most powerful subsect in the Ozo priesthood.

Igbo People: All people who spoke the Igbo language including the Nri clan.

Uwa People: All non-Igbo people.

NIGERIA

IGBOLAND IN NIGERIA

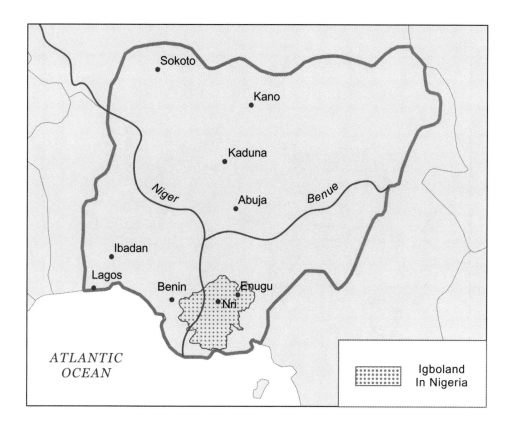

IGBOLAND

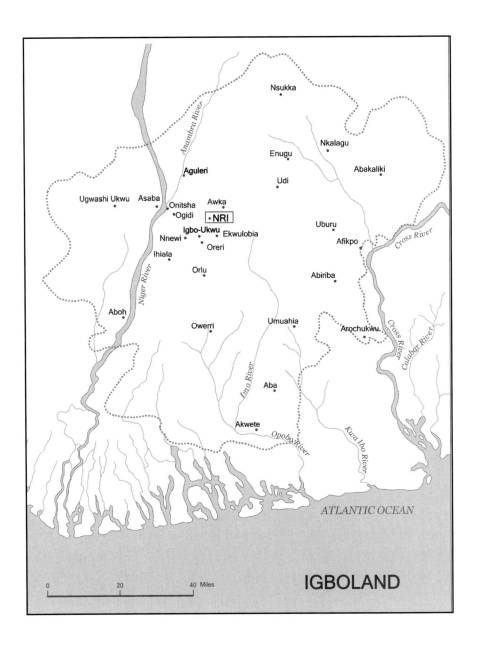

IGBOLAND

Author's Introductory Note

Toward the end of my undergraduate education at the University of Washington, the instructor of my Civilizations class, Dr. Constantin Behler, passed around a book to his students. We had just finished reading Chinua Achebe's *Things Fall Apart*. Dr. Behler thought that an *Igbo Arts and Cosmos* by Chike Okafor and Herbert Cole would give us more background about the culture described in Achebe's book.

As Dr. Behler lectured, the students browsed through the book, passing it on to the next person. Most of them looked at the pictures of carved arts and masquerades. I have no idea what the other students got from that book, but I know what it did for me.

I would later check it out many times from the University of Washington arts library. After studying the Okafor and Cole book, I gained more knowledge of Igbo culture and history, and I also saw beyond the Igbo culture of the 19th century described in *Things Fall Apart*. I saw Igbo bronze artifacts dating back to the ninth century. Those artifacts were much older and more sophisticated than any other metal castings that have since been discovered in West Africa. They could only be produced by a well-organized and fairly sophisticated culture. This insight raised the questions: Could it be that a civilization existed in Igbo land many centuries before the coming of the Europeans and then suddenly disappeared? If so, who were they? How did they live? What were their motivations and activities? And, most important, why did they disappear, leaving so little behind?

I went through the book's bibliography, did more research, and read the referenced books. And I was dumbfounded by what I learned about those ancient artifacts. I knew about Nri because I am from there. I knew about the Nri peace-making and abomination cleansing practices from my childhood and youth. Old men called these activities Ifu-Ije, meaning the outing mission. Each individual or group usually had a particular route of towns. And, yes, I knew that my ancestors made rounds in Igbo villages to make peace and to prescribe and interpret taboos, and I also knew they were respected priests in Igbo land. But I didn't know how elaborate those traditions were and that they went back to the ninth century and, perhaps, even earlier than that. I did not realize that they had built an elaborate and sophisticated culture that can rightly be called a civilization.

From my research, I learned that the most extensive study yet done about Nri civilization was by Professor M. A. Onwuejeogwu, a distinguished Nigerian anthropologist. In his book, *An Igbo Civilization: Nri Kingdom and Hegemony*, Dr. Onwuejeogwu chronicled the history, religion, philosophies, humanities, and political activities of the Nri civilization. That book was an epiphany for me. But perhaps the most eye-opening and most passionate writings on Nri civilization were by a British government designate to West Africa, M. D. W. Jeffreys. Dr. Jeffreys was a district officer in the British Cameroon during the 1930s. He wrote extensively on Nri culture, which he usually called Umundri (Umu-Nri), meaning children of Nri. Here are some excerpts from his article, "The Holy Grails of Africa," which appeared in the October 1936 issue of the *West African Review*.

Everyone knows about the legend renowned in the song and story of the Holy Grail; how it was brought to England; how it remained for many years in the land of its adoption. So sacred was this vessel that it vanished at the approach of anyone who was impure in word or deed. A grail also appeared in Africa, but it has not vanished...

He then explained how the vessel vanished in England and how the knights led by Sir Galahad were sent to find it, but failed. He described the grail's appearance and the origins of the word grail, stating that its Low Latin origin, *gradalis*, meant a twin vessel with two compartments. He continued

...Among the Umundri group of the Igbo tribe a high degree of religious ceremonial culture is found. When their priests make oblation to their Sky-God, Chuku, they do so through the medium of a communion meal. The meal is consumed by the priest. One compartment contains the wine and the other the food. The conclusion is that this vessel repeats the earliest and the correct form of this sacred vessel, i.e., the original form of the grail, a vessel with separate food compartments, a vessel that combined in one the Chalice for wine and the Paten for bread, and thus confirms its derivation from the Low Latin word, gradalis.

Emphasis in the beginning was laid on purity, on at-one-ment, when worshipping, and the instance of Sir Galahad was given. This high standard is [sic] insisted on among the Umundri when they worshipped...

So holy was the communion meal regarded that when the Umundri divine king—the Sky God's delegate on earth, and therefore himself a semi god—is partaking of it, a bell is rung for silence. Should this silence be broken the rest of the meal remains uneaten, and what had been swallowed must be vomited.

Another aspect in which the African grail resembles the sacred vessels of the Christian communion is that it, like them is highly ornamented—far more so than any profane or domestic vessels are.

Thus, Africa presents clearly the original form of the grail: the grail which has vanished because of impurity. The grail which eluded the quests of the Knights turns up anew in Africa, retained there because of the insistence of a high standard of holiness.

Glimpses have been caught of a West African ritual which has many parallels with the Christian practice. As the African ritual is known to be older than the Christian, it cannot be derived from it, nor will it be suggested that the Christian ritual is derived from the African. The conclusion is therefore, that both rituals derive from a common source.

My interest was not in the politics of the Holy Grail. I could see that Dr. Jeffreys was impressed by the humanities and religious worship practices of the Nri culture. His enthusiasm for Nri culture is clear. He even inserted a photograph of the African Grail in his article. I must point out that his writings were done before the accidental archeological discovery and later excavations at the Igbo-Ukwu sites.

After this initial research and other discoveries, I had many questions. For instance, if all this information was available, how was Nri civilization left completely out of Nigerian and world history? Why did I have to come to the United States to attend a university before discovering the true history and legacy of my own Igbo people? Throughout my primary and secondary education in Nigeria, I had learned history and humanities in different stages. But absolutely nothing was taught about Nri civilization. Before I graduated from primary school, I could recite by heart all the major Obas and Onis that had ever ruled mid- and southwestern Nigeria. I could also recite the major Emirs of northern Nigerian and other kingdoms of western Africa. I remembered how my primary-five teacher gave me six lashes of the rattan cane because I could not match a certain Oba with his reigning period. I had recalled all the other Obas that had ever ruled the Benin kingdom but could not match this particular Oba with his reign. I could tell the stories about all the major wars the Benin Empire had fought. The Ekiti Parapi War, for some reason, always stood out in my mind. By the time I had finished secondary school, I could recite, without thinking about it, all the pharaohs of Egypt, all the emperors of Rome, and all the rulers of the Greek kingdoms. The Spartans were my heroes because we were told that they would rather die in battle than surrender. At that time, one of the national football clubs in eastern Nigeria, the Spartans of Owerri, was named after my heroes, the Spartans of Greece. Nigeria was and still is a very savvy culture when it comes to education, especially history.

How then was Nri civilization left completely out of the Nigerian academic curriculum? The answer is simple. If one made peace and not war, then one had no place in history. If one made peace and not war, then one's history was not as interesting as those who made war and fought great battles where human blood flowed like a river. But perhaps the more interesting question would be: How can the people of the world coexist in peace if the history books are filled with wars and blood-thirsty warriors?

Nri civilization remains a mystery simply because it has not been properly investigated. This story is an attempt to generate more interest and, perhaps, more scholarly investigation into the Nri civilization. It is also an attempt to delve into that civilization and bring my audience along in the exploration. After all, the history of peace makers does not have to be boring.

I hope that there will be a renewed interest in what was once the height of moral consciousness in West Africa.

— CA

PART ONE

Prologue

Husband of Fish

In the fortieth year of the Third Century B.C., Okolo, a fisherman of the Igbo tribe, whose homeland was south of the Sahara Desert and a few day's walk by foot north of the Atlantic Ocean, sat in quiet meditation at the bank of the Ama-Mbala River. His back was to the river, his eyes were shut, his legs were folded in front of him, and his breathing was even. He saw nothing and thought of nothing. His senses were voluntarily silenced.

The Egbenu sect he belonged to jokingly called this mind-suspending technique hanging, for that was what it sometimes felt like. It was like being suspended in nothingness where time and space had no value—the border between the human and spiritual world. The Egbenu believed that if one hung in this void often and for long periods of time, one would learn to float and, someday, even fly. The purpose of this mystical practice was to reach amam-ife (wisdom) and acham-akwu (enlightenment).

The Egbenu were a guild of full-time hunters who had adopted this technique and customized it to their liking. Egbenu men had been hanging for many years, but none had yet floated or flown. But the practice certainly relaxed their nerves when they went after the wild bulls. Okolo was not a full-time hunter, but he enjoyed the fellowship of the other men. Egbenu men were considered the wise men of their time, and Okolo enjoyed their association. Also, he reasoned, fishing was not so different from hunting.

Okolo had no way of knowing how long he had been in this state of mental suspension. That was why he always faced east so that when the sun rose it would remind him that the soul had been fed, and it was time to fish so the body could be fed as well.

This particular morning, he had not been long in meditation before the sun rose with full force. Okolo opened his eyes and was temporarily blinded. This was not unusual—it happened all the time. He knew he just needed to wait until his eyes adjusted. He closed his eyes for a few moments, gently opening them again. The sun must have moved closer, because it was now right in his face. It seemed as if it was only a few footsteps away, and he could see nothing but the sun. Now that was unusual.

Okolo could not move. He tried to see the big ball of light before him. He felt like a wild bull looking at a hunter's lamp on a perfectly dark night. He could feel the sun's warmth all over his body and found it comforting.

Then, in the middle of the light, he saw a figure. It hung in the air. He shivered. It reminded him of the ghost tales he had heard as a child. Maybe if he rubbed his eyes and wiped them, his nightmare would end and no one would ever hear a word of it. He rubbed his eyes, wiped his face, and opened his eyes again. His eyes were clear all right. Before him stood a male figure who appeared to be between the ages of twenty-five and forty. He looked young but, at the same time, ageless. He smiled and spread both arms outward. *Was he the sun?* He radiated the light from the sun. Even his garment radiated light.

"Greetings to you, Okolo, the son of Nwanna," the figure said in perfect Igbo. That was real.

In an Igbo story, the lamb said that he was not gifted with the art of dancing, so he did not go around looking for music to dance to. If, however, the music missed its way and ended up at his doorstep, he would do his best, even though it meant simply jumping up and down. Like the lamb, Okolo had to do something, so he spoke.

"Chineke! (God!) Is that you?"

There was silence.

"Chineke! I said . . ."

"Call me Anyanwu, Light. I am not Chineke. Chineke is the Creator and Father of all. He is the Origin and the Destination. He is everywhere and yet nowhere."

"Well, it is nice to meet you—Anyanwu. What do you want of me, a poor fisherman?" Okolo asked confidently, knowing that if Chineke, his creator, was everywhere all the time, He was watching this drama.

"I came to tell you that I like how you devote time to rest your mind every morning. It is a good habit. I watch you every morning."

"Thank you very much. I enjoy it myself. It makes me feel good," said Okolo, now proud of himself.

"It is more than that to you. You do not miss it because it helps you catch more and bigger fish. You have learned that the days when you do not keep a quiet mind before a fishing trip, you catch far less. So you have to do it."

"So you have been watching me and know me that well."

The Light moved his arms for the first time. He pointed at Okolo with his right index finger, saying, "I know you more than you know yourself." Then he folded both arms across his lower abdomen like a wise teacher.

"Now you have my attention," said Okolo. "What else do you know about me?"

"I knew you would ask that because you are curious about things. I know also that you are not a fisherman, but a teacher. You are the teacher and leader among your people. You see yourself as a perfect fisherman. They call you 'Di-Azu' (Husband of Fish), and you enjoy that title. But this is not your true talent. You must lead your people to total freedom. You must prepare yourself. Before you engage in a quiet mind, instead of visualizing a big fish, see instead a happy, healthy, and peaceful community."

"Then what?"

"It is only then that you can float and fly just like I do. It is only then that you can teach your people to float and fly."

Then the Light started to retreat farther and farther away. A chill came over Okolo's body. He was usually tongue-tied and nervous around people, always searching for the right words to say, but sitting in front of the Light, he felt powerful. He also felt a peace he had never had before. He felt at one with the Light and was filled with an abundance of energy. Thoughts and words came naturally and freely. But now the Light was withdrawing, and he felt like his old self again—empty and powerless. When the Light was present, things happened in slow motion. When the Light lifted its hand and pointed at him, it had taken forever, and Okolo saw every detail of the hand lifting and pointing. He saw the spark of light leaving the finger and entering his heart. Then he felt the connection. But now the Light was leaving and he felt empty.

"Wait! Wait for a moment! Come back here! When can I expect to see you again?"

"The Light can come to you only once. After that, you must seek the Light by your own efforts. I will send you the perfect spirit to guide and counsel you. Call it 'Agbala,' because it will make you agile and give you wisdom. You will recognize it when it comes. Agbala will guide you to the Light. It is the giver of insight. It will give you wisdom and guide you all the way to the Light."

When Okolo awoke from his vision, he looked around him. The other fishermen were pointing at him and laughing at the loner who kept to himself.

"Now he is talking to himself, too," one of them said while others burst out laughing.

Yes, Agbala had come fifty years later, and led Okolo to the Light. Standing in front of the Light, Okolo had seen the vision very clearly, but at ninety-six he was too old to act on it so he put all his children, both male and female, to the test. Uyanna, his seventh son, did better than the rest, so Okolo gave Uyanna the nickname "Nri" meaning manifestation (of the vision, of the ideal). He changed his own name to "Eri" meaning manifestor (manifestor of the vision, the ideal). Okolo (Eri) shared the vision with Uyanna (Nri) and gave him his blessings, sending him on his way.

Uyanna, now known as Nri, moved south and settled at an uninhabited lake. He called his community Nri, meaning the ideal (or at least the beginning of it).

🦋 🦋 🦋

ONE

Turning Points

On an Nkwo market day, Okoye Nweri, a thirteenth generation descendant of Nri, walked home happy and proud of himself with a basket on his head. In the basket were his hunting club, a machete, and seven dead animals: three squirrels, four full-sized nchi (grass cutters or beavers), and one live baby ogini. The animals were his share from an all-morning hunting adventure at Ofia Okpukpo, a small wilderness belonging to his village, Nri-Agu, one of the fourteen Nri villages.

Okoye had since bade farewell to his three hunting partners, three brothers, the twins and their elder brother, from his maternal village of Nri-Ejiofor. He was particularly happy because the brothers had let him have the only living ogini any of them had caught. The ogini was a small animal that can easily be mistaken for a big rat if not for its beautiful spotted skin. It was rarely caught alive, and Okoye was looking forward to showing it off as a pet. The brothers had let him have it because he was the trip's organizer and had invited them to hunt in his own backyard wilderness. But this was not the only gift they had given to Okoye.

After giving him the ogini, the oldest of the boys dipped his hand into his basket, took out the biggest nchi, and dropped it into Okoye's basket.

"That one is for Our Big Sister."

The boy, Nweze, was sixteen years old, only two years older than Okoye, but he called Okoye's mother their Big Sister, making the boy look and sound more mature than he really was. Okoye was a little intimidated. He knew the brothers' mother was much younger than his own, but it was Nri custom to refer to all males in a mother's birth village as Symbolic Uncle and, in turn, every male in that village called the birth mother Big Sister. Even men twice her age called her Ada-Anyi-Nwanya. So Okoye felt a little uncomfortable whenever the boys asserted their rights as his symbolic uncles. It was very thoughtful and nice of the boy, though, to hold his mother in such high regard, and Okoye knew he would enjoy passing the gift along to his mother. He was sure she would be thrilled and would talk about it all day long. She always talked about the people of Nri-Ejiofor, her birth village, as some special breed of Nri people and she would use an event like this to her advantage, making sure that everyone around her knew about it. Okoye adored his mother and was always happy when she glowed while talking about her birth village and her youth years.

The time was inching into the first hour of the afternoon as Okoye came closer and closer to his home. The sun was still sweet on his body. Okoye could feel it on his neck and shoulders as he turned a corner and entered the Ebe Nri-Agu. As soon as he saw the old udala (apple) tree covered with yellow fruits, pleading to be eaten, he became hungry. Surely there would be children sitting all around the tree as usual, waiting for udala fruit to fall. Certainly they would give him one. Okoye wondered if he should show the ogini to the children. He decided that he would not unless the animal made noise and someone asked about it.

There were many legends and taboos about the udala tree at Nri. Its fruit must never be plucked. It must be allowed to fall on its own accord. Udala trees were native to the area, but were not planted by humans. They just showed up in big compounds or public squares where there were lots of children. Almost all of the public squares at Nri had one or two udala trees, and children at Nri knew which one had the sweetest fruit. Children and their baby watchers usually gathered around that one to play and wait for the fruit to drop. Then they would have a group chase to retrieve the udala; only one person would win the race. Because the udala dropped frequently, many children would be winners. The Nri believed that spirits hung around the udala trees when humans were not there. So it was taboo for a person to sit near an udala tree waiting for falling fruit. Nri were suspicious of anyone who did this.

As Okoye stepped into the square, no one was in sight. On an Nkwo market day, young mothers commonly brought their children to the square's communal child watch while the parents went to the market to buy or sell. Okoye wondered if he had mistaken the day, but he had not. His mother had mentioned leaving early for the market to sell a goat.

As he walked into the square, he was temporarily shielded from the sun by the udala tree which shaded most of the square. Then he heard a pleasant sound. An udala was falling from the tree! "Kpa-cham! Kpa-cham! Kpam!" It sounded as the fruit fell, touching leaves and branches, dropping finally on the ground in front of Okoye, "Kpooo!"

It was a good omen for an udala to greet someone by falling in front of him. With the basket still on his head, Okoye bent halfway down and picked up the fruit without looking at it. When he stood up, he saw it was filled with fruit bugs. He quickly dropped it on the ground. This was a bad omen. In the old days, his highly spiritual forebearers would have pointed the fruit to the sun and prayed that any misfortune it might bring be taken away. But Okoye did not know this.

As he walked towards his home past his uncle, Ozo Ikezuo's compound, he saw his uncle standing there with three other men; all of them had crossed their arms on their chests. The three men were all from his village. He saluted his uncle as he approached them.

"Ozo Nwayoo!"

Ozo Ikezuo did not reply but bent his neck to the right and sighed, a sign of frustration, of surrender.

"Ozo Nna-anyi!," Okoye saluted again and this time raised his voice to be heard.

"My Son, rain has beaten the elephant and has entered its eyes."

Okoye stopped, not knowing what to say. Two of the men headed toward Okoye's father's compound. The third man, Nwangene, invited Okoye to come into his uncle's compound. When they reached the front of the obu, Nwangene took the basket from Okoye's head and put it on the ground. Okoye's heart started racing. He did not need to be told that something terrible had happened, but what? Ozo Ikezuo sat down, looking very resigned. Then Nwangene, too, sat down and invited Okoye to join them.

"What happened?" Okoye asked.

"How many years are you?" asked Nwangene.

"Ten and four years," replied Okoye, more puzzled.

"That is a grown-up age," said Nwangene. "But you look and act even more mature than your age. Everyone, including your father, says that you act older than your age. Your father always says that. He is always very proud of you, and I think you should know that."

Ozo Ikezuo shook his head. "They cut off my ikenga arm (right arm)."

"Nna-anyi, what happened?" asked Okoye. There was no reply from his uncle who rocked back and forth on his ikpo (daybed).

"Rattlesnake bit your father three days ago during their trade journey," said Nwangene.

"Did he come back then? Is he at home now?" asked Okoye.

"My son, an abomination has happened! My eyes have seen my ears. Darkness has fallen in the day. They cut off my ikenga arm," said Ozo Ikezuo.

"Your father is no more. The poison killed him before they could get him to the closest herbalist. They brought him back very early this morning and everyone is waiting for you," said Nwangene.

"Abomination!" yelled Ozo Ikezuo. "Taaa! Taaaa! Abomination happened! Tufia! Taaa! Taaaa!" he shouted as he rocked back and forth on his ikpo.

"My ikenga hand is gone. They cut off my ikenga hand!"

Okoye froze. He heard his uncle's yelling and raving as from a distance. He faintly heard what Nwangene was saying to his uncle.

"How do you expect the boy to behave if you don't hold yourself? Look at him, see how calm and composed he is, taking it like the big man that he is."

Of course what they said could not be true. It could not be true because Okoye could not picture his father dead. His father was not the dying kind. He was full of life, always talking and laughing. Okoye sat dazed, almost in a trance. He could almost hear his father talking and laughing in his big voice. His father spoke his mind all the time, not holding anything back and people always said that Okoye took after his father. Okoye felt Nwangene patting his back.

"You are a good boy. Make your father very proud. Show all Nri-Agu what a brave son he has. We are going to your father's compound now.

Everyone is waiting for you. You must see him before he is put in the ground. When we get there, you must act like a grown man and make your father proud."

These were indeed Okoye's thoughts as they walked into his father's compound where all the men and women of Nri-Agu were gathered. The grave had been dug, and the young men of Nri-Agu village sat around it waiting to perform their last duty to the dead. The women of Nri-Agu sat inside and all around the outside of Okoye's mother's hut.

"O-batagwooo! Nwa-anyi-abatagwooooo! (He is back! Our son is back!)," a woman's voice yelled somewhere near his mother's hut.

Instantly, there came cries from all around. Nri-Agu men surrounded his father's big obu and filled most of the compound. Shades of bamboo poles and palm leaf had been made to shield those who sat outside in the sun. Okoye imagined that his father was sitting somewhere in the obu and that, as soon as he walked in, he would wake from his dream, and his father would smile and greet him. As they walked towards the obu with Nwangene leading the way and Ozo Ikezuo trailing behind, the men of Nri-Agu made way for them to pass.

"Our Son, we are sorry!," they said as Okoye passed them.

"Our Son, take heart!"

"Abomination happened!"

All of the men of Nri-Agu were saying this to him and some touched him as he moved past. Others, who had no words, simply sighed and crossed their arms across their chests. Okoye's heart beat so fast and loud that he thought others could hear it. *Chineke, let this not be true,* he was saying to himself.

The walk to his father's obu seemed to take an eternity. *Chineke, I promise to be very good to others. I will stop talking smart to others. Let this be a dream and nothing more and I will be a good man for the rest of my life.*

As they entered the reception area, people sat all around and on the short mud walls. Okoye looked for his father. They were all familiar faces, but none was his father's.

"Our Son, sorry!" greeted him.

"Our Son, have a strong heart!"

"Our Son, take heart!"

"Abomination happened!"

"Tufia! Tufiakwa!"

"Abomination has happened!"

Okoye saw his father sleeping on his ikpo. Nwankwo, Okoye's older brother, sat on a stool next to his father. For a brief moment, Okoye stopped, watching his father as he slept, waiting for him to wake up. He always did when Okoye walked into his obu, even if the boy tried to sneak in. His father always felt his presence and woke anyway. Then it hit Okoye like an udala fruit would hit someone on the head, "Kpoii." *Wake up from your daydream.*

His father's lips were not moving. Even when he slept, his mouth always moved. His father talked and laughed even in his sleep. Only then did Okoye know that his father might be dead.

"Nna-anyi, wake up!" Okoye yelled, rushing towards his father. "Wake up for all Nri-Agu is here waiting for you. Wake up and give them kola-nut. They think you are dead. Tell them you are not dead. Wake up! Wake up and tell them yourself!"

Now Okoye was sitting next to his father and shaking him. He did not cry. He only talked to his father. Nwankwo started to cry aloud. Before long, crying and lamentations were heard all around the compound.

❦ ❦ ❦

The burial, funeral, and mourning for the dead were very serious business in Nri and all of Igbo land, especially if the deceased was a well-established family man or woman. The funeral rites and official mourning for the dead lasted up to seven market weeks, twenty-eight days. Then family members and close relatives would try to ease themselves back into their regular routines. In those days, people lived long and died old. They usually did not die in their forty-plus years like Nwa-anyanwu, Okoye's father. So, although he was not widely known beyond Nri-Agu village, most people in Nri heard about his death and came because it was such a tragedy. It was always a tragedy when a man or woman died in the prime of life.

Sympathetic visitors were still coming, even into the seventh week, when the final rites were performed. That was another reason why Ozo Ikezuo waited to call a meeting. He called for it on the morning of the first day after the seven-market-week ceremony. The meeting was partly to assure Okoye's mother and her children of his support and partly to give his final formal condolence advice.

"There is nothing more to my calling you together except to tell you that our life will go on despite what happened. We will take life as we see it because no one can send a query to Chineke. Even if we have the power, we don't know how to send it to him. Nwa-Anyanwu was my only brother. I have many sisters, but they are all married and away now. Nwa-Anyanwu was like my right arm. Now it has been cut off from me. But, as I said, we cannot send a query to Chineke, and we will continue to live. Nchi (the grass cutter, beaver) says that even if all his kinsmen suddenly disappear from the bush leaving him by himself, he will continue to cut the grass in the bush because that is his destiny."

Okoye's mother was still dazed. She sat, trancelike, on the comfortable rattan chair in her late husband's obu. She held her chin in her right palm; her elbow rested on her lap; her eyes were fixed on the wall. She was a passive and sensitive wife who usually didn't say very much. The tragedy had hit her the hardest. Nwankwo, Okoye's older brother, took after their mother. He, too, had not recovered. He sat on a stool next to his mother, staring at the red-waxed terracotta floor as if the key to his future was buried there. Okoye had accepted the tragedy by the fourth day after his father was put into the ground.

His father was no more—true. He had been a good man and everyone who set foot in his father's compound said so. Okoye knew that Chineke listens to human testimonies and takes care of good people, so he knew Chineke would take care of his father wherever he was now. But Okoye's mother was still alive, so Okoye and Nwankwo must take care of her and their sisters. These were Okoye's thoughts as he pulled himself out of grief. Okoye was the only one really listening as Ozo Ikezuo spoke. Okoye was the only one who heard what was said and what was not said. So when Ozo Ikezuo finished his long speech telling the family to accept what had happened and to look to a future without their father, Okoye was listening. When Ozo Ikezuo assured them of his support and that he would treat them like his own children, Okoye listened. He was the only one who knew that his uncle had finished speaking, and, since neither his mother nor Nwankwo responded, Okoye did.

He thanked his uncle for what he said and all he had done to give his father a burial and funeral and all he promised to do for them in the future.

"I cannot speak for my mother or my brother, Nwankwo, but only for myself. I ask only one more favor from you. If you do this, then you have done everything for me. I would like you to find me a good trading group that I can join and trade with. If you do that for me, then you have done everything."

There was a long silence. Okoye did not dance around what he wanted but was very direct and blunt, just like his father. Nwankwo shifted on his stool. His younger brother had reminded him that there was a tomorrow. Their mother, too, turned her gaze from the wall and looked at Okoye. After a long reflection, his uncle replied.

"You know that I can do more than that for you when the time comes. But now you are only ten and four. To join a trading group as your own man, you have to have your own Otonsi Nri because that will guarantee your safe passage in all communities outside our own. And you have to become a Nze priest before you can get your own Otonsi. You have to become the age of two tens before you can become Onye-Nze and get your Otonsi. You will wait for another six . . ."

"But my father promised I could start next year. I know other people who started before they were the age of two tens."

"Your father did not lie to you," said Ozo Ikezuo. "One can travel under one's father's Otonsi before one gets his own but not under anyone else's; not even under mine if I still traveled. And you know that I don't travel anymore. Now you have to travel as your own man, and you need your own Otonsi. Nwankwo is now over ten and eight years of age. After another two years, he will get his Otonsi and do what he wants to. But for now, you two will take care of your father's yam crop until each of you reaches two tens and becomes independent. You will help attend to your father's yam crops until you reach the age of two tens."

There was disappointment in Okoye's face, but there was nothing he could do about it. He knew that his uncle meant well and spoke the truth.

❧ ❧ ❧

Two moons later and about five days' foot journey from Nri in the village of Umu-Uwakwe in the Amoko family, another young man, three years older than Okoye, also went hunting when tragedy befell him. His name was Erike and he, too, had lost his father, but it was not the same tragedy that Okoye had experienced. Erike's father had died when the boy was only five. This was a different kind of tragedy, more like losing one's own life.

Erike was a more serious hunter than Okoye. He did not hunt grass cutters, squirrels, and oginis but deer, antelope, and monkeys. And, unlike Okoye, he did not go hunting with a band of friends. He usually went by himself because when he was a young child, Erike had overheard others say that a serious hunter must never go hunting with casual friends. Things can happen in the wilderness that may demand perfect loyalty. Partial loyalty during hunting was as good as none. Erike had not found a perfect hunting partner. He was a loner who hunted by himself and he was a good hunter. But this fateful morning in the seventh moon of the year, he had made an exception and taken his cousin Ogu along.

Though it was no longer raining that morning, the bushes were still soaked from the night before. The path was so narrow that one person could barely fit, so it was almost impossible to avoid the rain-soaked bushes. Ogu was doing his best to push them aside as he walked along. Erike didn't mind the shrubs. He appeared indifferent to them.

"But is the rain good or bad for hunting?" Ogu asked Erike as he ran to catch up with him.

"It depends on what you are hunting for," Erike replied. "It is easier to hunt for antelope when it is raining. They do not like the rain, so you can find them in groups under some big trees. With monkeys, it is much more different because they hide in trees and don't make much sound."

Erike, who was seventeen and much older than Ogu, was teaching the youngster how to hunt. This was the first time they were going to hunt antelope. Erike had shown Ogu how to set traps for squirrels, fish, and other small animals in the past, but they had never gone on a live hunt. For the first time, Ogu was going to have this experience.

"I am looking forward to killing a deer. I will leave the skull with its long horns in front of our entrance gate so that our visitors can see it when they enter our house," said Ogu.

This brought back the memory of Erike's first killing of a deer. There was something exciting about creeping up to the animal or lying in ambush and jumping out at just the right time and striking. But this could also be very dangerous and one must always be on guard.

"I must warn you that hunting is not always easy and fun. It can be full of dangers. I have had such moments in the past. I don't mean to make you afraid, but you must know what can happen so that you will be ready to react."

"Is it true that you once fought and killed a lion?"

"It was a baby lion, but it was dangerous. It gave me this mark on my face," said Erike and turned to show off his scars.

Erike had been out hunting on his own when the lion attacked. As he tried to ambush a group of antelope, an inexperienced young lion had charged at Erike from nowhere. The beast seemed twice his size. Erike knew he had no chance with this devil. Quickly he pulled out his hunting knife and decided to go for the lion's stomach. It worked. He could not believe his eyes when the lion tried to run away, but could not. The animal was still fighting death when Erike climbed the closest tree and watched the beast die. He stayed in the tree until he was sure the lion was dead and that no others were in the area. He had been in the tree for only a few moments when he noticed blood stains all over his body. In addition to injuring his arms and leg, the lion had given Erike three identical marks on the left side of his face, just below the eye. When the marks healed later they looked like a partial ceremonial scarification. His playmates said these marks were free scarification. Erike still had dreams about this incident and would do anything to prevent something like this from happening again.

"Did you keep the skull?" asked Ogu as he tried to catch up with Erike who was walking very fast and had just turned a sharp corner.

Erike did not reply, and Ogu noticed that his cousin was slowing down. He heard the voice before he saw the man in front of them.

"My Chi has delivered you into my hands," the man said to Erike. "I told you that I would get you some day."

Ogu recognized the voice before he could see the face. It was Oduenyi.

"This is trouble," Ogu said to himself, but he didn't know how much trouble. Oduenyi was the village bully. He always meant business. Ogu did not know what the problem was between Erike and Oduenyi, but he knew that Oduenyi did not bluff. Oduenyi was much taller and larger than Erike. Everyone in his age grade seemed to be afraid of Oduenyi.

"I do not want trouble," Erike said to him as he made his way into the rain-soaked bushes so Oduenyi could pass. Instead of moving on, Oduenyi laid down his palm wine calabash, rope, and knife.

"I was only expressing my mind at the meeting. It was only my opinion, and I hope that you will not hold it against me."

"When I finish with you, you will have no opinions left," Oduenyi replied with a big, deep voice as he walked towards Erike.

For a moment, Erike thought about running away from the "crazy cow" as they called Oduenyi. But then he thought about Ogu. What would he think of him? Would he think him a coward? Wouldn't he lose respect? He must not run. He must stop and fight if it came to that, even if it meant taking a beating. No. He must stand and fight, even if it meant scaring the bully with his hunting knife.

Yeah! Pull out your knife and scare the son of a wild beast away. Show him you are serious, the voice inside his head told him. He jerked his sharp hunting knife from his waist.

"I do not want trouble," Erike repeated. But even with the knife, he looked and sounded scared.

"If you don't put that knife away, I will give you a free scarification with it," warned Oduenyi. He was now an arm's reach from Erike.

Did you hear that? He said free scarification. Just like the one you got from that wild beast a while back. Don't you remember? The beast was after your life, wasn't it? The man is serious. Look at him. Isn't he as big as that beast? To be twice fooled is bad, really bad!

As Oduenyi lifted his right hand, Erike saw the lion clearly. He saw its long claws, its piercing long teeth, and its bloody eyes. Even the beast's stinking urine-soaked smell was present.

Erike did what had worked before. He went for the stomach. As Oduenyi reached out to hit Erike, he ignored the hunting knife. Nobody had stood up to him for so long that he had forgotten that people could actually fight back.

Erike's uncle's advice had saved him the first time. "In a crisis, you must not panic. You must breathe in and out to keep calm. You must then do what you have to do," his uncle had told him many times.

Erike took a big gulp of fresh air and exhaled. *Yea, the stomach! Don't forget the stomach,* the voice reminded him.

Oduenyi fell hard on the knife that stuck out from his stomach. He did not struggle the way the lion had. He made a sound, but nothing Erike could understand. He bled like an animal.

Erike had killed a man! If Oduenyi hadn't fallen on the knife, Erike would not have been sure. If blood hadn't flowed freely from his mouth and nose and stomach, Erike would not have been sure. From the corner of his eye, he saw Ogu flee down the path. He wanted to call him back, but he had no strength left. He wanted to reach out to Oduenyi, but he was too scared. Besides, he knew it was hopeless. He started toward home. His first instinct was to go there and find a good strong rope to hang himself before anyone could ask questions and make judgments.

As he approached home, he saw villagers. They were asking the same questions. "What happened? Where is Oduenyi? What happened?"

Erike knew Ogu had told them. "Look at Erike's hands. He has blood on his hands," one of them said.

Then he saw what he most dreaded—his beloved uncle, Ogu's father. His uncle did not speak. He did not ask what had happened. He just followed Erike who knew then that his plan of hanging himself had been foiled. He knew that his uncle knew what he was thinking of doing.

Erike had not grown up in this village. He had been raised by his maternal uncle (his mother's brother), who was a professional hunter. Erike had come back to his village less than two years before, and, ever since he came back, he had been trying to avoid any problems with Oduenyi. There was a saying that an adult does not run away from a crazy cow, but uses diplomacy to avoid a fight. Erike had chosen diplomacy to avoid Oduenyi, but Oduenyi, who enjoyed intimidating his peers, had not seen fear in Erike's eyes. He knew when people were afraid of him. Erike did not seem to be afraid and avoided him instead. So Oduenyi had been looking for an opportunity to put fear in Erike's eyes so he would be put in his place.

One day in their peer group meeting, Erike had made a suggestion to reach a consensus through voting; Oduenyi took offence and berated him. Erike did not argue back. After the meeting, Oduenyi blocked the exit pretending that he was talking to some people. He made way for everyone except Erike. When, after a long diplomatic delay, Erike tried to pass, Oduenyi gave him an elbow. He claimed that Erike had pushed him. But there were many witnesses who came to Erike's side. A fight, or rather a public beating was avoided, but Oduenyi had told Erike that he would get him eventually. This had happened about five days before the encounter in the bush. But to the elders of Umu-Uwakwe village and the selected representatives of the entire Amoko family, the case was simple: Erike had used a knife to fight a man who had laid down his own knife. It was murder and murder has consequences.

The three options were equally distasteful. At the moment, public hanging was more attractive than the others. If he were hanged, he would have paid his debt in full so he could join his ancestors, and none of his family members would pay any other penalty for his actions. He could reincarnate in his own village as a full member. But if he chose to go into exile, he would live and die in exile. His descendents could never come back to the village. All his landed properties in the village would be given to the victim's family. When he died in exile, he would not reincarnate in his own village but in some foreign land. The third option was to take refuge with Ngwu, the village deity, and consecrate himself as an outcast. That way he could live and die in his village. But then he and his offspring would always be outcasts and slaves to the deity.

🌿 🌿 🌿

His uncle had sold Erike on the idea of going into exile. He had gone to Nri where he had done well with his second life. Now, Erike, like Okoye, wanted the Otonsi. But he wanted it for a different reason. The Otonsi would not only solidify his Nri citizenship, but it would give him something else—immunity to visit his birth village and see his mother without any harassment from the villagers. Erike was also fascinated by the Nri culture—its energy, pride, and the awe it struck among the Igbos. He wanted to know all the secrets and there was something new to learn every day.

Nri was the land of peaceful warriors and this was what Erike wanted to be.

TWO

Quest for Otonsi

"When dealing with your neighbor, you must always ask yourself, 'What is fair?' Do not ask, 'What is a good deal?' For a good deal to you may be very bad for your neighbor. You must always speak the truth. It must never be compromised. Telling the truth is your perfect guard against bad behavior. Look at it this way: If you know that you will tell the truth when the time comes, you will most likely not engage in bad behavior, because, if you do, then you will have to confess and receive your punishment. You must always speak up for what is right and just. You must shun 'Ochaa-Gbute Ochara-Gbute' (mediocrity). A Nze priest must think and act like a shepherd all the time; he must think like a leader and act like a host at all times," Igwe Nwadike said looking around at the young faces that surrounded him.

It was the second moon in Nri land, the month of the dawn of creation. The Eze Nri, Igwe Nwadike, sat like the rest of the men on a mat on the mud floor of the Agbala Temple in the holy forest. It was late in the evening and darkness would be descending at any moment. The sky was clear and light breezes streamed in between the big log pillars of the temple. The yellowish red rays of the late evening sun that filtered through the pillars of the temple were fading fast. Most of the men listened with keen interest to the old bald-headed King, or at least they pretended to. He had a reputation for repeating himself, and the thirty-seven young men had witnessed this first hand. They had just been on a twenty-eight day (seven week) retreat with him and had heard the same sermon every day. They enjoyed the stories of heroism. Igwe Nwadike was a master storyteller, and, for the past twenty-eight days, he used this skill to drive his points home. That was the good part, but the retreat was dominated by chanting, quiet meditation, individual counseling, and fasting. They ate only uncooked fruits and vegetables and drank only water.

Igwe Nwadike was feeling as holy as holy could be. After twelve years as the Eze Nri, he had learned to enjoy retreats and whatever happened to go along with them. He enjoyed these times even more when he was leading a group of curious young men who would soon be adopted into the Nze priesthood as his new agents of goodwill.

"You are the future of Nri. You cannot fail us, for all our hope is in you. You must make the Nri and all Igbo people proud."

He continued for what seemed like another hour before the moment the young men were waiting for finally arrived. After twenty-eight days in the holy forest, they were to be dismissed. The waiting seemed like torture to most of them, and it was not really over yet. They still had another day before the process would be completed. But, at least, they could sleep on a bed in their own homes for this night. They could take a good bath with palm-oil soap.

Okoye stood up just as soon as the old man finished. He could not wait to enjoy his freedom. He stretched and stretched again. He waved to his friend Erike Okolo and pointed to the exit. Erike looked at the old man. Igwe Nwadike was not looking back at him. He was busy talking to three young men. Erike continued to watch the old man, attempting to avoid eye contact with Okoye.

Okoye waited for a few moments, then went over and tapped Erike on the shoulder.

"Do you want to leave or not?" he asked.

"Or not," Erike joked. But Okoye did not find it funny. The old man might change his mind. "You don't want us to be the first to leave do you?" Erike added.

"And what is wrong with that?"

"It just doesn't look good. It gives a wrong impression."

"Wrong impression?" asked Okoye as he choked with laughter.

Just then a group of four headed for the exit, followed by two others.

"And what about those people?" Okoye said, pointing at them.

Erike knew that he was beaten. He got up and grabbed his worn-out, white-and black-spotted goat-skin bag. He was hoping to ask Igwe Nwadike a question or two. Not that he really needed an answer. He just wanted more time with the old man whom he had always seen from a distance, and he wondered when he would have another opportunity to be this close to him again.

Darkness was creeping in as the two young men left the retreat grounds and walked out the palace exit, both wearing the traditional Nri casual outfit, a loin cloth and a piece of garment wrapped from the right armpit and knotted on the left shoulder. All the young men carried a single palm frond in their mouths, a sign that they were in a state-of-holiness. Anyone who saw them when they carried fronds in this way would not attempt to speak or interact with them.

The downward-sloping road was rocky and paved with chunks of stone, but erosion had taken the better part of it. As they descended the hill, Erike admired the view. He saw the mystic Nri Lake glowing at the far right at the bottom of the hill. He saw several footpaths meandering to different villages. After six years at Nri, he could tell where each village started and ended. He could see the group of huts that made up family lineage of a village. But, apart from the Lake, the footpaths, and the group of huts, the rest of the Nri landscape was dense forest populated by iroko, cottonwood, achala (bamboo), arabah, akpaka, and sweet ugili fruit trees.

Okoye, who seemed to be celebrating his freedom, jumped from stone to stone as gravity pulled him down the road. They were barely one hundred footsteps from the palace, which Nri people called Nne Obu (Mother of Obu at Nri), when Okoye took the palm frond from his mouth and spoke.

"I will run away from Nri if I have to do this all over again."

Erike, who still had the frond in his mouth, said nothing.

"I said that I will run away if I have to do this all over again," Okoye repeated.

"We are not supposed to talk. We are in a holy state," Erike reminded him.

"The man skinned us alive for seven weeks."

"We are not supposed to say negative things or think negative thoughts, at least not until the ceremony is finished tomorrow. That is why we are not supposed to talk at all. Remember?"

"He is living in the past. I heard that our people used to be holy people. Now we are just acting. It is all an act, and he is taking it too far."

"I really like the man. I think that he is the nicest man I have ever met. He means well for all people."

"I like him too. But I will still run away from Nri if I have to do this again. The man is so boring. Could you imagine living the rest of your life like him?"

"You had better be careful of what you say. I heard that he can hear things you say in his absence. He may decide to disqualify you tomorrow."

"Well then, if he is that good, he will also know that I am only joking. He is a very good man. He is a holy man. He is our great King, the holy one of Nri! We marvel at his sight. He is Igwe, the heavenly one!" Okoye chanted as he danced from stone to stone. He chanted verses from the Odozi Obodo Women, (Keepers of the Town Women) praise song:

"He is the perfect savior and protector of his people. He is . . ."

"I truly marveled at his sight," Erike interrupted. "It was an honor to meet him. I used to see him from a distance. Now that I have met him, I think he is everything they say he is . . ."

"Sheeee! I see someone coming. We are in holiness. Remember?"

As the middle-aged woman carrying an ukpa basket on her head passed, both young men had palm fronds in their mouths. The steep hill had been a struggle for the woman, and she stopped to catch her breath. She turned to admire the two young men returning from the holy ground and saw Nri's future. She had heard about the ordainment ceremony to be held the next day. Her first son would be due for Nze priesthood in only five years.

Time goes by fast. It seemed like yesterday when he was a baby, she thought to herself.

The young men were about fifty foot-steps past her when Okoye reached for the palm frond, but at the last second, he decided to play safe. He turned around to see the woman staring at them, so he removed his hand from his mouth remembering he was supposed to be in holiness. That was how it was done in the old days when the forefathers were holy people. Now it was just an act, and Okoye Nweri was just playing a part.

❧ ❧ ❧

They walked silently down the rest of the hill path. During this time, Okoye had time to ponder their conversation. He admired Erike's innocence about Nri culture—how he took everything he heard about Nri at face value. Okoye had often wondered why immigrants were so eager to embrace the image of perfection that Nri projected. Maybe they tried so hard to believe that Nri must be better than whatever they were leaving behind. Maybe if they embraced Nri, Nri will embrace them back—making a contract with their new home. Or maybe they just did not know the true history and politics of Nri that the natural born citizens were privy to. Whatever the reason, Okoye felt obligated to share some truths with his immigrant friend.

"There are some things I think you should know about Nri," Okoye said, then stopped at the foot of the hill just before they were to bid each other goodnight and take separate paths to their villages. Erike stopped, too, the palm frond still in his mouth.

"Do you know about Ozo Oganiru priests?"

Erike nodded, and took out the frond. "I have heard about them, but I don't know any of them yet or what they do."

"They are big merchants and they hold Nri together. They are not happy with Igwe."

"Why? What has he done?"

"They think that he is holding Nri people down and stopping progress. My father told us that about ten years ago—four years before he died. At that time, there was tension at Nri. There were meetings everywhere and people were whispering as if something terrible was about to happen. One afternoon, five men I have never seen before came to our house and spoke to my father. They spoke mostly in proverbs and in low tones. I had never heard any of those proverbs before so I did not know what they were talking about. When they left, I asked my Father what was happening—what they were talking about. He asked me to go and call Nwankwo, my elder brother. When we both came he told us that the Ozo

Oganiru priests wanted to divide Nri into fragments so they could rule the villages. He said that they wanted to do this because Igwe was holding back progress and keeping everyone down."

"How is he stopping progress?" Erike asked, shifting his weight from his right to his left, his arms folded across his chest.

"That is another thing you should know. Before he became Eze Nri, Nze priests were ordained at their villages by the lead Ozo priest of each village—not the Eze Nri. Seekers of the Nze priesthood did not go through this rigorous purification that we did—I call it torture. As soon as he became Eze Nri, that was one of the first things he changed. He took charge of the Nze priesthood. The Ozo Oganiru priests did not like it. They thought that Nze priests were created to submit to Ozo priests and not directly to the Eze Nri."

"What difference does it make where Nze priests are ordained? Is it not petty to make it an issue?" Erike wondered aloud.

"It would not make a great difference if they believe in the same things, but they don't. Ozo Oganiru priests believe in trading and building the Nri economy. They want to make Nri the biggest market in the world. Nze priests are their arms and feet that they use for that purpose. Do you know about Ozo Mkputu priests?"

Erike shook his head.

"Ozo Mkputu priests are very few in numbers, but they too are very powerful. They believe in Nri ancient spiritual traditions. They believe in going to different places, preaching, and spreading the message of Aja-ana—the message of peace and non-violence, of kindness and holiness. They too believe in using Nze priests to do their work. In fact they believe in using every Nze priest for their work. Igwe Nwadike was their leader before he became Eze Nri. So when he took over the Nze priesthood, most Ozo priests, especially the Ozo Oganiru, did not like it. The Ozo Mkputu, of course, welcomed it. Somehow they made peace then and Nri stayed together. But the Ozo Oganiru still resent Igwe for taking control of the Nze priesthood, and they are still planning something. I don't know what."

"Who do you support? Who does your uncle support?"

"My uncle is neutral, but he is fond of Igwe. As for me—to tell the truth—I support no one. I just want to trade and take care of my mother and sisters and see the world. But in Nri, if you want to trade, then you have to deal with Oganiru priests. They hold the yam and they hold the knife. And your level of loyalty determines how big a piece they can cut you."

"But it looks like the Ozo Mkputu hold the Offor Nri," Erike countered.

"That is true—it makes it more interesting, does it not?"

Just then, there was a big commotion in the thick forest. All the trees started to rattle and shake. Nwangene creek monkeys began jumping from one tree to another, wailing as they leaped. There was a belief at Nri that monkeys do not like nightfall so they protest at the final moments before dark. They preferred to eat utu fruits and play and then eat and play some more. They preferred that cycle better than the cycle of night and day. It is said that utu fruits were so sweet to the Nri monkeys that they sometimes lost their senses while eating it. There have even been accounts of some monkeys falling to their death while eating utu fruits. The commotion reminded Okoye that he most hurry across the narrow Nwangene creek bridge before darkness so that he wouldn't have to crawl over it.

❀ ❀ ❀

Later that night, Okoye stood alone at the center of his late father's obu. He usually shared the room with his brother, Nwankwo, but this night Okoye had it to himself. Nwankwo had been gone for over three weeks and was not expected back for another two. He was now a three-year veteran trader. Okoye was happy for him, but, at the same time, he was jealous that he had not yet started trading. It was sibling rivalry and Nwankwo did not make it easy for Okoye when he returned from his trading trips. He would tell Okoye stories of his adventures at every opportunity. Okoye gave a sigh of relief. All the waiting would finally be over tomorrow. By the time Nwankwo came back, Okoye would be an Nze priest with Otonsi Nri, ready to go places.

Okoye was a little taller than average. He had chocolate-colored skin and the face of a Nri male over the age of thirteen—full scarification that resembled the rays of the sun. Nri people worshipped the sun, the dwelling place of Anyanwu and Agbala. All males over thirteen wore this scarification—single facial marks that started from the nose and covered each section of the face. The lines lay next to each other to pattern the sun's rays.

Okoye had big brown eyes that did not seem to blink. The rest of his body appeared to be nothing more than nerves wrapped around big bones. He had open upper-teeth that everyone had to notice because he smiled a lot. His was not an evil smile, yet it reminded his peers that he could not be taken advantage of. His was a confident smile, the smile of someone who was in control of his destiny, and who knew what he wanted from life.

Okoye walked to a far corner of the room and picked up an old hole digger made of a long arabah wooden handle with an iron tip. The digger was not quite his height. With his right hand, he grabbed it in the middle and lifted it in the air. Didn't it look like an Otonsi? He smiled broadly. Then he remembered the past twenty-eight days of torture. Hadn't Nwankwo warned him that it would be pretty bad? Hadn't he thought that Nwankwo was trying to discourage and scare him from doing as he, Nwankwo, had done? But the retreat had been worse than anything he had heard.

Okoye recalled the times that the old man had made them drink the gui, a bitter liquid he said would cleanse impurities from their bodies. The taste and smell had lasted for days. He recalled the time they fasted for two days in a row, drinking only water. But it was the chanting that nearly drove him insane. For the first two weeks, eight days, they chanted nonsense for half a day every day. He had no idea what those chants meant, for they were nothing close to the Igbo language he spoke. But everyone was supposed to chant while Igwe Nwadike was leading and watching. The quiet meditation, when everyone was to think and see nothing, was supposed to be worse, though, but Okoye had used these times to catch up on his sleep or think about his future. That was before Igwe Nwadike caught a young man sleeping and sent him home.

But the torture would all pay off tomorrow when he received his red cap and the Otonsi. Okoye let the hole digger rest where it belonged. He sat on the bamboo bed and thought about his future and how he could not wait to join the ranks of those who told stories of their travels. Girls loved those stories and the wealth the travelers brought home. Wasn't he himself fascinated by the travel tales of Ojemba? Over the years, Okoye had developed a picture of Ojemba, the legendary traveler who was supposed to have lived at least three generations before their time. There were supposed to be many others of Ojemba's kind in those days, but Ojemba became a legend because he had told stories of his experiences in words, songs, and poems. He was a legend's legend because he had discovered the elusive city of Iji-putu that others before him had told about but could never find.

It was said that the trade city of Iji-putu, where human beings of all shades and colors came to trade, had been like a fairy tale until Ojemba discovered it. Legend had it that Ojemba made his will before he embarked on the expedition to solve the mystery of Iji-putu. He failed, though, not because he did not discover Iji-putu, but because he did not come back in thirteen moons, one year's period, as Nri rules prescribed. One year after his disappearance, full funeral rites were performed for Ojemba. A descendent of Nri must never remain on the road for more than thirteen moons. If he must be gone longer, a credible witness would have to have seen him alive during that time. No one had seen or heard from Ojemba in three years. Two moons after the third year, Ojemba returned on an Nkwo market day. And it was not just any Nkwo market day, but the last Nkwo market day before the new yam festival.

There were many routes that Ojemba could have taken to enter Nri land but Ojemba, the dramatist, entered Nri city through the Nkwo market. Of course, the trading stopped because everyone followed Ojemba to hear stories about Iji-putu, the end of the world.

Ojemba told tales of men whose hair ran from their heads to their waists. The women's hair ran to their knees and sometimes almost touched the earth. He told stories of a lake that sometimes froze during the cold season, and human beings could walk on it.

"One could crack a nut on the surface of the lake. Imagine that!" he said.

He told of an evil wind that went in circles and was so fast and strong that it uprooted everything in its path, including houses and iroko trees.

Ojemba might have solved the mystery of Iji-putu, but he created two more. He had made a stunning discovery at Iji-putu about the city of Timbukutu to the far north of Nri and another city called Fakadus to the northeast. According to Ojemba, the city of Timbukutu was more fascinating than Iji-putu because it had the largest market in the world, and it really was the end of the world. If one made any attempt to go farther, they would fall off the cliff. But the city of Fakadus was also special because it was the city of unlimited knowledge. It was called the city of magicians and wizards.

Okoye Nweri had absolutely no interest in magic or wizardry, but as he lay on his late father's bamboo bed, he imagined what the city of Timbukutu looked like. Would he be the one to discover it? Would he be the next one after three generations to stop Nkwo market from trading the way Ojemba did? Imagine that.

꙰ ꙰ ꙰

Okoye wanted what a typical young Nri man of his time wanted—to see the world they called Uwa lands. He wanted to acquire lots of wealth. This was the accepted way at Nri. The best minds were in trade and had been to exotic places like the land of Iji-putu. These travelers displayed trophies at their obus to prove where they had been. A priceless accomplishment was to discover an Uwa land where no Igbo man had been before. Okoye believed it was his destiny to discover one of these places. But ambitious young men like Okoye must conquer one obstacle first. They had to obtain the Otonsi ceremonial spear carried by Nri holy priests. It was their passport to the rest of the world.

In addition to their facial scarification, the bronze ceremonial spear identified the Nri priests as authentic agents of Eze Nri, for there were many fakes in those days. The Otonsi was a staff of immunity and their passport to all Igbo lands and Uwa lands. As an agent of peace, the holder of the staff was free from harassment and persecution wherever he went. But the staff meant even more in the business community. The Otonsi-holder's word was his bond. His words were taken at a face value, unquestioned. The Otonsi was an instant guarantor of credit. The holders of the staff were given credit even when the rest of the world had cash and was willing to pay a little bit more for the same goods.

To obtain the Otonsi, a young Nri man must become either an Ozo priest or the lower Nze priest. The cost was minimal to join the Nze priesthood, so most ambitious young men would rather do that. But it was the hard initiation training, the twenty-eight days of isolation with Igwe Okoyeocha Nwadike in the holy forest that discouraged many. During the initiation, Igwe Nwadike, now a desperate old man, would throw everything he had at them, hoping to mold his perfect emissaries of goodwill in those twenty-eight days. But most of the young men who graduated would never participate in a goodwill mission. Half of them would be on the road when their services were needed. Many others would make up all the excuses known to man as to why they must be excused. Only about ten percent would actually serve. The percentages were not good and were getting worse every year. Most of those who actually took part in goodwill missions were not native-born citizens. They were what Nri people called transplants—Nri people who gained citizenship by migrating to Nri after they were born and were deemed "Nri-want-to-be's" by the natives. They were brought to Nri mostly by unfortunate circumstances. Erike Okolo was one of them.

THREE

Call to Duty

The mood was festive the next day as the soon-to-be Nze priests gathered, wearing their ceremonial dress. An Ufie musical orchestra entertained outside the big Nri Temple of Justice. Ufie music was listen-while-you-work, soft but quick-paced and rhythmic. It did not require a lot of one's attention, remaining in the background as one was conducting business. The music had a way of building demands on the listener so that at some point the listener had to give in to it. One had to dance to it and get it over with. The older men and women had learned from experience and knew to go straight to the group and yield to it before trying to conduct important business. The Ufie music was sure to supply a festive and distinguished atmosphere while allowing the business at hand to go on.

Selected Ozo priests and Nze priests filled the Nri Holy Temple of Justice, some of them sponsors of the young men. Just outside the temple, a handful of people were dancing to the Ufie music. The big temple was filled to capacity and spectators stood all around it. It was a colorful, vibrant scene full of music, dancing, and noisy talk.

Just before noon, moments before the event was to start, Okoye Nweri stood at the entrance with his mother and Ozo Ikezuo, his paternal uncle. Okoye had on a blue robe and worn-out, but expensive, leather sandals that had belonged to his late father. But his neck beads, tourmaline beads, were borrowed from his mother. He held a palm frond in his mouth. He looked at the middle of the hall where the candidates sat on stone seats. Just then, Erike waved at him and pointed to the vacant seat next to him in the first row of seven. Okoye looked at his mother who motioned for him to go on. Only then did he notice that his uncle was already heading to the Ufie musical group to dance.

"You are almost late," Erike said as Okoye sat down.

"And I call it good timing."

"You look good," said Erike, admiring Okoye's outfit.

"So do you."

"Did you borrow your nice outfit from your uncle?"

"Don't tell the whole world what you did. They know already."

Just then the bronze bell started ringing. It was exactly midday and the sun stood directly overhead. The spectators who stood outside could no longer see their own shadows. The Ufie music had stopped. All eyes were on the King.

Igwe Nwadike was escorted into the temple by his chief priest and two male dwarves. One of the dwarves rang a bronze bell while the other carried Igwe's ceremonial spear. Igwe Nwadike wore a white vest. A large piece of white cloth was wrapped around him from his right armpit over the left shoulders. He wore a tall red hat with eight white-eagle feathers sticking out around it. His Alo-Nri, a human size long ceremonial spear, was stuck in the ground in front of him as he sat on his throne. Igwe Nwadike looked like a different man. He had a circle of white chalk around his left eye and he glowed. He was not the bald, bare-chested old man the young recruits had spent seven weeks with in the holy forest.

Okoye looked up just in time to see Igwe Nwadike pointing a lump of kolanut (a highly caffeinated fruit, the shape but half the size of an avocado seed) to the sky.

"Chi-Ukwu Keluwa (Big God, the Creator), come and share kolanut with us," he started. "Anyanwu na Agbara (God of Light and God the Perfect Spirit), come and share kolanuts with us. Igwe na Ana (the Heavenly Host and the Earthly Host), come and share kolanut with us."

He then called on all the major deities in Nri land to come and share kolanut. They were many, for each of the twelve villages had at least one. He called on Nri Menri (the council of all the ascended Nri Kings) to come and share kolanut. He called on the spirit of departed Igbo and Nri elders (Ndi Ichie) to come and share kolanut. But this was more than an invitation to share kolanut. It was an invitation to preside over the event that was about to happen. It was also a prayer meditation and chant designed to put everyone in a ceremonial mood and to uplift their spirits. Then he made a wish since all the holy spirits were present. He wished that all the evil spirits would be chased away into the evil wilderness so that the ceremony could go forth without hindrance. He wished for long and healthy lives for the participants and their families. He wished for many good things for the Nri clan and Igbo nation and their Uwa friends. He wished that there would be enough land and resources in Igbo land and Uwa lands so that everyone would be happy and no one would have cause to fight another. It was over half an hour before the kolanut was finally broken and shared among the participants. He peeled off the hearts of the kolanut and threw them on the ground. Those were for the invited spirits.

"It has been a very productive seven weeks," Igwe Nwadike began as pieces of kolanut were passed around. "Personally, I enjoyed it if for nothing else than to give me an opportunity to lose some weight."

This drew laughs from the audience because Igwe Nwadike was a very skinny man and one could not imagine his losing more weight.

"I know that you soon-to-be Nze men are not used to this kind of prolonged retreat. You will, with time, get used to it and even come to enjoy it. I can assure you that no one starts out liking it, especially the fasting part. But it is necessary in order to get in touch with your Chi (the God in You)."

"In a moment you will be ordained as Nze priests, and you will be able to enjoy all the privileges that come with that in Nri and Igbo land and beyond. But the real benefit is the place you will hold among the elders thereafter. But before that, you will be their agents on earth. Agbala will work through you. You must manifest its perfect nature here before the hereafter. That is your responsibility. You must embrace your responsibilities, and your rights will come to you naturally. Agbala will make sure that all your rewards are given to you. If anyone tries to deny you your rights, when they pay you later, which they surely will, they must pay with interest. Your pay is inescapable when you have done your work, for that is the law. That is not all. If your brother or your neighbor ignores his responsibilities, you can assume his too. Do not seek his rights, but I can assure you that he will slowly lose his rights to you. There is nothing you or he can do about it. It is the law of nature. You cannot say that it is your brother's responsibility, therefore you cannot assume it. An adult cannot be in the house while a she-goat gives birth while on its tether. You must free the goat whether or not it is yours or your brother's or neighbor's."

He told them to have a just attitude at all times. He told them to live a modest life. He told them to be fair to others but, at the same time, to not neglect their own needs. He told them to speak the truth at all times.

"Truthfulness is the number one virtue of the follower of Agbala. Agbala said that its follower may compromise on other virtues, but he or she may not and cannot compromise on truthfulness. That is how Agbala values honesty. You cannot be an agent of Agbala if you are a liar. As an Nze priest, you will be issued a free red hat. The color red symbolizes fire, and fire symbolizes Agbala. It is not a coincidence that Nze men wear red hats. So whenever you put that red hat on your head, you must remember that you are an agent of Agbala. You must remember that the red hat is not for fashion, even though it will look good on you. May the collective spirit of our ancestors, the spirit that is pure and holy, abide with you. May the Agbala, the spirit that is perfect, guide you and help you to conduct yourself to its liking."

"Iseee! (amen)," the congregation concurred. "Igwe! Igwe! Igwe!" the congregation kept shouting.

"Igwe" was used to address the Eze Nri. It meant heavenly one, the most high, or his highness. It was used to show his distinct position among ordinary men, the combination of his wisdom, his righteousness, and all that a human can be as a spirit in the flesh. He was the heavenly being on earth.

The chief priest blew on his horn, a black musical instrument made of a wild-bull horn. "Pu-Pu-Pu-Puuu! (Igwe!). Pu-Pu-Pu-Puuu! Pu-Pu-Pu-Puuu!"

The chanting of "Igwe!" filled the void while the Eze Nri made a transition to another phase of the ceremony. The next phase was the actual ordination of the new Nze priests.

A male dwarf, half the size of Okoye, rose and motioned to the first candidate to go forward. It was Okoye Nweri. Okoye stood up and waited for Ozo Ikezuo, his uncle, who was also his sponsor. Together they moved forward. The dwarf escorted Okoye and his uncle to the Isi Nze, the head of the Nze priests, who was sitting to the right of Igwe Nwadike. Okoye knelt down in front of Isi Nze. His uncle knelt beside him at his right side. As the Isi Nze took some ukpah leaves from one of the bowls and dipped them in the palm wine bowl, Okoye opened his mouth and stuck out his tongue.

The Isi Nze cleaned his tongue, saying, "The Agbala absolves you from all the lies that you may have told in the past. Go forth and tell no more lies."

He then dropped the used leaves in a basket on his left. The basket would be taken to the Evil Wilderness where both the baskets would be burned.

Okoye and his uncle stood up. The male dwarf escorted them to Igwe Nwadike where they knelt. Okoye opened his mouth and stuck out his tongue again. A male dwarf sat on his right holding two bowls.

"Are you willing to accept the Agbala and become its agent?" Okoye nodded in agreement.

"Speak!" his uncle barked.

"Yes! Our-Father, The Heavenly One," Okoye agreed.

Igwe Nwadike reached into a basket carried by another dwarf and took out a fresh bamboo ruler. Okoye stuck out his tongue again. Igwe Nwadike scraped some saliva from Okoye's tongue then spread the saliva on the Nne Offor Nri, the Nri log of justice.

"This is an agreement between you and Agbala. You must be its agent. You must be an agent of peace wherever you find yourself and at all times."

He lifted the Nne Offor Nri and gently tapped it on Okoye's head saying, "You are now the agent of Agbala. You must never tell a lie. May Agbala abide in you and lead you."

"Igwe!" Okoye and his uncle hailed simultaneously.

As they got to their feet, Erike and his sponsor, his adopted father, were waiting to take their place. It was only when Okoye sat down again that he noticed the Ufie music had been playing all the time. He felt like dancing. It was finally almost over.

The second and final phase of the ceremony had the same order as the first. Okoye was led to Igwe Nwadike by one of the dwarves. This time he went without his sponsor. He knelt down in front of Igwe Nwadike who placed a red cap on Okoye's head. Igwe jokingly told him to use his money to buy another hat if he wanted a spare. He gave him one Offor stick, the smaller version of the staff of justice—a stick half the length of his arm. But it was the third object that Okoye wanted more than the others—the Otonsi, the ceremonial spear of immunity. After giving him the Otonsi, Igwe Nwadike patted Okoye on the shoulder.

"You've done well, my son!" he said.

The congregation clapped.

"Igwe!" hailed Okoye with a broad smile on his face. He felt like dancing to the Ufie music and he felt like shouting. He turned to leave and saw Erike approaching with his father and lifted his Otonsi in salute. Erike managed a smile of congratulations.

Food and drinks were served after the last candidate had received his ceremonial items. Igwe Nwadike left as soon as he finished with the last candidate. But the Ufie music group continued to entertain the crowd who danced, ate, and drank into the late evening.

※ ※ ※

Four days after Okoye became a full member of the Nze priesthood, the male dwarf came knocking at Ozo Ikezuo's door as he was having supper.

"Igwe would like to see you," he said.

"Does he want me to come with you?" Ozo Ikezuo asked.

The dwarf said, "No, but he would like to see you."

Early in the morning, Ozo Ikezuo went to Igwe Nwadike's personal quarters, arriving even before Igwe had finished his daily morning meditations.

"I should have been more specific," Igwe Nwadike apologized. "It is nothing urgent."

"It is all good. I have nothing else planned for this morning."

"I have some questions about your nephew. I noticed him during the retreat. He seems like a good young man."

"Of course he is. He is my son."

"Tell me about him," Igwe said as a male dwarf handed him a wooden tray with two kolanuts in it.

"Is there anything in particular you would like to know?"

Igwe washed his hands in a calabash bowl and said a short prayer, holding up the kolanuts. He chewed on the kolanut and some alligator pepper as he spoke.

"Okoye did well at the retreat. He and his friend asked a lot of interesting questions. They seemed to have enjoyed the whole thing. Okoye has good manners."

"Of course he has good manners. He has our family blood in him."

"Does he have a giving heart? Does he like attending to others?"

"He has a good and generous heart if that's what you mean. I have not given it much thought. For this generation, I guess it depends on the level of giving. They all want to get rich and travel. He is no exception."

"I think that we can use him around here. He and his friend can welcome visitors and direct them."

"I will ask him about it. I think that he will make a good candidate for that. He is good with people and he does not hide his feelings. But it depends entirely on him."

"Of course it depends on him. He should not agree to what he is not comfortable with. But he and his friend seem to have enjoyed the retreat. It says a lot about a man's priorities."

"And what does it say about me?"

"Ozo Nwayoo, you are fine," Igwe said as he burst out laughing. "You are a fine man."

The Gentle Ozo was his title name. But he was not so gentle when it came to the annual retreats for Ozo priests conducted by Igwe Nwadike. He was one among many who always chose to pay the hefty fines rather than to attend. But he was also among the very few who could still be counted on to lead a goodwill mission.

❊ ❊ ❊

Igwe Nwadike had not noticed the two young men at the retreat until the third day. From then on, however, he watched every move they made. At first, he could not tell them apart. He thought they were twins. They were the same height and build, and their facial features were similar. But it was not long before he found the basic difference. Okoye had open teeth. He smiled a lot and it was a confident smile. Erike was introverted and looked almost sad. But he was the one who asked all the intelligent questions. So when Igwe Nwadike later found out that the two were not twins, he was not surprised. The real shock was that the two young men had met for the first time at the retreat. They acted as if they had known each other since birth. It was amazing.

Erike had definitely enjoyed himself at the retreat, and he must have inspired Okoye who appeared to have enjoyed it too. Igwe Nwadike was happy for the young men. He wished them the best of friendships. It was not until the installation event and seeing them together in their ceremonial dress that he started having ideas about them. What if he called both to duty? They could be his front people. They could receive and direct people at the entrance. They would be perfect for the position. And who knew, when they got older and learned the protocols, maybe they could lead delegations on holy missions. It was then that Igwe Nwadike started asking the questions that led him to Ozo Ikezuo.

❦ ❦ ❦

Why was it always Ozo Ikezuo who brought life-changing bad news and why was it always on an Nkwo market day? Okoye thought. It was also Ozo Ikezuo who had called him on an Nkwo market day, in the morning to be exact, and told him that Igwe himself was interested in him. Before Okoye could say anything, Ozo Ikezuo told him to sleep on the idea for one full week. Okoye was to give an answer on the next Nkwo market day. As Okoye left the meeting with his uncle, he saw a pattern. Right then and there, he vowed never to meet with his godfather/uncle again on an Nkwo market day, only on the day before or after.

It was very early in the morning on an Eke market day, one day after his uncle had expected an answer. The birds were already having a feast on an ogbu tree in front of Ozo Ikezuo's main entrance gate. They were singing their morning songs or their thanksgiving prayers, who knew? Just by their songs, Okoye could tell what kind of birds they were. He counted at least three different species as he tiptoed towards his uncle's main gate to avoid the bird droppings and whatever might be falling from the big tree. The moment he pushed on the heavy mahogany gate, carved with scarification patterns, he knew that someone had beaten him to the first meeting or, worse yet, his uncle had already left. He had hoped to be the first to meet with Ozo Ikezuo before any distractions. A few steps into the big compound, he heard his uncle's voice in conversation with another man.

"I have to go now. I will let you know how it went," the second voice said. Okoye recognized the voice before he walked into the obu. Nwangene was already standing as Okoye walked in. Okoye greeted both men and sat down.

"Sorry that I could not come by yesterday," Okoye started as soon as Nwangene left.

"No need for apologies, my son. Yesterday and today are still the same."

Okoye stood up, picked up a piece of kolanut from the bowl, and took a bite.

"About what you told me the other day," Okoye started, looking down at the floor. "It is good that you gave me time to think about it."

"It is always good to sleep on a big decision, because once you commit yourself it becomes difficult to eat your words."

"It was a very tough decision to make. But during our retreat with Igwe, he talked about fairness. He talked a lot about making compromises. I think that I will be able to serve him for some years, and then I can do what I would like to do. I think that it is fair. You said that you would like it to be my decision, but I would still like to know what you think."

"What you have said is good," said Ozo Ikezuo. "How many years do you have in mind?"

"I think that four or five years is good. I can add more. But the big issue for me is having a good understanding about the time. I would be free to do what I really wanted to do after that time, knowing that I would still be young enough to do it and enjoy it."

"Say no more. Four years is good, my son. You speak just like your father. Your father spoke his heart all the time. And I loved him for it. Our people loved him for it. He was ten years my junior, but I learned that from him. You have spoken your heart, and I will let Igwe know this evening. To tell you the truth, I think that he does not need someone really badly. I have a hunch that he developed some liking for you and your friend, Erike, during the retreat. I think that he just wanted to spend more time with you and give you his blessings. It is good that you are willing to spend that time. You did well! Congratulations!"

FOUR

The First Warriors

Erike had a special relationship with Ozo Okolo, his adopted father. Others in his age grade at Nri had their own huts. But at the age of twenty-three, Erike still slept in the hut attached to his father's obu; the hut served as Ozo Okolo's working area.

Ozo Okolo was a tall, very dark-skinned man with a long face and a big bold nose. He was known all over Nri for his ivory and woodcarving work. He had two other sons who were in their forties, but neither of them showed any interest in his carving trade until Erike came into their family. Ozo Okolo had had many apprentices, but now in his early seventies, he knew that Erike would be his last one; besides, Erike was his own son and considered the last child of the family so Ozo Okolo was inclined to teach him everything he knew about carving. Though they were attached to each other, both father and son had taken Igwe's request gracefully and Erike was actually looking forward to his first day as a servant at the palace.

The night before he was to go to the palace, Erike was lying on his bed but had not gone to sleep when Okolo knocked on his door with his walking stick.

"Are you asleep?" Ozo Okolo asked.

Erike said, "No," and opened the door.

His father held a palm oil lamp in his left hand and supported himself with one of his carved walking sticks in his right hand. In the middle of the stick he had carved what looked like his face and people always teased him about this. Some asked him how he knew what his face looked like. He usually reminded them that he didn't need to know, that he just needed to remember his father's face.

"I will be leaving very early in the morning to Nri Okpala village. I may not be back before you leave for Nri Ejiofor. You have already heard all I can tell you. You must be careful there. It is like a public square and everyone knows what is going on. I will not have to remind you to conduct yourself well because I know you will. The only thing I will add is to be careful how you relate to Igwe. He is an easygoing man and sometimes people close to him do not give him all the prestige due to the Eze Nri. I have seen that on some occasions. They treat him casually—like one of them. It did not please me when I saw it. Don't let his easygoing nature confuse you and take away any prestige due to his position. That is all I will add to the other things we talked about before. I will come up in the evening to see how you are doing and where you will be sleeping while you will be there."

"I heard what you said," replied Erike and wondered if it was too late for some other discussions.

"I have a question or two I would have liked to ask you before going, but since you will rise early, they can wait."

"No. I am not feeling sleepy at all. We can talk," replied Ozo Okolo, leading the way to the obu reception area. He shuffled his right foot twice on the floor to shake off dirt before placing the oil lamp on the dwarf wall. Erike, who had trailed behind, sat down first.

"I want to ask you about the Ozo Oganiru and Ozo Mkputu groups. Okoye Nweri told me about them. He said that Ozo Oganiru do not like Igwe and disagree with him all the time."

Then Erike told about the discussion he had had with Okoye the night before they were ordained Nze priests.

Ozo Okolo sat on his mud daybed leaning forward, supporting himself with his walking stick as Erike spoke. Ozo Okolo put the walking stick on the floor and leaned back, resting on the wall behind him. He drew a long breath and exhaled.

"Your friend is somewhat right. Ozo Oganiru priests are mostly big merchants. I am surprised that you have not heard about them before your friend told you."

"I have heard about them, but don't know what they do. I have never heard about Ozo Mkputu."

"Ozo Oganiru is like an association of Nri merchants. They seek to create abundance of wealth at Nri. Ozo Mkputu priests want to live the way they believed our forefathers lived—to go around to Igbo and Uwa lands and make peace and preach good behavior. They think that is what an Ozo priest should be. Igwe Nwadike used to be the leader of the Ozo Mkputu before he became Eze Nri. Because of this, the Ozo Oganiru disagree with him most of the time."

"But what do you believe? During our purification month with him, Igwe told us a lot of good things about our ancestors and how they lived. He sounded very believable. Did he make those stories up?"

"I don't know everything he told you, but I will tell you what I know. What I am about to tell you, you can tell your children that your father told you so. I am telling you because my father told me with his mouth. He said that his father told him and his father's father told his father. That is how it is handed down from thirteen generations, for that was how long Nri clan has been in existence. Do you understand how I positioned my mouth?"

"I do understand," said Erike with a nod.

"You said that you are not sleepy"

"I am quite awake."

"Good! You are going to repeat this to your children someday. Our people came from the Ama-Mbala River. I am sure that you have heard that before. I am not sure how much you know already, but I will tell you everything and you can add it to what you know.

"Our great father was Nri. He came from the Ama-Mbala thirteen generations ago to find Nri. Before that time, this whole place was a big bush. He did not commit a crime at Ama-Mbala. He did not leave his father's place out of disagreement. He came here because he had a vision to come and to build an ideal community where people from all tribes could feel at home. You asked me what I think Ozo and Nze priesthood should be, so I am telling you what my father told me.

Nri inherited powers from his father, Eri, who was visited and given powers by the Sky Gods. Nri inherited the power to give peace and wisdom to all people—Igbo and non-Igbo. Seven years after he came, the

Sky beings made him Eze and Igwe. Eze (King) is the supreme leader of all and Igwe means that he is the Sky beings' designate on earth. Through the instructions from the Sky beings, he created the Ozo priesthood. They would become his hands and feet and take peace and words of kindness and wisdom to all people because the Eze Nri couldn't leave his domain. He did not create them to build a market. But at the same time, he did not say to them, 'You cannot feed your family because you are a priest.' Do you understand how I positioned my mouth?"

Erike nodded. "I understand what you mean."

"Yes, priesthood is not an excuse to starve one's family. The first Ozo priests were his four sons and eight of his students. Twelve of them became the heads of the first twelve villages. Now we have fourteen villages, but it was originally twelve. Initially, he trained over one hundred Ozo peace warriors in ten years. But after that, it was said that old age was catching up with him, and many Igbo people were still coming to be trained and to be part of the new humanitarian movement. Because of this high demand, he created the Nze priesthood.

The Nze priests were to be Ozo priests-in-training. But Nri did not train them by himself. Every Nze priest was apprenticed to an Ozo priest until he was qualified to become one himself. Those men who did not wish to become Ozo priests because of the rigorous and difficult responsibilities could remain Nze priests for life. They would also remain the Ozo priest's lifetime disciple. They were ordained at their villages by Ozo priests, and all their priestly services were supervised by their Ozo master. His goal was to make every adult male living at Nri a priest of some sort. According to my father, the Nze priesthood was consecrated to Agbala, the God of Service, because they were considered servants of the people. And Nze meant guardians or protectors or shepherd."

"Is it true that Ozo means savers?"

"Yes. I was getting to that. Ozo means savers or saviors, and they were consecrated to The Light, Anyanwu. They were a brotherhood of high mystics—some called them magicians because they controlled what seemed uncontrollable. They were not herbalists, but they could use their spoken words to cure a disease. They could even cause disease if they spoke out of anger. In those days, Ozo priests were like Eze Nri and one could pick an Ozo priest at random. They could perform the duties of the Eze Nri without additional training.

This is what my father told me of our origin and about Ozo and Nze priesthoods. If I added or subtracted something, I did so out of error. What I am about to tell you is something I witnessed for myself. After thirteen generations, Igwe Nwadike is now the Eze Nri, number twenty-one. As you can see, we are far off from what I described to you because of a lot of misinterpretations. The association between an Ozo and his Nze apprentice today is economic and no longer spiritual. Most Ozo priests today cannot perform a single ritual—most employ someone else to perform the simplest ones. That is why Igwe wanted to change things when he became Eze Nri about twelve years ago. He knew that Ozo priests are too arrogant, so he decided to reshape the Nze priesthood first. He wanted to train and ordain Nze priests himself. He was desperate, but the Oganiru priests deceived everyone. They raised an unfounded alarm—saying that Igwe was planning to become a dictator." Ozo Okolo gave out a big mocking laugh.

"The man does not even dictate to his family and servants. I was just telling you how easygoing he is and people close to him take advantage of him. The Ozo Oganiru deceived everyone because, as we found out later, they were afraid that if Igwe ordained Nze priests, he could influence who chooses to become a merchant Nze priest or who chooses to become a traditional Nze priest. They deceived everyone and Nri nearly broke into fragments. But they met their match in Igwe Nwadike. Igwe is a sophisticated thinker and a master negotiator. He was the best diplomat we had before he became Igwe and those who wanted to break Nri up met their match. That is why a lot of people who knew what happened are worried because when he is gone, the next Eze Nri may not be as sophisticated in diplomacy and thinking as he is and Nri may break up. Some selfish people among us still have the desire to break us into pieces."

There was a long moment of reflection and Erike detected his father's uneasiness. He had never seen it before—it was like someone terrified of the future.

"Their selfish plans will not work," Erike assured his father.

"We all pray—we hope. You must go and sleep my son. This is enough for tonight. You should look rested tomorrow—your first day at the palace."

FIVE

Okoye Meets Nri Lake

It was noon. Okoye was all by himself at the entrance to the palace. He heard the bullhorn announcing that the noon hour had arrived. He gazed at the sun which stood directly overhead. He said a brief prayer, a phrase of thanksgiving, and three wishes. He lifted his right hand to heaven and opened his palm so it absorbed the sunlight. Then he rubbed the warmth around his chest. This was one of the few devotional practices he had learned since he started his training at the palace. It was supposed to warm his heart and inflame deep compassion for his kind. For another few moments, his vision was impaired by the sun, so he did not see the two men as they approached. They were already only a few steps away when his vision cleared.

They rode on separate horses. The dwarf dismounted first. He was smiling just like Okoye and he even had open upper teeth. Though he was half Okoye's size, when he spoke, the guards' shack seemed to vibrate. Like that of a bad masquerade, his voice was intended to intimidate.

"Do you know me?" The big-headed dwarf asked as his friend dismounted his horse.

It was then that Okoye realized who he was. The big voice and the fat head covered with four feathers gave Ezu away. Okoye had seen him just once before.

"Ezuuuu!" Okoye saluted. The man smiled.

"What is your name, son of Nri? You must be new around here, aren't you?"

"Yes, my name is Okoye, the son of Nwa-anyanwu Nweri of Nri-agu village. We are related to Ozo Ikezuo Nweri of Nri-agu."

"I know Ozo Ikezuo. I knew your father. May his soul rest in peace. I was at the funeral. He was a good man. What a tragedy it was."

"Yes. It was." His handsome partner spoke for the first time.

Okoye did not need to be introduced to his partner, Ugocha Nwoye. There was a saying at Nri that "If you give Ezu the first cup of wine then you must give the second cup to Ugocha Nwoye." They were inseparable.

"What are you doing here?" Ezu asked him.

"I am working for Igwe now. He hired me a few weeks ago. I am still in training though. Sorry it took me awhile to recognize you."

Ezu looked at his partner as if to say that the young man did not have a clue. Then he turned back to Okoye. Ugocha Nwoye smiled, a smug smile intended to belittle.

"He must be one of those," Ugocha Nwoye said.

When Ezu spoke again he looked straight at Okoye. There was no smile on his face, and his voice was deeper and even more intimidating.

"You are full of life. Don't waste it." He turned and started walking toward the Igwe's quarters.

"You are a native-born citizen," Ugocha Nwoye added. "You are not transplanted. You are the son of the land. You should be doing better with your life."

Ezu must have felt some compassion for the lost soul because he turned around and came back.

"I will be here for only four years. That was the arrangement," Okoye said apologetically.

"He reached a contract. The old man made him reach an agreement," Ugocha Nwoye said as he burst out laughing.

"Nwa-Nnaaa (lineage boy), your father is no more," Ezu stated. "You should be providing for your family. What you are doing is for people who do not have a future in Nri. You have a bright future. You are an authentic son of the land. Have you ever handled a horse before?"

"Yes. I have tied a horse before."

"Good. Go and tie my horse. It is an expensive horse. Don't lose it."

"Yeah. With what you are doing, you will work for thirty years before you can buy one," Ugocha Nwoye joked.

Okoye tied the horses as the men went into Igwe's private quarters, but he could not take his eyes off the dwarf. He was particularly interested in the way he walked. It was the famous Ezu walk. Even children who had never met him knew the Ezu walk—short, but very quick steps with arms swinging freely. But anyone could do that. It was the head nodding with every step that was unique.

The pair spoke to Okoye Nweri again after their business with Igwe Nwadike, and Ezu was even more specific with the young man.

"A man must honor his contract. But when your said contract with Igwe is up and you are ready, you should come to see me. I help people who are not even Nri people, how much more for an authentic son of the land."

"Yes. When you are very rich like your peers, you will bring expensive gifts to the Igwe. You will help pay for some of his upkeep. That is how it is done around here. Igwe will appreciate it more." Ugocha Nwoye added. Okoye could not wait! The most admired men in Nri land spoke his language!

🐦 🐦 🐦

Nkwo market was one of four in Nri land. Just like every other market in Nri and, indeed, Igbo land, the Nkwo market had a personality and a reputation for being loud and full of eccentric people. And it had its share of homeless drifters just like other markets. But what set it apart was that those drifters (or madmen, as some chose to call them) did not actually beg for food or money. They preferred to earn it. This was probably a tradition started by a handful of earlier drifters or perhaps one person, but it quickly became the norm at Nkwo market.

On a good Nkwo market day, one could hear the intermittent clamor. And a brand new visitor to the market who wanted to know what was going on would see a circle of shoppers being entertained by one or two drifters. The entertainment ranged from joke telling to singing to dancing and even to magic tricks. Some entertainers worked in groups.

The Nkwo market traded every fourth day, and the drifters had to make enough tips to last them between market days. No one really cared to know where these people came from. They were mostly Igbo and Uwa people who made no trouble. They just found it necessary to earn their living in this way instead of begging for it.

Another invention of the Nkwo market was a bar where palm wine was sold in cups. Nri People used to buy palm wine in pots and share it with friends or customers if they must drink in the market place. But a Nri man named Mengine decided to sell leftovers in cups at a highly discounted price instead of taking the extra wine home. He had no idea what he was inventing. On an Nkwo market day, people looked forward to the late evening activities at the palm wine section of the market. It was not the wine that drew them, but the politics and light gossip. Most of the patrons were new immigrants or visitors who had no network of friends in Nri, but some Nri people were drawn there too.

Today was an Nkwo market day and darkness was descending. The market was almost deserted. Bamboo and palm frond shades lay all over. The handful of traders still there scrambled to beat the inevitable night-fall. Homeless drifters moved to reclaim their territory for another three days, each selecting the best of the bamboo shades. Three half drunk men sat in one of the bars. One of the men was the bar owner and the only woman present was his wife. She seemed to be in a hurry like everyone else to beat the darkness. The men were not. They were in a heated discussion.

FIRST MAN: Ndibia-Ndibia (immigration) is not good for Nri people. It is bad for our culture.

SECOND MAN: But that is who we are. We accept anyone who is not an active criminal. We accept them even when everyone else rejects them. It is who we are.

FIRST MAN: A lot has changed since our ancestors laid down the rules. They certainly did not anticipate madmen filling our market places. They surely did not anticipate that one day the population of immigrants would be more than that of genuine citizens.

SECOND MAN: It depends on what you call genuine citizens. Anyone who is not causing trouble looks genuine to me.

FIRST MAN: That is wrong. Nri land should belong to Nri people. That is why we are losing respect all over. People don't know what to call us anymore.

SECOND MAN: You are completely entitled to your opinion, but that is not the majority opinion. That is not the opinion of our leaders, including the Igwe himself.

FIRST MAN: And who are the majority? Immigrants! Immigrants!! They are the majority. They populate the villages and they own the markets.

THIRD MAN (the owner): You are both right. There is always a common ground. There is always a compromise.

His wife reluctantly lit an oil lamp.

WIFE: I have to go now! I will send the kids to help bring home the rest of the items.

The third man helped his wife put a basket on her head. The first man refilled his cup. The second man filled his nostrils with tobacco powder and then sneezed.

THIRD MAN: Your life. Bless your life. Someone is invoking your name.

FIRST MAN: We should be doing better than we are doing at Nri.

SECOND MAN: It depends on what better means to you.

FIRST MAN: First, Nri land should be for Nri people alone. Then, we should be building big houses. We should be building big temples in every village and huge sumanga (large huts) for our leaders. Pave the roads with stones. Build big temples to honor the deities and the gods. Build them with the finest clays and stones and woods.

SECOND MAN: That is what you think. It is okay. But it is not the way of our people. We make peace among people. We cleanse abominations. We prescribe taboos and interpret them. We welcome all people and host them and make them comfortable. We do goodwill. Goodwill is us. That is our footprint. That is our destiny. That is our agreement with Chineke. We are responsible for all people.

FIRST MAN: Great temples and castles: they testify to great minds and great civilizations. They endure for a long time. They guarantee respect for our offspring. They guarantee respect for us from our offspring. Our offspring will say to their friends, "Look, our forefathers built this and that. They were great men." Charity and goodwill fade fast. They are forgotten as soon as one can provide no more. Generations of goodwill are not only forgotten, but the former benefactors come with vengeance. They are the first to point accusing fingers. They are the first to sack villages and burn houses. They are the first to take captives and make slaves of your offspring.

SECOND MAN: Then that is another reason not to stop. If we have the will, Chineke will surely provide the way.

FIRST MAN: I tell you, we should build great armies. We should impose heavy taxes on the Igbo and Uwa people who benefit from our wisdom. Big houses and horses for every Nri man.

SECOND MAN: And where would Chineke be in all of that?

FIRST MAN: Chineke is in heaven. He is always in heaven. There is peace and order in heaven. But we live in a jungle and we have to survive. Survival is the game. Survival! Survival!! Survival!!!

THIRD MAN: There is always a middle ground. There is always a compromise. Can't we have both? We surely can have both.

SECOND MAN: But our agreement with Chineke is first. Our blessings and respect are tied to it. So far we are doing a good job of keeping to the agreement. There is peace in Igbo land and with our Uwa neighbors. That is more important.

FIRST MAN: Forget Igbo people. It is even possible that we are not Igbo. I heard a rumor the other day, that Nri people may have come from somewhere else. We came from somewhere far off.

SECOND MAN: And where might that be?

THIRD MAN: From heaven, I suppose!

All three burst out laughing.

SIX

He Killed a Man

Okoye and Erike's training at Igwe's palace went well for both of them, but it went especially well for Erike. While Erike did his very best, Okoye did as little as he could get away with. Erike followed every instruction with precision. He put his heart and soul in his training. The only time he did not was when he did not understand what was expected.

Their training began with palace protocol. They learned what they could and could not do. They learned the classifications of different power groups and what each group could and could not do. They learned who could see Igwe and on what occasions, and who could interrupt Igwe's retreats and for what reasons. After completion of that part of their training, they progressed to spiritual instruction, starting with cosmology. In just three months, they could identify by name all of the major stars and their characteristics. They understood how those stars related to events at Nri. They were told the religious history of the Nri people and the Igbo people. They knew the relationships between Chineke (Creator God), Anyanwu (Light of the World), and Agbala (Perfect Spirit). They learned of other important stars that appeared once in awhile and that might bring judgment or healing.

The most advanced training took longer. It was about themselves as individuals and as spirits. They were taught different ways of meditating and what each type would do for them. They learned advanced chanting techniques and the art of star watching. They were shown how to pick a particular star, watch it, and romance it (think about it and nothing else for a long time). They practiced gazing at clouds and thinking about nothing at all for a very long time. They watched a single dot on the wall and nothing else for long periods of time. They practiced different ways of breathing to feel fresh and relaxed.

Erike did not need to be told what all that meant for himself, for he could feel it. In less than six moons of training, Erike knew the difference. He was a changed man. He understood that the twenty-eight days of retreat were nothing at all. He enjoyed every bit of it. At the seventh moon after he had started, he had gained so much self-confidence and calmness that he was beginning to wonder how people could live without daily meditation. Okoye was changing, too, but his mind was somewhere else. If given a chance, he knew where he would rather be.

It was late afternoon around the ninth month. The sun was going down. The breeze was sweet on the body, and Erike was alone in the holy forest. He had just completed what seemed like a two-hour meditation, and he was relaxing for awhile to collect himself. The wind was blowing hard enough to move the leaves around. Out of habit, he was staring at a bunch of leaves and a particular leaf grabbed his attention. He had no clue why. He must have stared at that leaf for several moments or so before he realized what had happened. All the other leaves had blown away except the one he was staring at. As soon as he took his attention away from it, the leaf started to move. He zeroed in on it again and it stood still. He looked away again and the leaf started to move! Erike repeated this little experiment several times and the result was conclusive. Then he started thinking about events that had happened in the last few days.

First was the palace monkey which was friendly to everyone except him. He had tried all sorts of tricks to win the monkey's friendship, but nothing worked. A couple of days before this, he had wished the monkey would just disappear. He was surprised the next morning to learn that Igwe had decided to give the monkey to one of the Ozo priests. When Erike asked why, he learned that the animal had become too big and that Igwe wanted a smaller monkey. And there were other incidents like the day before when Ozo Mmaduabuchi was coming towards him through the palace gate. The previous day Ozo Mmaduabuchi had given him an urgent message to give to Igwe and had told him that he would come back the next day for a reply. The next day, as Ozo Mmaduabuchi approached him, Erike realized he had not given his message to Igwe. Erike felt embarrassed and wished he could switch the time back so he could deliver the message and save himself. Suddenly, Ozo Mmaduabuchi turned around like someone who had forgotten something and did not come back until the next day. There had been other strange events.

Erike concluded that something was happening around him. He wanted to talk to the Igwe's chief priest. He had become friends with this priest who knew a lot about such happenings. But things did not work out as Erike had planned. Instead, he found himself alone with Igwe that evening. Since Igwe was in a light mood, he encouraged Erike to tell him about these occurrences. Erike did.

❦ ❦ ❦

With arms folded, Okoye stood outside the small guards' hut. The huge iroko tree provided shade from the late afternoon sun. It was one of those afternoons when there was little traffic to the palace compound. Okoye was deep in thought. Erike smiled as he snuck up behind him. If Erike had imagined that Okoye was thinking about some Uwa land where he would rather be, he would have been right.

"Okoye Udo!" Erike teased.

"You killed a man," Okoye replied.

Erike said nothing. Okoye did not like the name Okoye Udo (Okoye Rope). It was given to him by a wrestling rival he had thrown in a fight. It had been about ten years back when Erike and his rival were both in their teens although the other boy was older, heavier, and more skilled. Okoye had thrown him anyway. Okoye had not given his opponent a chance to use his skills. He had wrapped around him like a rope so they would go down together, but when they were falling, Okoye slipped free, leaving the teen to fall hard. His opponent nicknamed him Okoye Udo out of revenge. The name was given for his wrestling tactics, but it stuck with him for a different reason.

Okoye's body was all muscles and bones, or more like muscles wrapped around bones. In later years, everyone had forgotten about his wrestling. The name became all about his body. He hated his physique so he hated this name. He fought many times against it, but his peers still referred to him as Okoye Udo behind his back. He knew this, but he could do nothing about it. But those who dared use the name to his face made him swear that they would see their God while they were still living.

Erike was the only one who called him this name to his face, but only when no one else was around. Okoye wanted him to stop, but he didn't. Okoye decided to make Erike respond in anger, but he wouldn't.

Erike had made peace with his past.

"Didn't you hear me? I said you killed a man."

"I killed a lion too. With my bare hands, I might add."

"I heard that you used a knife," Okoye said. Erike chuckled.

"I heard also that you did not have a witness to that one . . ."

". . . and the man was not just a man. He was a giant," Erike said as he went into the guards' hut.

"OK, so you killed a giant. I will remember that next time."

Erike did not reply. Reflecting, he sat on a stone in the hut. Okoye finally joined him.

"How did it go?" he asked.

"I finally realized what it was."

"What?"

"I told you about the ticklish sensation that I feel whenever I am in Igwe's presence. I finally realized what it was."

"So, what was it?"

"I used to feel it as a baby only when I was in my mother's lap. I finally realized the connection between him and my mother."

"What is the connection?"

Okoye had practically forced him to tell Igwe. So that afternoon Erike had done so.

❦ ❦ ❦

"It looks like you are developing a wish power," Igwe Nwadike told him after hearing his story.

"It is good that you told me about it. It is not unusual with the type of training you are having. But it is unusual to develop this power in such a short time. It usually takes about two years of serious training. You must have been working very hard. But even that alone will not make it happen so quickly. I think that you have a very kind spirit. It takes a kind spirit and lots of hard work to achieve this so soon. I usually tell trainees how to handle wish power when they are close to two years of training, and still a lot of people do not attain it at all."

Erike didn't know what to say.

"It is a good thing. But you must never use it unless you absolutely have to, and you must never use it for selfish reasons. If you do, you will lose it, and a bad thing may happen to you. You must also abstain from making careless statements because they may come true. You must mean things when you say them," Igwe Nwadike advised him.

Erike always felt some bodily sensation, a tingling all over his body, whenever he was in the presence of Igwe Nwadike. It was the feeling he had when he was a child in his mother's arms, a feeling of comfort and security. He had always wondered about the connection between Igwe Nwadike and his mother. As a grown-up, Erike no longer had those feelings in his mother's presence. He felt them only when he was with Igwe Nwadike. On this occasion, the feelings came on strong, starting from his forehead, going down his spine, and then to the rest of his body. For a split second, Erike was a child again sitting on his mother's lap. He turned around to embrace his mother, but she was not there. Instead he saw Igwe Nwadike sitting across the room. And Erike was nowhere near his lap. The man was a good five footsteps from him, but Erike could still feel his magnetic force. Then Erike realized that the connection between Igwe Nwadike and his mother was the selflessness that both radiated. He realized that he was in front of a man who thought about the welfare of others more than about his own. This was the source of the deep comfort and security he felt—the kind that only a child feels while sitting on his mother's lap.

The question came out before Erike realized what he was saying. It flowed out of the moment.

"Can I ever achieve half the level of selflessness and care that you have for other people?"

He did not know a better way to ask the question. Erike wanted to know what motivated the man.

"I would be lying if I said that my actions are completely selfless. I am happy when our people are happy. I am sad when they are sad. So it is not completely selfless, because I am looking for personal happiness, too. But, unlike most people, I have deliberately tied my happiness to that of the people. That is the only way to guarantee that your happiness does not depend on another's pain. Have you ever seen someone who was sad and you made him happy?"

Erike nodded.

"If you do that, next time this person will be happy to see you. It is a feeling that I cannot describe to you. You get this feeling when you know that a lot of people are happy because of you. They will always look forward to seeing you. You know that you genuinely care about them and you know that they know that. You also know that they genuinely like you and the liking is mutual. It is almost addictive, so you want to keep them happy so your own happiness will last. It is something that you have to feel to understand. It is like the love between a mother and child. You have to feel it to understand it."

Did he say mother and child? Erike wondered.

"But I must tell you that there is a small percentage of people you can never make happy. You will do everything you can, but you cannot succeed. You will be very disappointed to discover that their happiness comes only from your unhappiness. It is very disappointing. There is nothing you can do for those people because they deliberately tie their happiness to your unhappiness. If you can identify them, sometimes you can fake being unhappy so they will be happy. But at other times, you just can't help them. There are very few of them. Some people call them bullies and others call them antisocial. I call them troubled spirits."

Erike nodded, allowing this information to flow in freely.

"There is one more thing you must understand, Our Son. If you are making people happy who would otherwise be unhappy, you must be spiritually strong. This is because people who are sad are usually sad for a reason. There are forces that want them to be sad. So if you make them happy, those forces will come after you. The more people you try to make happy, the more negative forces you will have lined up against you. That is why we try to be in holiness state or spiritually strong at all times. That is our armor against those negative forces."

Erike was nodding all the time. He did not know about negative forces yet, but he definitely knew about bullies.

꙰ ꙰ ꙰

"You must miss your family. I mean your mother," Okoye said to Erike after listening to his account of his meeting with Igwe.

"I do miss my homeland, if that is what you mean. I do miss my blood people. But Nri is my home now, and I have a new family who cares about me as much as my other one. It is my akalaka (destiny) that brought me here. You have to follow your path, you know."

It was indeed destiny that had brought Erike to Nri seven years before. Since coming to Nri, Erike had played out different scenarios of the unfortunate event that made him an outcast. One scenario looked as distasteful as the other. So he had come to accept his akalaka. Erike had done well with his second chance at the holy land. He had a full-face scarification that brought him honor instead of the partial scarification that had brought him the wrong kind of attention. He had the Otonsi Nri staff of immunity to prove that he had done well at Nri. And he had unrestrained access to every door in the most respected compound in Igbo land. He had done well with his second chance at life. The man had every reason to be thankful.

SEVEN

The Needy

Every morning, come rain or haze, a group of Ozo priests met at a small temple in a forest behind Ozo Nwabia's compound. Sometimes the assembly would be as small as five. But a very good turnout could number as many as fourteen. Most of the time, Ozo Nwabia, their leader, whom everyone called Akalaka (Destiny), led the morning chanting and meditation. When the meditation was over, the men blessed and shared kolanuts. Then they told old stories about creation or ancestry or heroism while they ate.

They were all Ozo-Mkputu priests, a sect within a sect. They were the fundamentalists among the Ozo sect for they practiced the middle ways. They were spiritual but not so spiritual as to neglect their physical obligations. They were successful farmers, craftsmen, and traders and, yes, even long-distance traders. But whatever they did to keep body and soul together had to accommodate their commitment to goodwill. Their trade revolved around their obligations to the King of Manifestation.

Right after Nri, the founder of the Nri clan, died thirteen generations before, many schools of thought emerged at Nri among the Ozo priestly sect. Some preached total spirituality. There were many in this group, but the most notable, and perhaps the most extreme, were the Ozo-Mkpaa priests. They preached imitation of Nri. They believed an Ozo priest must marry as early as possible and have as many children as possible. He must then abandon all his children to his wife or wives and Umu-nna (Communal Family) and go into seclusion for the rest of his life. In seclusion, he must dedicate himself to total spirituality and goodwill missions. He must own no barn or farm but live on gifts from clients. At first, the Ozo Mpkaa sect flourished among the rest of the Ozo sects, but it died a quick death after less than two generations.

The elders believed that one extreme gave birth to the opposite one. They said that this was nature's way of finding a balance. This was very true about the Ozo-Mkpaa sect. Just as Ozo-Mkpaa was dying, a new school of thought emerged. It was even more radical, but it was the complete opposite of Ozo-Mkpaa thinking. Its members called themselves the Oganiru (Forward-moving or Progressives). Ironically, the Oganiru sect was founded by an abandoned son of an Ozo-Mkpaa priest. His name was Okeke Igodo, the son of Igodo Abba. Okeke Igodo preached a message of providence and abundance. To him, those things testified to his neighbors that he was doing something right. It was abundance, not poverty, that proved the Gods were with him and that he had peace within. To Okeke Igodo, the peacemaker did not have to wander for weeks like some homeless lamb. A peacemaker did not have to neglect his family in the name of spirituality or goodwill. All he needed to do was live in abundance and peace, and his lifestyle would resound far and wide so his neighbors would then seek to imitate him.

At first, his preaching was considered absurd, perhaps a joke. But Okeke Igodo practiced what he preached and his disciples practiced what he preached. It was they who discovered horses and who wore shiny, imported exotic clothing that made the news among the Igbo people and their neighbors. It was they who lived in style, and not the ones who wandered like homeless lambs, who invoked reverence among their neighbors. It was they who took good care of the material needs of their children, thus attracting the attention of the younger generation at Nri.

The Ozo Mpkaa sect did not stand a chance, so it died quickly. The only real remaining competitors were the Ozo-Mkputu priests. Their message of balance was classic as well as doable. So, for about ten generations, the psychological warfare between the Oganiru and Ozo-Mkputu raged on. But, by looking at the numbers, one could tell who was winning. The Ozo-Mkputu had fourteen members. The Oganiru had fifty-eight and could easily have doubled that figure if they hadn't raised their membership requirements. The rest of the Ozo men, about sixty percent, seemed to be neutral, content Ozo priests, though they were actually pawns used by both sides to get at the other.

The Ozo-Mkputu sect was home to Igwe Nwadike. He had been their leader before he became Eze Nri. Just before his coronation journey started, he had handpicked Akalaka, his former student, to lead the Ozo-Mkputu. So, as Eze Nri, Igwe's most trusted allies were Ozo-Mkputu priests. At a time when Ozo men were full of themselves, Igwe Nwadike could count on Ozo-Mkputu priests to deliver for him. But the Eze Nri must be above preferences and partisanships. He must not appear to favor anyone. So Igwe Nwadike kept his distance from the Ozo-Mkputu priests. Once in awhile, however, he would come across a young man who might be a good fit as a student for an Ozo-Mkputu priest, and he would arrange for an introduction. That had been the case with Okoye and Erike. Their introduction to Akalaka came in the form of an Ifu-Ije (missionary field work). They had heard enough about the needy. It was time to go to into the field with Akalaka to see, touch, and feel what the work was all about.

❋ ❋ ❋

Igwe Nwadike called Okoye and Erike "the twins" and sometimes pretended he could not tell one from the other. He would walk up to them at the palace main entrance or at their quarters and ask "Which one of you is Okoye?"

Okoye would point at Erike and Erike pointed back at Okoye. If a third party was in their midst, Igwe Nwadike would ask this person to tell him the truth because he knew those two were fooling him again. The third person sometimes decided to get in on the joke and pointed at the wrong person. When this happened, Igwe Nwadike would bend his head to the left and stare at the third party out of the corner of his eyes for a few moments as if he was not sure if he should trust him.

"Nwokie (Their Man), are you fooling me too?" he would finally ask.

He called almost every male Nwokem (My Man) when he was pleased with them and Nwokie (Their Man) when he was not pleased. Likewise, he called almost every woman Ada-anyi (Our Big Sister) when pleased, and Ada-fa (Their Big Sister) when he was not.

So, this mid-morning, Erike was walking up to the palace entrance when he and Igwe passed each other.

He greeted Igwe with "Our Father, Igwe."

"Eyee, my son," he answered.

"You will live long."

"And you will live longer than your Father."

Erike had walked several steps past him when Igwe called him "Nwo-ken." Erike turned. "Go and call your twin and come with him," Igwe said without turning.

Erike and Okoye found Igwe sitting on one of the ogwe that visitors to the holy forest sit on to reflect. He looked like a statue of an Ikenga in thought. He wore a deep blue cloth loosely wrapped around his body and running across his shoulders. He munched on something. In his left hand was a small cocoyam leaf which he carried like a bowl. "The twins" did not have to be told what he had in the cocoyam leaf. They knew his favorite snack. When they reached Igwe and Okoye greeted him, Igwe extended the cocoyam leaf the way one would offer kolanuts to his visitors. Erike took two small garden eggplant and one fresh green hot pepper, avoiding the red pepper. Okoye took one garden egg pulp.

"Pepper is good for you," said Igwe Nwadike. "It helps your digestion."

"I don't have a digestion problem, Our Father," Okoye said as he chewed on his egg pulp.

"Do you know what Ifu-Ije means?" Igwe asked Okoye.

"Of course, it means going on a trip," Okoye said looking at Erike in surprise at what seemed like a stupid question, or, more likely, a question meant as a trap. Everyone at Nri should know that Ifu-Ije meant going out on a trip.

"Going on a trip, going on a trip," Igwe Nwadike repeated twice to himself as if trying to make sense of his answer. "Going on a trip to do what?"

"It means going on a trading mission," replied Okoye.

Igwe Nwadike shook his head, not in disagreement but in amazement, before pointing to the seat on his right for Okoye.

Turning to Erike, "Nwokem, what does Ifu-Ije mean?"

"I think it means going on a peace mission," said Erike.

Igwe nodded in half approval and pointed to his left for Erike to sit. Okoye folded his arms. The air was cold and, although the morning fog was disappearing, one could not make out a face twenty footsteps away. Okoye did not fold his arms because of the cold but was bracing himself for another round of unending lecture.

Will it ever end? he thought. And just like a true twin, Erike knew what Okoye was thinking. He smiled in his mind.

"Nwokem, your answer is too broad. Ifu-Ije is a peace mission, but it is a specific kind. It is a non-quick-feet goodwill mission. It is a routine mission, sort of a touching-base mission. It is different from a Gbata-Oso mission. Gbata-Oso is a quick-feet-response mission. In Ifu-Ije, you may meet an emergency and you will attend to it, but it is not an emergency mission. In the old days, each Ozo priest and his Umu-Ukwu (disciples) would choose their favorite villages. They would routinely visit those villages, staying at least one week there. When leaving, they would usually tell the people when they would came back for another visit. Sometimes they might meet an emergency and attend to it, but that was not the purpose of the mission. During the visitation period, they would perform various services before moving on to the next village, and they would answer any questions the villagers might have.

Sometimes they would settle a dispute between a husband and wife or within a family or a village. Sometimes they would interpret moral laws or prescribe a new one in the face of a unique situation. This experience is especially good for young men like you because you will hear some personal stories and learn some things about yourselves and your heart, and you will be touched."

There was a brief moment of silence while Igwe Nwadike paused to reflect.

"When I was a young man like you, I believe it was during my second or third Ifu-Ije mission when I was a disciple of Ozo-Mkputu Nwana at Adagbe village, a whole village was distressed over what had happened a month before we came. Before that, I had known very little about childbirth. It happened that a young woman was having a baby and the baby came out sideways. One leg and one arm came out first and the rest of the body got stuck and could not come out. The poor woman was in labor for two days. By the end of the second day, she was barely alive. They decided to kill the baby so the woman could live. They killed and dismembered the baby before bringing it out. But, after that, the whole village was distressed and divided. That was when our people still had a conscience. Anyhow, when we arrived, they wanted to know if they had offended Earth Goddess by this action.

"Of course, they had done the right thing based on the options they had. But killing a human being, even under humanitarian grounds, is forbidden by Aja-Ana so we had to perform a cleansing ritual to appease Aja-Ana. That one incident changed something in me. I thought for months about the child who had been killed to save the mother, wondering if there was anything they could have done differently to save both mother and child."

Igwe Nwadike was a crafty storyteller, knowing when to pause and allow his audience to reflect on his story. As he paused, he wondered what Okoye was thinking.

"You will be going on an Ifu-Ije mission with Akalaka. He was one of my disciples. He learned well. You may be gone for a month or more. You will hear very personal stories and you may be touched. He will tell you when to be ready. He will give you at least one week to prepare."

As they walked back to their quarters, Okoye was excited about the Ifu-Ije and was looking forward to it. After so many months at the same compound, he needed anything that would take him away for awhile. Besides, in all his life, he had never slept away from Nri. He looked forward to seeing the Igbo mainland.

❦ ❦ ❦

Okoye was to soon find out that going for an Ifu-Ije had a bad name and reputation at Nri. When a perfectly good and noble tradition, such as the Ifu-Ije, was about to die off, it was sometimes given a bad name by those who opposed it. But the phrase had gained an even more demeaning stigma in Erike and Okoye's generation because it suggested a manual chore (a no-brainer). In the villages, they called it Kwa-Nkwo (every Nkwo). The phrase was invented for those teenage boys who had to baby-sit their younger siblings while their mothers shopped on the Nkwo market days. Because those boys were not free to do anything else on market days, their peers called them Kwa-Nkwo or Ore-Nnwa Kwa-Nkwo (babysitter every Nkwo). Over the years, the Oganiru, who had transformed the meaning of Ifu-Ije to mean trading mission, had to invent another name for this mundane missionary work. They nicknamed it Kwa-Nkwo and it stuck. The name suggested not only unexciting routine, but also lazy, un-heroic, and half-brained for those who ventured into it.

Oganiru priests did not disapprove of all missionary work though. They approved of the Gbata-Oso missionary work because it was good for their trading business. To them, the emergency response was as heroic as teenage boys who dare to put out a house fire during the harmattan season. It was a quick and brave chore and took as little time as possible and, most important to them, it involved no long-term commitment. On top of that, the teenagers would become instant heroes all harmattan season long or maybe all year long or even for life. The family whose house was saved would be eternally grateful. People who heard about the event would talk about the son of so-so and so or the children from the village of so-so and so who fought and subdued a house fire during the harmattan season, just as Igbo people talked about an Nri priest who put an end to full-blown warfare.

"How did they do it?"

They would lift their shoulders and lower them in amazement.

Having heard about the sharp contrast between Ifu-Ije and Gbata-Oso missions, Okoye secretly wished for a Gbata-Oso mission and was looking forward to the adventure that would take him out of Nri for awhile. But he also figured that if he must waste four years of his life, he might as well make the best of it. Serving as a personal assistant to Igwe would be good for business in the future. It would definitely add to his credibility, but actually participating in a holy mission would be invaluable. It was one thing to carry the Otonsi Nri around as an agent of peace, but it was quite another to actually participate in a peacemaking mission with the best that Nri could offer.

Yes. It would be invaluable. Okoye rehearsed different scenarios in his head. He imagined how he could slip his adventures into a trading conversation in the future. He would casually mention the peace he helped make in so-so and so village. *Nothing big though, just one of those side chores Nri holy priests did and still do.*

It would be good to learn all the procedures and secret languages. As a child, Okoye had heard that there was a secret process and particular coded language those "backward moving" old men used to fool or intimidate their clients into accepting a compromise for peace. Of course, he knew that some of them were just "maybes." But he also believed that there might be some truth behind them. Okoye could not wait to learn those secret languages.

When the long-awaited assignment finally came fifteen days after they were told to prepare for it, his prayers were answered, for it came as an emergency mission. But it was not the kind Okoye wished for. Okoye expected a dramatic beginning of full-fledged warfare, warriors to warriors, eyeballs to eyeballs, spears and arrows and machetes drawn, each side ready for full-scale combat. He visualized the other warriors, the warriors of peace (Okoye included, of course) coming between the savages and waving their magic wands, the Otonsi, and saying the magic words: "Stop it! Right now!" He visualized them speaking in some coded language. In his mind's eye, he saw both sides dropping their arrows and machetes, the warriors of peace having once more saved the savages from mutual destruction.

Okoye's daydreams were not to be, for when their assignment came, it was in the form of a cleansing ceremony.

The stupid cleansing ceremony! The undignified cleansing ceremony! The stinking feet-washing cleansing ceremony! Did it get lower than feet washing for an Nri priest? And if his facts were correct, it was the newest priests among the peace delegates who did the actual washing! When their assignment came, they did not say it was regarding a he or a she but they. *And "they" did not mean a family but an entire village! That was definitely too many feet to wash!*

Their Gbata-Oso assignment was to the village of Umuaku who believed their ancestors had killed a medicine man two generations before. The medicine man, according to them, had the most powerful Omalanko shrine as his patron deity. Omalanko deity, "The Bone Collector," had killed six people already and had vowed through divination revelations to kill two more every other week until its demands of two human sacrifices were met. Akalaka and his disciples were to perform a cleansing ceremony for the entire village, and part of this reconciliatory ceremony was to wash the hands and feet of everyone in that village. This would absolve them of their forefathers' sins and shield them from Omalanko.

EIGHT

The Adventures

Their entourage to Umuaku village included Akalaka; two long-term disciples, Ike, a dwarf, and Nweke; and two temporary disciples, Okoye and Erike. The clients from Umuaku who had invited them were Umeadi, Okpala, and Ayoh. Their three-day foot journey to Umuaku started before the cock's crow on an Eke market day.

Their first break stop was at Oye market at Akamkpa. After walking all morning, Okoye was hungry and tired. The Oye market was large and connected to many trading routes. Trading was supposed to take place every fourth day like other markets, but, because of its strategic location, this one traded every day. It had become a preferred resting place for many travelers.

Akalaka and his men had just settled down under a mmimi tree (sweet pepper tree) close to the market's entrance. Okoye wanted to lie down on his back and rest for awhile. He had just lain down and covered his face with his raffia hat that served as his sunshield when he heard the greetings, "Nri-is-Holy! Nri-is-Holy!" Okoye did not move until he heard the strange conversation that followed the greeting.

"I have very good news for you," the voice said. "The spirit wants me to tell you that your journey will be without any hindrance. You will have obstacles, but they will be nothing to worry about."

When Okoye opened his eyes, the speaker was already sitting next to Akalaka. He did not look like a madman so Okoye was still trying to make sense of it all when the man introduced himself.

"My name is Nwama," he said, stretching out his hands. "The spirits put me in charge of this market to make peace. Can't you see how peaceful it is? Can't you see that we are brothers in peace? Now I hope you don't mind if I share in your lunch. I have not eaten since last night. I feed off of people's goodwill because the spirits do not pay me, you know. They just tell me what to do. And now they want me to eat with you and receive your blessings," he concluded.

Okoye covered his face with his hat again so that Akalaka would not see him laughing.

"You certainly can join us for lunch," Akalaka replied. "And you also have all my blessings. Since you are a brother in peace, may peace follow you wherever you go, and may the spirits who sent you continue to protect you and show you where to feed."

Okoye felt a little guilty for his initial reaction and wondered if anyone had noticed it. Since Ike was bringing out the food, Okoye got up to help him. They had planned to rest a little before eating and then rest again before moving on to the next village. But, because Nwama asked and Akalaka agreed, they would have lunch before resting. This arrangement sounded better to Okoye.

Ike brought out the wrapped balls of food which Okoye opened—three wraps of roasted yam tubers and one of dried fish. Erike mixed the palm oil sauce with salt and lots of powdered red-hot pepper. In the middle of all this, Ayoh, the youngest of their clients from Umuaku, rose quickly like someone who had suddenly remembered his yam tuber was over-baking in the fire. He headed towards the closest shrubs but never got there. He threw up along the path. When he finally reached the shrubs, he bent down and threw up a little more. Okoye was the only one who went to him.

"Are you not feeling well?" Okoye asked, patting him on the back.

"I will be fine," he said.

Okoye was the only one who did not know why Ayoh was vomiting. He did not know because he had not seen Nwama approaching them. When Okoye had finally removed his raffia hat from his face and gotten up, Nwama had already sat down for lunch. His right ankle was covered by his garment so Okoye had not seen the open sore that covered most of Nwama's ankle. Okoye did notice all the flies but did not make a connection until the middle of lunch. When Nwama adjusted himself he accidentally exposed the ankle. Then the flies besieged him. Now Okoye understood the rotten odor that had intensified when he escorted Ayoh back to the group. Okoye had accidentally changed his seating position and ended up next to Nwama. Even though the smell was coming from human flesh it was like that of an animal that had been dead for weeks. The sore had been untreated for a very long time. The Igbo people called it lifetime sore. But the fact was that it did not go away because it had not been properly cared for.

Okoye became nauseated and could not fight it. He had just eaten so his vomiting was much more than Ayoh's. He threw up next to his food and in front of everyone. This was the end of the long-awaited lunch for everyone except for Nwama. He finished eating as if nothing had happened. And, indeed, as far as he was concerned nothing had happened. He had been living with this sore for years. The sight of it, the flies that followed him, and the smell were all normal to him. This had been his life and he believed it probably always would be. Most people with this kind of sore usually died eventually from it.

Nwama finished his food in silence, then got up quickly. "Nri-is-holy! Nri-is-holy! I thank you for your kindness. I wish you a very safe journey. As I said, there will be danger on the road, but it is not meant for you. Nri-is-holy! I greet you."

Nwama turned to leave, but then hesitated and scratched his head.

"Do you mind if I take the leftovers? I know you don't need them."

Ike was quick to respond. He waved at the food, a gesture for Nwama to take it. Erike dumped sand on top of Okoye's mess to cover it up. Nwama helped himself to the abandoned food that was right next to the vomit.

He had already walked several steps away when Akalaka spoke. "It is always good to share a meal with a stranger, especially when they ask for it. It is a good omen."

When he looked up, Nwama was already disappearing into the market. Only then did it strike Akalaka. It was not compassion because compassion struck Nri people at the lower left of the chest. It was guilt. Guilt struck Nri people at the lower right of the heart. It felt like a big hole had been drilled below his heart and the juice was emptying out through it.

How had he not thought about it until the last moment? Since when had he become so hardhearted? What had gone wrong? He used to help every single person in Nwama's condition that he had encountered. That used to be the standard for all Ozo and Nze priests. Maybe there were just too many people in need or maybe there were too few of his kind left at Nri.

"Go and call him back. Our Brother in Peace, call him back," he instructed Erike, making a hand gesture in the direction where Nwama had disappeared.

When he returned with Erike, Nwama was holding tightly to the ball of food which he had wrapped up in fresh green banana leaves.

"Sit down," Akalaka told him, pointing to the space next to him. Nwama sat down, but his eyes shifted from face to face as if he were searching for some clue. He pointed to Ike.

"He said I could have them. I knew you were going to throw them away. He said I could have them."

"I will show you how to dress your wound," Akalaka stated pointing at Nwama's right ankle.

There was a pause. Nwama looked at his ankle as if he were seeing the sore for the first time.

"What I will show you, you must do every morning, and your wound will heal very soon."

"It does not bother me at all. It is not a problem to me. Nri-is-Holy! I thank you for the food," Nwama said, making some movement to get up.

"Sit down!" commanded Ike.

"I promise that it will not be painful," Akalaka assured him.

Nwama nodded in agreement.

"How far is the stream from here?"

"It is not too far. Just down the valley."

"Good. First you must rinse the wound with water every morning. Do not rub it. Just go to the stream and pour some water on it to rinse the surface."

"Do not put your feet in the drinking water or the villagers will kill you," interrupted Ike.

"Fetch some water and then go to the dry ground away from the drinking water. Do you understand?" said Akalaka. Nwama nodded.

"Good. After you pour water on the sore, find this leaf." Akalaka went to the shrubs and fetched some leaves. "Can you recognize them tomorrow? This particular leaf?"

"Yes. My people call it the 'night plant.'"

"Good. Some people also call it 'shy plant.' The leaves open up at night, but as soon as daylight comes they shrink. You should grind them between your palms until you see foam and liquid coming out of them. Squeeze out the liquid and cover the entire surface of the wound with it. If you want to, you can throw the chaff away. But you can also cover the surface with the chaff. That is all you need to do and it is not painful. Today we are going to cover it with the chaff. Any fly with patches on it will die instantly. So you do not have to bother about flies any more. Can you do this every day until it heals?"

"I will do it if you promise that it will go away," said Nwama.

"And I give you my promise. It will heal in the name of Agbala!"

"Nri-is-holy! I thank you for your kindness," Nwama said as he got up.

"And next time I will find you and we will share lunch together. OK?"

"That's right, Nri-is-Holy. That's right." He adjusted his ball of food beneath his left armpit and made a half bow to Nri-is-Holy. He made another bow to the dwarf who had given him the food. Then he disappeared into the market.

Akalaka washed his hands and dried them on his garment. Then he sat down next to the mmimi tree and leaned his back and head on the trunk. He closed his eyes for a needed rest. But his own words came back to haunt him. *And I give you my promise. It will heal in the name of Agbala!*

But he made me do it, he thought. *He made me commit in your name, Agbala. Please do not disappoint this poor son of yours, Agbala. He has enough problems already. Please heal his wounds according to his agreement with your servant.*

It would take a few more moments before Akalaka dozed off.

He heard the voice in his dream first. He dreamed he met Nwama wandering at a stream. Though Nwama was in the stream, he was dirty and smelly and complaining of thirst. Akalaka gave him water and he drank. He washed Nwama's body and dressed him in fine clothing, but Nwama did not seem to like his new look.

"What have you done? What have you done to me?" he yelled.

When Akalaka opened his eyes, Nwama was rushing at them from the market.

"What have you done? What have you done? What have you done to me? What have you done to me?" Nwama kept yelling.

A crowd of market women and men were behind him. Okoye, who had also been awakened by the noise, did not understand the reason for the commotion. None of them understood until Nwama stopped in front of Akalaka and pointed to his right ankle. "What have you done to me?"

The chaff from the green leaves had fallen off and what had been an open sore was dry and shiny and a slightly lighter color than the rest of his skin. It looked like a scar from a healed fire burn. Akalaka seemed to be in shock himself, even more than Okoye. Akalaka got down on his knees to get a closer look. He touched the surface of what had been the open sore.

"Can you feel it? Can you feel pain as I touch it?"

"Just a little."

"Did you feel pain before now?"

"It used to hurt like hell when wind blew on it. Now I can hardly feel it even when you press hard."

"This is magic!," a man yelled from the crowd that had circled the mmimi tree.

"No," said another. "It is called a miracle. It is a miracle."

"What is the difference?" asked a woman. "The man is cured, is he not?"

"That is the difference. With a miracle, you cure people. With magic, you entertain people," said the second man.

The travelers did not get their needed lunch or rest with the crowd watching their every move as if they were open-market magicians. So they had to leave in haste. As they were walking out of the market, Akalaka had no doubt that this mission would definitely be his last. In over fifty years of being a missionary, he had seen a lot of miracles. After his blessing, he had seen barren women become pregnant at a very old age. He had seen hopeless illnesses healed—lots and lots of them. He had seen breakthroughs in peace mediations when all hope had failed.

A critic would attempt to explain each of these incidents. They were all miracles that only believers could recognize as so. But he had never seen one that even a non-believer would recognize even though that person might call it magic. *He had never seen one that would qualify as magic! Yes, magicians!* That was how critics described their forefathers. He had often wondered what he was not doing right. He had lived the way he had heard that the forefathers lived but had never seen any of the magic he had heard they performed.

"How did you do it?" One of the temporary disciples interrupted his thoughts. It was Okoye.

"Do what?"

"The magic, Our Father. Can you teach us how you did that one?"

Akalaka lifted his red cap and wiped sweat from his bald head. He smiled. "When for fifty years you have done all the things we will do in this mission and enjoyed every bit of it then no one will need to tell you how to do it. Some things require no explanation."

❦ ❦ ❦

They had walked for half an hour when they saw the huge snake. At first Okoye thought it was a big tree branch sticking out of a bush on the side of the road. But as they approached, it kept getting longer and longer. By the time they were several footsteps away, the snake covered half of the wide road. Then the creature saw the intruders for the first time. It stopped and lifted its ugly head, gazing at the men for what seemed like an eternity. Though its head was huge, its body was even bigger. Its eyes gleamed like those of a monster in a terrifying nightmare. The red crown on its head reminded Okoye of a mature village rooster. The rest of its body was as dark as ebony wood and as shiny as a marble gravel stone from the Ama-Mbala River. Okoye could tell from its diameter that much of its length was still in the bush. But it seemed to have no reason to attack the strangers. Lowering its head, the snake moved into the bushes on the other side of the road.

The men waited, but not for long. As soon as the snake's head disappeared into the bushes, Ayoh, the one who had thrown up in the market, took out a long machete from his waist and moved forward towards the place where the snake's head had vanished. Without saying a word, Akalaka reached out and held Ayoh's garment. The creature took its time as if it owned that part of the world and finally disappeared into the thickly-wooded forest. Only then did the men cross quickly like trespassers.

"What were you trying to do?" Akalaka asked Ayoh after they had crossed over.

"I was going to cut it in half. It was no longer a threat at that point, and it had no chance," Ayoh replied.

"Then that is another reason why you should not kill it," said Akalaka. "Do you know that animals do not kill unless they want food or are threatened? Only we humans kill another creature even if we don't want it for food and it does not threaten us. It is not a good practice to kill an animal unless you absolutely have to," he added.

Then Okoye remembered what the madman had said at the market. "There may be an obstacle on the road, but it will bypass you because it is not meant for you."

"This could be the obstacle the crazy man was talking about," he said.

"It could be," replied Akalaka.

⚶ ⚶ ⚶

After three hours of walking, the men were ready for another break, but they still had another half an hour to go before they reached the next market, their resting place. They had to reach the market before they could rest, not only because they needed to purchase more food and possibly some wine, but after about an hour's rest, they still had a two-hour walk to the next village where they would pass the night. They had to stay on schedule or they would have to pass the night at a marketplace. So they struggled up a steep hill that separated them from their resting-place. It felt as if the hill was there to squeeze the last bit of energy from them before they could rest. This was a test of will and Okoye, who had never walked this far before, was having a hard time. He was the last in line. Akalaka, Erike, and Ike were at the front.

As they neared the top of the hill, Okoye saw that Erike and Ike had stopped. Everyone else behind them also stopped except for Akalaka who overtook them.

Another snake? Okoye asked himself.

Then he saw five men coming out of the bush and at least seven more sitting on a fallen tree. As Okoye caught up, the seven men rose up and came out of the bushes. They were all young, in their twenties and thirties. Okoye thought they were performing some ritual because their faces were painted and they wore raffia around their waists. They held machetes in their hands and at least three of them had spears. The tall one, who seemed to be their leader, stopped in front of Akalaka. Two others stood at his side. Everyone else stayed behind him. The leader stuck his spear in the ground and put his machete in his waist.

"Nri-is-holy!" he greeted. "We have no problem with you. You can move on," he said.

"I greet you and I greet your chi," Akalaka replied, turning around and waving at the men behind him. "All of them are with me," he added. The man seemed to be disappointed.

He spoke over Akalaka's shoulders, saying something that sounded like "Admi Kef" as if he was speaking to Okoye. Okoye was puzzled at the strange word and looked back to see if there was someone else behind him. He was right. Another seven men were approaching from the back. They stopped several feet away.

"Admi Kef!" their leader said again.

The men behind Okoye started to retreat.

"Nwa-nshi (Son of Nri), give us kolanut," the man said to Akalaka.

Akalaka dipped his hand in his goat skinned bag and brought out two pieces of kolanut and handed them to him.

"Bless it," said the man in a commanding voice.

"It is already blessed," said Akalaka.

The man took it from him.

"You people are doing great work. Keep it up. But we have work to do too," the man said as he made way for Akalaka and his men to pass.

"I greet you and your chi," Akalaka replied as he moved on.

"Who were they?" asked Okoye as they were still a few feet away. No one replied. They walked in silence until they reached the top of the hill and could no longer see or hear the men.

"Who were those men?" asked Okoye again.

"Have you ever heard of Uwa Men?" asked Ike.

"No," replied Okoye. "Are they fighting warriors?"

"They are wilderness robbers," said Ike. "They rob travelers, especially traders."

"The man speaks Igbo without an accent. I think he is an Igbo man," said Erike.

"Who said that he is not an Igbo man?" replied Ike. "Do real Uwa people bless kolanut before they eat? I think that we just like to deny that those men are from Igbo villages. I find it hard to believe it myself," he added.

Akalaka ground his teeth, but said nothing.

NINE

Umuaku Case

The people of Umuaku village just wanted to live in peace. But to bullies, like the men of Umu-Mgbadike village, peace was a big luxury, just like a potbelly. To them, it was not much fun when there was peace between the two villages. They enjoyed things more when they had to make up a reason to whip out their signature machetes, the Obegili, and brandish them in front of an Umuaku victim. Killing did not thrill them, but publicly humiliating the victim did give them enjoyment. They loved to see fear in the eyes of husbands and fathers who knew they were about to die. When they saw family men weep in public like babies, some even wetting on themselves while begging for mercy, the bullies' thirst was quenched. Umuaku men who did not blink almost always died. Those who cried like babies and wet on their garments lived. But it was the latter that the warriors of Umu-Mgbadike talked about in their meetings and dramatized in the marketplaces. They amused themselves by telling about the cowards from Umuaku who called themselves men.

For five years the Umu-Mgbadike had invaded and terrorized Umuaku as often as they wished. They invaded for reasons as absurd as that one of their young woman felt threatened by the way some teenage boys from Umuaku had looked at her in the marketplace. So they would invade without notice. They would loot and burn houses and take hostages to be exchanged for money. After six years of constant terror and slaughter, the village of Umuaku had finally had enough.

For one week, the elders gathered and deliberated. On the fourth day, they reached a consensus. They agreed on what was to be a lasting solution to the problem of Umu-Mgbadike. They would hire a reputable medicine man, fondly called Nwa-mmo (The-Son-of-Ghost). They would pay whatever it took for his voodoo charm to produce peace. The most eloquent of the elders explained their specifications to Nwa-mmo. These were voodoo-charm functional specifications.

"We want to live and live in peace, and we want the families of Umu-Mgbadike to live in peace as well. We want no more war. But if the clan of Umu-Mgbadike must fight and shed blood, then let your medicine turn their necks to the west, for there they will find their match and destiny. If they ever rise for war and look east towards our village of Umuaku, let them see nothing but a big lake with crocodiles and hippopotami in it. Let them see a body of water that cannot be crossed. Let them turn in the opposite direction for there they will meet with Ndi-Dike-Afor-na-Nkwo (the Warriors-of-the-North-and-South) and their destiny."

Nwa-mmo pondered the work they proposed before giving an answer.

"I can do more than what you have asked for, but it will cost you."

"Just speak your price," the elders told him.

Nwa-mmo gave them a very long list of many cows and goats and other things that money could buy. But there was one item on the list that money could not buy that concerned and scared them. It involved a human sacrifice.

"You must sacrifice one head to save many," Nwa-mmo told them when they voiced their concern.

The elders of Umuaku took another day to deliberate some more. When they came back, they offered Nwa-mmo three times what he had asked for if only he would remove the human factor. Nwa-mmo refused. The elders of Umuaku had no choice.

"Do what you have to do then," they told him. "Give us your medicine for peace. We will bury it as you said with a human head when we find one."

Nwa-mmo manufactured his peace concoction and gave it to the elders. That was his last action. His head was buried with his concoction at the border of Umuaku and Umu-Mgbadike. It may have been a coincidence, but for over two generations, the village of Umuaku had peace. And the warriors of Umu-Mgbadike did, in fact, meet their match and demise with the Warriors-of-the-North-and-South. The Umuaku enjoyed peace until Omalanko, the patron deity of Nwa-mmo, was ready for full-fledged revenge on the village.

The revenge of Omalanko started as a marriage ceremony between a young and hopeful couple. The bride was from one village and the groom from the other. The in-laws from both sides agreed to agree. No rain spoiled the event. Food and drinks were plentiful. The young Umuaku woman's Opanda music was good and there was lots of dancing and celebration. All of the in-laws poured out blessings on the new couple. They wished them longevity and lots of children and wealth. An elderly man wished them six male and six female children, the ideal in those days. Later that evening, on their very first night together, a tree fell on their house killing the couple. Eyebrows were raised and heads scratched. But at the end of the day, after the burials, the Umuaku blamed the tragedy on bad luck.

It would be exactly two Igbo weeks, eight days, before the next incident.

He was a honey hunter with his only wife as his partner. He was not attacked by bees, as was usually the cause of accidents in his trade. A tree branch gave under him and fell on his wife. She died first. He died three days later from multiple broken bones.

Umuaku was evenly divided. Some believed in a spell, while the rest were still wondering when ten days later two innocent children became the next victims. The boy was only eleven. His sister was nine. On a windy evening, they were returning from the stream with five other children and an adult. A tree gave way in the wind and fell on the children. Although three others were severely injured, only the boy and his sister were killed.

Even a fool could see the pattern: couples and trees and funerals. After an emergency deliberation, the Umuaku elders agreed that men and women must not be seen together until the riddle had been solved. In the next two days, all trees that stood next to a home were cut down. When the women, men, and children of Umuaku had to walk close to a tree, they looked to the sky for what else might be falling. The diviner they hired to reveal the underworld only confirmed what they already knew. There was a curse on the whole village of Umuaku. But he also told them the part they did not know and dreaded to hear, their spell was from a horrible deity, Omalanko, the collector of bones.

Omalanko wanted two human sacrifices from Umuaku to atone for the sins of their forefathers. Of course, there were no volunteers in Umuaku. How could they make such choices? Should they choose through random selection or by election? The oldest? The youngest? The most marginal human among them? In the middle of their confusion, an in-law suggested they call an Nri priest. He mentioned that Nri priests had dealt with Omalanko before and could deal with him again. Good inquiries led them to none other than Akalaka himself. This would definitely be a spiritual warfare. Akalaka, who was in his early seventies, was a veteran of those wars. He had dealt with Omalanko five times in his lifetime. When he accepted this challenge, he believed it would be his last mission. But then, he had been saying that before every long-distance mission for the past six years. And he believed this in his heart each time.

The people who were familiar with Omalanko did not call him "The Collector of Bones" in jest. His victims were not buried, but must be dumped among the other skulls and bones at the deity's shrine. The skulls were there for one purpose only, to testify of Omalanko's power.

᛭ ᛭ ᛭

Akalaka stepped into the rattan ring that was big enough to fit four people. He invited Ichie Onuoha to join him. At ninety-two, Ichie Onuoha was the oldest man in Umuaku. He was one of the very few who had heard about the killing of Nwa-mmo by his forefathers before the divination.

Ichie Onuoha stepped into the rattan ring outlined on the sandy ground. Nri priests called it a holy circle. There was a clamor and some handclapping around the public square of Umuaku village. Embarrassed by the unwarranted attention, Ichie Onuoha looked around the big open square and smiled at the nearly 4,000 spectators. Out of politeness, he giggled and turned his attention back to Akalaka who was waiting. Although they had met the evening before, because of protocol Akalaka had to ask:

"What is your name?"

"My name is Ichie. Ichie Okonkwo Onuora."

"Ichie Okonkwo Onuora, what do you wish for yourself today from Agbala?"

"All the things I wish in life?"

"I mean, what do you wish from Agbala regarding the emergency problem at Umuaku?"

"I wish to be separated from the sins of my fathers and their fathers, if they committed any."

Akalaka lifted the Offor club of justice that he held in his left hand and reached behind Ichie Onuoha and gently tapped him on the back with the club. Then Akalaka said, "What you do not know will not know you."

Next he placed the club on Ichie Onuoha's left shoulder for quick moments and on his right shoulder for another two quick moments while saying, "Okonkwo Onuora, through the power of Agbala, I separate you from the sins of your fathers and their fathers. I separate you from any sin they may have committed against Aja-Ana."

Akalaka then asked Ichie Onuora to pick up the second and smaller Offor club that lay on the ground with his left hand and repeat after him. As Ichie Onuora bent down to pick up this club, the symbol of justice, there was complete silence in the public square. Only a newborn wailed somewhere in the crowd, but not even that could take away from the awe that the process invoked. The silence first came because of the offor club that Ichie Onuora was about to lift. Anyone with a dirty hand could not touch it. Its reputation for justice was well established throughout Igbo land, with a lot of exaggeration, of course. Then there was the Omalanko deity they were about to fight. Would it fight back? What if the process didn't work? Would its anger boil out all over Umuaku? But the biggest reason for the silence was curiosity about this process that none of them had seen before and that was unfolding before them.

"Repeat after me," said Akalaka. Ichie Onuora nodded.

Akalaka: What I do not know will not know me.
Ichie Onuora: What I do not know will not know me.

Akalaka: I am responsible for all my mistakes.
Ichie Onuora: I am responsible for all my mistakes.

Akalaka: Each and every one is responsible for their mistakes.
Ichie Onuora: Each and every one is responsible for their mistakes.

Akalaka: My fathers and mothers are responsible for their mistakes.
Ichie Onuora: My fathers and mothers are responsible for their mistakes.

Akalaka: My forefathers and foremothers are responsible for their mistakes.
Ichie Onuora: My forefathers and foremothers are responsible for their mistakes.

Akalaka: I am completely responsible for my judgments and mistakes, so everyone else should be responsible for their judgments and mistakes.
Ichie Onuora: I am completely responsible for my judgments and mistakes, so everyone else should be responsible for their judgments and mistakes.

Akalaka: What I do not know will not know me.
Ichie Onuora: What I do not know will not know me.

Akalaka: Through the power of Agbala, I cleanse you of any offense you may have committed knowingly or unknowingly against Aja-Ana. Aja-Ana absolves you and cleanses your feet from the sins of your fathers and forefathers. Go in peace and commit no more offense against Aja-Ana.

Akalaka dusted Ichie Onuoha's body with fresh ogilisi leaves while he said this last statement. When he finished, he held Ichie Onuoha's right hand, escorted him out of the ring, and led him to a chair in front of Okoye. While Okoye washed Ichie Onuoha's hands up to the elbow and feet up to the knees with an aged palm wine highly diluted with water, Akalaka was already processing the second candidate, the second oldest man in Umuaku. After drying Ichie Onuoha's feet, Okoye walked him to the chair in front of Ike, the dwarf. They walked on banana leaves so that Ichie Onuoha's feet did not touch the sandy ground. Ike scraped some particles from the holy chalk and dusted Ichie Onuoha's feet and legs up to the knee. He told Ichie Onuora not to wash for at least one full day. "You may go now in peace," he finally told Ichie Onuora.

The entire village of Umuaku had come out the first day. They soon found out, however, that not all would be processed in one day. It would take nine days to process the entire village. All the married men went first in order of birth. All the married women went next in order of date of marriage at Umuaku. Everyone else went in order of birth. On the tenth day, they celebrated at the public square with lots of food and drink and music. During their few days' stay at Umuaku, the men from the holy land had fascinated everyone. By the time they left, children were acting out the cleansing and separation ritual on their playgrounds. But they were even more awestruck by Ike, the dwarf.

Among the Umuaku people, the story of Nri dwarves had been more like a fairy tale until they actually saw Ike. Women of childbearing age and, especially pregnant women, were strongly warned not to look at him twice. "That is how you bear a dwarf child, by staring at one," they were told.

The wise advisers had themselves never seen a dwarf before. The Nri dwarf fascinated men, women, and children alike, but Ike, a veteran missionary, had seen worse in other villages. He was not bothered one bit by the staring. The villagers were even more puzzled that he was acting so normal.

As one woman said to another weeks after the missionaries left, "Could you believe it? He was even acting as if nothing had happened." She was pregnant.

Akalaka received payments of one he-goat and one she-goat, one bag of cowry, and a small basket full of kolanuts. That was the official payment. However, individuals also gave them gifts. By the time they left, the missionaries had received a total of five goats, fifteen chickens, and a lot more cowry money. Most of the gift items would be sold at the closest market outside Umuaku Village. Only the initial he- and she-goats would make it back to Nri. The he-goat and one third of the money would go to Eze Nri, the King of Nri. The mission lead usually took one third and one third would be shared among his disciples.

TEN

One Woman Warrior

During their stay at Umuaku, they camped at an abandoned house that was waiting for nature to gradually demolish it. The roof and walls were old but still strong and the house habitable. It suited Akalaka and his disciples well because it would have been unsociable for them to stay with a family yet cook their own food.

The abandoned house was a typical Igbo family compound of above average quality. A well-to-do man had abandoned it, not because it was in terrible shape but because his family had grown. It was clear that at some point he had planned for and had two wives, for there were only two Mk-puke (wives' quarters) in the red, mud-fenced compound. He must have decided to get a bigger place after marrying his third wife.

Akalaka and his disciples did their own cooking because their diet was limited and did not include meat of any kind. Only Ozo-Mkputu priests followed this practice. Akalaka would eat fish but only selected species. He had a very long list of things he did not eat, so the group brought their own pot and cooked for themselves at every mission. Doing their own cooking was not about trust or pride; it was about being fair to themselves and to their hosts. The priests were not willing to compromise their physical and spiritual health out of politeness. On the other hand, it would have been unsocial and outright selfish to make a long list of what their host must include or not include in cooking at his own home just because they happened to be staying with him.

Yes, an abandoned house of any kind was always a better arrange-ment. It was suitable for quiet meditation and perfect for chanting. Akalaka loved both. And if he chose to fast, which he did very often, he could do so without apologizing or explaining to his host.

On the evening of their third day at Umuaku, Akalaka sat with his four disciples around a fire in the obu close to the entrance gate of the house. They were roasting and eating yam tubers dipped in freshly squeezed palm oil mixed with salt and ground dried red pepper and ukpaka. This was dinner and their private time. Nweke, the second disciple, was teasing Ike, the dwarf, about how the women of Umuaku stared at him. Ike was the humorous one. He laughed loudly first before responding.

"Too bad that I am already married. Too bad." He shook his head as if he were disappointed in himself for being married. Ozo-Mkputu priests and their disciples could only marry one wife except in extreme cases.

"Tell the boys about your wife. Tell them how you met her," Nweke urged.

Ike laughed again. He loved to tell the story about how his tall, beautiful wife had followed him home during one of their missions. It sounded like a fantasy tale, but it was true. The missionaries were eating dinner at one of their host's homes when a young woman walked in looking for the dwarf named Ike. He invited her to come to Nri and she did. The rest was history.

"Too bad I am already married," he said again.

"Tell the boys how she followed you home. Tell them about the day she came to Nri for the first time."

Okoye moved closer to Ike, but Erike pretended that he wasn't listening. He picked up a piece of yam and buttered it with oil.

Akalaka got up and headed toward the inner building. *Time to let the children loosen up.*

Ike laughed again and shook his head. He was about to say something when the thick wooden gate squeaked open and Ijego (a tall, young, and beautiful woman) invaded their privacy. All eyes turned to Ike. He smiled.

❅ ❅ ❅

The cleansing ceremony had attracted a lot of spectators from neighboring villages in the larger Akuma family. Some people came to watch and see how it was done. Others came to see what Nri priests looked like. But many came, especially children, to see the all-powerful Nri dwarves whom they had heard many tales about. One woman came for all of the above reasons and more. She wanted to get any information she could about Nri people. Her name was Ijego Echika. Ijego was not there the first day of the ceremony because she did not know it was happening. But when she heard about it on the second day, she came and stayed until the end of the day.

"Akalaka!" she saluted as she moved towards the men.

"Whom do I greet?" Akalaka asked as he turned around and moved towards her.

Ijego smiled shyly, as if she did not know how to respond, and, for a brief moment, she truly did not know what else to say. She was overpowered by Akalaka's personality. Ijego was not usually shy or intimidated by anybody's presence, but on this occasion she had intruded into these people's private moment, and she did not know if they would be offended.

"I just need some advice, and I think you can help me," she said.

"Please come and join us. And what is your name, my daughter?" said Akalaka.

Ijego told him her name and said that she was from Ezikwe Village. That got his attention because he was expecting her to say Umuaku Village.

"Is it OK if I talk to you alone?" she asked.

"Of course," Akalaka said as he led the way to one of the Mkpuke parts of the compound.

On second thought, Akalaka turned around and grabbed the only oil lamp and two pieces of yam buttered with palm oil. Ike touched Okoye and gestured for him to follow Akalaka and their visitor. As they walked towards the Mkpuke area, Akalaka offered a piece of the yam to Ijego, which she took out of politeness. Ijego had decided that she would have just one bite from the yam and take the rest home. Akalaka was the first to settle down on the red clay mud bench. He invited Ijego to sit. Just as she was sitting down, about three steps from Akalaka, she noticed that one of the young men had followed them.

"Can we talk alone?" she asked for the second time.

"He is a new student of mine. This is the only way he can learn to perform his future duties. Besides, my position forbids me from being seen alone at night with a young woman who is not my blood relation or my wife. I can lose credibility or even my position. I can assure you that whatever is said here will not be heard by any other ears. Isn't that true, Okoye?"

"Yes. It is true," affirmed Okoye.

"His name is Okoye, but just ignore that he is here."

Okoye sat on the dwarf wall that separated the open reception area from the outside. His back was turned towards the other two. There was no other seat for him in the open living room that served as a front porch.

"I am not going to take a lot of your time because I know how hard you worked today," Ijego started. "I just want to know more about your people."

"We are Igbo people—like you," Akalaka said.

"I have heard a lot of things about your people, and I don't know what is true. For instance, I heard that women have more freedom at your place than they have in other parts of Igbo land."

Akalaka laughed because he had his opinions about that.

"I have been to other parts of Igbo land, and I think that the relationship between men and women is about the same. It could be better. Are you having a problem with your husband?" Akalaka asked, trying to get her to be more specific.

"My husband died about five years ago. That was when my problems began," Ijego said.

Akalaka had given her the opening she needed. She promised again not to take much of his time. But this was a rare opportunity. She might as well get the help she had been wanting for the last five years.

🜪 🜪 🜪

She had been born Ijego Gbakweri in Amoko Village in the Ikwine family. Her father was a professional palm-wine tapper and maker and a part-time farmer. Her mother was a successful dried fish trader. Her mother provided for the family most of the time and was the key decision maker in her family. Ijego was the only daughter and her mother's best friend. She had grown up helping her mother in her dried fish business. Just before turning eighteen, Ijego fell madly in love with one of her mother's customers, Uwakwe. Her mother did not approve because the man was about fifteen years older and came from another village which was about three days' walk. Her mother did not want her only daughter to live that far away. Besides, in their village of Amoko and in the Ikwine family, women were more active in the economy and politics. But it was not so in the suitor's village which had more traditional attitudes.

Ijego was young and naïve, and she followed her heart. Ijego ran away with Uwakwe Echika to Ezikwe Village. Ijego did not have a chance with the people of the village of Ezikwe, who were already prejudiced against her village. They thought that women from the Ikwine family were overly assertive and, therefore, would bring instability to their village. They hinted to Ijego that she was not welcome, but Ijego was in love and did not see the early signs.

Just like her mother, Ijego was a hard-worker. She took over Uwakwe's dried fish trading and improved it. Uwakwe left it to her to manage the business. By the third year of her involvement, they had built a much bigger house. Uwakwe retired completely from the business and left it entirely to Ijego. But Ijego not only ran Uwakwe's business, she ran his life. He did not care. He was an easygoing man who was in love. He was having the time of his life. But his mother, his brother, and some of his cousins thought differently. Now they had another reason to reaffirm their prejudice against the Ikwine family. They thought that Ijego was too controlling of their son and brother. They also thought that after five years of marriage to Ijego without a child, Uwakwe should be looking for another wife. Instead, he would not allow the issue of another wife to be discussed. The family concluded that Ijego must have used a strong charm from her village to confuse their brother.

Back in Amoko Village where Ijego came from, the story was similar but from another point of view. Ijego's mother had given up on her. She had not only lost her daughter but also one of her major customers. She believed that Uwakwe must have used some sort of charm to steal her daughter from her. How else could she explain what had happened? Ijego was always in control of herself. How could she, who had learned directly from her mother, turn out to be a complete disgrace to her family by running away with a man? The few times that the mother saw Ijego in the market buying fish from a rival wholesaler, she refused to speak to her.

Life was not all bad for Ijego at Ezikwe Village. She was popularly known as "Ogene" (a Gong). Ijego was the lead singer in the Ezikwe Village women's singing group. Most of their songs were already part of their performance before she came to the village, but she brought a different tone and pitch to the music. It was hard to believe that she had never sung in an organized group before she married. But as soon as Ijego joined the women's singing group in the village, which was mandatory for all married women, Ochioha, the leader of the group, quickly discovered that the newcomer's voice was an asset and encouraged her to sing more often. She gave Ijego private coaching which, over time, perfected her singing. Alternate singers faded into the background. The village women genuinely liked Ijego, and, apart from her husband's brother and some cousins, the village men had nothing against her. Uwakwe adored her. So her life was not totally miserable.

Sure, Uwakwe had actually thought about a second wife a few times, but his love for Ijego was too great, and he did not want to offend her. Besides she controlled all the money. So it was Ijego herself who first brought the subject up. Uwakwe quickly dismissed the idea, telling himself that it could be a trap to test his love. Only after she brought it up for the third time did he agree to discuss this option.

"It is OK with me if you personally pick her to make sure she is someone you will get along with," he told Ijego.

They both agreed that the coming dry season after crop harvesting would be the right time. That was when most feasts and ceremonies took place in Igbo land. Uwakwe sounded like a reluctant participant, but he was very enthusiastic when he told his mother about his agreement with Ijego. His brother was happy too. But Uwakwe died mysteriously in his sleep before the harvesting season began. Then the real trouble started for Ijego.

First came the outrageous accusation that she had something to do with Uwakwe's death and that she had killed her only love out of jealousy. Okereke, her brother-in-law, argued that she could not stand her husband marrying a second wife so she killed him. Of course, most of the villagers did not believe that and, therefore, she could live with the accusations of a handful of people. But then came the death of her mother-in-law only six months after her husband's death. And there was also the illness of everyone in her mother-in-law's household a few weeks after that. Okereke concluded that Ijego was a witch who was using magic to kill everyone in his family.

So Okereke decided that Ijego had to go, dead or alive. First, he tried to gather the support of the village members. Although they had their suspicions, there was no evidence that she had done anything wrong, and they did not want to punish an innocent person. Okereke decided to act alone to put pressure on her to leave the village.

One morning, Ijego was going to the market with a very big basket of dried fish on her head. She was already running late, and she was usually one of the first to set up in the market. On that day the sun had already come out, which meant that the market was already at full activity. She was counting how many customers she must have lost that day and did not pay attention to Okereke coming in the opposite direction. By the time she saw him, he was only a few feet away. They did not speak to each other. She was trying to decide which side of the narrow road to use. It seemed as if they both went in the same direction at the same time. They did this three times before Okereke lost his patience with this witch. He pushed Ijego into the shrubs on the right side of the road, making the basket of fish fall on top of her. Half of the fish poured out into the bush. Ijego pushed off the basket and ran after Okereke who was still walking home as if nothing had happened. He turned around only when Ijego was almost at his back. Okereke was ready to slap her and push her into the bushes again. But he underestimated Ijego's strength. Ijego did the pushing this time around.

Okereke was surprised at her strength, and he fell hard into the bushes. Ijego was about to call it even but remembered that her basket of fish was all over the place, so she climbed on top of Okereke who was struggling to get up. She sat on his stomach and punched him in the face with all her strength. She was almost amused at how easily Okereke had fallen. He struggled to push her off but could not, so he grabbed her throat and held on. Ijego gasped for breath, but Uwakwe refused to let go. She punched him as hard as she could, but still he wouldn't let go. She tried to take his hands off her throat but could not. Okereke seemed determined to squeeze the life out of her. In desperation, Ijego grabbed his manhood and squeezed! Only then did Okereke soften his grip, but he did not let go completely. Ijego had to squeeze hard before he released her, but it was too late for him. He was bleeding from somewhere around his manhood. He yelled at the top of his voice that Ijego, the blood-sucking witch, had sucked the blood from him in broad daylight. Ijego saw the blood, too, and was not sure how badly he was hurt.

Okereke completely fabricated his version of what had happened, partly because he was ashamed that a woman could have that much strength. To the first people who asked him what happened, he said that he was walking home when he saw a black bat coming at him from the bushes. He was trying to fight it off when he temporarily lost consciousness. When he regained consciousness, he was on the ground with Ijego on top of him. Only when he started yelling for help did she get up and run away. But a witness had seen Ijego picking up her fish. When he was asked why the basket of dried fish was there and how did the fish come to fill the bushes, Okereke changed his story about the black bat. He admitted that he had pushed Ijego, but said he was trying to help her get up when she must have used a charm to knock him unconscious. But the elders of the village did not believe his stories. They were not as straight as Ijego's version. They imposed a fine on Okereke for starting a fight. He was very happy to pay it because a bigger fine was imposed on Ijego, but for a different reason.

The elders of Ezikwe fined Ijego more severely because they reasoned that it was a great insult to all the men of Ezikwe Village to hold a man by the testicles during a fight between a man and a woman. So her fine was almost three times that of Okereke's. Not only was she going to pay a hefty fine, she was to apologize in public to her victim with a pot of palm wine and one immaculate white rooster. And to the men of Ezikwe Village she was to give one immaculate white she-goat and five pots of palm wine during the public apologies.

Ijego, of course, refused to pay. She had the money, but she felt that she had been defending herself. She refused to understand the elder's reasoning. Many Ezikwe women did not understand it either, but they were afraid to protest. Ijego was given three market weeks, twelve days, to accept the verdict or incur more penalties. Male admirers and women friends flooded her house, begging her to accept the verdict. A few even volunteered to pay some of the fees. But it wasn't the penalty that got to her; it was the public apology. The women's singing group, which had earned a lot of money, volunteered to pay all of Ijego's fines so that they wouldn't lose her. But the public apology was something she must do by herself. Ijego, however, could not do that. To her it was a matter of principle. She believed that nothing she did was wrong, that when a man grabbed a woman by the throat and would not let go, anything that she decided to do to save her life was fair. So the women of Ezikwe Village withdrew their offer.

After twelve days, the fine had doubled, and it continued to double every twelve days until not even the whole village could raise that kind of money. So Ijego was not only a childless widow, but an outcast in her village. No one would talk to her. She no longer had anything to do with the village apart from living there. Ijego was a prime candidate for a heart attack or suicide, but somehow she lived on. She would wake up in the morning singing loud abusive songs using the names of every man in Ezikwe Village. The voice that had once been an asset to the village became a nightmare. Ezikwe men deliberately avoided passing through her compound because she would start singing abusive songs using that person's name. She was gradually going crazy, talking to herself all day and all night.

Ijego had come to have the lowest opinion of men.

They will do anything to protect each other, she thought.

So when she came to meet with Akalaka, the head priest from Nri, she did not know how to behave. She did not want to project her hatred for men onto Akalaka. At first she was uncomfortable with him, but, as they talked, he seemed more like a father. She felt she could trust him to make a fair judgment.

Ijego told Akalaka her own version of the story, adding ingredients and leaving out details that would reveal her own faults. She left out that some close friends, mostly women, had taken a big risk and tried to sneak in at night to socialize with her. But Ijego not only refused their outreach, she raised her voice, calling them by name and asking them to leave so that the villagers would know who her visitors were.

Akalaka knew that there are always three sides to every story—his side, her side, and the truth. He was a very experienced man and could sift through her story to piece together the truth.

"It is a very sad story, indeed," Akalaka said. "I would love to help you, but at this point, I don't know how you would like me to come in."

"I have heard some good things about your people, and, if all the things I hear are true, then I would like to come and live there," Ijego replied.

"First of all, I don't know what you have heard about our place, but I can tell you that it is not all true. Igbo people have a way of making us look perfect, which we are not. We not only absorb people into our family, but we also mediate peace between people. I would love to mediate between you and your village. In fact, in a case like this, mediation would be a high-ly-favored approach because you have a network of friends and support in your village. All we need to do is to find a way to help you live in peace among your own people. I will use my influence to make that happen, and if that is not enough, I will use the men of Umuaku Village, whom I am helping, to make that happen. At this point, they will do about anything for me if I ask them. If you, however, come as a newcomer to Nri family, you will be received well. But, on the other hand, everyone is busy with their business, and it will be difficult to make a lot of new friends. Our place is ideal for newborns that will grow up knowing no other place. It is also good for runaway slaves or outcasts. But for someone in your situation, you need not be that extreme," he concluded.

But Ijego had had enough of Ezikwe Village men. She needed some fresh air, a new start.

"I don't think I could ever live in peace with the men of Ezikwe. There has been too much bad blood between us. Even if they say that they forgive everything and apologize, I don't know if I can ever trust them."

"As I told you, our place is not perfect. Men are men all over. Igbo men are the same even at Nri. They will flex their political muscles to get whatever they want. I believe that it is the same all over the world. But I have come to believe that these are not really men's problems, but human problems. Human beings will take advantage of you if they have some opportunity. It does not matter whether they are men or women. It is the same all over. But at Nri, we have put ourselves in a unique position because we know that Igbo people are watching us and looking to us for direction. Because of that, we have an obligation to try our best to do things right. But we are not perfect people. The younger generation at our place does not have a strong sense of obligation to the Igbo people and our people. They just want to make money and live their lives, and that is what scares us," Akalaka said philosophically.

This speech was meant to persuade Ijego to manage what she had instead of looking for something new and unknown. But it gave Ijego another reason to want to go to Nri. She reasoned that if this man could speak with such wisdom and fairness, wouldn't Nri leaders also do this?

It had been nearly four hours since she walked into the compound. Akalaka did not show any sign that he wanted her to leave. He wondered how someone, especially a young woman, could live for over five years without social support. As they walked to the outer part of the compound, he was not surprised that his assistants were already asleep and the fire had been put out. He woke them and together they escorted Ijego all the way to her village and into her house. Over the course of their eleven day's stay at Umuaku Village, Ijego visited Akalaka two more times. She even brought some dried fish. During those visits, she had gathered all the information she needed to move to Nri. Since Akalaka was not sure when they would return from this current mission, he asked her to meet Ichie Idika, a very good friend of his. Ichie Idika had the time, the knowledge, and the heart to give her all the help she would need.

🦋 🦋 🦋

Ijego brought a basket full of the best species of dried fish to Akalaka and his disciples the evening before they were to leave Umuaku. On that evening they finished arrangements for Ijego's journey to Nri. Akalaka, and his men would be on three other assignments for another seven weeks. Their Gbata-Oso mission had turned into an Ifu-Ije mission. So Ijego was to meet Akalaka's wife who would take her to Ichie Idika's home where she would be staying. This would be a perfect place for her to get a new start. Ichie Idika had plenty of land, most of which he loaned out.

It was still daylight and Akalaka decided that Ijego did not need an escort this time. So, when Ijego got up from the mud dwarf wall that also served as a visitor's sitting place, Akalaka did not gather the entire crew.

"I will see you off at the entrance," he said

"Don't worry about that. You people have a long journey tomorrow. You need all the rest you can get."

"You are right. But I will still walk you to the entrance."

Ijego bent down to go through the low exit from the hut. Akalaka did the same. As they reached the entrance gate, Okoye joined them, trailing behind like a bodyguard.

"Whatever you do, don't travel alone. The road is not safe these days," said Akalaka.

"You have said that ten times already," Ijego reminded him.

"Have you ever heard about Uwa Men?"

"Everyone knows about Uwa Men."

"They are no longer the Uwa Men you may know about. Right now they are everywhere, and they are becoming more aggressive."

"That is what I heard from my suppliers. Word goes around very fast."

"They used to wear masks and mimic foreign tongues. But these days they paint half their faces and speak perfect Igbo. They used to be shy and nervous when they saw Nri people, especially an Ozo man, like me. But the other day, one of them had the nerve to ask me for kolanut. It took all my energy to give him one. Then he asked me to bless it. Can you believe it?"

Ijego could not have asked the question ten days before. Then Akalaka and his men were complete strangers. But after nine days of watching them and four days of personal counseling from Akalaka, Ijego had enough trust to ask a troubling, but sincere, question. It was a question she would have asked her biological father if they had been on good terms.

"Why is it always men? Why is it always men who cause trouble everywhere? From the villages of Umuaku and Ezikwe to the seventeenth wilderness, wherever there is trouble you will find the handiwork of men. There will never be an 'Uwa Woman.' Chineke will forbid it!"

Okoye, who was a good five footsteps behind them, took a step backwards and closed one ear. Akalaka smiled like a father who had been confronted by a daughter troubled about the crimes of men. He lifted his red cap and wiped his forehead, then put the cap back on, thinking, *What do you tell your daughter when she confronts you about the sins of men? Do you deny your own kind and tell her the truth about the nature of men? — That men are power-grabbing bullies who will use every advantage they have for their own selfish goals? No! You do not tell her part of the truth. You tell her the whole truth. That is how you stitch together a broken heart.*

Akalaka smiled again.

"Perhaps we should not make it a man or woman problem," he stated. "What we have is a human problem. Conflicts are not because of gender. An oppressor could be a man or a woman, an adult or a child. This problem transcends cultural or clan boundaries. If human beings have an advantage over others, they often use it to serve their own selfish interests. Some people like to call these conflicts misunderstandings, but, most of the time, they are not. Usually the situation is simply a human being or a group of human beings trying to get away with something, not because it is fair or unfair, but simply because they think they can. Is this good? No! But you have to understand raw human nature before you can change it. That is why we ask people to be fair at all times. We say to people, 'Do not think about what you can get away with. Think instead about what is fair.'"

"But you must know that most of the time fighting brings more problems than you already have. What you did was to commit social suicide. When you are outnumbered you do not commit suicide. You appeal to the other person's conscience. This works miracles."

"So now it is entirely my fault? I should have fallen on the ground and begged for mercy?"

"I never said that. It is not weakness to appeal to someone's conscience. You are not only helping yourself, you are giving a precious gift too. You are giving a heart, a heart to feel with. When people are strong and secure, their consciences are active."

There was silence for another five steps.

"You are a young woman, and you will have a very good life at Nri. Don't forget the name Ichie Idika. He is a good man and a good friend of mine. Tell my wife to take you to him. He will give you whatever you will need to be happy at Nri."

ELEVEN

Ichie Idika – The Maverick

Ichie Idika was trouble. Everyone agreed about that. But whether he was good trouble or bad trouble would depend on whom you asked. He stood up and told truths that even the bravest would rather cover their heads with a basket than tell. And he did this in public for all to hear. Most people wanted to hear the truth, just not in public. Even his admirers sometimes wished that they could somehow control him.

He had been born into wealth but shunned it. As the first son, Ichie Idika inherited most of his father's wealth, including the Ozo priesthood. But he had one little problem with inheriting the Ozo priesthood. The inheritor had to go through the cleansing to make the priesthood his own. The cost was a fraction of the original price, but Ichie Idika refused to accept the Ozo priesthood if it was not based on personal achievements. But that was not all. He believed also that the Ozo priesthood should be based on moral and spiritual strength and not the economical might of the seeker. Therefore, he shunned what had become the sect of the elite. He had not yet given away all the wealth that he had inherited, but he was close to doing so. He had loaned most of his crops, lands, and livestock to immigrants and the less privileged in Nri and Igbo land. They shared all of the proceeds. The terms were most favorable to peasants. His only wife managed these arrangements. Ichie Idika was so busy philosophizing that most of the time he forgot to whom he had loaned what.

He had been known to go to Ozo men's meetings uninvited, especially when they were having a feast. No one dared ask him to leave because they all knew that he was just looking for trouble. They would give him a complimentary share of any loot they happened to be dividing. An Ozo man once approached him after a meeting he had crashed and offered to sponsor the cleansing ceremony for him so that he could become a legitimate member. Ichie Idika laughed so hard that the man was embarrassed for asking.

"Do you know how many Ozo men have made this proposal to me?" he asked. Ichie Idika was having fun. He enjoyed giving people trouble, especially Ozo men. He liked to cause trouble. Good trouble anyway, some would say.

As soon as Erike saw Ichie Idika, he knew he was in trouble. Erike was manning the entrance to Igwe's quarters because it was his turn. Even if Erike had had a chance to avoid Ichie Idika, he was not sure that he would have.

"Ichie!" Erike called out in greeting as the man approached. Ichie Idika meant "elder."

"Ichie!" He called out again.

Erike was laughing after the second greeting, and Ichie pretended he did not hear it. He pretended to be angry at something, and Erike was laughing at his fake anger.

"What is it that went into the bush single and came out with lots and lots of children?" he asked Erike maintaining his gruff voice.

"The mother chicken?" Erike answered.

"Wrong! Wrong!! It is the cocoyam."

The question was a child's riddle, and Ichie Idika had deliberately put it to Erike. Only people raised at Nri could understand the riddle. For some reason, Ichie Idika found it necessary to educate Erike on the history and teachings of the Nri people each time they met. Sometimes this made Erike feel like an outsider, but he had also learned a lot from the man about Nri culture. So these encounters had become tradeoffs. But Erike didn't like to be lectured in front of other people. Something about Ichie told Erike that he was a good man and meant well, and also that he knew something about Nri that very few people knew. Maybe that was why they let him be, even when he crossed the line. Erike knew what Ichie Idika wanted. It was not fun giving it to him, but there was nothing he could do about it.

Ichie Idika did not come to the palace to see anyone but his old friend Igwe Nwadike. The King, however, did not want to be bothered when he was having a quiet time with his grandchildren. Ichie Idika was not anyone. He was Ichie Idika—one of a kind. Erike shook his head in amazement as Ichie headed to the king's resting place. He could not stop him.

☙ ☙ ☙

Igwe Nwadike was not just a great storyteller; he was also a good singer in the Ulaga masquerade, a musical group organized by his age grade when he was a young man. He danced as well as he sang. This day he was sitting on his favorite rattan chair in his private family room, surrounded by seven grandchildren and their babysitters. The youngest, only twenty months old, sat on her babysitter's lap directly in front of Igwe Nwadike. As he sang to his young audience, Igwe played his Une, the local guitar he had personally crafted. After a very long negotiation between grandfather and children, they had agreed on ten songs because there were seven grandchildren and three babysitters. Igwe was on his third song when Ichie Idika crashed their party.

Ulaga Masquerade went to learn a new song in a foreign land (Repeat)
He could not learn the song and was crying (Repeat)
He could not learn the song and was wailing (Repeat)

He called on his father to come and save him
His father told him to come home if he could not learn the foreign song.
We still love you

He called on his mother to come and save him.
His mother told him to come home if he could not learn the foreign song. We still love you

He called on his best friend to come and save him
His best friend told him to come home if he could not learn the foreign song. We still love you

He called on his big sister to came and save him
His big sister went and saved him

Nri Warriors of Peace

"You are doing it the wrong way," his sister told him
You don't go there with your jar of water and your baskets of food and
your mother tongue

You must first drink their native water
You must eat their native food and enjoy it
You must learn and speak the native tongue
You must learn their culture and respect it

Only then can you learn their music
Only then can you sing and dance like the natives

He could not learn the song and was crying (Repeat)
He could not learn the song and was wailing (Repeat)

There is something else you should know
You must come home and sing it for our people when you learn it
You must come home and dance the new dance for our people
You must come home and teach us the new song and dance
If you don't, then your quest has failed

He could not learn the song and was crying (Repeat)
He could not learn the song and was wailing (Repeat)

Take the foreign gift you bought for your father and give to your sister

Take the foreign gift you bought for your mother and give to your sister

Take the foreign gift you bought for your friend and give to your sister

He could not learn the song and was crying (Repeat)

He could not learn the song and was wailing (Repeat)

"Igwe! Igwe!" Ichie Idika saluted as Igwe Nwadike completed the last song. The children seemed to get the hint. The party was over.

"Is that how you treat your best friend giving my gifts to your sister?" Ichie Idika asked, referring to the song.

"Hey, whoever gives me the right answer gets the credit. It is that simple," replied Igwe Nwadike.

"Fair enough. Fair enough. Take your best shot then."

"I was just thinking about you moments ago. It is amazing how that works out."

"I was thinking about you, too. That's how I found my way here. That makes two of us. That's why we are best friends, remember?"

As the old-timers went for a walk in the holy bush, the babies cried and complained about the broken contract they had had with grandpa. Grandpa would pay. He would pay with interest next time.

"What a good man you have recruited as your front person," Ichie Idika said as they exited the private quarters.

"Why would he not be a good man when he allowed you to invade my privacy?"

"Not even he could stop me from seeing my nnaochie (uncle)."

"You only remember the nnaochie business when you want to take advantage of me. Where is the kolanut you brought for your nnaochie?"

"I know you have plenty. Besides, caffeine is not good for your health. It wouldn't prevent us from sharing one though." Ichie Idika dipped his hand into his goatskin bag and produced a healthy ivory-colored kolanut. He was the greatest eater of kolanut in Nri, and he ate only "Oji Ugo" (eagle premium kolanuts) which were identified by their ivory color. He handed one to Igwe Nwadike to bless and share.

"We will all live long, healthy, and productive lives," Igwe Nwadike said and then broke the kolanut which fell into two pieces.

"I agree," Ichie Idika said.

"So what brought you to my place this late in the day?"

"I know that you are a lonely man. I thought that you might use some adult company."

"You made some little people very unhappy. The spirits may not be pleased with you. I hope you know that."

101

"Oh, believe me when I say that the spirits sent me to talk with you, so you don't have to worry about me."

"What brought you to my place?" Igwe Nwadike asked again as they stepped into the holy bush. Igwe Nwadike led the way, heading towards the vegetable garden, his favorite part of the bush.

"We have to talk. The Ozo men's annual meeting is only four weeks away. We have a lot to discuss."

Igwe Nwadike filled his left hand with garden egg leaves, his favorite snack.

"My ears are with you."

"The very first thing that I want to get off my chest is about the new immigrants. It would be very helpful if transplanted citizens were formally taught our culture and history. Your front man knows a lot, but that is only because he is working for you. He is only one out of many. At the rate transplanted citizens are now coming into our family, we cannot continue to leave it up to them to learn our ways on their own. The reality is that they will learn from what comes their way by accident and that will be very little. If they are formally taught what we stand for and why we stand for those things and how it all started, they will be willing to defend our ways. But if they don't know, they will be quick to want change without knowing what they are trying to change. Change for the right reasons is good, but you have to know what you are changing first."

"That is a very good thought. It is noted. What else do you have?"

"I am only an Nze priest, not that my opinions matter much. But I will express them anyway."

"Please go on."

"I have heard the Ozo men talking about the issue of expansion. If it means annexing an uninhabited forest in some other part of Igbo land, we should go for it. But if it means assimilating some other Igbo family against their will, that is not acceptable."

"Of course not. No one is talking about that. At least I have not heard that. What some people are suggesting is that we ask other Igbo families living close to us if they would like to have a common union with us. The problem is that we then have to change our name and some of the ways we do things. What you suggest is more practical for now. What I really like about this idea is that if we find two or three other uninhabited locations and send our people there, they will be much closer to more Igbo communities."

"That is true. Besides, just asking other communities to join our family will not produce the farmland our people need."

"Correct. What do your think about Nze men's status in our community?"

"I don't understand what you mean."

"Their status as a decision-making body? They could make minor decisions about Nri families instead of leaving all the decisions to Ozo men."

"Actually, that is one of the things I was going to talk about. If it were left to me, Nze men would be making all the decisions. They are actually the ones who know more about our people. Besides, all Ozo men are automatically Nze men too. So you will not be taking anything away from Ozo men. The only difference is that more opinions will be heard."

Igwe Nwadike had finished the garden egg leaves pill and was busy getting more. But this time he was also adding some red hot pepper. That would really wake him up. Ichie Idika was not a big fan of fresh vegetables, but he needed something, too. He reached into his goatskin bag again and brought out another lump of kolanut. This one was for him alone and it needed no additional blessing.

"That would be going too far. You don't want to do that. You start with a little and then you can always add more to their basket. The almighty Ozo priests have great pride, you know," said Igwe Nwadike.

"That is true. That is true."

"I was thinking of including Nze men in the year-counting ceremony, which is part of spiritual matters. Now Ozo men would not care about that, would they?"

"And that brings me to the next point—women. How can we as a community achieve our glories if women do not have a strong spiritual movement? Yes, Iyom women were meant to achieve that, but almost all of them are the wives of Ozo men. They are all rich women. To them, it is all about who owns what. A strong spiritual movement should be created for all women. It should not be based on what people own."

"There are just too many things to talk about and very little time."

"That is another reason why decision-making responsibilities should be shared between Ozo and Nze men and women, too."

"I am in favor of women being admitted as Nze women, but they must be over the age of childbearing. Women who are still bearing and raising children are the foundation of a strong and healthy family. If someone is admitted into Nze society, she should be able to respond quickly to the needs and demands of her position. There must be no compromise."

"Yes. But they can also be made associate members while they are still raising children. After that, they could become full members with full Nze responsibilities. That is only fair."

"I think you are right. It is not on the agenda for this meeting though. There are just too many other things to talk about. What do you think about Uwa men?"

"Which ones? Uwa men as in real Uwa men or Uwa men as in Igbo men?"

Igwe Nwadike gave out a big laugh. "I have never heard that one before. But you put it very nicely. Indeed, I mean Uwa men as in Igbo men."

"Well, we have to speak the truth. Then we can talk about it. If not, we will get nowhere. We have to accept the fact that they are indeed Igbo people from our Igbo villages before we can even try solving anything. If we keep calling them Uwa men, we will never solve that problem."

"Then what?"

"Well, I suggest that the full Ozo meeting adopt an agreement that they are indeed Igbo people. Once that is done, you can use that as a base to tell all Igbo people that Uwa men are indeed from their villages. Once that is done, the Igbo people can cooperate with our efforts. Only then can they come forward with information about those people. But we have to take the mask off first."

"I am very worried about the Uwa men. They are the biggest threat to our Igbo communities. I used to think that I could make peace with anyone. But it occurred to me that you can never make peace with some-one who is hiding behind a mask. You can't make peace with someone unless you know their true identity and what they really want. My last encounter with those people was a good fourteen years ago, but it is still fresh as if it happened yesterday. I can still hear their voices and see their faces."

"Maybe that's why our ancestors chose you to lead our people. You are one of the very few Ozo priests who still complies with the old way. But I am afraid that Uwa men are becoming bolder and bolder each day. They are beginning to harass even Nri priests."

"It is terrible and I want something done right away."

"I wish I could help you more on that, but the only lasting solution is one that you cannot accept."

"Of course, we can never engage in violent behavior or encourage Igbo people to do so. It is strictly against our beliefs. It is against Aja-Ana."

"Left to me, I would see nothing wrong with self-defense. Besides, those people are bullies. They bully peaceful Igbo people. Unfortunately, violence is what they understand. Sometimes that is the only option you have. You can never make peace with those people."

"That is what worries me."

"It is a test of our philosophies. Sometimes, philosophies ought to be modified, you know, to suit the present need."

Igwe Nwadike pondered this for several moments. He had thought about it many times before, but each time he always got the same answer.

"What the Nri stand for is the ideal. The Nri stand for a lasting solution and not a quick one."

TWELVE

Nri Lake

It had been said that Nri people did not think with their heads but with their hearts. And nowhere was that saying revealed more than in the way they described leadership. The male quarters, which was also the leadership center of the family, was referred to as the heart (obu or obi) of the compound. To Nri people, one used one's head to survive and one's heart to live a life of purpose and of service and fulfillment. The rest of the body did not serve the heart. Rather, the heart served the rest of the body with life-saving blood. It was the heart that recycled and cleansed any polluted blood and made it usable again. The heart understood how much blood was needed and where and when to send it. To Nri people, a leader must be ruled by the heart. A leader must reason well. He must live in isolation most of the time, like Eze Nri, so that his reasoning would be sound and his thinking deep. But he must also be ruled by his heart. To the Nri, a leader who could not feel with his heart was not worthy of leadership. So it was little wonder that they called the king's palace "Nne Obu Nri" (The Mother of All Hearts at Nri).

꙰ ꙰ ꙰

The congregation filled the huge temple that was the second largest obu in Nri. They were waiting for Ezu, the leader of the affluent Oganiru sect. Some people stood outside, chatting in small groups. Those who had come early had been waiting nearly two hours. Those who arrived on time had been there for an hour. Those who knew Ezu well came one hour late, or, maybe, right on time. The man did not wait on anyone. He would come out only when the house was full when he could have a maximum effect on the waiting crowd.

Ezu must have been told that the house was full, for he finally emerged from his personal quarters smiling broadly. His red cap had a total of four feathers, the most any Ozo priest wore. He wore a blue agbada robe like most men in the big compound, but his was shiny velveteen. His red hat was longer than most people's. His neck beads were at least ten strands and some of them reached his mid-body. He wore elephant ivory bracelets on both wrists. His brown sandals were made from some exotic animal and definitely imported. If he had been of average height, close to ninety percent of those in the compound would have qualified as giants. But he was not of average height—he was a dwarf.

"Ezuuuu! Ezuuuu!! Ezuuuu!!!" the entire crowd shouted as they rose to their feet.

Ezu started from the left side of the huge compound and walked his way to the right, then into the temple, hugging some and shaking hands with the rest. One could not miss the smile on his face or in his voice. The smile was genuine. He was completely happy with himself. But if the smile did not convey his contentment, then the voice was sure to do so. It was deep and loud and filled the whole compound. His voice was that of a man who had lots of confidence and was at peace with himself. He must have been saying something very funny to each of the men he shook hands with or hugged, for most of them immediately burst out in laughter and they laughed really hard. But Ezu himself laughed even harder and louder. When he was through welcoming his guests—about one hundred and fifty men—he settled in his special chair at the front of the congregation in his obu which had been turned into a temple. His carved mahogany chair with its armrest was higher and more decorated than the other chairs in the temple. Everyone else sat after he was seated.

"Ooh, ooooooh, oooh! The house is full," he announced as he surveyed the crowd once more. "The people who were invited have come. Do you have something for us?"

He spoke so that all could hear, but he was actually speaking to "The End" (Ejechee Ogwu). She was his sixth and youngest wife. She was twenty-two years old and stood at least twice his height—taller than most men. He called her The End, but that was what he had called his fifth wife before Ejechee Ogwu came around. His queen, standing at the entrance, motioned to a brigade of servants to bring baskets of kolanuts. It was a little past midday on an eighth moon day and an Eke market day. The sun was at its peak.

The congregation was the "Who was Who" of the Nri economic upper class. They were really more the Nri merchant class, for they were all big merchants. Ezu, their self-appointed leader, had called the meeting.

The group had existed for generations, but his father, Nweke Ubaka, was credited with founding the political Oganiru. Nweke Ubaka had sharpened the group as a political force in Nri. He had started the tradition of holding a meeting before the big meeting. They always met on the first Eke market day at the eighth moon of each year, their official meeting day. This timing was very convenient and offered them a chance to officially affirm their positions before the Ozo annual general meeting, which was only two market weeks away. They would examine every issue coming up at the general meeting and plot strategies for the outcomes they desired. Ezu made the decisions most of the time. He would provide the men with the finest brands of kolanuts, palm wines, and, sometimes, foreign wines, and the best exotic roasted meats and food. He knew each of the men personally, and he should because he traded any available commodities with each of the Oganiru men.

They ate kolanuts and the first round of roasted meat and drank wine before Ezu made his opening remarks. This was deemed the most important part of the meeting for he was a good orator and usually came up with a handful of new proverbs. He stood up on his chair, gave a fake cough, and cleared his throat. He had not invented this way of getting attention, but he used it quite often. There was silence in the nameless temple.

"Ana enwe obodo enwe (A town does not just exist. It is owned)," he started. "I am looking at the owners of Nri. I am looking at the people who have real interests to protect at Nri. We Oganiru have interests that can be seen, touched, and felt. Our ancestors have been protecting our ideas for generations. I have yet to see where that has led us. They were quick to invoke the ideal behavior. They called it heavenly or holy living. Unfortunately, we do not live in heaven. We live in the forest. We must wake up to the reality that we live in the forest."

"Oganiru Kwenu!"

"Yeaa!"

"Oganiru Kwenu!"

"Yeaa!"

"Igweh-Enyi Kwenu!"

"Yeaa!"

"There are two sets of laws that I know. There are the laws of sky (heaven), and then there are laws of the forest. Umu-nnaa (Brethren), it is with a heavy heart that I tell you that we do not live in heaven. We live in the forest. Yes! We live among lions and hyenas, jackals and hawks. So we have to play by the rules of the forest. In the forest, the rule of life is survival. It is that simple. In the forest, for instance, a frog that does not swallow another frog does not grow and may not survive. But if it swallows other frogs, it will become so big that its chances of being swallowed by another will be slim to none. That is the secret of survival in the forest, Umu-nnaa. We are told that everyone in heaven is equal, that food is rationed, and that there is perfect order and harmony. But then again, Umu-nnaa, we do not live in heaven. How I wish we did."

"Speak!"

"Ezuuuu! Ezuuuu!!"

There were applause and standing ovations from every section of the nameless temple.

"Our Eze, Igwe Nwadike, follows the old ways. He would like everyone to engage in meditation half of every day. To me, Umu-nnaa, this is encouraging laziness, nurturing laziness. Our generation cannot afford to nurture laziness. That kind of meditation symbolizes how we close our eyes to all the dangers that surround us. We want people who produce with their eyes wide open. We want people who build. The days we are not meditating, Eze would like us to be in some Igbo village trying to tell the people why they should not fight one another. Do you know that business is good during times of war? Do you know that then we sell the most arrows and machetes and spears? Do you know that Umu-Nri are more valuable to our neighbors during war than during peace? We become very rich and are hailed as warriors of peace. Do you know that those communities listen better to a peacemaker when the natural war hunger has been purged? Do you know, my friends, that the absence of ill will diminishes the value of good? Peace can be valued only when people have seen war. It is only when they have seen body parts lying everywhere that they ask themselves, 'Why are we fighting again? What are we fighting for?' But before people see the horrors of war, it is just like another game. A peacemaker is looked at as if he were a parent preventing his children from playing the game of life and learning from experience."

"Nri people must think for themselves and become very rich for themselves. It is only through our riches and not through our kind hearts that we are valued and respected. We should not be the peacemakers to all Uwa people (the rest of the world). We should not be playing the role of mother hen to the rest of the world when we have enough problems at home to keep us very busy. Hohohoo! Hohoho . . . ."

He gave out his signature baritone laugh which filled the temple. His faithful followers knew what was coming—perhaps some new sayings.

"Ezuuuu! Speak," someone yelled from the crowd. "Speak to your own people!"

"Speaking about mother hens, Igwe is a good man with a very good heart, and we love him for it, but he reminds me of 'Abonoba's chicken.'"

It was then that the roof seemed to come off the obu.

"Ezu! Ezu!! Ezu!!!"

He did not have to retell the story of Abonoba's chicken. It was an Igbo folktale that the men knew well. It was about a chicken farmer named Abonoba. He had really bad luck with his chicken which would lay lots and lots of eggs, but, out of selfishness, would open the eggs one by one and suck out the juice. Then she would lay more eggs and feast on them. Months turned into years and years rolled by, and Abonoba still had no proceeds from his chicken. He went to a local oracle and offered sacrifices. The oracle asked him to make a wish so Abonoba wished that his chicken should be selfless instead of selfish. And so it was. His chicken had many chicks. She would fetch food and give all of it to her chicks. She ate very little herself. Her chicks kept growing bigger and bigger, and the mother kept getting smaller and smaller. One day a hawk came from the sky looking for food. It confused the mother for her chicks and lunched on her. This story was told to selfless individuals to encourage them to take care of themselves too.

As Ezu continued speaking, the basic foundation was set, and soon everyone present was thinking along the same line. Nze associates, women, servants, and children stood around the outside of the temple. They watched and listened. Ezu's ideas would be repeated in small groups, including in the palm wine bars in Nkwo market.

❧ ❧ ❧

Ezu was one of the highest positions an Ozo man could hold. Just like the Eze Nri, the Ezu Nri title could be held by only one person at a time. It was a lifetime position. The holder wore four feathers on his red cap. But, unlike Eze Nri, who was appointed by the spirit of the departed Nri kings called the Nri Menri council, Ezu Nri was appointed by living Ozo men through voting. One year after the holder of the Ezu title died, any Ozo man in good standing was free to seek the position.

The position had been created ten generations ego. It was meant to be the highest spiritual position next to the Eze Nri. Ozo men were supposed to vote for whoever seemed to be the most spiritual, selfless, and humble. The position was created to make up for what the Eze Nri was lacking—closeness to the ordinary people. The Eze Nri, because of his spiritual position and practice, saw very little of his Nri subjects and Igbo clients. In the Igbo language, Ezu meant "lake," and Ezu Nri meant "Nri Lake," the symbol of all giving. Nri Lake was the perfect selfless entity, the perfect host where every living creature around Nri at one time or another had received some form of blessing, directly or indirectly. So, when the selfless ceremonial position next to the Eze Nri was created, they called it Ezu Nri. But that had been ten generations before. A lot had changed since then.

The affluent Oganiru priestly sect had adopted the Ezu Nri position as their own and had produced the position holder for the past seven generations. They reasoned that since the holders of Eze Nri position had mostly came from the Ozo-Mkputu sect, then the Ezu Nri must come from the Oganiru. This had become an unwritten arrangement. In ten generations, the role of Ezu Nri had slowly changed from the most spiritual and altruistic to the most wealthy and famous. And famous, of course, meant whoever was the loudest.

A different line of thinking had emerged to justify the change: Nri Lake (Ezu Nri) had never dried up and would never dry up. So the wealth of the Ezu Nri titleholder would never dry up. That was the new line of thinking.

In the old days, when a new Ezu Nri was chosen, the selected Ozo priest was put to a test. He was sent into one year of isolation in the holy forest. During that year, he would see no one and speak to no one. He would eat only uncooked food. If he could stand a year of lonesomeness, of fasting and meditation and prayer, then he was good enough.

With the new philosophy came a different kind of test. In fact, the new appointee was not put to a test at all, only his wealth was tested. When the Oganiru men talked about the old days, they meant only four generations ago. At that time, when a new Ezu Nri was selected, he was taken to Ugwu Owele (Backyard Hill), a small but long and steep hill at Nri. At the peak, the finalist would slaughter hundreds of cattle. The blood was poured over the hilltop and the slaughter continued until the blood reached the foot of the hill. The whole city would wait there for the blood to reach them. When it did, the representatives at the peak would hear the clamor.

"Ozugwo! Ozugwo!! (Enough! Enough!!)," the observers at the foot of the hill would shout. Then they would begin singing and dancing. The first test had been passed.

The second test was a feast. The position seeker must feed the whole Nri clan, all twelve villages, for twelve days in a row. If one single person complained about not being fed a single meal during any of the twelve days, the deal was off. There were other minor tests like giving expensive gifts to appease important Ozo priests.

One generation before Okeke Ubaka, the current Ezu Nri, was selected, Ozo men finally became more enlightened and changed the test. Killing the cows and feeding the whole clan for twelve days was considered too uncivilized. They decided to estimate how many cattle it would take to feed everyone and just share them among the villagers. And, instead of feeding the whole clan for twelve days at thirty cattle per village, they decided to just estimate the monetary value of the cattle and share that among the villages.

But when Okeke Ubaka was chosen a generation later, he made history. He insisted that he must do it both ways, the old way and the new way. He slaughtered cattle at Ugwu Owele and fed the Nri clan for twelve days. And he also estimated the monetary value of the whole process and gave the Nri people money as well. He did this to erase any doubt in anyone's mind that he was the greatest man to ever hold the Ezu position. He instantly got the full respect of the rich and famous in Nri and Igbo land. He had seized the moment and recycled the wacky ideology of the Oganiru group into a perfect political tool. When Ezu Nri, Okeke Ubaka, spoke, Oganiru men listened.

❧ ❧ ❧

Ichie Idika sensed something was in the air as soon as he walked into the palace ground. But not even the wise man could figure out what it was. For a very long time, he had always been the one to disturb Igwe's private time. He was always inviting himself. But for the first time in a long time, Igwe Nwadike had sent for him. He was treated like an Eze Nri by everyone as soon as he set his foot in the palace grounds. Igwe Nwadike and Ichie Idika had a relationship going back to their childhood. Igwe Nwadike had been about seven and Ichie Idika about five when they first met.

Ichie Idika's mother was from Igwe Nwadike's village of Nri-Ejiofor. Igwe Nwadike could recall that when he was nine, Ichie Idika would come to his village by himself just to play with other kids. Then Ichie would go back to his village to eat lunch and return to Nri Ejiofor after lunch to play some more. Most of the time, he would not even set foot in his maternal compound. At the time, none of the kids at Nri Ejiofor knew his real name. They simply called him Nwadiana (Sister's Son or Sister's Child). It was a sacred relationship to be someone's Nwadiana. Ichie Idika, the Nwadiana, knew more people in Nri Ejiofor village than Igwe Nwadike himself who spent more time serving his father's business associates outside of Nri than he spent at his village.

"Nwadiana, welcome," Igwe Nwadike said as soon as he joined him in the big private living room.

"That's it. I knew it. I knew that all this pampering had something behind it. And this Nwadiana business just confirmed it. When did you last call me Nwadiana? I know that you are just fattening the cow so that you can slaughter it. Prove me wrong then. Prove me wrong."

"I do not intend to. I need you."

"Okay . . . , please continue . . . ."

"Why again do you not want to take the Ozo title?"

"You know very well why I do not belong to the sect. They are too political for me. There are some Ozo men I respect very much. But most of them I simply cannot stand."

"No one is perfect. Even Eze Nri himself."

"What is the purpose of joining a group that is more interested in making laws to suit their personal interests than in making our place better? Igbo people and Uwa people look up to us for direction. I amuse myself at the thought of an ordinary Igbo man coming to witness an Ozo Nri meeting. And yet Ozo Nri priests were supposed to lead Nri and Igbo people to The Light. It saddens me to know that every Ozo man at present is a potential candidate for the Eze Nri position. It saddens me because it shows what lies ahead for our people if things do not change."

"So how do you hope to bring about that change? By running away from it?"

"There is not much I can do in my capacity to affect the kind of change I would like to see. I am not a wealthy man. I have the right to inherit my father's Ozo priesthood. But I cannot do that because I do not believe that people should inherit the Ozo priesthood. They should earn it through personal achievement. So I cannot inherit my father's Ozo priesthood and then turn around and advocate that people should not inherit it. Ozo priesthood should be based on proven personal discipline, spiritual development, and the ability to seek the greater interest of Nri and Igbo people. You have done a very good job with Nze priests. I have no doubt that you can do the same with Ozo priests."

Igwe Nwadike knew that Ichie Idika was telling him the truth that he needed to hear. But he had himself been an Ozo man before he became Eze Nri. He knew how the politics were played. A majority of Ozo men thought that money and alliances would get them any law they wanted. He knew what needed to be done, but he had to have a very strong alliance with the right people.

"I would like you to attend the coming Ozo meeting."

"But I am not an Ozo priest."

"Congratulations, Nwadiana, you are now one, compliments of your wisdom and our-best-friendship."

"I would not like to be abused for speaking my heart."

"That I will guarantee you. No one will abuse you. And I am also giving you an honorary and full membership in the Ozo priesthood. You spend nothing and you inherit nothing. I am giving it to you because you have proven your personal discipline and spiritual development and what else you said it should be."

"And I thank you very kindly for your wisdom and courage, 'Holy one.'"

"Now all you have to do in return is to go there and speak your heart."

"Speaking my heart will be a lot of work. It will cause me great pain. I hope you know that."

"Then enjoy it."

THIRTEEN

The Mission

The first day of the twelve-day annual general meeting was Eze Nri's day. He would use it to set the tone for the meeting. Igwe Nwadike had a message and was motivated to share it. He was more passionate about this particular meeting than any other since he had become Eze Nri. Most Ozo priests also felt strongly about the annual meeting because the major issues of discussion would define the future of Nri and how it would be perceived by everyone around Nri. The key issues were admission of new citizens to Nri and expanding the Nri territory. They seemed to be two different things, but they were not. In fact, they were two different solutions to one problem: over-population at Nri land. Over-population had been a problem for a long time. But everyone had been avoiding discussing it because Nri was evenly divided on the best solution.

Oganiru priests wanted to scale down on admitting new citizens and, if possible, stop immigration altogether. Ozo-Mkputu priests wanted to expand Nri land. That way they could admit and reach more Igbo people. Was not this the goal of Nri? "What was the Nri mission without this?" they would ask.

To Ozo-Mkputu priests, being Nri was a state of the heart and not really the purity of Nri blood as Oganiru priests would like to think. In fact, at the heart of this meeting seemed to be the question: "Who is the correct citizen of Nri?"

Igwe Nwadike had his own views, but this was not an autocratic community. He did not even have a vote in the matter because he was Eze Nri, a neutral entity, a spirit who must let humans decide their own future. But he must guide them by appealing to their conscience. That was his role as Eze Nri, and Igwe Nwadike was skilled at doing this.

Finally, he stood up to face the Ozo Nri council. The temperature was right—the sun was rising, but the air was cold. There was complete silence in the room. Igwe Nwadike understood Ozo priests, even the most difficult ones. He knew how to get what he wanted from every one of them while leaving their pride intact. Sometimes he even added something to their pride. He was popular. He was one of them. He had played their politics before he was chosen as Eze Nri. The temple of the light was full, and he enjoyed a big audience.

"Umu-Nri (Children of Nri), I greet you!"

"Yeaa!" they answered.

"Umu-Nri, I greet you!"

"Yeaa!"

"Nri bu Nri (Nri of Nri), I greet you!"

"Yeaa!"

"Ozo Nri, I greet you!"

"Yeaa!"

"Igwe!" someone yelled from somewhere. It was contagious. "Igwe!"

"Igwee!!! Igweee!!!!" Everyone stood up and some raised their red caps. Igwee had not said a thing, but somehow they knew what was coming.

"Looking at the number of people who have come, I have no doubt that you feel as strongly as I do about this particular meeting. It is very important to us because a lot of decisions will be made for our people. It is true that we have different views about the matters at stake, but I am very pleased that a lot of us are interested in these questions. It shows our commitment to the good of our people. I must confess that I have my own personal opinions about some policies that we are going to discuss in the days ahead. But, according to our customs, I will act as a neutral figure, guiding and mediating between your views. You are the people who walk the villages of Igbo and Uwa families. So you see what I do not see. You are the people who till our lands and conduct your business with the rest of our Igbo and Uwa people. You are the ones who serve our people. So you should know what works and what does not work. You should know what needs to be improved and how we can best do this."

"My position at this meeting as always is to be first a mediator between your different views and to seek a compromise if it is necessary. It is also my role to constantly remind you that your opinions should not reflect your personal interests but the collective interests of our entire people and our ancestors. Because of this, I will remind you of our destiny as a people. I hope that I will make good on that so that those who betray our course as a people by placing their personal interest above our people's interest will do so because they have chosen to and not because they are ignorant of their actions."

He said that their first duty as the Ozo sect was to make the people happy and that this can be done by creating a community that is free from discrimination. He said that happiness is worthless if it does not translate into service and that it is the duty of all Nri people to serve Igbo and Uwa people.

"Our mission as Umu-Nri is to serve Igbo people and our Uwa neighbors. This is our purpose. Yes, we want to be happy as Umu-Nri people, but if we do not convert that happiness into goodwill on the earth we have failed. We are a unique people as Umu-Nri. You can say that we are special people, but then, all communities are special in their own right. They just have to discover their talents as communities and then use them to serve the earth and other people. We cannot tell any community what their gifts are. They must discover them for themselves and then choose to use them. We must understand that Chineke did not put us on earth, so that we would be happy. Yes, Chineke (God) wants us to be happy and have fun, but Chineke also wants us to contribute to the condition of the environment for him."

"I will not tell you the history of our Nri people. As Ozo men, you should know that. We all know what we mean to all Igbo and Uwa people. But, once in awhile, especially at a time like this meeting, we have to remind ourselves so that some people will not claim sudden forgetfulness regarding our purpose."

Igwe said that it is their first duty to accept anybody who walks into the Nri community seeking to have a new life. It does not matter if their former communities rejected them or if they willingly left their communities as long as those immigrants respect Nri laws. He said that the second duty Nri people owe to their environment is to actively spread the message of peace, tolerance, fair play, and non-violence as Agbala and Aja-Ana had shown them. He reminded them that the third duty of the Nri community to their environment is to prescribe and interpret moral laws according to Aja-Ana (the Earth Goddess) and to cleanse whoever had offended Aja-Ana.

He said that "Contrary to what some believe, it is *not* part of our duties as Nri people to break up fights. It is part of our duties as human beings. As human beings, we are as guilty and uncivilized as the parties fighting each other if we do not attempt to break up a fight. We may be peaceful today, but that is not guaranteed tomorrow. When emotions run wild in our part of the world and punches fly in every direction, we cannot expect monkeys to get down from the trees and call us to our senses. We will expect other human beings to come and break up the fight. They may get bruised in the course of doing that though, but it is part of their duty to humankind."

He stated that the fourth duty Nri owe to the earth is to continue to explore what it means to be a perfect human being and, therefore, a perfect society and then make those discoveries a reality in the world. He said that Ozo status has turned into something unintended and many Ozo priests do not even know what Ozo means. He said Ozo means saver or savior. It does not mean a wealthy person.

"You are the spiritual and moral saviors of all people. But a human being cannot really save another. Agbala saves people. We must, therefore, make ourselves available so Agbala can save people through us. We must make ourselves available to Agbala by speaking the truth all the time. Agbala values truthfulness above all things. This requires a heart that tells the truth. Agbala also values humility, so we must be humble."

At this point in his speech, there were murmurings and feet shuffling in a particular part of the temple. Igwe Nwadike must have assumed that his message of humility was not popular to certain people and decided to speak more on that.

"There is something about humility that you must understand. You can choose to humble yourself and follow the will of Agbala. When you humble yourself, humility is achieved willingly. But if you do not humble yourself, then Agbala will humiliate you. Then humility is also achieved, but without your will. It does not matter to Agbala how humility is achieved. If you are destined to be used by Agbala, you cannot escape humility."

Igwe Nwadike made a long list of the benefits that would come from Agbala if Nri people do a good job and perform their duties to the earth. Those included respect from the rest of the world, wealth, peace, and intervention of the Gods when Nri people call on them. But he also made what seemed like a longer list of calamities that would befall Nri people should they fail to perform their duties. Some were very frightening like being deserted by the Gods and being invaded by other nations who would impose their Gods on Nri people. He also said that if Nri people did not serve other nations willingly, other nations would take them as slaves and make them serve in chains. He stated that this would be part of the humiliation from Agbala. The only way to get out of that captivity would be to willingly serve our world according to our agreement with Agbala.

He concluded by saying that "Everything we say about Nri people is also true for all Igbo people. Umu-Nri came from Igbo people, and Igbo people come from Nri people. But when a fire starts, it starts from one spot and then spreads."

"There are no shortcuts to the tasks that lie ahead of us. Our duties to our community will be done and they will be done to suit Agbala. And we will be abundantly blessed. During the breaking of the kolanut, we invited God the Creator (Chineke), God the Light (Anyanwu), the Perfect Spirit (Agbala), the Heavenly Host and the Earthly Host (Igwe na Ana). We invited all our ancestors (Ndi Ichie) and all our deities. They are all still present here with us. Let them bear witness that I have at least tried to do my duty by giving you all the information you need to make a good decision for our people and our world. Our deities will remain with us throughout the duration of our meetings, twelve days. They will bear witness that I will do my best to guide you to make good decisions for our people. They will bear witness as to who among us will try to add pepper to the medicine we are making for clear eyes. I wish that I could make all decisions for our people. It would be very simple. But I cannot because if I make the decisions I would be feeding them. I would rather show you how to take care of yourselves so that when I join our ancestors you will continue to feed yourselves.

You must make good decisions for our people and our environment even after I join our ancestors. You must learn from your mistakes. You must make the decision to either humble yourselves or be humiliated. It is your decision and not mine to make. You, Ozo men, are the adults in Nri land and Igbo land. You must behave like adults. You must save Nri and all Igbo people from what is coming. It is coming and not very far away."

"Umu-Nri I greet you!"

"Yeaa!" they answered.

"Ozo Nri, I greet you!"

"Yeaa!"

"Ozo Nri, I greet you!"

"Yeaa! Igweee! Igweee!! Igweee!!!" Different individuals were shouting. All stood up. The chief priest was also giving praises with his bullhorn trumpet.

❦ ❦ ❦

It was Oduh's duty as Head of Ozo priests to reply to Igwe's opening remarks and to introduce the agenda for the meeting. Isi-Ozo Nri Oduh stood on his stone chair because he was not a very tall man. Oduh, a perfect bureaucrat, was not one to make a big speech. He had tried many times and knew he didn't have this skill so he took the safe route. He shouted greetings to the congregation then thanked Igwe Nwadike for his inspiring words. He reminded the congregation that "He whose name was being called frequently had something very special to do that touches all of us. We hail 'Igweee!' all the time, and we do not hail his name for nothing."

Oduh said that Igwe had proven again that those who called on him all the time were not mistaken. He said that the state of Nri, not to mention Igbo land, was in a very bad state and that their generation had not performed to the standard of their founding ancestors. He appealed to all Ozo men to set examples for the entire Nri people. He said that it was common knowledge in Nri that Nze priests were more organized and focused than Ozo priests. He said that Ozo men, an advanced form of the Nze sect, should be the ones better organized, the ones setting examples. He said this reversal was a bad omen.

"It is a bad omen because when the stream is corrupted from the source then it is only a matter of time before the rest of the stream is corrupted. The Ozo council must make very major attitude changes so that the community can count on them to make good decisions."

He thanked Igwe Nwadike again for his good examples for all of them and for his care for their cause as a people. Oduh then officially stated the questions to be dealt with during this current meeting.

Isi-Ozo Oduh cared very much for the cause of the Nri people. He would do anything to achieve the objectives clearly stated by Igwe Nwadike. The only problem was that he did not introduce new ideas. He was not a charismatic leader of the Ozo men. He was a good manager, but not a good leader. He could manage what was but could not lead Ozo men to have new ideas and goals. He had earned his position by not holding any extreme ideas and, therefore, he did not step on any toes. He said the right things at the right time but did not follow up with action. Anyone who knew him could have predicted his speech.

Isi-Ozo Oduh was giving his greetings to indicate that he had finished his response to Igwe Nwadike's speech. Then the inevitable happened. There was supposed to be a brief break with refreshments after Isi-Ozo's reply. Instead, Ichie Idika stood up on his chair. Like Oduh, he was not very tall. It was clear to everyone that he wanted to speak. However, it was against Ozo protocol for anyone else to respond to Igwe's speech other than the Isi-Ozo. Everyone was clearly against Ichie's speaking at this point. Though all were objecting to Ichie's move, some were particularly afraid of what he had to say. They stood up in order to intimidate him into sitting down instead of allowing Isi-Ozo to quietly explain that Ichie's move was against the Ozo's meeting protocol.

"Sit down! Sit down!" could be heard all over the temple, especially in a particular section. Some of those who were yelling at him were now standing on their chairs.

Ozo Ikezuo, Okoye's uncle, sat near the back of the temple. He bent his head and leaned towards his right and touched Ozo Umeadi. Lowering his voice almost to a whisper, he said, "I knew that this would happen, but not this soon. Can't he wait for the meeting to start? Is your man that anxious?"

"I thought he was your friend?" said Ozo Umeadi "If he waits for the meeting to start, then Igwe would be gone, and he would not get the attention he is looking for. Ichie is only looking for attention, that's all."

"I agree with you on that. However, I don't like this type of intimidation, especially when Igwe is still here. It makes me uneasy. What he wants to do is against our tradition. However he does not deserve to be shouted at by young men half his age. Since he is a new member, they should let Isi-Ozo explain to him the Ozo traditions."

Ozo Umeadi sighed. "Don't you see where all that shouting is coming from? Oganiru priests are afraid of what he may say. I think that they may have had a meeting and agreed to shout him down and not let him speak."

Ozo Ikezuo laughed. "Then, they don't know your man," he said. "You can only reason with him. You can only get something out of him with a low tone. You give him more strength when you try to overpower him. What they are doing may turn against them."

It was as if Isi-Ozo Oduh was listening to their conversation. *You cannot shout at a grown man like a child, especially in front of Igwe!* He thought to himself. *They should have respected the presence of Igwe in our midst!*

Oduh stood on his chair, visibly angry now. It was as if a forest full of overfed monkeys suddenly realized that a lion was in their midst. The transition from full blown turmoil to complete silence was like the wave of a magic wand. Among the Ozo priests, Igwe Nwadike was revered for his position, but Isi-Ozo Oduh was feared for his. He was very much liked and respected by many, but he was more feared than respected because of his quest for justice and orderliness. He had been known to impose a fine of ten cattle on an Ozo priest for speaking out of turn. And he was also known to order that the red cap be taken off until the fine was paid. Many Isi-Ozo before Oduh had done the same. It was the only way to handle the Ozo priests.

"It is against our tradition to respond to Igwe's opening speech by anyone other than Isi-Ozo," Oduh said looking at Ichie Idika who was now sitting down.

"We have this tradition because we do not want to create a door for anyone to disagree with what Igwe has said to us. He is a spirit and brings internal wisdom to us. Some of that wisdom we may not understand now. I will allow you to speak if what you will say is not in disagreement with Igwe's advice to us."

Ichie Idika stood up before responding. "I agree completely with what Igwe Nri has said. What I am about to say is not to Igwe, but to the Ozo Nri (Ozo council)."

"Then, I give you permission to say it this one time because you are a new member to the Ozo council. However, if you have something to say to Igwe about his speech, you must address it to me, and I will interpret it to Igwe. And, remember, if you disagree with Igwe, that is a very serious offense."

Isi-Ozo Oduh sat down, leaving the floor to Ichie. Ichie came out into the open space and paused to reflect on what he was about to say. Everyone in the temple held his breath. Sometimes Ichie Idika looked haggard and even unkempt. If a stranger was to observe him on this occasion, he might seem like someone who had very little to lose. Their assessment would have been right. Ichie Idika was not attached to anything or anyone. He was known to have big arguments with people, only to show up at their houses the next morning asking if they had any fresh palm wine. He did not care much about his clothing and could get by with one set of clothes for a long time. He would argue to his wife that he was already married; therefore, he was not afraid that young women would reject him for not wearing new clothes. He had no known trade. He had inherited lots of lands and livestock from his father who was a wealthy Ozo priest.

After his father died, Ichie loaned most of the land to farmers, mostly immigrant citizens. They, in turn, gave him some share of the harvest every season. He also gave people in various villages his cattle, goats, and lambs to take care of. Of the offspring of every cow, female goat, or sheep, the caretaker would give Ichie the first one and keep the second. His wife would go from caretaker to caretaker collecting whatever was due to them. So it was his wife who kept count of what was owed them. The only thing that Ichie Idika was attached to was his kolanut. He ate kolanut as if it was a snack. He would bless a handful of kolanut and put it in his sheepskin bag. Then he was good for the day. A friend teased him once that if the holy ancestors were with people when they were eating a blessed kolanut, then Ichie was continuously in the presence of the ancestors. Ichie believed that as long as he spoke the truth as he saw it without being violent, he was completely protected by Aja-Ana (the Earth Goddess).

One thing everyone agreed on about Ichie Idika was that whenever he stood up to speak, one must be ready for trouble. But the type of trouble depended on whom one asked. To those who had different opinions from Ichie's, it was bad trouble. To those who shared his opinions but were afraid to speak up, it was good trouble. Also, everyone agreed that eventually one would feel nothing but respect for the man. This was because he could make his point whether one agreed with him or not. He would simply wait until everyone realized Ichie was right. That was probably what scared people most. It seemed that his mere expression of an opinion made it right. He was known to boast that what he saw while sitting down, the average man would have to climb an iroko tree to see, meaning that he had more insight than the average man.

"Igweee!" Ichie Idika hailed as he bent down, touching the ground in respect. Igwe Nwadike nodded in acknowledgement.

"Isi-Ozo Nri!" he saluted Oduh.

Oduh nodded.

"Ozo Council, I salute you!" he hailed, waving to the whole congregation. A handful answered with their throats and not their mouths.

Turning to Isi-Ozo Oduh, Ichie said, "I thank you and the Ozo council whom you represent for giving me this opportunity to speak my mind. It is not my intention to offend Igwe or Ndi Ozo by insisting that I should speak. I must express a very important opinion before we can move on. You can ignore my opinion after I have expressed it, but please do not ignore my person, the messenger. Our elders said that if the bird learns to fly without perching, then the hunter must learn to shoot without aiming. There should be an exception to every rule. I thank you very dearly for making this exception."

"Please thank Igwe for me for making the duties and destiny of our people so clear that no one can claim to be unsure about them. If anyone claims to be confused, I will have the pleasure of explaining to them what they don't understand. I am, however, beginning to understand the consequences that await our people if we fail to perform according to expectations. This started me thinking that maybe our people have been doing things the wrong way. How can we allow a few people to make decisions without the formal consent of everyone? I would not even have been here if Igwe had not granted me an exception. As an individual, I would not like to suffer the consequences for a decision I did not make."

Some people were already shuffling their feet to show their discomfort. There were fake coughs in a particular section of the temple. All these distractions were desperate moves to buy time. But they were only delaying the inevitable. If Ichie's presence was a bad dream, then it was one that was slowly turning real.

"I have two problems with the current arrangements," he continued. "One is that our people should be involved in making decisions on policies so that if they pay the price of bad decisions, then they will be able to accept the consequences. If they formally select people to represent them, then they will also be better able to live with the consequences if bad decisions are made. So our people should either make decisions collectively or formally select representatives to do so on their behalf. The second concern I have is this: If for some reason—some reason that is beyond my understanding—Ozo Nri must make critical decisions for our people, then Ozo Nri membership must be based on spiritual advancement and not on economic power. If membership is based primarily on the wealth of its members, the decisions they make will inevitably be motivated by money. And, according to Igwe himself, manifesting wealth is not our primary mission as a people. This is only my personal opinion. As I said, you can throw away my opinion, but please do not throw away my person."

Ichie did not shout greetings to formally hand over the floor because he knew that only a handful of his ardent friends would care to reply to him. At first, no one knew how to react to Ichie Idika's latest challenge. They were all speechless. It was one thing to disagree with or attack a policy the almighty Ozo council had made. It was something else to attack the legitimacy of the Ozo council as a decision-making body for the Nri clan. And no one living at the time knew how or when the tradition had started.

As Ichie Idika sat down, Ozo Ikezuo and Ozo Umeadi exchanged glances. Ozo Ikezuo showed Ozo Umeadi his palms, which meant: "I don't know the answer to your puzzle" or "I don't know what you want."

"This is good for Igwe who invited him," said Ozo Umeadi. "Didn't the elders say that the young man whose father sent him to steal did not jump the fence but rather kicked down the main gate with his bare foot."

Ozo Ikezuo reached for his snuff box. "He will not last in the council. You can say that I told you so."

It was Isi-Ozo Oduh who responded. He assured Ichie Idika that nobody would throw him or his opinion away as long Isi-Ozo Oduh was still alive. He said, however, that they must take a well deserved break so they could digest what he had suggested to them.

During the break, Ichie Idika was the topic of every discussion. Everyone avoided him. He did not care. He was busy sniffing his tobacco. That was his favorite way of killing time when he wanted to be alone in a room full of unfriendly people.

FOURTEEN

Ozo Meeting

Okoye Nweri watched the whole drama of the opening speech. He absorbed every word and analyzed every phrase. He had never been to an Ozo meeting before, and he thought it was quite an experience. What he saw was not completely alien to him, but he was beginning to understand more about the priesthood and its importance. The events at their outing mission had given him a growing awareness and made him question more things about the Nri people. Every event in that mission had touched and challenged his previous beliefs. Even the Uwa men (wilderness robbers) had respected them and even sought the missionaries' blessing. The madman had paid his respects, given his blessing, and sought and received theirs. Even Ijego (the lone woman warrior), who did not like men very much, had made an exception when she saw the missionaries. The whole village at Umuaku had looked at them with awe as if they were sacred beings who had fallen from the sky. Akalaka believed in the mission, and the people who had been touched had believed in him. Was it all an illusion? Was it an act in which everyone played his or her part too well? Or was it something much more, something real?

Before attaining his position at the palace, Okoye had gone to the year-counting and keeping ceremonies, the biggest community event at Nri, where he heard Igwe Nwadike's speeches. But he had never really listened to what the bald old man was saying because he was prejudiced against him. Okoye had believed the village gossip that he had heard about Igwe—that he lived in his own world, a world of fairy tales. A world in which everything was perfect and everyone was saved from suffering. A make-believe world in which everything was possible. But with his new awareness after the outing mission, Okoye realized that the old man they all called "Our Father" was talking to the wrong crowd. He needed to take his message to ordinary people who were thirsting for it.

It was only during the mission that Okoye had come to understand why Nri people do not kill certain animals. During their second night at Umuaku, Okoye had confessed to Akalaka that he had never thought about sparing a snake simply because it was not an immediate threat.

"Why do you think that our people do not kill the gentle python?" Akalaka had asked. "Why do you think that our people do not kill the Nri Lake crocodile? The python has never been a threat to us, so we don't kill it. The crocodile is different. Once the crocodile understood that we do not kill it, it stopped attacking our people. Therefore, we have a mutual understanding that the crocodiles should live and we should live. There is nothing more to our relationship with the python or the Nri Lake crocodile. They are just symbols of the animals that we do not need for food and are no threat to us. So we don't kill them and they have nothing against us. There is nothing more to it."

Okoye had seemed puzzled by this new idea about the Nri Lake crocodile and the python. Until then, he had believed there was some form of secret relationship between the "Sacred Python" or the "Sacred Crocodile."

Akalaka saw that puzzled look, so he continued, "In fact, in the old days, before our people killed a goat, a cow, or a chicken, they would say a prayer for it and wish its spirit well, because they have nothing personal against it. They just need it for food. Sometimes the owners hired a stranger to kill the animal and would not be around during the slaughter. Today some of our people still pray for an animal before they kill it for food, but only a selected few perform that rite."

The sudden ringing of a bell brought Okoye's attention back to the meeting. He looked up and saw Oduh rising from his seat. Akalaka was seated behind Oduh. Their eyes met and Okoye felt a chill over his body. He recognized the feeling. It was the same thing Erike had described that he felt when he was in the presence of Igwe Nwadike. Okoye wiped tears from his eyes.

"Are you feeling well?" asked the palace Chief Priest, who was sitting to his left.

"I am just tired. But I will be fine."

"Maybe you should go to your quarters and lie down. Go get some rest."

"No. I will be fine. I am fine."

True to his word, Igwe Nwadike had left after the break. It was the group's decision to make. He must remain a neutral fatherly figure. They could consult him if they needed advice or clarification. He was gone, but his eyes and ears remained behind. Oduh would brief Igwe Nwadike every evening for the twelve days of the meeting. That was protocol and everyone knew it. Very few knew about the other eyes and ears present at the meeting. They belonged to Nwoye Nwana who was quick to smile and painfully honest. He had to be honest.

Nwoye Nwana was the youngest member of the Ozo-Mkputu and a former student of Igwe Nwadike. He saw what no one else saw and heard what no one else heard in Nri. He knew when a child was born in Nri and which family it was born to. He knew when a transplanted citizen was admitted and who was behind the admittance. He knew when any citizen or visitor died in Nri. He knew who said what and to whom and when. Knowledge was his food and invisibility his armor. He was the Isi Ogbadu Eze (the Head of the King's Forerunners).

The Ogbadu Eze secret sect had always been around. It was as old as the Ozo or Nze or Iyom sects. It was not political, just informational. It was a secret sect that gathered information for every Eze Nri who had ever been. Every adult in Nri had on one occasion or another heard about the Ogbadu Eze sect. But most people thought the group was a product of someone's clever imagination, just something they talked about, letting their imaginations run wild. Very few nonmembers knew how organized or widespread the sect was. They did not know its structure. Not even the Eze Nri himself knew, nor did the members know each other. They did not know who else was in the sect. The Eze Nri had not recruited them. They did their recruiting by approaching every new Eze Nri and offering their services. But this was not necessary since most Eze Nri had come from the sect. Every leader had been from the Ozo-Mkputu sect. Eze Nri knew very few of the members. Only Nwoye Nwana gave him information and what he provided was appropriate only for the ears of the Eze Nri alone. Very few members of Ogbadu-Eze knew who Nwoye Nwana was because he did not deal directly with lay members of the secret sect. Okoye was one of the few who knew him personally because Ozo Nwana had recruited him.

Like most people, Nwoye was a palace regular. With each visit he had become closer and closer to Okoye. He would tease him and pick his mind. Sometimes he would reveal a secret or two to the young recruit-to-be. This continued until Okoye had total confidence in Nwoye. Then Nwoye recruited and initiated Okoye by administering an oath.

The initiation took place on a cold, rainy evening in the planting month. Nwoye had sent for Okoye, and when he arrived at the Agbala temple in the holy forest, several other men were present. Okoye knew them all because they were regulars at the palace. He made the connection and was ready for what was about to happen. When Nwoye had invited Okoye to join and serve the sect, the young man had accepted. Nwoye warned him that his word was not enough. There had to be initiation rites in front of witnesses. There had to be promises made and oaths taken. Okoye accepted all of this.

The sect encouraged travel so Okoye had told Nwoye of his plans for the future. "I don't want any commitments that will tie me down at Nri. I want to be able to travel and see the world like my peers."

Nwoye smiled. "Our organization encourages people to travel. We frown on our core members who do not travel. The farther you can travel, the better. We encourage you to go to the Uwa lands that have not been discovered by our people. All we ask is that you bring back knowledge. Bring us souvenirs that will help us understand those people and their way of life."

"Then I am the person you want," Okoye said.

Nwoye smiled. He knew his man. He was everything they said he was.

At the initiation, Okoye greeted the men by their title names.

"Ideh!" (pillar-of-the-house).

Ideh was a member of the Oganiru. He was a wealthy man and sponsored most of their activities.

He greeted Nwoye, "Onyinalo!" (If-Diplomacy-Fails...! ...Should we then use our fist?). He greeted the third, "Onuora!" (the-voice-of-all), then the fourth man, "Ifennamgwalum!" (my-father-told-me-a-secret). The men did not waste time.

Ideh spoke first. "We have a lot of confidence in you, Our Son. The rites we are about to perform must not be heard by anyone else. Our organization is secret, but what we do is not evil. We cannot ask you to kill or hurt someone or tell a lie. All we do is get information and give it to Igwe and our leaders. What they choose to do with it is their own decision. It is important to keep the nature of the business secret. That is the only way you can get good information. Almost everything we learn is common knowledge but when we put it together it can tell us a lot. . . ."

"I told him many things already," Nwoye interrupted.

"Good. Good. Do you have any questions?" Ideh asked Okoye.

"No. Not at this moment."

"Good then. Onyinalo is the one to ask if you have any questions."

The initiation was as quick and simple as their conversation had been. Okoye was given an Offor club of justice. While holding the Offor, he swore an oath of secrecy and allegiance. He promised to always tell the truth to the sect. After the oath was taken, Ifennamgwalum, the youngest of the four men, filled a cup of palm wine from a small jar and poured it on the ground. Then he filled the second cup and gave it to Okoye. Ideh, who seemed to be in a hurry, left after guzzling down his cup of wine.

Okoye and Nwoye Nwana saw each other many times after that, but nothing was said about that evening or the sect. Three moons later and ten days before the Ozo meeting, Nwoye told Okoye to cover the Ozo annual meeting. He was to observe who said what. During the breaks, he was to mingle, chat, and listen. Then he would meet with Nwoye Nwana every evening and report what he had learned. That was his first assignment, and it was as simple and straightforward as the initiation had been.

※ ※ ※

The meeting in the big hall was getting rowdy. Someone was making a speech in favor of Ndi-bia Ndi-bia (immigration). Okoye did not care about Ndi-bia Ndi-bia because he was hungry, and it was past time for the break. Okoye was not expecting to see Erike in the hall when he noticed his friend bending down and talking to someone. Okoye had not seen him come in. As Erike got up to leave, their eyes met. Erike smiled. Okoye pointed to his stomach and shook his head. Erike shrugged and showed Okoye his two palms. Suddenly there was a loud outburst of laughter in the hall. The speaker must have said something very funny. Everyone rose from their chairs. There was some applause. It was break time. Okoye was the second to exit the hall following after Erike.

"Nwune-ozu! Nwune-Ozu!!" (Brother of the Helpless Corps) he called after Erike who was already several foot-steps. "How can I repay my debt to the stomach?"

"I heard that lunch will be provided all," Erike said as he turned around.

"Don't count on it. I heard that about breakfast, but I did not see one."

"Maybe not breakfast but lunch for sure."

"Don't count on it. Besides they may decide to feed us cocoyam."

"Cocoyam at an Ozo meeting?"

"Anything is possible these days. I heard that . . . ." Okoye felt someone grab his right hand from behind. He was pretty sure it was a dwarf. He could tell by the grip. The hand was small but strong. Definitely one of his dwarf mates at the palace.

"Whoever you are, you'd better have something for the stomach," Okoye joked without turning around.

"Your stomach, is that all you care for?" asked the masquerade voice.

"I am very sorry, Our Master!" Okoye said as he turned facing Ezu.

"There is no need for an apology. Just follow me and you will never go hungry again," said Ezu, leading Okoye away who laughingly obeyed. He followed like a little child. Ezu stopped three times to make short conversations. All the time he kept a very tight grip on Okoye's right hand. At one point, Okoye wondered if what he'd heard about Ezu was true—that Ezu was only thirty-one years old (only nine years older than he was). Because Ezu was very dominating and intimidating, he looked and acted at least fifty.

It had been said that Ezu was Oganiru and Oganiru was Ezu. He was a typical member of the merchant club, young and very wealthy, and he had not created his own wealth. It had been handed down to him through five generations. Most Oganiru men inherited their wealth and, therefore, had never known hardship. They had never been abandoned at a seven-way crossroad. They had never been forced to choose between bad and worse. Their canoes had never capsized in the middle of the ocean, forcing them to make a deal with their chi. They had never had the privilege of making a deal with God for one more chance—for a last chance to be good. They had never seen tough times and they preferred things to remain that way. They believed the best way to ensure their position was to hold on to whatever they had and maybe add to it.

Igwe Nwadike was different. He, too, was rich and had inherited his wealth from two generations back. But he hadn't seen any of it until his father died. Igwe lived outside of his father's house most of his youth. It would have been better for him if he had lived with a relative or a wealthy friend of his father's, but this was not the case. He lived with his father's business servants in the Igbo mainland where he became the servant to his father's servants. And they did not seem to notice or care that it was his father that they worshipped. Igwe was insulted and abused by most of these servants. He had always wondered why his father hated him so much. He once asked his mother if this man was his real father, and his mother broke down crying. It had been during one of his mother's irregular visits when he was at the age of ten and four that Okoyeocha Nwadike put the question to her. She had just finished telling him that his age group had learned a new dance. Okoyeocha Nwadike had asked her who their lead singer was and his mother told him it was his namesake, Okoyeocha, the son of Nwuche. Okoyeocha was outraged.

"The idiot cannot sing! He cannot sing! The son of a wild animal took my position."

"The son of an Ozo priest cannot say unkind words about other people. You cannot call people bad names," his mother had reminded him. It was then that he asked the question that made his mother to go back fifteen years to when he was conceived.

"Is he my real father? I mean, is Nduluo my blood father? You must tell me the truth."

His mother stared at him for several moments before responding.

"I swear by the sun that he is your father," she said. Then she wept. Okoyeocha did not feel guilty for asking but was puzzled at her answer. He made no attempt to console his mother. It was after she had wiped her tears with her waist clothes that she said something Okoyeocha would never forget.

"Your father likes you more than the rest of your brothers. He thinks you are more persistent than the others. He says that you are as strong as a rope, and he likes you for that. You should trust your father. Whatever he is doing is for your own good."

Okoyeocha welcomed this new information but still did not understand his situation. His mother told him that he could always come home if he wanted to. But Okoyeocha did not want to disappoint his father. Besides, the humiliation was even worse at home. One incident always stood out in his mind. His father had never taken him to the Ozo feast that other Ozo priests took their first sons to. His father always took his younger brother, Nwude. But for one year-ending feast Nwude was sick and could not go. His father told Igwe the night before to get ready to accompany him. The boy was so excited that he could not sleep all night. Early in the morning he bathed and put on his best new clothes so he would look like the proper first son of an Ozo priest. Usually his father would choose one of the servants to carry the huge pot of palm wine whenever Nwude accompanied him to a feast. But, after looking at his clothes, his father put the pot of foamy palm wine on his head. The smelly foam soaked his clothes before they got to the feast. He smelled like a palm winemaker all day.

The humiliation did not end there. When they arrived at the big temple hall, his father went around the hall greeting his friends and introducing Okoyeocha with the pot of palm wine still on his head. The other boys, his peers who accompanied their fathers, were laughing and pointing at him, and Okoyeocha was sure that his father saw them. It took the goodwill of one of his father's friends to help him take the palm wine pot from off his head. He was forced to spend the rest of the feast outside the temple since the other boys, who had formed their own little feast down the hall, complained that he smelled like palm wine. One boy jokingly called him "palm winemaker."

Exactly two weeks after his mother's visit, the answers to Okoyeocha's questions came. He had just finished cutting firewood for his master's wife and had been rewarded with roasted plantain buttered with palm oil. After he finished eating, he drank two cups of cold water. The day was sunny and his master was not at home so he sat down in his master's obu and dozed off. He was awakened by the voice of his master's wife. At first he thought he was dreaming.

"Run, Oyeocha. Run!" she yelled.

Everyone called him Oyeocha, the short version of his name. Okoyeocha opened his eyes, and there he was—Azubuike, the madman, was standing three footsteps away, looking down at him. Azubuike was known to be violent and had attacked villagers in the past. Everyone was afraid of him, but no one had dared touch him because he was Nwadiana, chased away from his own village and free to return to his mother's birthplace. There he was, a violent and crazy sacred cow, only a few feet away and breathing down on Okoyeocha.

"Run, Oyeocha. Run!" the master's wife kept yelling. Okoyeocha made a useless attempt at getting up from his master's rattan chair.

"Do not run," Azubuike said in a commanding but low tone. "I am not here to harm you but to give you a message."

Okoyeocha said nothing, his eyes nearly popping out of his head like a cornered antelope.

"I will not hurt you" Azubuike assured him again. "I was just passing by and met some people who said that they were Ndi-Gboo (Ancient Men). They told me to come by and give you a message. I told them that everyone runs from me. They promised that they would put you to sleep so that I could reach you."

Okoyeocha Nwadike had nothing to say.

"They said that you have been chosen to lead your people, and that you should never blame your father for making you live a humble life. He did it so you may be a good leader," Azubuike said. Then he turned and walked away.

"What did he say to you? What does he want?" Okoyeocha master's wife asked him holding her waist cloth, ready to flee.

"He said that he would not hurt me and then he said other things that I did not understand," Okoyeocha told her.

❊ ❊ ❊

They sat around an apple tree in the big compound about two hundred footsteps from the Offor Nri temple. They were the who's who of the Oganiru priests though they would rather have been called the who's who of the Nri holy priests. There were about forty of them. Some sat down while others stood. Ezu was one of the few who arrived last. He liked to appear when the congregation was full so he could make a pronounced entrance. Instead of joining the rest, Ezu went to the front of the group. With a dramatic gesture, he raised Okoye's right hand the way one would with an unknown kid who had just thrown the reigning champion in a wrestling match.

"This is Okoye Nweri. His friends call him Okoye Udo," the baritone voice announced. "He is a future member of Oganiru."

"Welcome to the real world," someone yelled.

"He is mine. I will make him very rich and very wise," Ezu added.

"We want men who will produce!" another voice said.

"Of course, he will produce. They call him Okoye Udo," Ezu replied.

"Then he is good," the voice said again.

"But right now Okoye Udo is hungry. I said to him, follow Ezu Nri, and you will never go hungry again."

"And I say to you: watch your step, young man," the voice said again. It was Ugocha Nwoye.

Ezu knew how to entertain them. The group came to life. They told jokes in every corner. One was about how Ezu would milk the lifeforce out of a young man if he dared serve him. There were jokes about poor people who needed to be fed. There were jokes about "money-missed-roads" (Aku-Fulu-Uzo), people who spent their lives accumulating great wealth in hopes of joining the Oganiru affluent club some day. They were to find out that they were not welcome in the tightly knit group. Oganiru men called them money-missed-roads because wealth must have missed its intended destination, an Oganiru man's house, and landed at the wrong obu. The Oganiru group was only for wealthy germinated-citizens (natural born) of Nri. But those were not the only qualifications. Only those who had inherited their wealth were welcome, and their wealth must have survived at least three generations in order to count. By those standards, Igwe Nwadike was not qualified to join since his family wealth was only two generations old.

Ezu took Okoye behind the big, old udala tree to a different group—ten, imported young women who wore short waist and chest cloths. The rest of their bodies were decorated with uli. The End, Ezu's youngest wife, had hired them to provide the finest food for the Oganiru men during their meeting.

"Provide lineage boy with whatever he can eat. Serve him first before anyone else. Today, he will eat with the wealthy and the wise. Today he will see how real laws are made."

Okoye ate pounded yams which were soft as cotton-wool with bitter leaf soup. He ate fresh and dried fish, goat meat and ram meat. It was all delicious and he loved everything. It was the kind of food that made a young man grow hair on his chest. And, better yet, it was all familiar but the wine. He would talk about the foreign wine for many weeks. It was as red as blood, but sweet as honey. The jar that contained it was as unique and foreign as the wine. It was not made with ordinary clay but some much stronger material. It was shiny and had the image of a beautiful woman carved on both sides. Ezu poured the wine himself. It reminded Okoye of human blood. Once Okoye saw the color, he felt nauseated. He did not want any part of it, but Ezu was watching.

"It is the best wine you will ever find in Uwa land. Go ahead, taste it," Ezu said.

Okoye sniffed it. It smelled like some flower's dew. Then he tasted it. It was like honey, but with ticklish bubbles that ran down his throat. He could feel them even in his stomach. The wine was refreshing and gooood.

"What is it called?" Okoye finally asked.

"They call it 'Konya' in Uwa land. But I call it 'Nkwu-ana.' It is not tapped from the tree. It is manufactured from certain Uwa fruits on the ground. The more it ages, the better it tastes. Do you like it?" Ezu asked.

"It is just like you said. It is the best wine I have ever had and probably ever will."

"Once you get past the bloody look, it is the best wine in the world. I must admit that our people seem to have a problem with the color."

"So they had to make it look that way?"

"Yes, it is actually a love drink in Uwa land. The color looks like a certain love flower and smells like it too. Women love it in Uwa land. If you give it to your wife, she will be truly yours. It has twice the alcohol of an aged palm wine."

Okoye guzzled down what was left of his drink and thanked Ezu for the food and wine. "I encourage you to sit and listen to wise people deliberate. It is the start of your own wisdom." Ezu left him to join his faithful followers. Okoye could not miss the friendliness coming from the man who had personally served him the love drink, the man who most young men at Nri admired so much that they would do about anything for the opportunity to shake hands with him.

The group of wise men talked about policies and reaffirmed their beliefs while they ate. Those Okoye already knew. He knew where they stood. What he did not know was how far they were willing to go to get what they wanted. The talk was unguarded. The Konya wine was taking its toll. Ichie Idika, Okoye learned, was the biggest threat. But the wise men had a solution for him, too. They appointed a man named Isika-isi, himself a maverick. Isika-isi was bald and small like Ichie Idika. He was to challenge whatever Ichie had to say. He must talk philosophically, like Ichie Idika, sometimes using his fist to compliment his words and, at other times, pausing in the middle of a sentence to reflect as if he were listening to the gentle whisper of the Ancient People. That way he would lessen some of the awe associated with Ichie Idika.

The wise men also talked about twisting arms. Everyone chose an Ozo subject or two outside of the Oganiru to work on. They would be responsible for how their subjects voted. How they chose to do this was their business, but they must deliver their votes. Their reputations and their places in the affluent sect depended on this.

Just when Okoye thought he had heard it all, Ezu rose from his seat. He thanked everyone for the parts they were about to play in the annual meeting. He told them that Ichie Idika was a problem, but he was not the only one. In fact, he was just a nuisance who craved attention.

"At worst he is a distraction," Ezu said. The real problem was the Ozo-Mkputu priests. They had always been the problem at Nri. He called them a bunch of Abonoba's chickens who thought they could solve the world's problems. He said they locked themselves up half of every day to dream.

"The only problem is that they still have to wake up to reality, to the real world."

"They call it meditation. I call it laziness. Nri people cannot afford to nurture laziness. That was not the intention of our forefathers. They did not intend for us to drift off into some magic land or to look for another fight to break up. The founders of our clan wanted us to live. They wanted us to survive."

He said that Ozo-Mkputu go out of their way to invite people to come and live at Nri.

"They tell Igbo people that we have plenty of land to accommodate the rest of the world. Instead of settling a dispute, they encourage one of the parties to come to Nri and live."

Ezu said that the Ozo-Mkputu priests were responsible for the lack of progress in Nri land and, probably, in Igbo land. He predicted that they would probably die off in the next forty to fifty years. He said that without new recruits to replace them, their generation would see the end of the Ozo-Mkputu priesthood once the youngest of them had died. Then the rebuilding process would start at Nri and Igbo lands.

The Konya was taking its toll on Okoye and he nearly missed the joke. In fact, he had missed it until the crowd of Oganiru priests, the giant black elephants as they were known, roared and shouted praises to their pathfinder.

"Ezuuu! Ezuuu!! Ezuuu!!!"

Okoye mustered enough focus to think about what had been said and what was funny about it. What was funny about a human being looking forward to the death of others simply because they had different ideas about how things should be? What was funny about that? If they were looking forward to someone else's death, would they cause it if they could get away with it? Had they done this in the past? Were they doing it now? Was that the plan? It must be the Konya. It was supposed to be a love drink, but it was making Okoye think evil thoughts and taking his thinking too far. Okoye rose from behind the Group of Giant Elephants. Ezu was in the middle of some enlightened philosophical talk.

"Keep the young generation away from the Ozo-Mkputu priests. That is how you cut off their life source. Just keep the young generation away from them and then wait them out. They will die a peaceful death."

It took several hours, but Okoye finally slept off the Konya. Two cups of cold water helped, too. Later that evening, Okoye sat by himself at the Offor Nri temple. There was no love drink confusing his mind. Now it was just Okoye and his chi. But the evil thoughts were still in his mind. Okoye realized that he could not rationalize away what he had heard or blame it on himself or on the love drink. No, it was not his fault. One of the paintings on the temple walls caught his attention. It was of an ascended Eze Nri. He was sitting on a stone, and standing in front of him was a man, an Igbo visitor. Eze Nri was handing a lump of holy chalk to the visitor. A long line of visitors stood behind the first person. Okoye remembered what Igwe Nwadike had said about the ascended Eze Nri when he had shown them around the temple.

There were also paintings of six of his predecessors, but Igwe Nwadike had stopped at this one and talked about it the longest.

"He is considered the holiest ever. His name is Nwora (Son-of-All), Igwe Nri Nwora. His young wife died while he was on a one-year-seclusion during his coronation. He never married again. He had no children of his blood. But he had many adopted children from Igbo villages, most of them unwanted dwarves from Igbo and Uwa lands. He lived to be one hundred and twenty-one years old. It was during his reign that dwarves flourished in Nri. Before him, they were considered evil and bad luck in Igbo land, but Igwe Nri Nwora raised their status higher than ordinary people and made them sacred.

As Igwe Nwadike walked, he joked about it.

"When I am a grown man, I want to be just like him."

Okoye knew that he was joking, but it was not really a joke. Igwe Nwadike adored Igwe Nwora. Gazing at his painting, Okoye swore an oath to himself. He would never take an Ozo title. If what he had seen was what it was about, he would have no part of it. If what he had heard was their heart, he did not want it. He would be a very rich man, and he would also perform his goodwill duties. Without politics he could do both and do them well. For the first time, he noticed that the painting of

Igwe Nwora was actually smiling. Yes! He would travel to the ends of the earth. He would accumulate as much wealth as he could without soiling his hands. But he must also make Igwe Nwadike and Akalaka proud. He must discover exotic Uwa lands and bring back souvenirs for Ozo Nwana, his Ogbadu-Eze boss. He must live his dreams, but he must also contribute his share. That was only fair to him and his community.

FIFTEEN

Year Counting

Igu Aro (the year-counting and keeping ceremony) was one of the ties that bound Eze Nri and Igbo families and solidified his influence over their communities. Based on the official year recordings of Eze Nri and his officials, Igbo people observed special days and communal events. In return, they sent representatives to pay tribute during the year-counting ceremony to show their loyalty and to receive blessings on behalf of their people. It was one of the rare services that Eze Nri personally performed rather than one of his Ozo or Nze emissaries. It was one, if not the only, regular event at which he could speak directly to all Igbo people. He took this time to reflect on the end of the year or the century, as the case may be, and to count blessings from the past, to reaffirm the Igbo mission and philosophy, and to share his new vision or any spiritual messages he had received. So the ceremony was not only the official counting of the year's ending, but a time to tell the Igbo people about the state of their nation.

Because Eze Nri's status was considered half-human and half-spirit, he did not speak to non-Nri priests outside of his own family. If he must speak to non-Nri priests, he did so through an interpreter. The year counting was different, though. It was a rare occasion where he could speak freely to the whole audience (invited and uninvited, Igbo and non-Igbo). Therefore, he had to be at his highest capacity as a holy man and a holy spirit. He prepared himself with much fasting, meditation, reflection, and visioning. Only through this preparation could he get a clear message for his people, attain a spiritual height guaranteed to override any bad spirits that might come to cause trouble during the festivity, and harvest enough blessing to spread to Igbo land and beyond for the coming year.

Igwe Nwadike was in his seventh Igbo week (twenty-eight days) of retreat when people began arriving in record numbers. They came— the not-so-good, the good, and the best of the best—all the Ozo priests in the Nri family. They came to welcome him home from his spiritual journey. Even the not-so-good among them were on their best behavior because they had to attain a certain level of spiritual goodness before they could be eligible to participate. There was really no way of knowing how decent each man was, but unprepared people had been known to fall ill after receiving the King. So at the back of every Ozo man's mind the potential for death guaranteed that each of them would make some serious effort. These efforts ranged from full courses of purification to fasting and meditation, and sometimes something as simple as abstaining from certain acts, like sex, for some period of time. For Eze Nri Nwadike, it was always good to see his men at their best and to commune with them when he was at his best. It was always good, too, to eat prepared food (even though uncooked) after twenty-eight days without it.

"Igweee! Igweee!! Igweee!!!" the crowd thundered as he emerged from the one-room bamboo-pole and thatched-roof hut in the Ofia nso (holy bush) behind Igwe's official quarters. But it was the sound of his chief priest's bullhorn that moved Igwe the most because it stood out above the roar of voices. There was something mystical in its coded messages that communicated directly to his spirit.

The legend could only wave his white ceremonial horsetail in reply, without smiling. This was done partly to acknowledge their greetings and partly to bless his people. Igwe Nwadike did not smile very much. Many of his predecessors hadn't either, perhaps because of the responsibilities of their position. But it would have been difficult for anyone to smile after twenty-eight days of serious retreat, twenty-eight days of living on uncooked garden egg (egg plant) fruits and leaves.

Led by his chief priest who continued to blow his bullhorn trumpet, Igwe followed the procession. After him came two male dwarves, one ringing a bronze bell and the other holding the king's ceremonial spear, and Okoye Nweri. Two more male dwarves followed Okoye. One carried a terracotta bowl of water and the other a ceremonial chair. The rest of the Ozo men trailed behind in order of their importance. Igwe Nwadike did not speak until he had settled down on the ceremonial stone chair. After all the Ozo men and the palace officials were seated in what seemed to be prearranged positions, the Isi-Ozo Oduh made a short welcoming speech. Then he presented Igwe Nwadike with a tray of kolanut. After washing his hands, Igwe selected a kolanut. Next Oduh passed the tray around to all the Isi-Ozo from each of the twelve villages. Igwe blessed the kolanut, and, as he was breaking it, the rest of the Isi-Ozo men broke theirs as well. As they ate, Igwe started his short and somewhat informal speech. He thanked everyone for coming to welcome him, and, jokingly, thanked them for not causing trouble while he was away. He told them that every year's retreat was always different and that this one was not an exception.

"This retreat was particularly eye-opening. But the package that will be opened does not need to be viewed by poking holes in it," he said. He was referring to the New Year's speech he would be delivering the next day. He joked that he hoped they did not come to welcome him with kolanuts only. It was a sign that he had nothing more to say and that it was time to eat.

Oduh, the chief priest, and some other officials went into the inner room and brought out wooden trays of salad and catfish. Oduh presented Igwe Nwadike with the first tray. Igwe climbed down from his stone throne and settled on his informal carved mahogany seat in front of the big salad tray. As he began eating with his bare hands, he was joined by Oduh, Okoye, two male dwarves who were themselves Ozo men, and one other official. The six men circled the big tray and ate as if it was the most delicious meal they had ever eaten. The food had been prepared by the chief priest himself with the assistance of Okoye and the male dwarves who were eating with them. The salad was made of chopped garden egg pulp and leaves mixed with a fresh squeezed palm oil, then sprinkled with salt and pepper. It was accompanied with dried catfish. The garden egg pulp and leaves had been harvested from the holy bushes planted by Igwe Nwadike himself with help from some of his officials. Attending to his vegetable gardens was one of Igwe's hobbies. His others were philosophy and playing his une musical instrument and singing (not in public, however). In groups of about ten, the rest of the Ozo men circled more trays of the same dishes.

Each group was made up of members from a particular village. Altogether there were fourteen trays. It was not long before the fourteen groups had transformed into many smaller ones scattered in different parts of the big hall and chatting informally. Even though Igwe Nwadike was not in his formal wear and not sitting on his formal throne, a stranger would still have identified him because he was surrounded by at least twenty men, each one trying to gain his attention. The first part of the ceremony ended late in the evening with most of the participants quietly departing, sometimes in small groups.

❦ ❦ ❦

About four Igbo hours before the Igwe welcoming ceremony, a young man in his twenties had been riding a brown horse heading east along the highway of the seventh wilderness. It was two hours past midday. The youth would have qualified as an average Igbo but for the horse. Racing at high speed, he nearly missed the old, spotted cottonwood tree. But he finally saw it and made an abrupt stop. He could see a piece of red cloth tied to a small tree behind the cottonwood tree. Only someone on horseback could see it, and very few people rode on horseback then. Without hesitation, the young man reached into his breast-covering and took out a matching piece of red cloth. He waved it in the air for a full two moments, then sped off again.

The leader of uwa men (the wilderness outlaws) who sat on a stump, reached into his waist bag and took out a half-eaten dried pulp of alligator pepper. Squeezing about twenty seeds from the pulp, he threw them into his mouth and chewed. Next he took out his tobacco box and emptied half of its contents into his left palm. He sniffed half into each nostril, then sneezed and sneezed again. Rising from the stump like a veteran performer about to entertain a familiar audience, he untied a black-spotted brown horse, mounted, and walked it a few steps to the old cottonwood tree in the rainforest. He stopped behind the tree and waited.

It took another half hour, but the traders came—about fifty in number. Only five were women. The women were not themselves traders, but part of the twenty person delegates from Erike's birth clan, Umu-Uwakwe, going to the year counting ceremony. Apart from delegates from Umu-Uwakwe, the traders who set the pace were healthy young men. They all carried uniform, long narrow baskets that the Igbo people called ukpa. Everyone was speed-walking, but they might as well have been running. They seemed indifferent to the blazing sun.

The first man in the group was the only one who rode on horseback, and he set the pace. His followers stretched about thirty footsteps behind him. The leader was several feet past the cottonwood tree when the world ended.

It started as a high-pitched whistle that could be heard a mile in each direction. It was a sound none of them had heard before. Their leader, who was a veteran trader, had heard stories about the sound and recognized it immediately. He made a hopeless attempt to run, but it was too late. He was the first to die. One of the fortunate people who survived said that they rose from the shrubs like locusts. Another said that they rose like ghosts from their graves.

The sound was like a chant sung by birds in the morning hours. "Do not run if you want to live. Do not run if you want to live. Do not run if you want to live. Do not run if you want to live . . . ."

When the carnage was over, fifteen men had died. All had tried to run. Two more would later die from bleeding. Those who gave up their baskets without resistance went home unharmed. Those who could not make up their minds quickly enough were persuaded by a stroke of the long narrow machete that shone in the blazing sun.

❧ ❧ ❧

The main part of the year-counting ceremony involved very few people, just the Isi-Ozo from the twelve villages of Nri, the Eze Nri, and his core officials. It was an all-night event beginning with informal chitchat in the big Temple of the Light (Okwu Anyanwu). Most was light gossip or talk about the August event. Igwe Nwadike stayed in the hall's inner room until midnight when he came out to lead an hour-long chant meditation. Then he returned to the inner room for a short nap while the rest of the men kept vigil and engaged in quiet reflection. At the mid-hour of the night, Igwe came out again to join the group. At this point, each Isi-Ozo priest, twelve men each representing the twelve villages, produced a rooster which was placed in front of the group. Because the Igbo New

Year started at cock crow, not at midnight, the first rooster to crow would mark the beginning of the final ceremonies for the night.

The first cock crowed at the third and last hour of the night. The cock had been brought by the Isi-Ozo from Nri-Ejiofor village. The palace chief priest invoked the Aro deity and then broke a kolanut which everyone ate, including Igwe Nwadike. The chief priest put a copper ring on the left ankle of the rooster that had ushered in a new year.

"Roam freely on the land," said the chief priest. "Remind us of all the blessings of the New Year."

Then he took the rooster outside. Isi-Ozo Nri, Oduh, and Isi-Ozo for Nri-Ejiofor village, Ude, who had won the rooster contest, joined him. Okoye looked around. No one seemed to notice him. Uninvited he went outside. The chief priest handed Okoye the lamp and motioned for him to lead the way. He led them to the path that went into the thickly wooded part of the holy forest. He wore no sandals nor did any of the other men.

When they had gone about one hundred footsteps, the chief priest said "Enough!"

Okoye stopped and turned around in time to see the chief priest raising the rooster up in the air.

"Aro! The God of All Seasons! Accept the offer that we give to you. Bring forth good seasons this year and bless your children."

He released the rooster and dropped a single kolanut on the ground. The rooster instantly became sacred. Because it wore a copper anklet, it would join the other sacred roosters to roam unharassed and free in the holy forest and beyond.

As the men entered the temple, Okoye knew instantly that he had missed something. Now, at the center of the assembly, three bronze pots sat on three stools. A fourth pot, smaller and with little inscriptions on it, sat on the ground. It was the only one covered by a folded piece of white cloth. The others had built-on covers.

The chief priest stood in front of Igwe Nwadike. With a piece of white chalk that he had brought from the forest, the chief priest wrote something on the ground. The inscription looked like "ELFE." It must have meant that their mission was good or accomplished because Igwe Nwadike nodded.

The priest dropped the chalk on the ground and moved over to the pots. He removed the white cloth covering the fourth pot and unfolded it. He spread it on the ground and emptied the contents of the first of the three pots into the cloth. The contents were ordinary but, at the same time, unique—shiny marble-like gravel that could easily be mistaken for precious stones. They were hard, dark, and glittery.

The chief priest knelt down and counted the pieces of gravel. Everyone in the hall watched. Oduh stood next to him. The priest counted aloud so that when he finished he wouldn't have to announce to the audience again how many he had counted. But he did, in fact, announce the number.

"We counted thirty-eight years!" He stood up and Oduh started counting the same stones. He, too, counted aloud and reached the same figure. The chief priest put the pieces back into the pot and placed it back on its stool. He repeated the process with the other two pots. The three pots each contained thirty-eight pieces of gravel.

After the last of the three pots had been opened, counted, and re-counted, the Isi-Ozo Nri, Ozo Oduh, called on the Isi-Ozo from each village one after the other. He asked them what figures they had counted from the pots at home.

"I now call on the Isi-Ozo of Adagbe," the Oduh would say. As the Isi-Ozo stood up, he would ask, "Did you count your village Aro pot as required by our customs before coming?"

After each Isi-Ozo had answered in the affirmative, Oduh would say, "Give me a number!"

He would then announce a figure. After it was confirmed that each of the three identical pots had the same number of hard gravel in each and that each Isi-Ozo man had counted the same number in his village Aro pot, Isi-Ozo Oduh took the fourth pot to Igwe Nwadike.

He held the wide-mouthed pot in front of Igwe Nwadike who dipped his hand into it and produced a single piece of gravel. He gave it to the chief priest who put this piece in the first of the three identical pots and sealed it. The same process was repeated for the other two bronze pots. After all pots had been resealed, Oduh called on each of the Isi-Ozo men and gave them each one piece of gravel which he obtained from Igwe Nwadike. The Isi-Ozo men would perform an identical process at their villages in front of selected Ozo men and the Aro deity's chief priest as soon as they got home. They were also to sacrifice a white rooster to their village Aro deity.

Even though three of the four pots in front of Igwe Nwadike looked similar in size and shape, their markings were different. The first one was decorated with Offor logs, the second with scarification marks, and the third with ceremonial spear figures. The pot decorated with Offor logs was to be kept by Igwe Nwadike or whoever was the Eze Nri. The pot decorated with scarification patterns was kept by the Isi-Ozo Nri until next year's ceremony. The third pot, marked with ceremonial spear figures, would be handed over to the Isi-Ozo whose rooster first ushered in the New Year. In this case, it went to the Isi-Ozo from Nri-Ejiofor village. The fourth pot with the wide mouth contained left-over gravel for the next year's ceremony.

Each piece of gravel in the identical pots signified one year. So the New Year they had just ushered in was the thirty-ninth year of the ninth century, and the ninth century after Nri, son of Eri, received enlightenment. That was when he had started keeping count of the years and had developed this simple process of year-counting. The process had now evolved into these elaborate ceremonies.

One Igbo century was forty years times three, or 120 years. After the current pots attained a maximum of 120, not more, not less, all would be welded shut and buried in a secret location which only members of the Isi-Ozo sect, the current Eze Nri, and the chief priests would know about. But each Ozo priest and a few laymen kept track of the years in one form or another, some by simply marking them on the walls of their inner rooms at home.

Someone touched Okoye on his right elbow. It was the Nwangwu, Isi-Ozo of Nri-Agu village, his village.

"Do you understand what we are doing?" he asked.

"Of course, we are counting the year. I was part of the team that freed the sacred Aro rooster too."

"What year is it then?"

"We are in the thirty-eighth year," answered Okoye, as if he himself had started it.

"No. We are in the thirty-ninth year. First we count the previous years, then we add one to it."

"OK, so we have thirty-nine. I missed it by one, right?"

"No, Master! You missed it by many. You forgot to count the centuries before the years."

"What is a century?"

Nwangwu gave out a big laugh, turned around, and touched the man next to him.

"He is living at Nne Obu Nri, and he does not know what a century is. We are in real trouble."

"Is that supposed to be a surprise? You are just now finding out that we are in trouble? I tell you the truth: One day our people will wake up after our generation is gone, and no one will know where the Aro pots are buried or what year it is. Now that will be trouble!"

"That would be a problem," agreed Nwangwu.

"Ask him the true meaning of Eke. I bet you he does not know that either."

"Hey! Is that supposed to be an insult?" asked Okoye.

"It could be if you know the answer. I can bet that you don't," said Nwangwu.

"Eke is the first market in Nri. After Eke then Oye, then Afor. Nkwo is the youngest and the last market day," said Okoye with enthusiasm.

"You are correct, but only partially. What is the first and true meaning of Eke?"

"Yes. What is its cosmological meaning?" added the other man.

Okoye's eyes rolled back in his head as if the answer were in his memory somewhere.

"He does not know it and it is not his fault. Very few his age will know that. They were never taught."

"But he is in the service of Nne Obu Nri. That is different," said Nwangwu.

"My son, Eke is the direction in which the sun rises (east), and the Governor of the eastern sky is called Eke. The sun sets at Oye (west) and the Governor of the western sky is called Oye. If you are facing the rising sun and spread both arms, your left hand is pointing to Afor (north) and your right arm to Nkwo (south). The Governor of the north is called Afor and the Governor of the south is called Nkwo. We use these guides to monitor not only space, but time. That is why we have four days in a week cycle. Naming the market by it is just a way to remember the day of the week that the market trades. All of these Governors or Gods are patrons of the market days. I hope that you have learned something because this night is for nothing else."

SIXTEEN

The Challenge

What an ordinary person at Nri or Igbo land knew about the year-counting ceremony was that there was an elaborate celebration that preceded the nearly secret event. People came from all parts of Igbo and Uwa land to take part. Some arrived two and even three days before the event. Almost all Igbo-speaking families sent delegates, mostly their community leaders. So the people came, not only with full delegations, but they also brought some kind of performance group. Delegates from the Akuta family came with a Mambazu masquerade group which was at least fifty strong. Because of their number, they could not fit into any family compound at Nri, so a temporary camp was built for the group. Selected families at Nri cooked and took care of their needs. The Akuta family was one of the largest delegations. The majority of the delegations, plus their performance groups, numbered about twenty each and easily fit in their host's compound. Neighboring families around Nri also hosted some delegates. Someone, like Nweze, the chief priest of Animba, had too many guests and had to assign some to his neighbors.

The Eze Nri officially invited all of the delegates, but there were many uninvited guests. These were mostly individuals who had come on their own to see the carnival of masquerades and the musical groups. But many of the uninvited also came to see Eze Nri and listen to his wisdom. It was this last group who camped at Igwe Nwadike's compound overnight so they could be assured of a good spot in the morning. What they didn't know was that when the events started in earnest, they would be asked to move because their campsite was reserved for some Igbo delegates.

Igwe Nwadike's compound was larger than that of most of his predecessors. He expanded it every year and yet there was always a Nri family
member who complained that the Igbo delegates they hosted were not giv-
en a spot inside the compound. Usually about a third of the guests did not
fit inside the compound by the peak of the year-counting event. Because
he was one of the wisest and most charismatic Eze Nri, Igwe Nwadike was
one of the most popular. His compound was about twenty times the size of
an average village square (about twenty acres). Half of it was the holy bush
where only the titled men and women of Nri and selected titled people of
Igbo could venture. The other half of the compound was divided into two
parts, one part being the open public square. The other part contained the
Obu Offor Nri temple which could comfortably fit two thousand people.
There were no walls around the temple, just log pillars and mud dwarf walls
where visitors often sat when the temple was full. This design made it possible for people to stand outside the temple and still participate in what
went on inside. Apart from the temple and a few small huts dedicated to
one deity or another, the rest of this section of the compound was empty.
The living section measured about nine hundred footsteps in each direction. One third was Igwe Nwadike's quarters, one third was his two wives'
quarters, and one third was the palace officials' quarters. The palace officials,
like Okoye, were all Nri people, so they lived there only half the time, and
the other half they spent at their regular village compounds.

Every section of Igwe's compound, except for the living quarters, had
a mud wall dividing it from the other sections. The living quarters had
carved wooden gates as dividers. The main entrance to the compound
had no gate, but an attendant guarded it constantly. All the year-counting
ceremony activities and other large events took place at the Obu Offor
Nri temple part of the compound while the entertainment took place in
the open public square.

Each delegation was assigned an Ozo or Nze priest as a host. The
priest and his family would take care of the group's lodging and food in
whatever way they chose. The host would lobby for his guests' sitting positions in the compound and for their place in the queue when the time
came to pay homage to Eze Nri. Each official delegate was required to pay
this homage as part of the ceremony.

The political skills of each Ozo or Nze host were very critical. Some delegates did not get to see the King until very late in the evening. And only those who saw the King and paid homage could go home the same day, thus gaining respect among the Igbo families. Where delegates stood in the queue to see the King signified the level of political connection they had at Nri.

In official groups, the political delegates began coming to Igwe Nwadike's compound about mid-morning. Most of the early arrivals were still not sure if they had good positions, so they came early to negotiate. Delegates from Aguleri, for instance, had nothing to worry about, for their position was always assured because they came from the origin place of the Nri clan. These delegates, and others like them, arrived just before the event would begin which would be at midday, when the sun was at its apex and a man could not see his shadow. Experience had taught everyone that Igwe Nwadike was always on time, so they knew that the event would start on time. Just before midday, the place was already filled with people. It was like ten markets put together, and so was the noise generated by the numerous conversations. At the public square, different groups were already dancing unofficially, but without their masquerades. Although masquerades were forbidden from performing at the palace because Eze Nri are not allowed to see masquerades, the public square was considered outside the palace compound, so many masquerades would perform and entertain at the peak of the event. The musical instruments and singing, added to the rising noise of the table conversations going on here and there, created a din that could be heard from distant villages. Over at the temple part of the compound, delegates were seated in a very orderly fashion and there was no dancing or singing. But people were still talking at the top of their voices in order to be heard.

❧ ❧ ❧

Erike had now been at Nri for seven years. He had not seen his mother for three years, his great uncle for five, and his cousin Ogu for seven. But all three were coming with a host of others from their village. It would be like a reunion. His village had never sent a delegate to the year counting. His mother had come with his uncle before, but this time they were to make the long leap forward. They would come with gifts and

155

probably a dance group as a delegation from the Umunta family. There was already talk of Erike visiting his village afterwards.

Igwe Nwadike knew about this because everyone else knew about it, so he had seized the moment. Erike was to lead the procession. He was to carry the Sacred Nri message board believed to have been carved by Nri himself and containing the summary of the Nri philosophy of peace. His people would be proud of him. It would be a testimony of his salvation. Igwe Nwadike was a holy man, but he was also a natural-born politician. He knew that Nri and Igbo people would point fingers and ask one another, "Who was that young man who led the procession?" He knew that the story of Erike's success would spread. And that was not all. Erike would lead his people to Eze Nri and introduce them in front of multitudes of Igbo delegates and spectators. It would make an interesting story. This was an opportunity that not even the holy man could pass up.

Okoye had teased Erike about it for weeks, calling him "Erike Nwa-Okpulu" (poor Erike), and saying "Erike Nwa-Okpulu will be the man of the event."

🐝 🐝 🐝

Like some big sacrificial scene, clouds of smoke drifted up to heaven from different corners of the big compound. One could hear the rhythm of pestles as they hit mortars. People of different genders, ages, sizes, and shapes moved around in the compound. Some were busy with errands, mostly last moment arrangements for the August event. Some just chatted with friends and acquaintances. Most of these were already fully dressed for the ceremony.

It was a colorful and memorable scene. Uninvited adventurers who had slept all over in the compound, mostly in and around the holy temple, were looking for water to wash their faces and feet and hoping that free food would be served early enough to count as breakfast. Some had already volunteered to cut firewood in exchange for bathing water and breakfast. Igwe Nwadike was somewhere in the holy forest. He was one of the few who memorized most parts of his speeches, and he was on the last round of practicing his New Year speech.

Okoye Nweri was at the Holy Temple of Justice. He was in charge of security and peace, whatever that meant. But part of his job was to do

156

the dirty work that no one else wanted to do. His was the face that told people to move down the line because where they had slept all night was reserved for more important people. After weeks of gathering information and misinformation, he had come to know by heart all of the major delegates, their leaders, and their Nri host families. He also had come to know the names of people he had never met and probably never would meet. At that particular moment, he was deciding the best way to approach three adventurers who had carved out for themselves the best seats in the temple. They were definitely adventurers, but they were also about his age. If the positions had been reversed, Okoye would probably have been more creative than these boys had been.

Ufie music was being played just outside the temple. It had been going all night and would continue most of the day. About two hundred footsteps to the west of the big temple lay the public square where Okoye had had his first taste of Konya, the love drink. Different musical groups who had rehearsed for the event temporarily owned the huge court.

About one hundred footsteps to the east of the Offor Nri holy temple lay the servant quarters. Those who served in the palace lived in the housing project. Most of the cooking was done there. It was there that Erike stood with Iyom, an oversized wife of one of the Ozo priests. She was in charge of all who cooked in the palace for the big event. She temporarily owned Erike because he had been designated to meet all her firewood needs. Finally, Iyom was no longer complaining. Erike and his men had produced twice the amount of the firewood she needed. Now it was Erike's turn to complain. His men had delivered, but Iyom had not. They had not been fed breakfast yet and were hungry. In the middle of prolonged reassurances from Iyom that his men would not be short-changed, Erike saw his adopted father coming through the main entrance of the servants' quarters.

"Finally. Finally," he murmured to himself.

They had not seen each other in seven years and yet Erike immediately recognized him. Because he was not expecting Emenike, he would not have recognized him except that he was with his own father, Ozo Okolo. He had not thought about Emenike for at least two years, and he was the last person Erike expected to agree to come, given the role he had played in the past. He was in the next age group up from Erike's. But he was the one who had made the most noise when Erike was judged for killing Oduenyi. He was one of those who had insisted that there was no option other than hanging. Yet there he was in the Mother of All Obus to receive blessings and to be introduced by none other than Erike himself.

Erike, the one who had killed a man, had made peace with himself. Destiny had brought him to Nri land. Those who bullied and those who collaborated with them and those who judged were just instruments used by destiny. The one who had killed a man flashed his perfect white teeth and reached out to embrace the guests.

"Our people! My people! Our people!" he called as they embraced.

It was more Erike embracing Emenike than the reverse, for Erike did not feel any warmth from his village boy. Ozo Okolo must have seen the disappointment that his adopted son felt and decided to explain what had happened.

"There has been a terrible tragedy, my son," he said. Emenike started sobbing. He had been crying ever since the tragedy at the seventh wilderness almost a day before. He was one of the lucky ones who survived. The family of Amoko lost six men. Four of them were from Erike's village of Umu-Uwakwe. Because the village of Umu-Uwakwe had organized the group, it had provided ten people of the twenty. The other five villages had each sent two people. All of them had joined with a group trading calm wood, ivory, and precious stone beads. In those days, one traveled by joining traders who provided security and set the pace. Plus the traders handed one over to a credible group when it came time to part ways. That way one was always accounted for.

"There was a tragic incident at the seventh wilderness, but your mother is safe," Ozo Okolo continued.

"And the rest? Ogu? His father? The rest?"

"Your cousin Ogu is also fine."

"His father?"

"I am very sorry," Ozo Okolo said.

"My uncle? My uncle? My uncle? What happened? Tell me! You can tell me. I am a man now. I can take it."

Crowds were already circling in the servant quarters of the mother compound. Erike was correct. He was a man all right. He was crying like one, like a mature adult. His crying voice was spiked with a loud cow-like sound. It was a perfect drama and the event would not have been better, for the palace was already partially filled.

"We have to go now. We have to go," Ozo Okolo said.

Okoye heard the crying voice of an adult. He instantly knew what it was. It had to be his dream last night. In the dream, one of the firewood cutters had accidentally cut himself.

There was already a big crowd when Okoye got there. As the officer in charge of security and peace, he fought his way to the center. He saw Erike wailing like a big cow, but there was no blood.

"What happened? What happened?" Okoye asked no one in particular.

"You were right. You were right."

"About what? About what? About . . . "

"The year! I am the man of the event! But why me? Why me? Why?"

SEVENTEEN

Warrior Parade

The trio circled around the public square and went through the temple and into the holy forest. Ringing the bronze bell as they walked, the dwarf led the way. The chief priest followed. He peeled pieces of holy chalk and spread them on the ground as they walked. Okoye carried several palm fronds in his left hand which he dropped one at a time on the ground as he went along, occasionally throwing a few into the crowd. He had no idea why he did this, but Okoye had been told to do so, and he had seen it done before.

Almost immediately after the forerunners completed their round, the actual procession began. The group had been assembled in the holy forest where they were supposed to meet Igwe Nwadike halfway from his spiritual journey. This meeting was to symbolize his absence for the past twenty-eight days, or one year, depending on the observer's calculation.

The Nze priests were first to emerge. Marching in rows of five, they totaled about fifteen thousand. They had on what at first looked to be uniforms, though actually they were not. All were wearing blue robes of different shades and patterns. They carried their ceremonial spears in their right hand, their Offor in their left hand, and goat skin bags slung across their shoulders.

The Odozi-Obodo (Keepers of the Town) women followed them. These were the wives and widows of Ozo priests, the who's who of Nri women. All of them belonged to the affluent Iyom women's sect. But not all Iyom women could belong to Odozi-Obodo. Not only were they affluent, the Odozi-Obodo women also had style. Eze Nwanyi, the king's first and eldest wife, led the group though she did not lead the chant. Another, a much younger woman, led their chant.

The Ozo priests followed their wives. They looked similar to the Nze priests except they had more potbellies. Also, they had more than one eagle feather sticking from their red caps. And their clothing was baggier than that of the Nze priests. They looked more relaxed and talked and made jokes with each other as they moved along.

There was a huge gap between the Ozo men and the Eze Nri entourage which was led by Okoye Nweri. Okoye walked by himself. Erike had requested that Okoye take his place of honor in the procession. Okoye wore the same outfit as the other Nze men, but he had no ceremonial spear or Offor staff. Instead, in both hands, he carried the sacred sign board that was shown once every year and only during the year-counting procession. It was about an arm's length wide and half an arm's length tall and made of dark brown wood. Nri people called it the "heart of peace" (Obu Udo) board. The sign was one of the oldest artifacts at Nri. It was believed to have been carved from the sacred Offor tree (Justice and Peace Tree) thirteen generations earlier by Nri himself. Words had been carved into the wood, and every year they were filled with white holy chalk so they could be seen from a distance. Okoye lifted the sign as high as he could. The inscription read:

**"The only debt a being owes another is fairness.
What is fairness?"**

The board was meant to be a philosophical clue to finding peace. Instead, it had become an enigma. The inscription that had helped to build the Nri kingdom was now helping to bring it down. It was not the first sentence that caused problems, only the second one. Even the most selfish people, like the Oganiru (the Progressives) invoked the question often to justify their selfish positions.

The chief priest walked behind Okoye. He continued to peel pieces of white holy chalk, dropping the particles on the ground. Right behind the chief priest were the Nri sacred dwarves, nearly two hundred of them—the tall, the short, the very short, the overweight, the skinny, the light-skinned and dark-skinned, men and women—all looking their best. All were Ozo and Nze priests. In the Nri clan, a dwarf was considered sacred and even superhuman, so women dwarves were ordained Ozo and Nze priests too.

Igwe Nwadike joined the procession behind the group of dwarves. He was glowing. His smile was authentic as he waved his white horsetail at the crowd on both sides of the procession path.

"Igwee! Igweee!! Igweee!!!" Men, women, and children hailed as he went by.

Others simply bowed or raised both hands in surrender. For most of them, seeing Igwe would be a once-in-a-lifetime experience. There had been testimonies of illnesses healed at the sight of the Eze Nri. There had also been witnesses to spontaneous confessions triggered at the sight of the "Holy One."

The eleven Ozo-Mkputu priests followed Igwe Nwadike. And behind Igwe were the Nze Ikenga priests who were the last in the procession, though definitely not the least important group. If Ozo-Mkputu priests were the saviors of the saviors, the Nze Ikenga priests were the guardians of the guardians or the shepherds of the shepherds. There were about a hundred Nze Ikenga priests. And, just as Ozo-Mkputu men were considered an endangered species of Ozo priests, Nze Ikenga priests were an endangered species of Nze priests. At the peak of the Nri kingdom, they had numbered above one third of all Nze priests. Now they were less than one percent. They could be considered "The-Old-Pride," ordinary men who, through the support and sacrifices of their wives, roamed the villages of Igbo people and their neighbors working miracles. Most of them could hardly afford the expensive fabric they had been made to buy in order to fit in with the other members of the procession. They chanted their signature chant as they marched, the words reflecting optimism. But deep down they knew very well the odds against them, ninety-nine percent against less than one percent. But, then again, they were miracle workers. Optimism, one could say, is a miracle worker's best ally.

Lead: *And what of Nnanyi Nnekwu (Big Father, Master), Nri?*

Chorus: *Big Father set an example for all of us*
He was the first priest and the first prophet; the teacher and
the peace warrior
He was the perfect manifester and the follower of the light
His holy deeds we remember; His footsteps we follow

Lead: *And what of Nri Menri Nwora?*

Chorus: *He too set an example*
He was a holy priest and a prophet; a teacher and a peace
warrior
He was the perfect follower of the light
His holy deeds we remember; His footsteps we follow

Lead: *And of Ichie Ozo Nweke Udala na Adagbe Nri?*

Chorus: *He too set an example*
He gave his life in service, as a peace warrior, a holy priest,
and a teacher
He was a follower of the light
His holy deeds we remember; His footsteps we follow

Lead: *And what of Nze Nwankwo Oraka na Nri Okpala?*

Chorus: *He too set an example*
He died at the ninth wilderness, a peace warrior between
two warring enemies
His lungs collapsed by a client's long sharp machete
His holy deeds we remember; His footsteps we follow

Lead: *And of Nri Menri Ejiofor?*

❀ ❀ ❀

163

The procession went around the big public square and then around the outside of the temple before entering it. Igwe Nwadike stood until all in the procession went to their reserved places. Then he sat down on his stone throne and everyone followed his lead. Two dwarves sat on stone seats on Igwe's right and two sat on his left. His chief priest, Okoye, and all the Ozo and Nze priests also sat on stone seats. Those who wore sandals took them off so their feet would touch the bare ground. This was as close to sitting on the bare floor as they could manage, and a sign that each was at peace with the earth. In the old days, everyone sat on the floor and was always barefoot in order to be at one with the earth.

A moment or two after all had settled on their seats, Oduh rose and, holding a small basket full of eagle kolanuts, he stood at the center of the hall. When he was sure he had Igwe's attention, he spoke.

"We welcome Igwe from his journey. We Umu-Nri and our friends thank you for bringing us the New Year and all the blessing that will come with it."

Then he presented the basket of kolanuts to Igwe Nwadike who took it, helped himself to a piece of kolanut, and handed the basket to one of the dwarves at his left. He took a piece of holy chalk from the dwarf on his right and gave it to Oduh.

"You people did well," he said as he handed the holy chalk. He sounded like a happy father blessing a well-behaved son. Oduh handed the big round lump of chalk to his second who stood behind him. Oduh had a brief low conversation with His Holiness while the kolanut passed around to the leaders of all the major groups and delegations.

Igwe Nwadike was well known for his long kolanut blessing. It sometimes ran over an hour. Some joked that he could make an entire speech just by blessing kolanuts. This year's blessing, however, was brief and to the point. The carnage at the seventh wilderness had become like bad-tasting water in everyone's mouth. Those who had come to learn some new saying were a little disappointed. After giving the blessing, Igwe broke the kolanut and used a small knife to separate each piece.

"Kolanut is now broken," he announced, as if to make the act official. He took a piece for himself and handed the knife and the rest of the pieces to the chief priest.

During the blessing, the heads of each group and delegation had held onto their kolanuts. As soon as Igwe Nwadike announced that the kolanut was broken, the leaders did as he had done, breaking their kolanuts and dropping the hearts on the floor. Then they each took one piece for themselves and handed the rest to their seconds who distributed them to the rest of their group.

"Papaa...puupuu...puuu!" blasted the chief priest's bullhorn. He wanted to entertain the crowd and fill the time gap while they ate their kolanut. To many assembled there, the sound of the bullhorn was sweet to their ears. It was a good alternative to the Ufie music. But to Igwe Nwadike and those who spent time around him, it was more than a sound. It was poetry that used words and images to lure its listeners and then take them back to places in the past and forward into the future. It told of battles won and lost and those yet to be fought.

Papaapu Papuupuupuuu! ("Beware!" it says).
Papaapu Papuupuupuuu! ("Beware!" it says).
Papaapu Papuupuupuuu Puupuu Pupupuuu
    (Beware of the lure of the great serpent).
Violence leads to more violence.
It leads to greater and advanced violence.
Ultimately it leads to total destruction.
Remember Nri and the green-eyed serpent at Ugwu Owele.
Remember its lure at Nri Lake.
Remember its lure at the fourteenth wilderness.
Remember the evil one that brings nothing but violence.
He brings nothing but bad news. Remember him?
Remember Nri, the great manifester and Akalogheli at Obu Nri.
Remember him? Akalogheli, the jester; the clown; the joker.
Remember him now? The snake monkey?
As comical as the monkey, and yet...
... And yet more deadly than his father.
Remember him?

The King and the trumpeter, his spiritual counselor, understood each other perfectly. Igwe Nwadike knew about Ekwensu, the green-eyed serpent. And he knew about Akalogheli, the serpent's perfect son, the jester, who finished what his father could not.

🜉 🜉 🜉

Twenty-five years after the visions were manifested, Nri, whom Nri people called Big Father, sat alone in his obu. It was nearly noon. The period before noon was his quiet time for reflection, and everyone around him knew and respected this. So when the wooden gate to his obu opened slowly, Big Father knew this was a stranger. For several moments after the gate opened, no one entered. When the visitor finally emerged, Big Father knew why. The stranger was so tall that he had to bend down to get through the gate. He was definitely an Uwa man. His skin was much lighter than that of an average Igbo, though not too light. His garment covered his entire body. He had a large pointed nose that caved into a long face. It was a face women might have considered handsome. His barely visible black sandals were so shiny they must have been painted with oil. As he approached, Big Father could see that most of his fingers were covered with gold rings.

The gold crown on his head gave him away as an Uwa prince, perhaps a young king. He could not have been more than thirty years old. Everything on his body looked flashy, but his mistress looked even flashier. Big Father said nothing, and the prince said nothing until his brigade of servants and bodyguards trailed into the compound. Big Father counted fifteen of them, excluding the prince and his mistress.

"Greetings to you, Nri the son of Eri, ruler of the earth," the visitor said in Igbo. Big Father recognized him as soon as he opened his mouth. It was not what he said but how he said it. He spoke exactly like his father, Ekwensu, had twenty years before.

"I am not the ruler of the earth. Do not address me with a false title," Big Father protested.

The young man did not apologize or argue or feel offended. Instead he burst into loud laughter that could be heard outside the big compound. As the man laughed Big Father noticed the small teeth that filled his mouth. That confirmed it. He had heard many tales about Akalogheli, the jester son of Ekwensu. He had heard that he sometimes posed as a Uwa prince and at other times as a merchant.

Big Father did not invite him to sit so Akalogheli sat himself down and invited his mistress to do so. They made themselves comfortable while his brigade of bodyguards and servants stood outside. Big Father did not offer him a single kolanut or any water, but the man did not seem to mind. Everything was funny to him. He laughed uproariously at every opportunity.

"Allow me to introduce myself, The Wise One," he said.

"I know who you are. Just say what's on your mind," Big Father interrupted.

"We have heard of your deeds and wisdom, and I was sent to come and bear witness."

"And who are 'We'?"

"My people and our friends all around the globe."

"And who are your people? Do they have a name?"

"We are the Kingdom of the North and South. We are all over. But you can just call us 'The Kingdom.'"

"Please continue."

"We want to make friends with you and your people and form a strong partnership. Where we come from we call it The Alliance. We watch your back and you protect our interests."

"And what exactly is your interest here?"

"Good question. Very good question, The Wise One. We have mostly commercial interests. But we also have some interest in cultural exchanges. We are fascinated by your culture, and we would like to know more about it. We want to have a mutual understanding with your people," he said as his mistress rubbed his back.

For a split moment, the stranger sounded reasonable, and Big Father nearly let his guard down. Maybe he had misjudged his visitor. He was even thinking of kolanut when the stranger started laying down the terms.

"But there is something you must understand, The Wise One," said the young man. "You have to prove yourself to The Alliance before you can join. You have proved yourself to be wise and that is why we came. But you must prove to The Alliance that you are prudent as well. The Alliance values prudent partners as well."

"The Alliance values prudent partners?"

"Yes. You must prove yourself to be prudent."

"Prudent is a new term to me. Could you explain what it means?" Big Father asked innocently, so Akalogheli started talking freely.

"It simply means to secure what you already have and then reach for more. First you need security; therefore, you should build a strong fighting army. We will provide the metal and metal support."

"You must excuse the ignorance of The Wise One, but what exactly is metal and metal support?"

"And I apologize as well if I am going too fast. Metal is a professional term we use to describe fighting objects, like spears and machetes. Metal support will include the initial training, weapon repair, replacements, and additional training. Those are the lay terms. But once you begin, you will find the professional terms more convenient."

"And what exactly are we going to do with all this metal and metal support?"

"Good. Good question. First you provide personal security. We call it bodyguards. Then you provide security for your holy city. When that is done, the real work will start. You will start with what we call 'consolidation.' Again I apologize for the new terms, but The Alliance values these terms. Consolidation means to gather together as one. You must consolidate your power in all Igbo land. When you have finished consolidating your power in Igbo land, everyone will know who the King is. It is not enough to get goats and chickens once a year from the Igbo people. They must pay taxes and submit completely to your authority. Your army will strictly enforce this. The Alliance will get some percentage. When you have established your presence completely in all Igbo land, then you will look beyond. You have complete discretion about where you go. The Kingdom likes ambitious people."

"After that, you will learn another term The Alliance calls 'acquisition.' The Alliance values consolidation and acquisition very much. They . . ."

"They value it more than metal and metal support?"

"Oh no! Metal and support are like the foundation. They are only tools, a means to an end, if you wish."

"Means and ends. I think that I have heard those terms before," Big Father said recalling his encounter with Ekwensu at the fourteenth wilderness twenty-five years before. During that meeting, Ekwensu had given him a full day of Nkuzi (lecture) which he had called "Means and Ends." It was the most persuasive lecture Big Father had ever heard.

"I am sure that you have heard those terms. They are common among The Alliance. Your people use expressions with special meanings, but The Alliance uses practical terms. Not that one is better than the other, but you can see the differences and similarities in both cultures. That is why cultural exchange will benefit both sides. Both sides can compare and contrast and then, in time, come to adopt each other's ways."

Big Father had a reputation for a long and piercing stare. Neighboring Igbo families frequently brought disputes for him to settle, and he was known for staring at the party he felt was distorting facts or hiding information. Under those searching and penetrating eyes, the lying parties usually changed their stories and told the whole truth. Even some innocent men, under the glare of those intimidating eyes, sometimes nervously dropped a piece of kolanut intended for their mouth.

Big Father stared at Akalogheli with those big eyes, not to intimidate him, but rather the way one would stare at a misguided youngster who was having fun playing with fire during the dry season. This time, his stare was longer and his eyes seemed bigger and more searching. Akalogheli did not melt under the rays of those eyes as most people did. He simply stared back the way a bad son possessed by a deep river demon would stare shamelessly back at his disappointed father. Then he gave out a long and loud explosion of laughter. Big Father wondered if Akalogheli was laughing at himself or his father, Ekwensu.

"The-Wise-One! The-Wise-One!" called Akalogheli. "I encourage you to come to 'The Kingdom' for a visit. I promise you will learn a few things to add to your wisdom."

Big Father knew instantly that sitting in front of him was a hopeless case. He knew that his young visitor was not laughing at his father but at his own fate.

"This 'Kingdom' that you talk about, this place where you came from, do they believe in the great Chi-Ukwu (Big God)? Do they believe in the supreme Chineke (Creator God) who gave life to all things, and who holds all responsible for their actions?"

At the mention of accountability, Akalogheli shifted on his chair, probably remembering that he was sitting on someone else's chair, in another's obu. He exchanged an 'I-told-you' look with his mistress who had not spoken a word yet, then he gazed in reflection at the bright sunlight outside. For the first time since he greeted Big Father with a false title, there was silence at Obu Nri. Akalogheli did not laugh, instead he was serious. Big Father folded his arms and held his breath, giving Akalogheli time to search his soul. This might be the moment in his long life when Big Father would personally witness Akalogheli confess all his crimes against Aja-Ana (Earth Goddess). *This will make for a good testimony in the great assembly of Nze and Ozo priests*, thought Big Father.

Moments later when Akalogheli emerged from his reflection and spoke, he seemed as cool and as calm as Nri Lake on a cold night.

"There is something you should know, The Wise One," he said. "Everything is relative to everything else. There are different forms of awareness or what some people call intelligence. What you call supreme is relative to what we call supreme at The Kingdom. As I said before, when you come to The Kingdom, you will see a different way of looking at things and how relative everything is."

Big Father lifted and lowered his shoulders in amazement at the young man's clever dancing feet. He had no doubt that this man truly had a big title at "The Kingdom." He wanted to dismiss his visitor at this point, but Big Father needed more information about the man and where he came from so he could share it with his children and children's children. He had no doubt that Akalogheli, who could sell a pig for a goat in broad daylight at Nkwo market, would come back in the future. Nri knew he must share his insights about the intruder's nature with the future generations so that they would recognize him when he came.

"I think that you forgot to explain what acquisition means."

"Oh. That means to seek out and absorb new territories and then consolidate them as one."

"But metal and metal support is the foundation?"

"You are learning very fast, The Wise One. The Alliance values people who learn quickly."

"You son of The Devil! I thought I recognized you the moment you opened your mouth. I knew your father even before you were born. I know his heart and desires completely. You did not tell him that you were coming, did you? He would have warned you that you were going to waste your time. He . . ."

"What are you talking about? There must be a mistake somewhere," the stranger said, faking embarrassment.

"You can pretend all you want. But you will get nothing from our people or from me. I have dealt with your father many times before you were born. I knew about metal and metal support before you were born. I knew about Mkpokota na Nwekota (consolidations and acquisitions) from your father before you were conceived. But I bought none of it from him, and I will buy none of it from you. My children and our people will buy nothing from you. You and your father bring nothing but bad news."

"What confidence!" said the stranger. "What confidence. But you should speak for yourself only. Do not speak for your children or their descendants. And you must certainly not speak for Igbo people. They may be more prudent than The Wise One. Speak for yourself only," the stranger said as he got up to leave. "You should think security for your people. The Alliance is security."

"Go away, jester!" said Big Father with a wave of his hand. "We do not spill human blood, so we will buy no metal or metal support from you. We are contented with what we have and who we are, so we will buy no consolidations or acquisitions from you. What we do is Nzofuta (liberation). Now here is a new practical term you will teach your 'Kingdom.' My children and our people will liberate all Igbo and Uwa people and set them free from your intentions. We will foil your evil plans for the world."

"Oh! What a waste! What a waste!" said Akalogheli as he stepped outside and adjusted his gold crown. "The Alliance will be back in the future. They will visit your descendants and your people many times. But they will visit Igbo people and their neighbors as well. Maybe your neighbors will come and acquire some territory for themselves, or should I say, liberate your people. Think security, old man! Think assurance. Think prudence!" Akalogheli laughed boisterously as the entourage left. The echoes of his laughter could be heard long after he was gone.

EIGHTEEN

New Year Blessings

People often wondered how Igwe Nwadike did it though anyone with a passion for talking and to be understood could do the same. It was difficult for Igwe to speak loud enough to be heard by a huge audience and still maintain his eloquence. But not only did he have a message, he was one with his message. The man was inspired, thanks to the man who sat behind him and supported him with the sound of his bullhorn.

"We have gathered to welcome the New Year!" Igwe began, then he paused.

"But . . . but we have first to give thanks. We have to give baskets full of thanks to Chi Okike for the year past." He paused again.

"The past year has been a remarkable one for all Igbo people and for our Uwa neighbors. We could not have asked for a better harvest. The weather was very good. It was moderate. When it rains, we complain about rain, and when sunshine comes, we complain about sunshine, but we need both. We asked Chi Okike to give us both in moderation, and last year was such a year. But good weather and good harvest were only part of the blessings that last year brought. Last year turned out to be the most peaceful year I have ever witnessed in Igbo land. We did not see new disputes between Igbo communities, and a lot of old disputes were laid to rest."

"Igwe!" someone yelled from the crowd. This was always contagious and soon almost everyone followed suit. The sound of bullhorns and elephant horns filled the air. The crowd was pleased with something. They all stood on their feet.

"I need not recite last year's blessings because you know them more than I do. I do not walk to Igbo communities myself. All the reports I get come from Igbo families and through other channels. And this year they were all the same. But I can assure you that the new year will be even better than the last.

"Igwe! Igwe!! Igwe!!!" the crowd exploded again.

"I am happy that you are happy and that the earth has been good to us. The land has continued to bless and enrich us. But there is one question I would like to ask. Have we been good to the earth? Our host has been good to us, but have we been good to our earthly host? Most Igbo people would say yes and mean it. However, a small minority continues to insult the earth. They hide behind masks and terrorize our people. We call them Uwa men. But we know better than that. We know they are Igbo people. They come from our villages and families, and their relatives know who they are but are afraid to speak up."

"I tell you today that if you do not speak up and expose evil, you are as guilty as the evildoers themselves. If you do not speak up for the earth then you do not have a right to blessings from the earth. We must speak the truth at all times, even when no one is watching. Truthfulness is the foundation of a good person and, therefore, the foundation of a good community. A community that does not speak the truth will not survive."

"Igbo people refer to Nri land as 'the Holy Land,' but the truth is that all Igbo land is a holy land and all Igbo people are holy people. All Uwa land is holy as well. So whoever defames Nri land, Igbo land, or Uwa land will answer for it. They cannot go free. We must turn away from Ochaa-ghute Ochara-ghute (mediocrity). We must earn our blessings, for that is the foundation of peace. Most conflicts come when people try to take what they have not earned or when they are refused what they have rightfully earned. We must promote rights and responsibilities and develop the ties between the two. We must embrace our responsibilities because that is the only guaranteed avenue for obtaining our own rights. Rights are never free. There is always a corresponding responsibility attached to them. If you embrace your responsibility, your rights will always find you. If your rights do not come to you on time, they must come with interest when they come to you later. That is the law!"

He talked about forgiving one another, but he said that forgiveness does not mean trust. "If someone deliberately hits you on the head with a big stick, you must forgive that person, but it will be foolish to give him another chance if the offender has not repented. We must be fair to our neighbors, but that is all we owe them."

He said that Igbo people must shun violence and that, at best, violence leads to nothing; at worst, it leads to total destruction. He stated that Igbo people have not seen new disputes but admitted that Igbo land has seen more violence than ever before. He wondered how that could be. "How can you have violence without a dispute? That, Umu-Igbo, is the greatest threat to peace. If you have a dispute with your neighbor, you sit down and talk, and you find a solution. But how can you talk with an enemy who has no face and with whom you have no dispute. Uwa men have no faces, and we have no dispute with their people. Yet they come with violence. They terrorize innocent, peaceful people. Because there is no dispute, we cannot talk or negotiate. So some would say that the only solution left is violence against violence."

"You may call it fire-for-fire, but it is not the only solution left to us. This is the lure of the devil that is bent on total destruction. It uses the most disgruntled among us to act against all of us. What we need is to expose these people. We need to expose them so we can give them counsel and heal their wounds. They are disgruntled spirits that need healing. I must repeat that violence against violence leads to nothing good. It is against the earth to engage in violent acts against other human beings or animals. We kill animals for food only, and it is okay to kill them in self-defense. The earthly host permits it. But we cannot torture animals or kill them for entertainment. It is against the earth. We cannot spill human blood under any circumstances. The earth is completely against it. A human being cannot own another human being. The earth forbids it. We must not only make peace with each other, but with the earth. We must be worthy of the blessings that we receive from the earth."

"Today is a great day for all of us, and we will celebrate it. Not even the massacres at the seventh wilderness will prevent us from celebrating the New Year. We shall give thanks for all the blessings we received in the year past. But, as we celebrate, we must remember the heroes who died at the seventh wilderness. Yes! You are a hero when you are not causing trouble for everyone else. You are a hero when you are sweating and going about your business under the blazing sun, and you are killed for no reason at all. You think that you have lost everything, but you have not. Whatever you think has been taken away from you will be given to you threefold. Yes, we are going to eat and drink and entertain ourselves because what we are celebrating is beyond any one of us. But I do make a request. I request that out of respect for those whose blood was spilled at the seventh wilderness, we dance today without the masquerades. No masquerade will be allowed to perform at Nri today."

"May the new year bring everything good to Igbo people and our friends. May the earth give us moderate weather and good harvest. May we gather here this time next year and give thanks for all the blessings that this year has brought us. May you meet your family alive and well as you have left them."

"Igwe! Igwee!! Igweee!!"

Now the chief priest opened the floor to acknowledge the end of the speech, and the rest of the crowd followed.

"Paapaa…puupuuu…puuuu!" (Igwe)

"Paapaa…puupuuu…puuuu!" (Igwe)

This much the officials understood. Most Ozo priests stood up and began blowing their elephant tusk trumpets in praise. The rest of the crowd hailed "Igwe!" "Igwe!! Igwe!!!"

All stood up out of respect for the man and his spirit. Odozi-obodo women began to sing, moving out to the center of the hall where they started dancing. Then the queen, Eze Nwanya, led them to Igwe Nwa-dike. They presented him with a bronze ceremonial knife and a large roll of cloth. Unceremoniously, a few representatives of the Ozo men came next. To save time, the Nze priests did the same since most delegates liked to go with a full delegation. The other delegates followed after the Nze priests.

Each delegate was led by their Nri host who introduced them to Oduh, head of the Ozo men. Then Oduh repeated the introduction and what they had brought to Igwe. Igwe acknowledged the group by lifting up his horsetail in a blessing. Then he took a large piece of holy chalk from his chief priest and gave it to Oduh who handed it to the delegation's leader. The leader passed the holy chalk and whatever was left of the kolanut to the rest of his group. Most delegates had brought gifts of money and rope. A big piece of rope tied together signified a head of cattle. A small piece signified a goat. A small white piece signified a ram. The rope meant that the livestock had already been given to their Nri host who would later deliver the animal to the officials. Some brought as many as five big ropes and some small ones. After the gift exchange with each delegate, the entertainment groups went to the big public square to dance as much as they wanted. Later, their hosts took them to private locations for food and drink. Some of them would return individually to the public square to watch other groups perform.

The procession for the exchange of gifts lasted late into the evening. The dancing and celebration at the public square went on into the night. By the end of the next day, most guests were already on their way home. And by the end of the third day, only a few who had some other business, mostly political, were still at Nri.

Among the many Igbo delegates who came to the ceremony were the Amauzo-Agu and the Ukwe families. They were nineteenth in the hall, a very high ranking. Though they were two separate families, they came under the umbrella name of "Amauzo-Agukwe" family. Their delegation was one of the few that Igwe Nwadike smiled at during the gift exchange procession. Their Nri host made no attempt to introduce them to Oduh. He simply smiled at Oduh, who turned to Igwe and smiled at him as if that were the introduction. And, as a matter of fact, this was enough introduction for the Amauzo-Agukwe family. Their meeting had put the smile on the faces of Igwe Nwadike and Oduh. The two families had brought gifts, but nobody cared about the number of cows or goats. What mattered was that the two families had come, and not only that they had come, but that they stood next to each other. And not only did they stand next to each other, they came as a union of families (Amauzo-Agukwe), a name derived from the Amauzo-Agu and Ukwe families. They brought gifts as one family to prove their unity. If anyone tried to tell which family was which, it seemed to be Igwe Nwadike, for he gave them two lumps of holy chalk. They were one of the very few delegations to whom he gave more than one lump of chalk. He meant this as a double blessing. It was not an attempt to tell them apart even though a bystander might have assumed this was his motive.

Igwe had made their union possible. Making peace between the Amauzo-Agu and the Ukwe families stood out as one of Igwe's greatest achievements. It was a testimony before all Igbo people of Igwe's wisdom and political skill, and, maybe, it included a little luck.

NINETEEN

The Union

The land dispute between the Amauzo-Agu and Ukwe families had gone on for four generations. All Igbo people knew this was a lost cause, a hopeless case. In some parts of Igbo land there was a saying that "If an Nri priest thinks he is so good at making peace, let him go to Amauzo-Agu and prove it."

There were different versions of the saying, depending on the particular dialect and it was, of course, said behind the backs of Nri people, even though no insult was intended. The saying simply meant that some disputes are too great for even an Nri priest to solve. Actually, this was a compliment to Nri people, but they did not see it that way.

The dispute between the Amauzo-Agu and Ukwe families was like a rotten egg on the reputation of every well-meaning Nri priest, and it was even more so for every Eze Nri who had reigned during the dispute, including Igwe Nwadike.

Amauzo-Agu meant "the people of the wilderness," but it could also mean "the road to the wilderness." The Amauzo-Agu people claimed both meanings. They claimed that they owned the road to the wilderness as well as the wilderness itself though they actually lived in, farmed, and hunted in a very small part of the huge thirteenth wilderness. The only time they saw more of it was once every five years when they performed a particular ritual. In this ritual, they made a procession that went around the entire wilderness. The ritual concluded in the heart of the wilderness with a sacrifice to their God. They had done this for many generations before the Ukwe people migrated from the west. The wilderness was so big and rich with streams and vegetation that no new immigrant could ignore it. And, over the generations, many made a try to move there. But the Amauzo-Agu were not only good fighters, they truly believed that the wilderness was given to them only. They believed that the spirit of their gods resided in the great thirteenth wilderness and that no immigrant should be allowed to desecrate it. So they had successfully chased away everyone who tried to settle there until the Ukwe people came along.

The Ukwe were not average immigrants. They were not fleeing political oppression, drought, or plague. They were migrating because Uda, their head deity, had told them to. They were a highly ritualized, non-Igbo people who followed the revelations of their deities without question. So, when their head deity told them to migrate to the east and to keep going until they were told to stop, they raised no objections. They crossed seven rivers, but Uda told them to keep going. When they stopped at the tenth wilderness owned by the Ndana Family it seemed to match Uda's revelation to them except there was no hill at the north. There was a huge valley with a waterfall at the south end that Uda had described, but no hill at the north. When their high priest consulted Uda, the deity told them to keep going eastward. The Ndana people were very friendly and asked the Ukwe people to stay and become caretakers of their rich tenth wilderness, but not even that offer could stop their search. Instead, they left their children and elderly women at Agu-Neli while they went looking for the perfect land. They kept going and began to feel that they would never get there. But when they reached the thirteenth wilderness, they didn't need to consult Uda. Everything fit the description. As a formality, the high priest consulted Uda who answered in the affirmative.

Uda warned them to expect initial problems with the local people. But things were far worse than they expected. The Ukwe were used to fighting people who were afraid of dying, but the Amauzo-Agu were not. The Amauzo-Agu were not only brave, but they fought with conviction. They were fighting to preserve the sacred dwelling place of their gods, and they outnumbered the Ukwe four to one. Their weapon of choice was the ogbuadana, an ugly-looking machete that could easily be mistaken for an axe. Some simply called it ugly-head, because its cutting tip was heavier and wider than its handle. A well fed fighter could chop off an opponent's limb with one stroke. But the Ukwe people were fighting out of desperation. And one simply does not challenge a desperate human being. One side may be fighting to win, but the opponent is fighting to stay alive.

The Ukwe had given up all they had to follow Uda, and there was no going back. They did not have the number of fighters that the Amauzo-Agu had, but they had the weapons to make up for it, their poisonous arrows, and they were very good with them, just as the Amauzo-Agu were good at machete fighting. The Ukwe had another advantage—their deity. Uda revealed to them when to expect an attack from the Amauzo-Agu, and the revelations were mostly accurate. The war between the two families had gone on for generations. It began with spiritual conviction and evolved into simple revenge for the last attack from the other side. Over the years, the Amauzo-Agu had come to adopt the arrow technique, and they, too, became pretty good at the use of this weapon. The Ukwe adapted to their hostile neighbors' moves by making it mandatory that every man must marry at least four wives and have as many children as possible. So, in one generation, just as the Amauzo-Agu were becoming good at arrow technology, the Ukwe increased in numbers. Each side had gained the leverage that the other side had previously held. Then the real slaughter began.

There was something about the Amauzo-Agu that said they would fight until the end of time. So it was the Ukwe who were always looking for an avenue of peace. Over the years, the Ukwe developed an annex house at the tenth wilderness. Their old went there to retire, and their young went there to grow up and have a normal life before moving to the "battle-field." The Ukwe old men living at Agu-Ndana, the tenth wilderness, kept in touch with Nri people. They invited Nri men to visit them, and the Nri men had done so ever since the war started. The Nri peace warriors had come in different groups, stages, and levels. Earlier on two Ozo men and their Nze associates came. They invited the leaders of the two sides to meet and quickly discovered that the dispute was much bigger than two men could handle. The Eze Nri at the time sent three high-ranking Ozo priests to settle the matter, but they also failed. After a year, with the war still raging, he made a third try by sending the best of the best, ten of the highest ranking Ozo priests. At that time, Ozo priests still had a reputation as peacemakers. But the priests came back empty-handed. Igwe Onuora, the Eze Nri at the time, invited the two sides to come together, but the Amauzo-Agu refused. To them, peace talks meant compromises. There was nothing to compromise. The Ukwe must move on or move back to wherever they came from. That was the only solution.

In a desperate effort, Igwe Onuora did what he had never done before. He sent three Ozo men to dwell among them to mediate peace on a daily basis. They were to remain as long as it took to find a solution to the mess at the thirteenth wilderness. Three months into their mission, an accident occurred.

One evening the Ozo priests were going from the Ukwe to the Amauzo-Agu side to consult with them. It was almost dark and the men standing guard at Amauzo-Agu attacked the priests before realizing who they were. The Amauzo-Agu killed one of the three Ozo men and the other two were badly wounded. So, even that effort brought no peace to the thirteenth wilderness. After that, Igwe Onuora withdrew all interest from the thirteenth wilderness. But the three Eze Nri who came after him tried in one way or another to bring peace, but all failed. When Igwe Nwadike became Eze Nri, he had little hope of resolving the feud. He, too, deliberately ignored the warring parties. He wanted them to believe that he did not care what they did to each other. He wanted to work on them when he would have the most impact. But he did not have to decide on when to work on their case. They came to him instead. It was not the Ukwe people who came as usual and neither was it the Amauzo-Agu people but a group of Nwadiana led by Akpaka.

Akpaka was a wealthy and influential young man from the Ndana family, but his mother had come from the Amauzo-Agu. He had fallen in love with a very beautiful woman from the neighboring family. When he found out that his lover's mother came from the Ukwe family, he vowed to do everything he could to bring the two people to the peace room again, and he did. Shortly after he married Unoma, he started a one-man crusade for peace. Working with Unoma's brothers, his brothers-in-law, he gathered all of the men outside of Ukwe and Amauzo-Agu whose mothers came from Amauzo-Agu or Ukwe and persuaded them that they could do something for the two families. In Igbo culture, no maternal uncle can refuse any reasonable request from his nephew or niece. When an organized group of Nwadiana (nephews and nieces outside Amauzo-Agu) led by Akpaka went to Amauzo-Agu to make their request, the Amauzo-Agu people listened. Not only did they listen, they agreed to meet with Igwe Nwadike. That was in itself a milestone. The Nwadiana of the Ukwe family did not have difficulties with the Ukwe people. They knew that the Ukwe had always wanted peace. They just did not want to have to move away.

The first day of the meeting with Igwe Nwadike was more like a welcoming ceremony. Igwe Nwadike spoke to both families through Oduh, Isi-Ozo Nri. He presented them with kolanut and thanked them for coming and for trusting that his people could help settle their dispute once and for all. He told them that he and his people had nothing to gain apart from seeing them living peacefully with each other. He told them touching stories about himself and about the Nri people and what his men had gone through to bring peace and harmony to Igbo land and beyond. He told them the humbling history of the Nri people. He shared with them what Nri, the founder of the Nri people, went through before he gained enlightenment, how he learned that the cost of achieving enlightenment was high and that using his wisdom for personal gain would never repay him for what he lost. He told about the harsh training he had received from his father and that he had lost his childhood and that he had had to be alone to learn how to build the ideal society his father had seen in a vision. He discovered that the only way he could ever make up for his losses was to use the wisdom he gained to benefit as many people as possible. He told them how many Nri men died every year trying to break up fights among communities.

"It is not worth it if this is done for selfish reasons," he concluded.

The second day was the Amauzo-Agu's day. They stated what they wanted. Igwe Nwadike asked them many questions to clarify their points. The Ukwe had some questions of their own, but they were not allowed to question the Amauzo-Agu. They met outside and gave their questions to Oduh who, in turn, presented the questions to Ukwe as if they were his own. By the end of the second day, Igwe Nwadike and his official knew what the Amauzo-Agu wanted and where they stood. On the third day, the Ukwe told their story. The fourth day was for Igwe Nwadike. By then, he understood well what was at stake, and he knew exactly where the problems were.

"I have listened very carefully to both sides," he began. "And I think I have a very good understanding of the roots of your dispute. What you lack is a little imagination, that's all. In my younger days, I had good friends in both of the Amauzo-Agu and Ukwe families. You are not the kind of people who are incapable of making peace. You are good people. And I mean that. People who are incapable of making peace are people who think like bullies. They are never satisfied until their opponents are cheated and in pain. They want everyone to be afraid of them, and they confuse that with respect. I have yet to see those kinds of people in the Amauzo-Agu or Ukwe families. It is not your nature. Igbo people want fairness, that's all. So I mean it when I say that what you lack is imagination. You think that what you have is yours and that is the end of the matter. It is not that simple. Amauzo-Agu, you say that the wilderness is your place of worship and that it was given to you by the gods. Well, the only problem is that the Ukwe claim the same rights. You must learn how to coexist. You must find a creative solution to your problems. And my role is to guide you while you are doing that. My role is not to render judgment. What if I give judgment and you do not accept? Then what? Nature itself is very creative, and we have learned a lot from nature."

"When you look at the Nri community, you see dwarves, giants, twins, and albinos. There are even people with six toes on each foot. Igbo and Uwa people reject them because they want things to be simple. But that is not nature's way. Nature is creative. So we must learn from nature to be creative as well."

"I can make suggestions about how you can coexist peacefully. But they will be simply to give you some ideas. You will have to explore some other options and find what is fair to both sides. The first option that comes to mind is that the Ukwe could become a village in Amauzo-Agu. That way, the whole place would still be Amauzo-Agu. The second option is that the Ukwe could be adopted brothers to the Amauzo-Agu, and the Amauzo-Agu could still come to the Ukwe part of the wilderness and perform ceremonies once every five years. You could also coexist as different families in one union. You could get rid of your old names completely and adopt a common name. All of these options I had not thought of beforehand. I just want you to know that the only limit to the possible solutions is your imagination."

"My second duty to you is to appeal to your consciences so that when you explore creative solutions, you will do so sincerely and in good faith."

Turning to the Amauzo-Agu people, he said, "You believe that your god resides in the wilderness. How are you sure that your god and the Ukwe people's god are not the same? How are you sure that Ukwe people are not your long lost cousins? How are you sure that their deity did not lead them all the way from far Uwa land to join their long lost cousins? Have you ever thought of that? Have you ever imagined that you may have been fighting and killing your own brothers all these years? I do not mean to be hard on you, but you are the adults in that part of Igbo land. And you must behave like adults. You have the responsibility of welcoming newcomers and making them feel at home with you. You must adopt a host attitude and mentality toward immigrants. You must have a fatherly relationship with them, and they, in turn, must come to you every year and pay their tribute and acknowledge your goodwill. That is how it is done."

He told them that the population of Nri was ten times that of the Amauzo-Agu, but that the Amauzo-Agu had five times the land of the Nri. "Nri people have no big wilderness and yet Nri people can never stop accepting immigrants." He told them that half of the Nri were not of original Nri descent, but that everyone had the same rights. He told them about the history of Ubom village in Nri which was founded by immigrants. They had the same rights as everyone else. When the entire village at Ubom invoked the forefathers they did not mean their blood forefathers. They meant the founders of Nri. "It is a sign that we are doing something good. You can learn from us, and you can also learn from the Ndana people. The Ndana welcome immigrants. This is only a test. Ukwe people could move on, but I guarantee you that someone else even more desperate will come along. I guarantee you that you will keep fighting until you pass that test."

Turning to the Ukwe, he said, "You must honor and respect the people who lived there before you and treat them as you treat your elders. You must consult them before making a major decision so they will know that you are not a threat to them, and they will have an opportunity to guide you. But, most important, since you think that you have the right to live there, you have the responsibility of welcoming future immigrants with open arms. That is the only way you can validate your right to live there."

For the rest of the fourth day and all of the fifth, Oduh supervised their negotiations. By the end of the seventh day, they had reached an agreement. They were to coexist as adopted cousins. The Amauzo-Agu people would have an unsupervised right to perform rituals in Ukwe territory anytime they wanted. The Ukwe would live and farm in a specific section of the wilderness and would ask for more if they needed it. The Ukwe people must never kill the wall gecko, a domestic lizard, as long as they dwelt at the thirteenth wilderness. The wall gecko was sacred to the Amauzo-Agu people, and their god forbade killing it. In the future, before admitting new groups of immigrants, both sides would meet and agree on the immigrants' rights. The two families were now free to visit each other and intermarry. They were to set aside a day every year to reaffirm and celebrate their agreement and cousinhood. But the agreement that made waves across Igbo land was the adoption of a new name for the duo community. They agreed on the Amauzo-Agukwe union though each family would retain its original name, but to outsiders they would be known as the Amauzo-Agukwe family.

On the sixth day, there was a big celebration at Nri. Igwe Nwadike gave them blessed planting yam, some special species of yam tubers, and many lumps of holy chalk. It was said that the Amauzo-Ukwe people became the greatest yam farmers from that year onward, abandoning their hunting profession.

So the sight of the two families standing next to each other at the year-counting ceremony was a special treat for Igwe Nwadike. Though he had achieved many other things, making peace between the Amauzo-Agu and the Ukwe people gave Igwe special joy.

PART TWO

TWENTY

The Big Meeting

Twenty-one years later

It had been twenty-one years since Erike lost his uncle to the robbers at the seventh wilderness. On the first Oye market day of eighth moon, the Nri annual general meeting of all Ozo and Nze priests was only three days away. At Ama-Ijedimma, south of the fifth wilderness, a group of thirty-five men was invading the Oye Ama-Ijedimma marketplace. At least, it seemed like an invasion. The men were salt traders from Nri and, having missed their target resting place, they had to settle for an open marketplace to spend the night. They could have crossed the fifth wilderness that late in the evening, but that was when accidents happened to Nri people.

Now it was getting dark, so the group had to stay at the Oye Ama-Ijedimma market. Their leader was not happy about this. The traders called the leader "Ochiagha" which translated to captain. Since the Nri people did not have an army, had never had an army, or had never engaged in warfare, the nickname Ochiagha was a polite way of calling the leader a slave driver, for that was what Okoye had seemed to become. He was a contract merchant, which meant that he did not take title for any of the products he traded. Wealthy Ozo men, mostly Oganiru types, contracted with him to lead their traders to long-distance markets. For this service, they paid him a fee or commission. His duties, among other things, were to foresee and eliminate obstacles on the way so the traders could deliver on time. His reputation of truthfulness, perfect judgment, and unadulterated bravery was long established. Most of the men he worked for were Ozo men who no longer wanted to travel themselves.

Any day short of the return target day would cut into Okoye's commission. So far this group had not missed a day, and they were nearing home. Okoye's only displeasure was sleeping in the open marketplace. In addition to fighting off bugs, they had to watch out for mad people who seemed to own the markets at night. So, even though there was always a designated person standing guard while the others slept, Okoye did not feel comfortable sleeping in this market. For one thing, it was unrealistic to ask one of his people who had just walked eight hours non-stop to watch while others slept. He had learned the hard way that this just did not work. So Okoye, being Okoye, would rather stand guard himself while everyone else slept. To him that was realistic because he had complete responsibility for the failure or success of each trade expedition. In addition to the responsibility resting on his head, he was the only one in the group who rode on horseback most of the time, so he was the least tired.

Each group Okoye led had a unique chemistry. This particular group happened to be one of the happiest and loudest. Even when they were supposed to be bone-tired, they still made jokes about each other and laughed loudly, thanks to an energetic group of young immigrants to Nri. Joking and camaraderie was always good for the team spirit, Okoye had initially thought.

It was not long after the men had finished eating their dinner at the marketplace that the young men began singing and dancing. And, as outrageous as it seemed, the young men still had made room for their musical instruments in the heavy loads they carried on their heads. Okoye disliked the noise they made. He did not object to the happiness that the singing and dancing brought them, but he disliked the attention it drew. Before long the villagers were aware of their presence. This attention was not always bad. It could sometimes prevent negative feelings being directed toward them once people understood who they were, but Okoye would rather have spent the evening unnoticed and moved on as early as possible.

His men finally went to sleep a little late because of all the attention from the village. Only two hours after the others had fallen asleep, Okoye began fighting to stay awake himself. A large dose of tobacco snuff always helped, so Okoye took out his tobacco bottle and sniffed the brown powder inside. After consuming the dose in his left palm, he started sneezing. This was a sign that he was awake, at least for the time being. As he was putting away the bottle, he saw two figures coming toward them. The figures were not coming from the walkway, but from the thickly-wooded area. In the dim moonlight, he could tell that they were men and that at least one of them had a machete at his waist. From the way they moved, he knew they were more scared than he was. So they could not be Uwa men, for Uwa men were always more organized and came in large groups to intimidate their prey. So these could be snatch-and-run thieves. There was only one way to find out. Okoye shuffled his feet and faked a cough, a way of letting the strangers know that someone was awake. The two figures stood still for awhile. Then one pulled back while the one with a machete came forward. Okoye stood up to eliminate any doubt that someone was awake and had seen the intruders, but the man kept coming though he would stop at intervals as if to make up his mind.

"Is it a human or a spirit that I greet?" queried Okoye.

"Are you Nshi men?" the figure queried back.

"We could be if I know what you want."

"We need your help."

"Then leave your machete behind and come forth," Okoye told him.

Half of his men were awake now and sitting up, while the others were struggling to wake up. The second figure had completely disappeared into the woods. The other one had managed to put his machete on the ground. As he came closer, the man picked up the oil lamp that was burning nearby. He was still about ten footsteps away, but Okoye knew exactly who he was—an outcast. Only an outcast or a madman would have that smell. It came from weeks or even months of not bathing. Madmen smelled that way, too, but they would not be as coordinated and forceful as this man was and certainly would not be allowed by any villagers to own a machete.

Only after the man had lifted the oil lamp up to Okoye's face and satisfied himself about his identity did he start talking. By the time he finished his story, his partner was out of the woods and standing next to him. Both men were outcasts consecrated to some local deity which made them more like slaves. In those days, outcasts did not mingle with normal people. They could not even go to the village stream to bathe when ordinary people would be there. They could only go at night, but most of the time they preferred not to which explained the terrible smell. They were forbidden any interaction with normal people, including speaking. They were also forbidden to go outside their village borders. So if an outcast was the only person in that village, he or she was doomed to madness. The individual might start off as normal but eventually the outcast would go crazy from the isolation.

The man standing before Okoye had been named Coconut-head by the villagers. He was a coup leader who had dreamed up an escape idea and sold it to his partner whom the villagers called Chameleon. The outcasts could be killed if the villagers found out what they were up to. Isiaki had been with the deity for only five years. Chameleon had been consecrated to the deity since he was six and had little recollection of where he had come from and absolutely no real motivation for a change of life until Isiaki came along eleven years later. Coconut-head was a prisoner of war purchased from a very faraway Igbo land. After his consecration to their deity, the villagers checked on him every morning. Later they asked Chameleon to spy on him. Isiaki knew very well that Chameleon was spying on him, so he gained his trust first. After a year he started putting pictures of the Nri fantasyland into his partner's mind. What started as a fairy tale had turned into a full-scale coup d'etat plan after two years. Isiaki could not go back to his home village because he had been consecrated to a deity. The only way out was to start a new life at Nri. For over a year, the pair had waited for a perfect opportunity, but none of the Nri men who had come through the village had spent the night until tonight. Isiaki had not actually seen the traders singing and dancing, but he had overheard the villagers talking about them.

Okoye did not like this situation, but he had no choice. He must attend to the two men even if it meant his own men would not get enough sleep and, therefore, not meet their journey target. As a Nze Nri priest, before any other business, Okoye must attend to anyone in distress. This was the second code of the Nze Nri priestly sect, which even superseded submission to the Eze Nri, the third code. The first code was telling the truth at all times. Okoye and his men had to perform a full cleansing ceremony on the two men before they could adopt them. This ceremony included shaving their hair and washing their feet. The traders did not sleep after that and had to leave much earlier than usual to avoid any confrontation with the villagers. They rested more frequently on their way but still did not miss their target. As they drew closer and closer to Nri, they merged with other groups going home for the big meeting. By the time they finally reached Nri they had merged with four other groups. Their group alone now numbered about two hundred people. Other Nri people were coming home in record numbers from all directions. It was two days before the general meeting and one day before the closed door meeting of the officials.

❧ ❧ ❧

By all accounts, Igwe Nwadike had done well. He had accomplished more than his predecessors and was far more popular than any of them. He was a household name. Under his leadership, the Nze priesthood had been conferred on the first non-Nri Igbo man. He had voiced the obscure ideas of the early mystics and made them understandable to lay people. Under his watch, the Igbo people had invented a war dance. With no real wars to fight, the communities had invented a dance to satisfy their human warlike impulses. Igwe Nwadike had achieved so much, and yet he lived in despair. He was a disappointed old man. He was disappointed in the philosophy that he felt had failed him, but he was also unwilling to change it.

He had repeatedly and clearly told the Igbo people to shun violence. Yet violence seemed to be the only answer to the problem of dealing with the Uwa men. Under his watch, the Uwa men had grown in numbers and their impact had spread like a terminal illness. Under his watch, Uwa activities had tripled though they were still limited to attacks on traders a few times a month. The worry was the copycat Uwa men. These people targeted ordinary Igbo citizens and ran off with whatever they could grab. Some gangs targeted farmers and one particular gang's signature was to rape women. The copycats worried people because their acts were senseless and had the signature of Akalogheli (a misguided and troubled spirit). So the Uwa men had become the biggest test of the Nri philosophy of nonviolence.

But that was not the only reason Igwe Nwadike was living the rest of his life in despair. He had long suspected that the Oganiru men, or at least some of them, knew something about Uwa men that they were not willing to share. But the Wise One had refused to nurture that idea until an Igbo man put it to him bluntly in public. Igwe had invited the family of Umu-Oke to a meeting with him and some of his cabinet members. At this meeting, Igwe accused them of knowing something about the Uwa men that they were not sharing. Out of desperation, he put it bluntly to the representatives of Umu-Oke.

"How could someone in your family not know anything when you own the seventh wilderness? You live and farm there and most of the robbery activities happen in the seventh wilderness. How could someone in your family not know or see something?"

Maybe the fact that Igwe put it so directly caused a young man to speak frankly. Or maybe it was the fact that Igwe had threatened to impose a sanction on their market. The latter may have propelled the young man to stand up in front of everyone and risk all. But, actually, he risked nothing because Igwe already knew the truth. The man spoke through an interpreter, but Igwe Nwadike understood every word.

"How could our community be responsible when we do not deal in elephant ivory or calm-wood or precious stones or salt? We are farmers and we sell food items only. Those people who rob innocent traders do not swallow their loot. They sell it through authentic dealers. If one is investigating a homicide, he should start with the ironsmith that manufactures murder weapons. Maybe he will lead to the people who bought his weapons."

The young man had not exactly said it, but he was pointing a finger back at the Nri people. He had pointed fingers at the self-proclaimed "stake-holders" of Nri, the Oganiru. Igwe Nwadike swallowed hard.

After this meeting and over the next several years, Igwe made frequent trips to the ironsmith, but each time he was met with sealed lips. Either he was talking to the wrong ironsmith or the ironsmith had lost his conscience. One thing was certain: Oganiru men, because of their flamboyant lifestyle, were not a good influence on the Nri and Igbo people. At best, they were not asking enough questions. And, at worst, they were doing the unthinkable—buying stolen merchandise directly or indirectly.

The Oganiru nicknamed themselves "Igwe-Enyi" (Herd of Elephants). The nickname came from their carved symbol of a giant herd of elephants, which symbolized their strength as pathfinders who cleared the bush and created a way in the thickly-wooded forests. But Igwe saw a different picture. To him, the Oganiru were a herd of giant elephants all right, but they were a herd that had gone to the source of the stream, not to drink, but just for thc luxury of bathing. They were so blind that they could not see that there would be no drinking water left after they had taken their baths. They were too stubborn to listen to the bald eagle that sat in the iroko tree and could see the origin, the middle, and the destination of the life-giving water. The eagle on the high plain knew that most of the elephants would probably die of thirst after bathing. But to the bald eagle who had spent his lifetime preaching fairness that would only be a fair price for their stiff-necked foolishness. What was not fair was that the innocent victims who depended on the stream would also die because of the foolishness of the few strong elephants.

The rest of the Nri and Igbo people drank innocently from the life-giving stream, oblivious of the corrupted water coming from upstream. What was not fair was that the eagle itself depended on that stream and its young ones depended on it too. The eagle had long gained total freedom and could easily fly to a distant land to drink its belly full then return if it had to. But its eaglets had no wings yet and could not fly away. The bald eagle wept for all the innocent victims who had no wings and could not walk far enough to find another stream. Those who could walk might travel forty days and forty nights to the closest stream. There, under the constant watch and distrust of the locals, they might negotiate for a small dose of drinking water to quench their thirst. But, most unfair of all, the elephants were among the few who could make it that far.

This unfairness propelled the bald eagle at the age of 104 to make one last desperate attempt to reach their consciences. It seemed a hopeless attempt because the elephants had not listened for the forty-eight years Igwe had presided. Why would they suddenly have a change of heart? But a miracle worker who lacks optimism has no job.

When a lay Igbo person looked at the clear night sky, he saw small glittering lights; some glittered more than others. They called all of them kpakpando (stars). When an adept like Igwe Nwadike looked up at the sky, he, too, saw kpakpandos, but they had names and personalities. When he looked at the sky on a clear night, he saw events now happening and about to happen. These were not just cosmological but earthly events as well.

On the third Afor market day on the seventh moon, Igwe Nwadike saw the big star for the first time. It had come from the north. He observed it for eight more days before he knew what it was—the star of renewal that called for atonement. This star visited earth every one hundred years and stayed for a full year before bidding the earth farewell. Immediately after the star's departure, something was supposed to happen, a big change of some sort. The change could be good, but it could also be bad. An optimist like Igwe saw the good part and ignored the bad. He scheduled a general meeting exactly one year from the day he had sighted the star of renewal. He declared the period in between the sighting and the general meeting to be days of purification and atonement.

There was a heavy fine for absentees from the meeting, but that was not why a high turnout was expected. The meeting was also only weeks before the New Yam (Harvest) Festival. Igwe considered this to be his last big opportunity to save his people.

One month before what he called "the Mother of All Meetings," Igwe went into isolation. During his younger years he had gone into the holy forest. But, at 104, he stayed in his personal quarters. There, on the first day of his official one-month seclusion, he started thinking of a message for the Nri people, but nothing came. He wanted a new message, a fresh one, something that had not been said in fifty years. He found none.

Just give it a week, maybe two weeks, and it will come, he thought. Sometimes he would seek out thoughts and find them. At other times, mostly during his isolations, wise and fresh thoughts snuck up on him, sometimes like a thief. Most of the time, these would become the valuable ones. He waited. Quietly, like a thief, something came, but it was not wise thoughts. What came was reality, and it came as an Owl.

❦ ❦ ❦

Ichie Idika was the first to arrive for the meeting. He was not an official, but Igwe had given him a special invitation to attend. He had also extended a special invitation to other people close to him, including his head wife and the two first sons of his two wives. Ichie Idika was two hours early. Igwe was bathing when he arrived, and Ichie had to wait. As they had gotten older, the two men had become closer and closer. So they were eating breakfast together and talking about their childhood when Oduh arrived. Only then did both men learn that the meeting would be held at Igwe's personal obu and not at the big hall. The men thought nothing of it since they had held quite a few meetings there in the past, especially as Igwe got older. Not long after Oduh arrived, others appeared. The big obu was almost full. People made jokes while they waited for the others to arrive. Igwe Nwadike seemed unusually cheerful and in high spirits. He was waiting for his head wife, who had not shown up yet, so he had to start a little late. As usual, he broke kolanuts which everyone was eating when he started his opening speech.

Igwe thanked them for coming and hinted that this was a very important meeting, perhaps the most important one they would ever have with him. Some were beginning to smile quietly for they had heard all of this before. Igwe always said that every meeting was very important. Then he gave them the first surprise. He would not be presiding over the general meeting tomorrow.

"By the time our meeting is over, you will know why," he said. Pointing in the direction of Oduh, he said, "I would like you to listen carefully to what I am about to say, because you will lead tomorrow's meeting. I would like you to quote me word for word during the meeting. If you fail to remember any of it, Ichie Idika will be happy to help you. He has a good memory."

Igwe adjusted himself on his daybed. As he had grown old, he had an ikpo (daybed) built for himself so that he did not have to walk back and forth all the time.

"Tell our people that we are failing. We have drifted away from our mission. A long time ago when our ancestors engaged in long distance travel, they went looking for knowledge to share with our Igbo people and our Uwa neighbors. Today we go to places our ancestors could only imagine. And what do we bring back? Just another shiny piece of clothing material to sell and make money. Nri land, which was once the knowledge and spiritual center of our people, has been reduced to a market where people come to buy the latest piece of clothing and jewelry. I need not say a lot about this because I was thinking the other day that whatever I was about to say to our people in this meeting, I have already said before. It is not that we have not said or done what we need to say or do, but that our people have chosen a very long and difficult path. Am I angry? No. Disappointed? Yes. I am disappointed that our people do not know what they have. What we have neglected today, our neighbors will adopt tomorrow, repackage it, and sell it back to us at a very high price. And another disappointment is that our people are happy to buy something because it is foreign, therefore, it must be good. I am terrified when I look into our young people's eyes. I do not see the fire that used to burn there. The few who have that fire do not have a sense of mission (vocation), and the ones that have a sense of mission do not have that fire."

"You may think that things do not look so bad, but I am looking at the next generation and the ones after it, and it does not look good. I meant this to be a happy meeting, so I apologize for being emotional. Our people came from the great Ama-Mbala River. When you are confused about what you ought to be doing, you should go down to that river and watch its activities. It flows into the great world ocean. It may not be the biggest river, but it contributes everything to the ocean. It feeds the locals and gives then drinking water. But most of it flows into the world ocean. Ama-Mbala does not create water. Water does not even originate from it. It is only a chosen channel for that energy. It is not about the water, but the flavor it contributes. It must contribute its own flavor and influence the taste of the world ocean. Nri people must never try to inhibit the energy that flows through us. We must let it flow freely into the world ocean and influence its flavor. Ama-Mbala is a holy place for our people, and we must not forget that. We will gain a lot by going there often."

He told again the history of the Nri people which they had all heard many times over in the forty-eight years since he had become Eze Nri. It was torture to some of the men in the room. They knew the history could be long or short, depending on Igwe's mood. He gave them the short version, but quickly turned it into a story of his own life and history. When most people tell their life history, they tell it from the beginning and progress to the end. Igwe told his from the middle back to the beginning. Maybe his life had ended after his servanthood, or maybe that part was just the most eye-opening or the most interesting, but it always started when he was finally coming back to his family for good after ten years of servanthood with different families. He had had seven masters, and all of them had been his father's servants at one point or another. The beginning of the story almost never progressed earlier than his first musical group, which was also his first age grade group. But this particular time it did.

Then something happened. Igwe's speech had been comprehensible, but now he acted as if he were hallucinating. He started talking about his first age grade and his first masquerade, which they usually danced at the age of ten. He had been younger than the others. "Could you believe that I was the youngest in the group, but I was their lead dancer. They had to cancel their first outing because I was sick."

Then he started singing and acting out the Ulaga dance. He talked about his infancy and how good it had felt. He said he wished to be born again, that it had felt so good in his mother's womb. "It was so comfortable, so peaceful in there." Then he started acting like a baby in the womb and rolling himself up into a ball. Everyone in the room thought he had gone crazy.

Ichie Idika understood first. "Odugboo! (Ancient One!)" he called. "What do you think you are doing?"

"I knew you would be the one. When we get old, we do not grow an apple tree on our heads, we join the elders instead. That is the proper way."

Just then the gray owl that visited him during his forty days of isolation came again and sat outside. But this time two other owls joined it. It was exactly noon. Igwe Nwadike nodded to the group of owls standing outside and said to the men in the room, "Our people hold the lamp for all Igbo people. We must never forget that. If that lamp ever goes out, it is our duty to light it up again."

He started to lie down on the daybed. As he put his head down and stretched out his legs, he said his last words: "The only thing that has substance is the truth. When darkness comes and all fails you, the truth you told is all you have."

Eze-Nwanya (the queen) was just coming in when he took his last breath. She knew something was wrong, but not what it was. All the men in the room were crying but made no attempt to save Igwe, not even his two sons. Eze-Nwanya was the only one who tried to do something. The basket filled with dried catfish fell from her hands as she rushed toward her husband.

"Get me some water! He is dehydrated from all this long fasting," she said to her son, who was only now coming forward to his dead father but only to close his open mouth. That was the only thing that Igwe had not been able to do for himself. He had bathed himself and eaten breakfast. He had even blessed and eaten kolanuts with his people and had done his job for the last time. He had laid himself down, stretched out his arms and legs, closed his eyes, and gone to sleep. That was how the holiest of them used to die, though not in public as Igwe Nwadike had.

In the confusion, no one knew when or how the owls left.

Eze Nwanya could not forgive herself for being late. That was the price she paid for being a "perfect wife." She had been separating bones from dried fish so their guests would not have to do it for themselves. She had many attendants, but she did many things herself, especially the task of removing the bones because she did not trust anyone else to do it well.

There was turmoil in the big room. The first person to recover from shock was the chief priest. That was his job. He began to blow his bullhorn in praises to his master. The sound of the horn made matters worse, for it sent chills down the spines of everyone in the room. The sound that had once been used to focus the attention of his master was now sending him on a journey, never to be seen again. It was an hour before Oduh recovered. He started making burial arrangements so the Legend would be buried during the general meeting at noon the next day. That was the date he had with his people.

When Igwe Nwadike had scheduled the meetings, and even when he had started his forty-day isolation, he had not known about his departure. Four days after he started his forty-day isolation, he heard the owl at midnight. From then on, every night it came closer and closer, until one night it was on his rooftop when he was alone in his quarters. In Igbo land, the owl was a mystical bird that brought messages from the underworld. In the middle of Igwe's isolation, the gray owl began showing up at midday. It would stand for a few moments and then leave. At the same time, Igwe Nwadike was seeing all his dead relatives in his dreams at night. He had learned to expect the owl at midday, but four days before the end of his isolation, just before midday, he had fallen asleep. He was awakened by a voice that he recognized as his late uncle's (his mother's brother). He could hear the voice and was quite awake, but he could not open his eyes. It felt as though they were glued shut.

"You must be ready on the first day of the meeting at noon. You must make your last speech before noon, for we will come at noon and take you with us. You have done well and have nothing to be afraid of," the voice said. He managed to open his eyes just in time to see the gray owl flying away. Then he understood.

TWENTY-ONE

Okoye Chosen

Those who cried during their facial scarification were labeled scream-ers for life. It did not matter how brave they might act or become as they grew up, they would always be reminded by their peers of how they had embarrassed their age grade in front of their guests. The young men beat their drums and blew their flutes and sang songs of encouragement. They took turns dancing to their drums. The singers invoked the young man's name and told him to make their age group proud. They told him that girls were watching. They called the names of their heroes, those who did their peers proud. But the young man cried louder than all the drums and the singing. His screaming turned into lamentations that could be heard all around Nri-Agu village.

Okoye Nweri shook his head and drank from his cup of palm wine.

"I have never heard this style of lamentation before," he told the man sitting to his right.

"Then we should call it lamentation original," the man replied.

All who heard him burst out laughing.

"In our day one would never recover from such embarrassment in front of his peers. But these days, it is common," said Okoye.

"That is very true," replied another man, who grinned with his teeth. He must have recalled his own scarification. In the Nri clan, it was the first introduction to manhood, or to womanhood for dwarf girls.

It was late in the evening and less than a day since they had come back from their three month trip. Okoye had many chores waiting for his attention, but he chose instead to attend a scarification ceremony. He was obsessed with scarification ceremonies. He had had his own scarification when he was eleven years old. Before his scarification, his elder brother was his father's favorite, and Okoye hung out mostly with his mother in the kitchen. During his scarification, he did not utter a sound. Even the bravest made some sounds, maybe non-verbal, but still vocal. At only eleven, Okoye had lain there like a piece of wood while the artists from Umudebe carved his face. He wanted to impress his father, and his father was more than impressed. The scarification artist would later joke that at some point he thought the young man was dead. It was at that event Okoye got his father's attention and since then, he was obsessed with scarification ceremonies. He would go just to prove to himself that he was still the best and relive his greatest childhood achievement. Even at his present age of forty-three, Okoye would rather go to a scarification ceremony than to an Ozo ordainment ceremony. He had yet to see someone who did as well as he had. As soon as the blade touched the young man's face, he started screaming. It was childish, but Okoye breathed a sigh of relief. This one had not held out for even a short moment. The young man's name was Chikadibia, and Okoye knew him very well because he was friends with his father.

Chikadibia lay on a worn-out mat with his back to the ground. His face looked up to the sky with his head pointing to the east. Both arms were spread so that his right arm pointed to the north and his left arm pointed to the south. Both arms and legs were pinned to the ground with metal hooks so they could not be moved. His chest and abdomen was also loosely pinned to the ground. His head rested on a carving board and was also strapped down. As a tradition, his peers (who were also his age group members) would keep him company during the scarification. His favorite uncles and aunts and cousins were only a few steps away. At intervals they called his name and offered words of encouragement. The scarification artists were from the Umudebe family, a non-Nri Igbo clan. They were themselves scarified, but their patterns were different. Theirs were just on the forehead and halfway down their faces. But the Nri people's scarification went all the way down to the cheek and chin.

In a standard Nri scarification, the artist would carve the first line to run from the center of the forehead down to the center of the chin. They would then carve a second line to run across the face, from the right cheek to the left. The second line met the first at the center of the nose, making it a perfect cross. The second cross was drawn with one line running from the left side of the forehead down to right side of the chin and another line running the opposite direction. This sequence and pattern was repeated until the pattern looked like the rays of the sun. Altogether it took sixteen straight lines, eight crosses, for a full-face scarification that mirrored the rays of the sun. It was their way of honoring the sun that they worshipped. But it was more than that. It was the face of service and another way of losing one's facial personality. There was a joke in those days that all Nri men looked alike. After each cut, drops of hot water were poured on the cut to sterilize it. After they completed the final cut, a bandage of Ogilisi leaves warmed in the open fire was applied to the open cuts to sterilize them. This would remain on the patient's face for about twelve days or until the leaves fell off. At the end of twelve days the wounds must have healed. On that twelfth day, his age-grade group would escort the young man to the marketplace as they sang and danced. Even strangers would present him with gifts.

The men from Umudebe had completed only the first cross, but songs of praise and words of comfort could not slow or suppress the boy's lamentations. There was a pause. It was a taboo not to complete a scarification once it had started, so they did what could be done only in extreme cases. They stopped to give the young man some dried palm wine. It was the only form of anesthetic available, but it was always discouraged because it tended to cause more bleeding. The alcohol seemed to help him though, for the young man did little screaming for the rest of the operation. So the ceremony progressed rather more quickly than they had anticipated.

When the two men from Umudebe started applying bandages to the young man's face, his relatives were relieved that it finally was coming to an end. The drumming and singing took a turn. It was definitely louder and more jubilant and seemed to invite all to dance. Now it was a song of victory. Okoye remembered this too well. He looked up to see Isiaki, one of the former outcasts he had adopted, dancing to the drums of the young men. Isiaki was drunk. Okoye admired him for a full moment, then laughed and shook his head. He was laughing at Isiaki's dance steps. There was something so innocent about the way he danced. He was off rhythm and uncoordinated. Okoye, who was himself a little drunk, started wondering who had invented slavery. *How did it start?* he wondered. It was then that the three men let themselves into the main gate.

Okoye knew that something was wrong as soon as they walked into the compound. They looked out of place. They were not in a festive mood like everyone else and looked tense. They quickly scanned the entire compound as if they were looking for someone. If Okoye had not recognized them as Nri men, he would have concluded they'd been invaded. The men were not only from Nri, but were themselves from Nri-Agu village, as were Okoye and most of the people in the compound. Without any other information, they summoned all the full-aged men to an urgent meeting. They were to go immediately. The three men had been going from door to door and did not have time to explain to everyone. Only at the meeting did Okoye learn of Igwe Nwadike's death. Igwe had been dead for almost half a day, a long time before the scarification ceremony had started. Okoye felt a sudden burden resting on his shoulders that he had never felt before. The effect of the alcohol was already gone. The men were to meet again at cock's crow to plan the burial.

Okoye felt burdened by the death of his master, not from sorrow or grief, for 105 years was a very generous age at which to die, especially if one had achieved so much. Different people felt a burden differently when it manifested itself in a physical form. To some, it felt like an invisible load lying squarely on the head. To others, it felt as if they could never breathe enough air, as if everyone else was in their space, sharing their air. Okoye felt it as a soreness in his neck that ran down both shoulders. It felt sore and heavy. When the meeting ended, the men of Nri-Agu village stood in groups and shared their surprise at the news and how they felt about it. Some were in tears. Those who left immediately went in groups. Okoye, too, left immediately but he was alone with his arms folded. He had a lot of memories of the old man, but one in particular came to mind as he walked out of the Nri-Agu village square. It had been twenty-one years ago and his last meeting with Igwe at the end of his palace servant-hood.

Igwe Nwadike had been alone in quiet reflection in his inner room when Okoye came in. Usually the palace attendants called him Nna-Anyi

(Our Father) because it was deemed too official to call him Igwe. Okoye had always called him Our Father but on this fateful afternoon, he had called him Nnam-Ukwu (My Master) for the first time. It was so spontaneous that Okoye would not have remembered it later if Our Father hadn't called his attention to it.

"I didn't know I was your master," the old man joked.

Okoye laughed and thought he could laugh it off, but apparently not.

"Do you know that in the old days, before you became someone's student, you came with two baskets full of white yams and some eagle kolanuts? You would come with a credible surety and witness. It would be your own father or your godfather/uncle. You had to get on your knees in front of your master-to-be, with your surety/witness watching, and beg him to accept you as his student. He might eat your yams and kolanuts and still reject you for one reason or another. But these days, it is the master that begs the disciple to come and learn."

It was right then and there and only three days before the end of his four-year contract, that Okoye knew for certain what he had been doing at the Nne Obu Nri. All along he had thought he was receiving training so he could become a good temporary servant. But it had always been the opposite. He had been serving so that he could receive training to become a good human being.

"I am troubled, Master, and I have come to seek your council. But now I feel worse off."

"Well, you should. That is what good medicine does to you. You first feel worse off than you were. Then you feel better and eventually you are healed."

Okoye needed no invitation to sit, so he did. There was a very long pause. Okoye said nothing. His new-found master said nothing. Igwe Nwadike was never bothered by silence and everyone knew it, so Okoye took his time.

"Sometimes I wonder if I have made the right decision," Okoye said finally, almost talking to himself.

"About what?"

"I mean my decision to actually leave Nne Obu Nri. It seems selfish of me to do what I am about to do. Perhaps I could be more useful here at Nne Obu Nri.

"Maybe, maybe not. It is for you to know what is in your heart. You must follow your heart," the old man said nonchalantly.

"As a child, I always looked forward to this moment. I looked forward to the time when I would get to see what the rest of the world looked like. It has always been my only aspiration. As a child, I wanted to be the one who would discover the end of the earth for all Igbo people. It may sound childish, but I still feel so at my age."

"A human being must always follow his deep burning desires. If he has a fair mind, it will lead him to his fate. Tender no apologies to anyone, but you must be fair to your wife when you have one. You must be fair to your children and be fair to your community. You must be fair to all the people you will meet on the way and all the people you will meet when you arrive at the end of the earth. That is how it is done."

❧ ❧ ❧

The moon had not come out yet, and it was dark. As Okoye got closer to his compound, he could see lights clearly. He knew they were not coming from the main gate. For a moment he thought he had gone to the wrong place. But as he got closer, he saw what had happened. A section of his compound wall had collapsed. It was less than three years old and had been built to last for a long time. He needed the sleep, so he went straight to bed.

In his dream, Okoye was in some Uwa land. His host's wife came to his hut and told him that he had a visitor. When Okoye came outside, he saw Igwe Nwadike. Standing behind him were many dwarves. Igwe showed him a piece of rope he had in his right hand.

"It is time to go home. We have to take you home now," Igwe Nwadike said. All the dwarves seemed to be nodding in agreement. Okoye woke up and sat up on his bamboo bed. He simply could not understand it. He decided to think about his last few days and recount all the things that had happened. Maybe there was a clue he had missed. He got all the way to the point where he had decided to accept the two outcasts. Then he went back to sleep. He woke up only two hours later with yet another dream. In it, Okoye was running, and Igwe was again running after him with a piece of rope. He had behind him a whole village of dwarves. The dwarves got to him first. They held him on the ground, and Okoye struggled to free himself. Holding the rope, Igwe Nwadike stood over him like a giant.

"You must accept your fate. You must willingly accept your fate. If you do not, I will tie you down with this rope. And the rope will not look good on you," he said.

"Why me? Why me?" Okoye screamed. He woke up with a pounding headache and a racing heartbeat.

Okoye was one of the very few Nri men who smoked tobacco, a habit he had picked up from his travels. He got up to have a smoke and catch some fresh air.

He could not believe what he saw when he stepped outside. All the walls around his compound had fallen! *How could it be? How could they have fallen without his hearing them fall?* Then he started thinking about the possibility of what was to come.

At their last meeting before Okoye had started his travel career that never ended, Igwe Nwadike had offered him lots of advice and later laid his hand on his forehead while he said a prayer of good wishes for him. He blessed him abundantly. But, as Okoye was about to leave the room, Igwe Nwadike asked him an apparently simple question.

"You said that you want to find the end of the earth for Igbo people?"

Okoye knew there was something behind the question, but he did not know what. He did not want to jump into that trap, so he walked into it slowly. He smiled first, then nodded.

Our Father laughed.

"Then you must be willing to travel very far. Everything goes in a circle and the earth is not an exception. If you travel far enough, you will find yourself standing here at Nne Obu Nri. Only Nri people who do not travel far enough do not come back."

Okoye had not understood then. He did not understand until he woke up from his dream that had turned into a nightmare and saw the handwriting on his collapsed walls.

※ ※ ※

Igwe Nwadike was buried at noon exactly two days after he died in a private but detailed ceremony. Okoye was one of the few lucky non-Ozo men in attendance during his burial. He had begged to be there, and Igwe Nwadike's sons granted his request. Igwe was buried at noon in front of his obu in a big tomb about twelve footsteps deep. He was seated on a stone facing the direction of the rising sun. His left foot touched the bare earth but his right foot rested on a wooden plank. It was a sign that he had fully ascended, but was still grounded in the affairs of his people on earth.

Igwe was buried in full ceremonial dress. He wore his red cap with the eight eagle feathers. A bronze bell lay in front of him. His crown would always remind him of his rights at Nri as the King, and the ceremonial bronze bell would remind him of his responsibilities as the leader of the Nri people. He had in his left hand an Offor stick, the symbol of justice. In his right hand he held his Otonsi ceremonial staff of immunity. He was buried in a six by six by six foot chamber that mimicked a coffin, though it was not. The four corners of the chamber and the top were padded with thick, carved mahogany planks. The rest of the tomb was covered with nothing but red earth. The only marking for the grave was an ogilisi tree at the position of Igwe's head. The tree would one day become very large.

The ogilisi tree was a replacement for Igwe's personal ogbu tree which had been cut down after his burial. The ogbu tree was a sign of physical life, while the ogilisi tree was a sign of a living spirit. Ogbu trees were usually planted in front of a man's quarters as soon as he became of independent age and had built his own compound. Every Nri woman, on the other hand, planted her own tree in front of her quarters as soon as she got married. Her tree was called the ogbuchi (life tree for the individual personal god). It was highly durable and survived all kinds of weather. It was a very bad omen for someone's ogbu tree to suddenly die before the owner died. Its death was followed by a special purification process performed for the owner before a replacement was planted. It was an act of sabotage to knowingly cut down a living person's ogbu tree. This act carried a very high fine, including the cost of the purification ceremony. The ogbu tree produced a small seed-like fruit that birds loved. It was thought a good sign when many birds came to a particular person's tree. It signified that the person had a very generous and good spirit. Usually people who would have been less generous took this sign as a cue and became more generous when birds preferred their tree over someone else's.

The ogilisi plant, on the other hand, was another way of honoring the departed spirit. Just like the ogbu tree, the spirit survived all seasons.

Most of the time, ogilisi played dead, but during the dry season, it wore a very beautiful flower that butterflies loved. The flowers seem to remind the living that though the person might appear dead, the spirit lived on. So the ogilisi would become the permanent marker of Igwe Nwadike's burial place. It would also become a reminder that his spirit lived on.

❧ ❧ ❧

Nri people believed that the sun was the dwelling place of Anyanwu (The God of Light) and Agbala (The Holy Spirit). They believed Agbala to be the collective spirit of all holy beings (human and nonhuman). The Holy Spirit was the perfect agent of Chi-Ukwu or Chineke (the big God or the Creator God). The Holy Spirit chose its human and nonhuman agents only by their merit. It knew no politics. It transcended religion and culture and, of course, gender. It worked with the humble and the truthful. They believed Anyanwu, the Light, to be the symbol of human perfection that all must seek. Anyanwu was perfection and Agbala was entrusted to lead us there. Since both Anyanwu and Agbala dwelt in the sun, they worshipped the sun.

In those days, it was fitting to watch the sun rise. In the morning, the elders and spiritual adepts would gather in groups in Umu-nna (lineage groups) in the villages. They would wait and wait and tell stories or socialize while they waited. When the sun finally emerged, they would celebrate with kolanuts. Then they would break kolanuts with prayers and wishes for the day.

Just as they welcomed the sunrise, the most spiritual of them would sit alone in the evening and watch the sun set. They would give thanks for the day and reflect on its activities. That was how it was done way back in those days when Nri people were Nri people. Very few remembered. Ichie Idika was one who did. He sat on a stump behind his obu, gazing at the sunset. At the eighth Igbo month, the sunset was spectacular.

Ichie Idika had absolutely no doubt that the spirit of Igwe Nwadike was somewhere in the beauty he was gazing at. It must be an illusion, but the sun seemed brighter. His friend's spirit must have added something to the brightness of the sun. He shook his head as tears ran down his cheeks.

"But the man died disappointed," he muttered to himself. "He sure did. But he was not alone."

They come once in a while.
They come to save the world.
They come with nothing but love and their fate.

They walk on their heads to bring peace.
They starve themselves to show their love.
They lose their freedom to tell the truth.

Then they get disappointed.
They go back very disappointed in us.
They say we don't understand.

We... don't understand?
No!
They . . . don't understand!

. . . That their hands are tied,
. . . That they can only tell us the truth and show their love and then
cross their fingers,
. . . That they can only remind us of what we already know...

. . . That gifts are not really for free,
. . . That rights are equal to responsibilities and responsibilities to
rights,
. . . That there are no shortcuts to whatever our hearts desire,

They still go home disappointed.

He wiped the tears from his eyes. He was not weeping for his friend, who was at the best place a being could be. He was weeping for the darkness that was sure to descend as he watched the sunset. The sun would surely shine another day, though not before the long, dark, cold night.

TWENTY-TWO

Okoye's Fate

Okoye finished a late supper and washed his hands. It was dark outside and the only light inside was provided by two palm oil lamps. One sat on the dwarf wall where it gave flickers of light to the outside and to the obu reception area where Okoye sat with his senior wife, Mgbafor. The second lamp was on a window ledge between the reception area and Okoye's sleeping quarters. The aroma of nchu-agwo filled the air emitting a dry, aromatic fragrance that most people used as incense. Actually it was a snake chaser.

"I like the soup. It reminds me of my grandmother's cooking," Okoye remarked and leaned on the backrest of his rattan chair.

Mgbafor smiled. "Everything good reminds you of your grandmother. I wish I had met that woman."

Okoye pondered. "She was a great woman. She did everything right. She was the only person I always looked forward to seeing when I was a kid."

"And after you grew up?"

"Then I got married to you," Okoye said, not looking at her. Mgbafor knew as soon as she asked that she should not have. Mgbafor knew that Okoye was lying. Enenebe, Okoye's second wife, was his favorite. Mgbafor had heard that Okoye compared Enenebe to his grandmother.

She put the last piece of goat meat in her mouth and munched as she washed her hands in the big calabash bowl.

"Ochiagha!" she saluted.

"Nwogo!" Okoye saluted back. Nwogo was her salutation name. It meant daughter of kindness or born out of kindness.

"You have done me well," Okoye added, to show his gratitude for the food. He stretched his feet and rested both hands on his head, his favorite relaxing position. Mgbafor got up, took the soup and the pounded yam foo-foo terracotta bowl, and put them in the big calabash bowl. Okoye knew that she was getting ready to leave for her hut.

"You don't have to rush after a meal with your husband. Besides, you can spend the night here," suggested Okoye.

Mgbafor said nothing.

"Why don't you stay the night here?" Okoye insisted.

"And then do what?" asked Mgbafor as she lifted the calabash water jug and, with her wet palm, wiped the wooden stool that had served as an eating table.

"We have things to talk about. Besides, I am still your husband. The elders of Nri-Agu will not deliberate over it if you spend the night with me."

Mgbafor hissed. "We are not looking for a baby. Or are we?" Okoye said nothing this time. She picked up the big calabash bowl, now containing the dinner bowls, covers, and drinking cups. "I will be back so that we can talk, but I will not spend the night."

There was finality to the last phrase that told Okoye that she meant it. But she was still his wife and she would be back. Okoye held out hope.

Mgbafor bent down to leave and emerged outside, carrying the dinner plates. Okoye did the same, holding one of the lamps. Enenebe, his junior wife, ducked behind the banana trees that stood in front of her quarters, her favorite spot whenever Mgbafor spent time alone with Okoye when it was dark. Okoye trailed Mgbafor to the middle of the large compound and lifted the oil lamp high above his head. He stopped and waited.

"I am okay now," Mgbafor said as she went into her hut. Okoye turned and went back to his obu. He sat and waited.

Mgbafor kept her promise. She returned soon carrying an oil lamp and sat on the dwarf wall at the entrance, a good five steps from Okoye.

"We can talk now," she announced. Okoye shifted uneasily in his chair. Enenebe smiled at the huge space between Okoye and his wife and turned her right ear in their direction.

"I think you must have guessed what I want to talk about. It is what everyone else is talking about at Nri-Agu."

There was a pause while Okoye reflected. "It is about our compound walls which fell down. Because they fell the same day Igwe Nwadike went home, people think there is some meaning behind it. I want to know what you heard and what you think about it."

"What do you think?" asked Mgbafor. "And what exactly did you hear?"

Okoye hissed to show his frustration. "Well . . . Well, I have been approached by quite a few people asking me if I know the significance of our fallen walls. One of them was Erike Okolo. That was why he came here this morning. I saw him at the burial, but prior to that, I had not seen him in six months. When I asked him how he had heard about the walls falling, he said that everyone was talking about it. I asked him what he thought the significance might be. He said it usually means that the owner of the walls is a candidate to replace the ascended Eze Nri."

He rested his feet on the wooden stool and rested both hands on his head again.

"I have heard similar rumors from a few people. But they are just rumors . . ."

"And you did not mention this to me?" Okoye said, shifting his position so that he was looking away from Mgbafor. There was a very long pause before Mgbafor replied.

"I did not mean to offend you. I was waiting for the right moment. I know whatever it is will come out in the open. I did not mean any offense at all." This seemed genuine, because she got up, picked up another carved wooden stool, sat next to Okoye, and began to rub his right arm. His anger did not last.

"So what do you think about it?" Okoye finally asked. He regretted speaking, because as soon as he broke the silence, the rubbing stopped. Mgbafor folded her hands on her chest.

"As I said before, I think we should wait and see what will happen next. Erike is your friend and he is a good man. He would not come to you if he did not think the rumors had deserved some merit. But I think we should wait."

"All right. We will wait and see, but I hope there is nothing to it, because it will not be a good thing for me."

"It is not for anyone, but someone has to do it. Someone has to be Eze Nri."

Cold air drifted in, touching Mgbafor's naked back and neck. It must have reminded her that the night was aging, because she shuffled her feet, a sign that if this was all there was to be discussed, she would be leaving. Okoye said nothing.

"I think I will be going to sleep now. Or is there something else we are going to talk about? I will be waking up early."

"You can sleep here," Okoye suggested again. Mgbafor did not reply. She made a movement to get up, but Okoye got up at the same time and grabbed her left arm.

"Spend the night here. I will wake you early enough," Okoye said, looking directly into her eyes.

Mgbafor looked away to the darkness outside. Okoye took her silence as a sign that she had changed her mind. He started to lead her towards the inner room. Mgbafor took two steps forward, far enough to grab one of the log supports that held up the hut. She clung to the support and would not let go. Okoye pulled some more. The whole hut started to shake. Remembering his fallen walls, Okoye did not want to give Nri-Agu village something else to talk about. He let go of her arm. Mgbafor picked up her oil lamp and ran outside. Okoye watched in disappoint-ment, as Mgbafor made her way into her hut. He could not understand her stiffness.

From behind the banana trees, Enenebe smiled and shook her head. "Human being too! Well, someone's loss is another's profit."

She would wait until Okoye retired into his sleeping room, then wait an-other half hour and tap on his door as usual. She would tell him everything she had heard during the day with salt and pepper added. Then she would ask the right questions and make the right comments, and Okoye would tell her stories of his travel adventures. Then . . . there would be a feast.

❊ ❊ ❊

They call her Enenebe which translated to "looking" or "if one starts to look." But the full meaning was that if one started to look, one (in this case a man) would abandon his work. She was not as tall as Mgbafor, but her beauty made up for her lack of height. She had a fair complexion. She

215

was not overweight, but she had a lot of flesh on her well-proportioned body. But her looks were not her greatest asset. She understood people—all people, but she seemed to understand Okoye better. It was as if they had one mind. The people of Nri Agu called Mgbafor "Okoye's Wife," but Enenebe was not just Okoye's wife. She and Okoye were one. Mgbafor was intelligent, but Enenebe was really the smart one though she played the fool in Okoye's household. She seemed to want only what Okoye seemed to want though it was Okoye who wanted what Enenebe wanted most of the time because he trusted her loyalty completely. Enenebe did not stand in front of Okoye pointing at his mouth and yelling at him like Mgbafor often did. Okoye had a very good heart, but he was careless with his mouth sometimes, and Mgbafor let him know this.

Enenebe once boasted to her closest lady friend that she and Okoye see things the same way. "It is as if we have the same eyes and mind and like the same things—as if he sees with my eyes and I see with his."

"When a man falls under a woman's spell he sees with her eyes," said Nwamma.

"You forget that I am under his spell too. It goes both ways . . . ."

"You people were meant for each other."

"People say that. But it takes a lot of hard work too."

"How do you do it?" said Nwamma, shifting her stool towards Enenebe. "All Nri Agu women would like to know."

"You have to merge with him first. During the merging time, you avoid any confrontation. That is when you build trust and confidence. He will know that you are but one breath with him. Men are like that—they talk very tough, but deep in their belly they are very afraid of their women. They think that women are interested in one thing only—in making their men look like big fools. They think that once a man falls under a woman's spell, she will put him on a leash like a goat and drag him out in public to show what a big fool he can be under her spell. So most men are scared and on guard all of the time. Very few women are really like that, but those are the ones that Nri men see. Once they know that you share their interest and that they can trust you, they usually fall under your spell. Then they will listen to everything you say as an insider in their life. That is the charm they say I used on Okoye."

Mgbafor was the perfect outsider in Okoye's life, always wanting the opposite of whatever he wanted. She could not understand Okoye's obsession with Uwa lands. Although Okoye had forgotten the argument he and Mgbafor had less than three moons after they were married, Mgbafor still remembered it clearly after twelve years of marriage. To Okoye it was a conversation, not an argument, between two newly married people who were trying to learn about each other. To Mgbafor, it was a big fight for Okoye's heart, and she lost it many years before Enenebe came.

They had been having supper in front of their new hut under the moonlight. At that time they shared one hut. Mgbafor wanted to tell Okoye the good news about their first pregnancy. But Okoye's eyes glittered and his face glowed under the moonlight as he talked in his loud voice about the desert tribe people of Kabuku; how the entire village eats supper together under the moonlight. How the village elders took turns telling stories while the entire village sampled each other's food. How the young women and men sang and danced after their supper in one big celebration of life. How he (Okoye) loved to be their special guest whenever he stopped by for a night or two. How they pronounced his name with their phony accent and how they giggled and laughed as he tried to speak their language with his strange accent.

Then and there Mgbafor knew that Okoye was under the spell of something. Maybe it was more an obsession to see and know other lands. If their marriage had not been arranged by Ozo Ikezuo, she would have known about that before they were married. But, according to Nri customs, they could not see each other and have a heart-to-heart conversation until they were married.

"Is that what you like about your line of trade?" Mgbafor cut in as soon as Okoye stopped to catch his breath.

"You mean besides providing for the entire village, our marriage will also produce?" It was Okoye Rope's attempt at humor. But Mgbafor did not find it funny.

"People who buy and sell at Nkwo market provide for their family too," she said. The fight was on. She had just registered her disapproval of Okoye's trade, but Okoye was not listening. To him, buying and selling at Nkwo market was not even a consideration.

"If that is what they like to do, Chineke will bless them."

"I had always wanted to marry a husband who does not travel. My father did not travel very much, and I wanted a husband just like him so that if someone knocks at the gate in the middle of the night, he would be the one to answer it and not me. We would raise children together, and they would behave well under their father's watch. And if there is a death at Nri Agu, I would like to do a condolence visit with my husband. If there is an Ozo ordainment ceremony, we would go together."

Okoye pondered. "That is how things should be in a perfect world. But the world is not perfect, and we should be thankful for what Chineke has given us and make the best of it," he said in reflection. "Sometimes I wonder what Nri would be like if everyone bought and sold at Nkwo market, and no one had ever heard about places like Kutunger and Ijiputu and Kabuku."

Mgbafor did not respond. She knew that she had lost the fight. She started washing her hands. Okoye paused to reflect some more, wondering what the world would be like if there were no adventurers like him to bridge cultures. What would the world be like if all clans farmed and traded in their own groups and did not go to see how others lived?

Okoye molded a big lump of pounded yam and dipped it in the onugbu soup his new bride had made as Mgbafor washed her hands and wondered, *what would Okoye be if he could not travel and mingle with the tribes of the world? Would his name still be Okoye or something else—Nwoye perhaps? What other trade could offer him such freedom of movement?*

Okoye left for his travels the next morning. Mgbafor was already four moons pregnant when he came back two moons later. Mgbafor did not have the satisfaction of telling him the good news herself because Okoye could tell himself and all Nri Agu had known before he did. When Obuka, their first son, was born, Okoye was on the road even though he had planned to return in time for the birth, but he was delayed by a rainstorm.

Mgbafor had come to despise Okoye and anything he liked even before they knew Enenebe. He had built Mgbafor the finest Mkpuke in the village and filled four big baskets with the best imported clothing. And he had filled her bronze jewelry pot with the best jewelry that Nri Agu women had ever seen. Many came quite often to borrow pieces for important ceremonies. So Okoye could not understand Mgbafor's stiffness.

Enenebe understood Okoye and accepted his obsession with travel and made it work for her too. In fact, she loved it. Whenever Okoye returned from one of his trade adventures, Enenebe wanted to know every detail. Okoye glowed as he talked about his travels. Then he would be delighted to hear the unending details about everything that happened while he was gone from his beloved. In this way, they shared the same memories and mind and liked the same things.

But Okoye was not the only one with an obsession. Enenebe, too, had one. If Okoye was obsessed with exotic places, then Enenebe was obsessed with people. She was a magnet for all kinds of people—men and women, young and old. Nri Agu women sometimes casually called her "Ndumodu" (counselor) because Nri Agu people streamed into her hut at all hours to receive free advice on relationships or marriage or about a troubled child. This conflicted with Okoye's love of privacy, but he adapted to it and gave Enenebe a free hand. At a time in Nri when other men would have objected to people streaming into his wife's hut, especially other men, Okoye understood because he knew his wife. Though it was considered a weakness to fall under a woman's spell, Okoye displayed his own acceptance of his wife's power as if it were an eagle feather on his red cap.

Now Okoye sat on his bed and wondered if Enenebe would come. She usually knew when Mgbafor was not with him. Would she knock on his door and spend the night with him? They could talk into the night. Would that not take his mind off his present problem with the fallen walls? How her presence lit up the whole room. How her face glowed as soon as he started talking about his travels. How could he ever watch that face become unhappy? No! He could only add to her happiness. He would kill himself before he would be the person who would take the light from that glowing, happy face.

But Mgbafor is my wife too, reasoned Okoye. *She deserves to be happy too.* Even though she was always trying to prove something, always being unnecessarily difficult, she was still his wife. He owed her that much. Wasn't she his first wife and the mother of his first two sons and three daughters? Was it really her fault that she was so stiff? Wasn't her father an Ozo-Mkputu priest and very conservative? Wasn't she raised to be idealistic like her father and mother? Wasn't Enenebe raised by her father, a core member of the Oganiru, to enjoy life? Wasn't she raised to be practical?

Okoye pondered his fallen walls and felt a cold chill rush through his body. What if the nightmare turned real and he became the Eze Nri? Wouldn't he be caught between the Ozo-Mkputu and Oganiru priests, always trying to appease both, just the way it was twenty-five years ago at Nne Obu Nri? Wouldn't he be caught between the ideal and the practical, just as with his two wives? But he must live in the present, not think about tomorrow. He must close his eyes and enjoy the now—wealth, good health, happiness. Okoye lay on his back on the bamboo bed. It was not long before he heard the gentle tap on the wooden door. Enenebe entered carrying a small bowl of roasted goat meat with palm oil sauce dip. They would eat supper and after the supper they would talk.

🦋 🦋 🦋

Two months had gone by since Igwe Nwadike had been buried and one month since the official grieving period had ended. Okoye should now be ready to go about his business. In fact, he should have been ready three weeks ago. Instead, he was battling a mysterious illness. He stood next to his barn behind his obu wearing only a loin cloth. It was close to noon, and he was surveying his outstretched arms, his chest, his legs, and the other parts of his body that he could see. The boils were all over and there were fewer spaces between each one now. It was unlike anything he had seen before. He could not imagine anything worse, yet he had been told by at least two different people that the ones on his upper back did look worse. The high fever seemed to decrease in the morning and afternoon, only to come back with full force at sunset. His nose was completely blocked so that he had to breathe through his mouth. He coughed every few moments. He felt pain all over his body because some of the boils were beginning to pop and peel, creating little sores. He had found it difficult to lie on the bamboo bed, yet he had to rest.

But all this was not his immediate concern, for Okoye Rope could handle whatever life brought to his body. His immediate concern was Enenebe. Just four days before, Enenebe, too, had fallen ill with the mysterious illness. It started just like Okoye's with a pounding headache, a little fever, and a few traces of boils on her chest and upper back. But yesterday morning when she had come by, the boils had spread and the fever had increased. It was agonizing for Okoye to see the damage done to her skin, especially her face. But worse still was her only son, Emenike. She had brought him over to show Okoye this morning.

"It is the boils, all right, and the high temperature too," confirmed Okoye, after surveying Emenike's body. The boy was only nine months old and Enenebe's only son. He had cried all night. It pierced Okoye's heart whenever he heard the boy cry, knowing that it might be the mysterious illness. After he had confirmed it this morning, Okoye had arranged for Mgbafor to take all her children to her birthplace. They were not to come back until all of the infected had been cured. Mgbafor and her children had not been infected. He had ordered two of Enenebe's daughters taken to their mother's birthplace as well. Then Okoye sent for Erike with specific instructions to bring the herbalist, Ikuku. This was extreme but conventional herbs had failed.

Okoye blew mucous from his nose into the gray sandy ground behind his obu. With his left foot, he covered the mucous with sand. He emerged into his obu, now visibly angry at something.

Erike hissed. "There is no reason to be angry. Illnesses come and go. It is a fact of life," said Erike, looking directly at his good friend.

"It is not the illness I am angry about. I am angry about what people are saying, putting their eyes and ears in other people's business."

"People are going to talk. That is why we are human. Besides, no one lives in isolation. 'People see, people talk.' Remember that?"

Okoye nodded in a mock agreement, "Yeah. It is more like 'people don't see, people talk anyway.'" There was a long chain of coughs ending with a sneeze.

Ikuku, the herbalist, laughed. "I am not laughing at you, but at what you said."

He adjusted himself on the stool before revealing his diagnosis. "This is efufu, so it is not a mystery anymore. It is completely treatable, and I will be sending the remedies this evening. One is a mixture of seven different leaves and roots which you will boil in water and wash your body with. That one will eliminate all the boils. The second. . ."

"How long will it be before I am completely cured, and I can go back to my work?" asked Okoye.

"I would say about two weeks, eight days. But you have to wash your body with the remedy morning and evening during that period," replied Ikuku.

"The same for the little boy?" asked Erike.

"Yes, the same for the boy. Not the second remedy though. That is for adults only. It will look and smell like coconut butter and it doesn't taste bad. The ingredients are mixed in a coconut cream. It will come in slices. Dissolve half a slice in a cup of warm water as close to hot as you can handle, then drink it morning and evening. You cannot give that one to the little boy. Once his boils go away, his fever will slowly leave, too."

Ikuku leaned forward to examine Okoye's back once more, as if to confirm that his diagnosis was correct. "As I said, this is not a mysterious illness. There is one mystery though. It is not an infectious illness, so I don't understand how it has infected more than one person in your household. That is something to think about, because it can only infect people who have traveled outside our area. It is not common here."

Ikuku left after promising to send the remedies through one of his apprentices.

Erike waited until Ikuku was gone before speaking his mind.

"I heard about the goats dying yesterday and the chickens that die almost every day now."

"Who told you about it?" asked Okoye, looking very angry.

"People hear, people talk. Remember?"

"Well, they will die no more and people will talk no more. I have made sure of that. I have ordered all of the goats and chickens sold." Okoye seemed to be proud that he had done something about it.

"That is good to hear," said Erike. "But what about your family? Are you going to order them sold as well? Or maybe give them away? Send them all to your in-laws and give some to your friends? I would love to have some. I am particularly interested in your two sons, Obuka and his brother. I would like to adopt them."

A long pause followed. Erike waited for a reply, but there was none.

"You cannot cover your head with a water pot so you don't see what is right in front of you. The least we can do is to ask questions. That is a place to start," Erike concluded.

"A man deserves to live his life and in peace. A man deserves to pursue and live his dreams," Okoye said, looking at the wall.

He turned to Erike. "Are you not doing what you chose to do? Why should my life be different? I do not wish to be Eze Nri. The wall falling and family illnesses and dying of livestock will not make me change my mind."

"Is that what you think?" replied Erike. "That Erike is living the life of his dreams, doing what he wants to, and that his life is better than Okoye's?"

He burst out in laughter. "Remember, I am the one who was banished from his village. When I was a little boy, my dreams were to become a great hunter and to live among my blood kinsmen. I dreamed of living close to my blood mother and cousins and uncles. I wanted to attend to my mother in her old age. Instead, what did I get? Sometimes one needs to take cues from the spirit guides that hide behind the clouds."

When Erike finished, Okoye had no reply.

"I will be leaving now, and I will invite a diviner to meet us here tomorrow morning. The least we can do is to ask questions about all these mysteries before a life is lost."

"He will not come to my house," Okoye said, not looking at Erike.

"Then I will invite him to my house. I will come at sunset and let you know what he said."

Erike got up to leave.

"I do not want to hear it! I do not want to hear it, and I mean it. You are a very good friend to me, and that is why I sent for you this morning. But do not do what you just said. I will not be pleased with it."

Erike simply shook his head and left.

TWENTY-THREE

Okoye Accepts

The second quarter of the morning was only beginning. Darkness was fading. Oduh, having exercised all his "this and that" small talk options, decided to get down to real business. He adjusted himself a couple of times in his rattan chair, but could not come up with the right opening. A seasoned diplomat, Oduh did not know how to approach the man in front of him. Oduh was quite cultured, perhaps too cultured for his visitor. Oduh believed that if one negotiated one could bargain on anything if one followed the right protocol. One must start with small talk and then use appropriate terms to give signals and pick up clues. Then, if the road was clear, bargaining could be started. Even then, one moved cautiously. That way one could avoid unnecessary confrontation.

Okoye Nweri hated diplomacy. To him, it was a dignified form of lying. He hated small talk. He was a straight talker. He laid everything on the ground and expected the other person to do the same. He thought that there was a way things should be in every situation and one could not get to that point by negotiation. When negotiating, one used all of the advantage at one's disposal to get whatever one wanted from the other side. He deemed this to be unfair to the less privileged. Laying everything on the ground was his favored choice. This way one could get to the truth only by each side laying everything on the ground, and then assessing the information to find the correct answers.

Oduh was at least forty years older than Okoye and had come across him more than a few times in his life. He thought that Okoye was rude or that, at best, he was impatient. So the men had their differences, but they had been brought together by an event neither could control.

Suddenly, Oduh realized something he had not learned in eighty-four years—that one talked straight to straight talkers and used diplomacy with people who would appreciate it.

"I have seen the signs myself. I think they are pretty convincing," Oduh started.

Okoye knew what he was talking about, but decided to play dumb.

"What signs?" Okoye inquired.

"Oh, come on! Your walls are falling. Your livestock is dying every day. You are constantly sick with mysterious illnesses . . . one after another. We do not need a diviner to figure that one out," Oduh said. *How good it felt to say what he felt without having to dance around it*, he thought.

"Why are we waiting for signs when we have better ways of doing things?" Okoye asked—referring to the divination process used to confirm the candidate for Eze Nri.

"Each process has its own benefits. When both are combined, we can be very confident that we have the right person," Oduh said.

"Well, the only problem with that is that by the time it gets to the second stage, the diviner's findings may be biased based on what we have already heard," Okoye said.

"That is so, if you don't have confidence in the integrity of what the diviners do."

"I have so much confidence in them that is why I said that they should have been consulted before waiting for signs."

"My son, your walls fell down before Igwe Nwadike was even buried. So even if we wanted to do what you are suggesting, we could not before his burial ceremony. It is true that you have traveled far and wide, but you still cannot beat the experience accumulated by age. I am telling you that I have seen things myself, and I am quite convinced that the Offor Nri has fallen in your lap. It is a big responsibility, but the spirits of our ancestors see what we don't see. They have seen something very good in you. I am telling you that you should prepare yourself," he concluded.

There was silence in the room. Oduh had laid it all on the ground. He had said all he needed to say. It was Okoye's turn to reply, and, for a brief moment, he could not. He could not because he was fighting tears. By the time he started to speak, the tears were running down his cheeks.

"All my life I have made it my business to stay out of politics as much as possible. I love people, but they scare me. People like to be chased around before they do what they ought to do to begin with. They think of it as some sort of hide-and-seek game. They like to negotiate even though they already know what the right thing to do is, and they know that you know it too. I had enough money to become an Ozo priest, but I did not want to because that is where the real politics are. That is where it gets really ugly. And now, after all these years of avoiding all of that, what do I get? A mandate that I must deal with every Ozo man in Nri and beyond! Not that I can, but that I must. And it is not for a set period of time, but for the rest of my life!"

"Welcome to my world! And you have to get along with each one of them too!"

"I will never again go to the marketplace like everyone else. I will never again go unescorted to ceremonies outside my house. I will never again go to a scarification ceremony! My life will be over."

"Why do you think that during coronation we mimic a burial ceremony for the candidate? You will lose most of your physical life, but you will get used to it. You will find ways to make yourself happy. Igwe Nwadike entertained himself and his family with his music. You will amaze yourself with how quickly you adapt. I have heard rumors that you smoke tobacco. You must give that up too."

"That is very reassuring and I appreciate that," Okoye joked, "even though I don't know what all this means. But if what you are saying is true, can you remain Isi-Ozo for awhile?"

"I will be around as much as you people need me to be. Isi-Ozo is not a lifetime position, but I will serve for life if that's what our people want," Oduh answered.

The two men spoke openly and honestly for the rest of the meeting. "I thought you disliked me," Okoye commented at some point.

"I can only dislike someone who is not dealing in good faith. You cannot dislike someone simply because he has a different approach than you have," Oduh replied.

❦ ❦ ❦

That morning as Okoye was walking home, he passed two young girls. He would not have looked at them twice except that one of them called him *Ochiagha* and smiled shyly as they passed. "And who might you be Ezigbo (Nice One)?"

"I am sure that you will not remember me. I am Nne-Amaka, the first daughter of Erike Okolo," she said, smiling.

Okoye froze. He used to carry her on his head and tell her and her sister stories. He had frequented their home, and he recalled her or her sister asking him once if he was their father's brother. Okoye had said, "Yes." The child asked him why he lived in a different village. Okoye had been thinking about the right answer when Erike rescued him.

"We are very good friends," Erike had cut in. "When you are very good friends with someone, they become like your brother or sister."

"How is your father?" Okoye asked to hide his embarrassment. The last time he had been to Erike's place was over a year ago and even then he had not seen Erike's children. It was always Erike coming to his house, or they would see each other at one ceremonial function or another.

"My father is well. He is at home right now."

"And your mother and siblings?"

"We are all doing well."

"Is this your sister too?" Okoye said, pointing at the other young girl. He asked before it dawned on him that she could not have been. Nne-Amaka was the older of the two sisters, and this girl looked a little older than Nne-Amaka.

"No, this is Nnem-Ochie, (my first cousin, from my mother's birth-place). That is where we are going."

"Is your father with someone? Does he have a guest?" asked Okoye.

"No. Right now he is at his workshop behind his obu. Are you going to see him then?"

"I will go and say hello to him before going home. It has been awhile since I came to your place."

"That would be nice of you," she said, smiling shyly.

"You look just like your mother, as beautiful as your mother."

She smiled again.

"Be well Umu-iru-ezigbo (you pretty faces)."

"Be well!" The girls responded.

※ ※ ※

Erike was chiseling on a piece of hard mahogany wood and did not notice Okoye's entrance into his workshop. Immediately he rose from his chair. "Okoye Nweri!" he yelled, coming towards Okoye. They embraced. "I was thinking about visiting you last night," Erike confessed.

"Well, that makes the two of us. It has been a long time since I have been here."

"It looks like it. More like six moons," said Erike, leading the way to his obu.

"I would say at least one year," Okoye said. "And I feel awful about it."

"You should not. You are always on the road. When you are at home, you are resting or getting ready for another trip. I completely understand."

"I saw Nne-Amaka on my way. She is a grown woman."

"You recognized her?"

"I did not at first. But once she told me, I disliked myself for not recognizing her mother's face. How is Nwamma?"

"She will be back in a moment. She went to her vegetable garden to fetch some okwulu (okra)," Erike said as he tried to lead the way into his obu.

But Okoye objected. "We can sit here. I don't wish to disturb your work. Besides, I would like to see what you are doing."

Erike agreed. They re-entered the workshop shed made of bamboo poles and a thatched roof. Pieces of wood were scattered everywhere. Erike pointed to the only empty chair in the shade. "Sit over there."

While Okoye sat down, Erike scrambled to clear some of the wood to make room for his guest's feet. A piece of half-carved stool caught Okoye's eye. He bent over and picked it up. "Good work!" he said.

Erike smiled. "Do you like it?"

"It is nice. Especially the carved image." Okoye admired the figure of the ascended Igwe Nwadike who was sitting on a stool, his right foot resting on the ground, and his left resting on a piece of plank. Okoye realized how skillful a carver his friend was.

"It was terrible what happened to us. I can still not get over his death," said Erike, referring to the death of Igwe Nwadike. "He was like a father to me."

"He was like a father to a lot of us. But those things happen."

"You are right. It is very true. So when are you going to accept?"

Erike's bluntness caught Okoye off guard. "You think I should?"

"I know you will. It is a matter of when," Erike said confidently.

Okoye smiled and looked outside. "What makes you that sure?" he finally asked.

"Because you do not have a choice. They could make you insane or a cripple for not accepting. It has happened before." He was referring to Nri-Menri, the ancestral spirits, who choose a king for the Nri clan.

"Then I will go insane or be crippled at my own home. Isn't that an option?"

"Or what is left of your house. Don't you understand? They start with your walls, but it does not end there. Eventually your whole house will fall. I just hope that no one will be in it when it does. I am not wishing you ill, but I am telling you what I know for sure."

"And I will have to accept before you can offer me kolanut?" asked Okoye, adjusting himself.

Erike tendered his apologies as he rose, but Okoye blocked him with his left hand. "I was only joking. I have had enough this morning. I am just coming from Oduh's place."

Erike stopped at the mention of Oduh.

"We had a very long discussion this morning," added Okoye.

"And you accepted, yes?" Erike was nodding as he asked as if answering his own question.

"Not officially yet."

Suddenly Erike ran into his obu. When he returned, he had a wooden tray of kolanuts in his left hand and a new stool in his right.

"Let me be the first to welcome you as Eze Nri." He handed the stool to Okoye. It was a completed version of the stool he was working on. It had a round seat and bottom and a side handle. On one side was a carving of the ascended Igwe Nwadike. One of his feet rested on the ground and the other on a plank. He held an Offor Nri in his left hand and an Alor Nri (kingship ceremonial spear) in his right hand. And on the other side of the stool was a carving of Igwe Nwadike as a living man. Both feet rested on the ground. In both carvings, he was flanked by dwarves. The stool was taller than most others at Nri.

"It is beautiful," said Okoye as he held it up and admired it.

They ate kolanut and chatted. Erike chiseled at the mahogany wood, revealing figures and images locked in it. Later they drank palm wine brought by Nwamma, Erike's wife.

As Okoye left Erike's compound and closed the heavy wooden gate behind him, he admired his first acceptance gift. It was beautiful, but very heavy. He realized it was a mistake to have carried it with him. Erike had wanted him to leave it behind so he could send one of his children to deliver it later. But Okoye had insisted on taking it with him. Now he realized that his family would ask questions about the stool and this would lead to his decision to accept. He would have preferred to have a meeting with his family first. But Erike was not just anyone. His family would understand. They knew that the two men used to be inseparable. Okoye shook his head as he thought about their past relationship. It was his fault for putting that big space in their friendship and letting it wane.

When Okoye had started his trading career, he had always looked forward to his return so he could talk and drink with Erike. Hadn't he looked forward to telling him every detail of his journey? Hadn't he looked forward to teasing him and having Erike tease him back? Hadn't he enjoyed hearing from Erike about what had happened at Nri while he had been away? Even when they both married, their relationship had remained the same. Maybe it wasn't entirely his fault. Maybe it just happened because they had pursued different interests and made little room for common ones.

The change in their relationship had started when Erike joined the Nze Ikenga sect, the most conservative part of the Nze priesthood. His personality had changed. First he stopped drinking alcohol and eating meat, except for lamb. That would not have made much difference if Erike's conversations had not been about spirituality and right and wrong actions. Okoye's travel adventures did not interest him anymore. When Erike asked questions, they would be about the religion of the Uwa lands where Okoye had gone. Okoye wanted to know the gist of all the major happenings at Nri while he'd been gone, but Erike fed him the activities of the Nze Ikenga priests.

So it was only natural that Okoye avoided him. But this did not stop Erike from visiting Okoye, who had been jokingly called his twin during their time at Igwe Nwadike's palace. From time to time, Erike would stop by or simply send his children to find out when Okoye was coming back. But this was not like when Okoye had actually visited Erike or sent for him as soon as he returned from his travels. Their relationship had become one-sided. Erike did not seem to mind.

One afternoon, Okoye had come back from one of his trips, and Erike was waiting at Okoye's obu. Chiaka, a business friend, was also there. They chatted for awhile, and Okoye escorted Chiaka halfway home, telling Erike that he was coming back soon. But Okoye did not return until dark. By that time, Erike had left. Although the lapse was not intentional, Okoye thought that Erike would be offended. But he was not. He came back the next day and accepted his apologies before Okoye could finish them.

As Okoye stepped onto the bridge of Nwangene Creek that separated Nri-Agu, his village, from Erike's village of Nri Ezune, he thought about the simple life his friend was living. He walked delicately on the five palm tree trunks that served as a bridge and recalled how contented Erike had looked as he chiseled away on the hardwood that did not earn him much cowry money. Okoye was surprised that Erike had drunk palm wine with him that morning. He must have done this to show happiness for the visit or maybe he was happy that Okoye had accepted his calling.

As Okoye climbed the small hill leading to the Nri-Agu village square, he recalled the day that Erike had made him shed tears in public.

After nine months away, Okoye had come back from his first trip to Timbuktu. It was supposed to have been a three-month trip, but, after six months, everyone thought that Okoye had died and was buried deep in the Sahara Desert or, worst yet, he had been eaten alive by desert hyenas. Erike was the only one who consistently said that Okoye was alive.

On that unforgettable moment when Okoye had just returned to his compound after nine months away, he kissed the ground. Erike was not around but the whole village of Nri-Agu was there in no time to celebrate Okoye's return. Some people touched him to convince themselves that they were not dreaming. The celebration quickly moved to the Nri-Agu public square since Okoye's compound could not contain everyone. That afternoon, when Erike finally came, the Nri-Agu village square was filled to its capacity. When Erike saw his "twin" for the first time in nine months, what followed was startling and dramatic. Erike picked Okoye up and put him on his right shoulder carrying him like a baby and running around the public square with the whole village cheering and running after them. It was embarrassing to Okoye, because it showed how much weight he had lost. But he was also deeply humbled by Erike's actions and he started sobbing in public.

Okoye later heard stories about how Erike had frequented his home while he was gone. Most of the time he would stay at Okoye's obu by himself, meditating or chanting for a long time before leaving, telling everyone that his "twin" brother was on his way home. He frequently told Okoye's wife that her husband was not dead because he had seen him in dreams.

"He has fallen sick and is recovering. As soon as he fully recovers, he will come home," he had said on one occasion. Erike had been right. Okoye had fallen ill during that trip. That dramatic incident temporarily rekindled their friendship, but it was not close to where it had been and had quickly declined again.

Okoye paused before opening his compound gate. He studied his stool again. Now Okoye Rope was back where he belonged, or at least where the ancestors thought he belonged. He would be happy to talk about spirituality with his "twin." He realized he must utilize all the knowledge Erike had gained about Nri spirituality while he had been out hunting cowry money across the desert. It would be humbling to ask an immigrant about the spiritual ways and laws of his forefathers. But that would be a small price to pay. Then Okoye remembered that he must go and see Akalaka the next morning. He had confessed to Erike during their chat that Erike would be his best source of information on spiritual affairs and he had meant it. But Erike laughed. "Why do you want to waste your time with me when you can learn directly from my source who is still alive," said Erike. "Nna Anyi, Akalaka will tell you everything you need to know about the spirits and about our customs. In fact, I recommend you see him first before you do anything else." Okoye promised he would visit with Akalaka the next day.

TWENTY-FOUR

Aja-Ana

Okoye took Erike's advice and went to see Akalaka. Okoye vaguely remembered Akalaka's face. It had been over twenty years since he saw him, and he had been to his house only once. Okoye entered two wrong houses before he finally arrived at Akalaka's obu, but Akalaka was not at home. Instead Okoye met a young lad who was taking an afternoon nap. It was the first hour of the noontime. Okoye had to wake him up.

"Where is Nna-Anyi (Our Father), Akalaka?"

"Nnaa Ochie (Grandfather) is not home," he replied while rubbing his eyes. Saliva dripped from the left side of his mouth.

"I can see that," replied Okoye. "Where did he go? When will he be back? Did he go very far?"

"I don't know when he will be back. But he did not go very far," said the young boy who could not have been more than ten years old. "I can take you were he is," he added pointing to the big forest behind their compound.

"Is he in the farm by himself?"

"He is at Aja-Ana Temple in worship. I think he is alone. I . . . I am not so sure, but he does not mind people coming to see him there."

There was clearly a path into the thickly-wooded forest, but it seemed to be rarely used because Okoye had to lift tree branches and push back shrubs and walk on high grass to get through. He wondered what kind of temple the path would lead to. He had in mind a small hut with a worn out and leaky thatch roof. He was wrong. The temple was quite large and well built. It could comfortably sit fifty people. The high roof was supported by huge log pillars. The building stood elegantly and defiantly in the middle of the forest, a classic Nri model temple surrounded by knee-high dwarf walls. Apart from the storage room area, the temple was open and had many stone seats inside it. The temple floor was slightly elevated above the forest ground. The red earth mud walls were decorated with scarification patterns, and it looked as if it had been waxed the day before. Ogwe (stair benches) were built all around the temple separating it from the thick forest. The remaining open space between the temple house and the ogwe was as clean as the inside of the temple. Akalaka sat on one of the ogwe benches as his grandson led the way towards him. His eyes were shut and his mouth moving. He was clearly in some sort of meditation.

"Nna Ochie! Nna Ochie! Someone is looking for you!"

Okoye introduced himself as Okoye Nweri from Nri-Agu village in response to Akalaka's questioning look. He was obviously trying hard to recollect the face. Now Okoye remembered Akalaka's face very well. It had not aged very much in the twenty something years since they last met.

"You cannot remember me. But I am Erike Okolo's friend. He sent me."

"He did well. He was a good Umu-Ukwu (disciple) of mine . . . one of the brightest."

Akalaka spoke in almost a whisper like Igwe Nwadike. Even his voice sounded like Igwe Nwadike.

"Now I remember you. Erike talked a lot about his friend from Nri Agu. He was very fond of you. He swore I would recognize your face when I saw you. Please sit down so I can see your face."

Okoye sat down as the young boy left the temple.

"You said your name is Okoye Nweri. That is not enough for me. Are you Okoyeocha (light-skinned Okoye) or Okoyeojii (dark-skinned Okoye) or maybe tall Okoye? There are too many people named Okoye these days . . . every family has at least one."

Okoye chuckled at the humor. Even Akalaka's humor was as low profile as if it had been delivered by Igwe Nwadike. Okoye insisted that he was just Okoye. Then he chuckled some more at the thought of telling Akalaka that his name was Okoye Rope.

"What is you true name?" the old man insisted. He would not give in. "What is your nickname? Mine is Akalaka (Destiny)."

"You may call me Ochiagha (War Leader). That is what Nri Agu people call me."

"That is a very good name. I like it. But may I ask what war you are fighting?"

Okoye scratched his head and wondered when the introduction business would be over.

"Some think that long distance trading is like going to war and call me Ochiagha because I lead and manage a herd of traders."

"I like that name very much. I like the warrior mindset. Nri need warriors like you. Do you know that Nri have never fought a war, but we are always at war? We are at war with ourselves and, if care is not taken, we will defeat ourselves. Can you imagine that? Someone defeating and taking himself captive before the real enemy comes? When the real enemy comes, he will only gather his fortune and thank his God because no one will put up a fight. Don't mind me. It is old man talk and you will not understand it. But I can tell you this: You may not have an enemy, but once you defeat and cripple yourself, you will invite all sorts of enemies. Even your closest friend will come to take advantage of your condition, and you will think it unfair and label him your enemy too."

"Our people do not have the warrior mindset like you do anymore. You do not have to tell me that you are a warrior because I can see it in your eyes. Very few have that fire in their eyes and almost all of them are fighting the wrong war. Those who are fighting the right war do not have that fire in their eyes. They do not have that zeal to conquer. Our situation is like the two knives you will find in a pauper's kitchen: the sharp knife does not have a handle and the one with a handle is not sharp. It is a true recipe for failure."

Okoye felt quite at home because Akalaka was speaking his mind, and Okoye was ready to hear it. He had already submitted to his new calling. Two moons before, he would have felt quite uneasy with the talk of fighting the wrong war. But he also felt comfortable for another reason. The man sounded very much like Igwe Nwadike. It was as if Igwe Nwadike had risen from the dead and was talking to him.

"Are you Okoyeocha or Okoyeojii?" Okoye repeated aloud and then burst out laughing. "You sound very much like Igwe Nwadike. That is how he would have said it."

"Good!" replied Akalaka. "It is a good thing when someone says you sound like your master. It usually means that you learned well as a student. That is the right way to learn. A student should keep his entire attention on his master just as a baby watches his mother or father and mimics everything they do. That is how you learn well. Do you know that in the old days students dressed like their master and some even imitated how their master walked?"

At this point Okoye told Akalaka why he had come. He told about his fallen walls and the mysterious illnesses and the different events that had been making the rounds in his household, including the dying of all of his livestock. He told Akalaka about his meeting with Oduh and the discussions with Erike and how Erike suggested that he see Akalaka before taking any further steps in the coronation process. Okoye admitted that he did not hope to learn everything in one day, but he wanted to know more than the average person about Chi-Ukwu and Anyanwu and Agbala and their relationship with Eze Nri.

"You did well to come. It is a very good step for you," said Akalaka who extended his hand. The two men shook hands. Okoye wondered if he should tell Akalaka now that he brought him a goat. He decided to let Akalaka discover this for himself after Okoye had left.

"Chi-Ukwu is the supreme God and the creator of all things. Without him, nothing will be, so all things bow to him. We follow Anyanwu because he is Chi-Ukwu's most perfect creation and closest to him. We aspire to be like him because he is the perfect light. Agbala is the God of Service and Vocation and the Giver of Insight and Wisdom. He does all Chi-Ukwu's work. We submit all of our talents to Agbala so they can be used to serve Chi-Ukwu. We should always ask Agbala for more wisdom and talent for one can never have enough. But I will tell you this, if you want to know yourself as Eze Nri and as Nwa Nri (Son of Nri), then you should understand Aja-Ana completely. This is what I usually tell new students because Aja-Ana will keep your hands and feet clean." Akalaka finished with a long, unblinking look at Okoye. Okoye shifted on his seat and showed his white teeth, now confused about the new importance given to Aja-Ana (The Earth Goddess) over the sky beings.

"Chineke created Aja-Ana too, but as Children of Nri, Aja-Ana is our direct boss. If you understand your master, then you will understand his master and his master's master better. As you know, Eze Nri is the supreme head at Nri. Then you have Ezu Nri, Ide Nri, Obah Nri and Iji Nri and Isi-Ozo Nri and others. They all do special things and are all leaders. But as Nze priest, if you want to understand yourself and your duties, you must understand your Ozo master completely. As Eze Nri, your Ozo master is Aja-Ana. You must strive to please her all the time because if she is displeased with you, then all the sky beings will be displeased with you as well . . . ."

"Then, Our Father, you must tell me everything about Aja-Ana. I want to know her and her nature. Tell me everything please."

At this point Akalaka apologized for breaking protocol and not offering kolanut first. He then asked Okoye to go into the storage area and get the small basket with a lid. When Okoye came back, they each took turns washing their hands while the other poured water from a calabash bowl Akalaka had fetched. Then they ate kolanut after Akalaka blessed it.

"Now we can have a long discussion, and I will not feel guilty," said Akalaka as he crunched on his kolanut.

"Aja-Ana is the most misunderstood among the Deities. Some people call her the Deity of Vengeance, but she is not. She is the Governor of the Earth and the Deity of Justice and Peace. You can say that she is perfect justice and perfect compassion at the same time. Some people call her Earth Mother, but we call Her Aja-Ana (Earth Dust) because she is one with the dust and sees through the eyes of the dust. She sees every footstep under the sun and hears every whisper, even your thoughts. And she considers all things at judgment. Aja-Ana seeks to protect the weak from the strong and to enhance the strong by making them humble because humility can only make one stronger and not weak. She is the host and the moderator between different players on Earth and we, Umu-Nri, are her helpers."

"To really understand and appreciate Aja-Ana, one has to imagine the Earth as a big market place which hosts many buyers and sellers and brokers and market officials. This market is a physical structure, but it has an intelligent being behind it. One can call this being the Manager, Governess, or Regulator of all that goes on in this market. Apart from the upkeep of this market, Aja-Ana, as the Governess, creates and enforces rules of fairness among all who buy, sell, and broker in this market.

"Aja-Ana places the safety and well-being of the market and all who are hosted in it above everything else. Therefore, it is a high crime for a human being to kill another under any circumstances or to kill himself or herself. A human being is considered sacred by Chineke, the Creator, so Aja-Ana is tasked by Chineke with the safety of the market and everyone in it. According to Aja-Ana, no circumstances can excuse homicide or suicide. In fact, according to our forefather's beliefs, it is an abomination to cause another human being to bleed in a fight. If another person is caused to bleed, even in an accident, the right cleansing must be done just in case there was any ill-will involved. According to Aja-Ana, a human being must never torture an animal or kill it without good cause. Good cause in this case would include killing for food or in self defense. According to Aja-Ana, a human being must never put a price on the head of another human being or own another human as a property because humans are free and sacred beings. The Aja-Ana Moral Codes are very long and mostly deal with fairness to oneself and to others and fairness to the earth (the Market). Are you following me?"

Okoye gave three quick nods.

"But breaking any of those codes should not be the end of the earth. The moral message of Aja-Ana also includes compassion and forgiveness. Should any of the taboos be broken, Aja-Ana forgives when repentance is followed by appeasement. This is where our people, Ozo and Nze Nri, come in, for we are the servants of Aja-Ana (part of the market workers). We should religiously preach these laws of fairness so that they are not broken. But when the laws are broken, our priests have the mandate and authority to cleanse the offender. The offender and his or her environment are deemed to have been contaminated. Anyone who deals with the offender before he or she is cleansed will also be contaminated and must be cleansed as well. This cross contamination will continue to spread if the contaminated ones are not isolated and treated. Are you with me?"

"Completely!" said Okoye, transfixed by the gleaming eyes of the old man. The passion was written all over Akalaka. This was his life and Okoye wondered how many disciples the old man had had in his lifetime.

"Aja-Ana punishes individuals in different forms, mostly illness of the body or mind, like a split mind or swollen legs and belly or isa-asisa (a trancelike public confession when someone is about to die for offences against Aja-Ana). But, most often, Aja-Ana punishes a whole community because, through cross contamination, the entire community can be polluted quickly. Looking at the earth as a market, Aja-Ana may deny a section of the market water (rain), or light (sunshine). But this moral contamination can evolve into a disease epidemic or a natural disaster like a flood or an earthquake or a tornado. One could see this as a punishment, but it could also be seen as a natural form of cleansing. Sometimes this natural cleansing runs its full course. When it runs out on its own, the community has been naturally cleansed. At other times, the community will take a cue in the middle of a calamity and ask our priests to intervene."

"Nri people and Nri priests are not immune to this contamination and collective punishments because contamination can come from neighboring communities or even from within ours. So our priests are not only acting as agents of Aja-Ana, but on behalf of our own good as well. If moral offences by neighboring communities are not treated, they will eventually reach Nri land. And we, too, will be included in these collective punishments or cleansing. So with the spilling of human blood, the highest crime against Aja-Ana, you can see why our priests tremble at the knowledge of an outbreak of war between two clans or villages. In ancient times, one could only imagine how distressed our ancestors were at the knowledge of an all-out war between two neighboring communities when tens and hundreds of people would be dying from another's spear or machete. Our people do not believe in those things anymore. That is what worries me and a lot of people who understand our duties to Aja-Ana. We do not tremble anymore at the knowledge of a homicide or suicide and that is why we are dying like chickens. There are all sorts of diseases in our place. We cannot even name them. Do you know that in some part of Igbo land today, someone will be killed for digging up a yam tuber from another's farm?"

"In the old days, our forefathers did not set a thief free. They made a first and second time thief pay a hefty fine and apologize in public. Then he is forgiven. But third time or habitual offenders were given an ogba-na-ajilija treatment after paying a hefty fine. Do you know what ogba-na-ajilija treatment is?"

"They are beaten up by their age grade," said Okoye, recalling one he had seen as a young boy at Nkwo market.

"They are not supposed to be beaten because beating rarely stops a thief from stealing again. Even a fine does not stop a thief from stealing again. But mind treatment like a public apology does work most of the time. That is why ogba-na-ajilija treatment was very effective in the old days. In this treatment, the habitual thief or child molester was handed over to his age group. They would shave his head, paint his face, and dress him to look like a thief. They would give him whatever he stole to hold or carry on his head. They would beat drums and sing for him. They would call his name in a song and say ". . . You are a goat thief" and he would answer "Eyee. I am a goat thief," while dancing to their drum. He would be paraded around the village while dancing. After that he was taken to the market to dance there. If he was married, he was led to his in-law's place and he would dance for them. Then he was led to his mother's birthplace where he would dance for them. If he had friends he would dance for them as well. He was beaten only if he refused to dance or refused treatment. After full treatment, offenders usually went through a deep conversion and became good (even model) citizens. Sometimes, out of shame, they might decide to go into self exile. They might move to the tribe of thieves where everyone is a thief and no one would tell another to stop. If the offender continued to live and steal among their people, then they had a mental illness and appropriate treatments—herbal and spiritual—would be given to cure the mental ailments. Today, we just club them to death on the spot."

"Just the other day, I heard that a mentally ill man was burned alive in the full gaze of market shoppers for stealing in the marketplace in Igbo land. I heard that they tried to club him to death, and he did not die quickly enough, so they set firewood on top of him and burned him to death! And some were sharing while watching it. And those people call themselves 'Igbo People' and bless kolanuts at sunrise and eat them! Do you know that even a chicken has more respect than a human being in Igbo land today? If one were to kill a chicken, for instance, one would at least run around first, sharpen a knife, boil water, find a container, and maybe dig a hole for the chicken blood. But human beings are killed instantly . . . squashed like a cockroach. Then we wonder why we are fallen like half-ripped, disease-infected udala fruits. How can Chineke give us a long life if we do not value life?"

All the while, Okoye was looking at the temple while listening to the tortured outcry of the old man. But now Akalaka stopped to reflect and Okoye turned to look at him and noticed tears in his eyes and he, too, began shedding tears.

"There was a belief among our people in the old days that Aja-Ana might become so angry that she would evict everyone in that section of the market or even the entire market (the whole Earth). If this extreme happens, that would be the end of human activities on earth."

"Nna Anyi, what do you think?" asked Okoye, adjusting himself on the bench. "You surely do not believe that?"

"Eyee vunu (of course), I believe it. You have to understand that Chineke is a trader too. If he is not getting profits from his investments for a very long time, he will close that market down. You are a trader, and you will understand this better than I do."

"I can see that very well. His patience can run out very easily if he is not making a profit, losing constantly instead. But what about the innocent ones like you? Why would they be punished for the sins of others?"

"That is a good question. At a first look, one might think that this collective punishment or cleansing by Aja-Ana is unfair. Why can't the offenders be singled out and punished? Wouldn't that end the story? One might ask as you did. But on a closer look, one can see that Aja-Ana wants humans to watch out for each other. Human beings should be their sibling's watchers because no one lives in isolation. Here one may borrow Nri people's phrase: 'When two individuals or communities fight, they should not expect a monkey to come down from the tree and break them up. Instead, they will expect another human being or another community to come and stop them.' This intervention by a third party (a bystander) is a moral obligation, and if they do not honor that obligation, the observers are as uncivil and probably as guilty as the parties who were fighting and destroying each other. This third party will, therefore, eventually partake in the consequences."

Okoye looked at Akalaka and wondered if Igwe Nwadike was speaking through him. Or maybe the ancient ancestors were speaking through him. The making of an Eze Nri had started.

TWENTY-FIVE

The Coronation Journey

After the early morning meeting between Oduh and Okoye, everything else in the selection process went more quickly than usual. Usually, it took at least two years before a new candidate was chosen and accepted. But in the fourteenth month after Igwe Nwadike was laid to rest, Okoye was unanimously accepted as the right candidate. The rest of the selection process was quite simple, but it could get complicated if there was substantial opposition. In this case, there was little. The result was eleven out of twelve in favor of Okoye which was even better than the vote for Igwe Nwadike who had gotten ten out of twelve in his favor. The divination process was very simple. Each village invited a diviner outside of Nri who was stationed at the village square at the same time and day. The diviners were unknown to each other. Each village sent a representative to the other eleven villages so every village had outside observers watching their process. Then the diviner for each village would reveal the chosen candidate. The divination process was a deductive one. The diviners, who were themselves servants for a particular deity, would inquire from their deity if a member of one village would produce the next potential candidate. The deity would answer yes or no through a set of divination beads. The count could be narrowed down to six villages out of twelve during the first round. After the second round, the count could be narrowed to two or three villages. The fifth or sixth round would narrow it to just one village.

After eliminating the eleven villages, a fresh inquiry was started centering on the chosen village. This second round would examine the lineage of each village until a lineage was chosen. Then the lineage was narrowed to a particular family, a broad range of extended families that still had a common last name. Once a particular family was chosen, every mature male who had taken the Nze or Ozo priesthood would be examined. The elimination continued until the deity, through its servant diviner, chose a particular individual. After watching the process at each village, the observers went back to their own villages to tell the result. If the divination process was still going on at their village when they returned, they would tell no one until it was over. In fact, they would not even go to the village square while this was happening. By the end of the day, each village would meet and assess the fairness of the process. The results were either accepted or rejected. If any village rejected the results, the whole process would be repeated.

After all twelve villages accepted the result, a date was set for all of the villages to get together to officially accept the chosen candidate. During the acceptance ceremony, a date would be set for the candidate to officially accept his fate.

ⵣ ⵣ ⵣ

Even before Okoye had officially become Eze Nri, everyone was already treating him like a king. His name was so common in Nri that children were already referring to him as Igwe Okoye. This morning, Okoye sat among his village members at Igwe Nwadike's compound. Each village group sat together. The compound was almost full. Almost all of the Nri people had come; most just wanted to catch a glimpse of the would-be king and hear his nnabata (acceptance) talk. Even though his name had grown like a wild fire since his selection, very few people outside of his village could recognize his face. He had lived a very private life, and, besides, he was not an Ozo priest. In fact, he was the first non-Ozo priest to be selected for the Eze Nri position.

Oduh spoke at length during his nnabata speech. He was frank about not knowing Okoye well before the selection process, but he had come to know and like him since the selection process had begun.

"From what I have heard and seen, he has a good mind and he cares deeply for the affairs of Nri and Igbo people. But who am I to tell you about him when the Ancient Ancestors have testified about him and have

244

selected him for us. It is therefore with a happy heart that I am pointing to you the next Eze Nri!"

He went to Okoye, who was standing up, and raised Okoye's right hand. The crowd went wild.

"Igwe! Igwe!! Igwe!!!" filled the air as everyone stood.

Unlike Igwe Nwadike, Okoye smiled a lot so as the crowd hailed his name, he smiled broadly the whole time. Anyone who did not know him would have thought his was a politician's smile, but it was far from that. It was the confident smile of someone who knows his heart and speaks it at all times, the smile of one who knows what he wants and cannot accept less. A lot of people did not know Okoye and were anxious to hear him speak. But few who knew him really knew him well. These were the wealthiest men in Nri for whom he had run his trading business. They had nicknamed him Ochiagha, which translated to fight leader. But some of them, especially from his village who knew him from far back, still referred to him as Okoye Rope.

This was the name he had earned as a teenager when he used to wrestle. Originally he earned it because of his wrestling tactics. But, later on, the name was used to describe his body of muscles and bones. Later, when he became an adult and was engaged in trade and community affairs, the name was about his strong will to accomplish and survive. Once he set his mind on a task, he did not back down.

So, just as a rope hangs on without breaking, even in adversity, Okoye never gave in. He was perhaps too strong-willed at times. Once he had a contract to lead an unprecedented expedition to Timbuktu, thought by the Nri people to be the end of the world. Okoye led fifty-six men on that expedition, and he must have driven them too hard and too fast because they revolted and went back to their village. Deep in the Sahara Desert, the heat was like an oven, and, as soon as the heat slowed down, an evil wind took over and blinded everyone. Their veteran guides from the desert tribe continued on, and Okoye told his men that they must as well, that those Uwa people cannot be tougher than an Igbo man. But the Igbo were not veterans at crossing the desert like "those Uwa people." They could not handle that level of heat, so they revolted and turned back, leaving him with only two of his assistants. Okoye decided to move on though he encouraged the assistants to go back like the others, but they refused.

Nine months went by and no one had heard from them. Everyone thought they were dead and buried deep in the Sahara Desert. Nine months later, like ghosts they returned with donkey-loads of all sorts of foreign merchandise. If they had waited another four months, making their time away a full year, they would have returned to their own funeral ceremonies.

When they arrived, they claimed that they had made it to Timbuktu. The men who had revolted against Okoye did not want to believe them. But Okoye and his assistants brought back many items to prove it, including some written materials that they were still trying to decode before Igwe Nwadike died. Okoye had proved that Igbo people could cross that desert and there were many trips to Timbuktu after that one. After that first expedition, Okoye earned the new nickname of Ochiagha (Captain), a polite name for calling him slave-driver.

But his strong will to accomplish was the least of the reputations that had earned him contract after contract from the richest merchants in Nri. His strongest reputation was his uncompromising honesty. If one wanted a second opinion from someone who would tell the truth, Okoye would be the man. If the stakes were high and the investment even higher, Okoye was the man to contract with because he would stay up at night (as the real owner would) thinking about ways to protect the owner's interest. He was not gifted with natural wisdom like Igwe Nwadike, but he had achieved wisdom through his personal efforts. His life philosophy was simple. If something was worthwhile, then it had to be achieved. Okoye Nweri, Okoye Udo, Okoye Apali (Okoye Wild-Rope), Okoye Ekwele (Okoye string), Ochiagha, and soon to be Igwe Nweri had earned every bit of money he had made and all of the reputation he had. Those who were jealous of his accomplishments called him "Ike-Kete-Olie" (He who became rich by his manual labor or another's). He had earned that too.

Okoye was still smiling when he reached the center of the open square. Most people in his position would have been just a little nervous. He was not. He was simply himself. The first impression that people who had never seen Okoye before had was of a calm and confident man. For the first time, Okoye realized how many non-Nri people were in the crowd. There were a lot of un-scarified faces. He had prepared a speech for Nri people, but he quickly realized that it was not about the Nri people anymore. It was about the Igbo people.

"Igbo people I salute you!."

"Yeaa!" the crowd answered back.

He saluted the Igbo people three times, the Nri people three times, the Ozo priests twice, and the Nze priests twice.

"The lamb says that he does not know how to dance, but if he is at his home minding his business and the music comes to his home, if he does not know what to do, he will start jumping up and down. The music has come to me."

There was a short pause. The entire place was so quiet that one could hear a leaf falling from a tree.

A gray owl took off from one of the trees, perched on the ground in the middle of the square and went to where Okoye was standing—a clear sign that Okoye was indeed the chosen one. But Okoye, who had known that a long time before everyone else did, read a different meaning into the visit of the mystical bird. To him, it was an answer to his statement. It seemed to be saying to him that the lamb was not alone after all, that if the lamb did not know how to dance, he would be taught how to dance.

"But our people say also that the red hot charcoal a parent puts into his child's palm cannot burn the child. I, therefore, accept the appointment to be Eze Nri."

He thanked the Nri people for choosing him and promised to serve them well. "But at the end, it will not be about the Nri people. It will be about the Igbo people. When we have lasting peace and understanding in Igbo land and all Uwa land, then our task will have been done," he concluded.

Those who were used to Igwe Nwadike's long sermons expected a lengthy acceptance speech. They were disappointed. Okoye had said all he needed to say. He had accepted the nomination, showed his gratitude for it, and promised to do a good job. He had even gone out of his way to tell the people what he thought were his duties to them and to all Igbo people.

"Igwe! Igwe!! Igwe!!!" the crowd hailed him as he went back to his seat. It might have been the sound of the crowd hailing the soon-to-be King that told the owl it had overstayed its welcome. It vanished into the bright sky as Igwe Nwadike's family served refreshments to the crowd. It was a tradition that the acceptance ceremony be held at the predecessor's compound, and it was a joyful thing that someone had accepted. Igwe Nwadike's spirit could rest well now.

⚜ ⚜ ⚜

Okoye's long coronation process started with visitations. He rested for four days after his acceptance and before the long journey. Then he visited all the temples of the ascended Eze Nri where he sacrificed a he-goat, a hen, a cock, and one eagle kolanut at each temple. Next he visited all the twelve villages in the Nri family and announced his acceptance of the position in each village's public square. He visited every major clan or family (town) in Igbo land. At each town, he made a speech in the public square and visited the family's major deity which was recognized by Nri people. He spent at least a night with each family who presented him with gifts. His journey through Igbo land ended at Aguleri, the place of origin of the Nri people and many other Igbo people. At Aguleri, he went to Obu Uga and received the blessings of Eri, the grandfather of the Nri people. He also obtained a large lump of clay from the bottom of the great Ama-mbala River. This clay would later be used to mold a clay pot for the shrine of Nri Menri (the Council of all ascended Eze Nri). The journey around Igbo land took him about three moons.

As soon as he returned from his visitations, Okoye went into seclusion for one whole year. He spent his seclusion in a small thatched hut in the collective holy forest of the Nri people called Abananwara. Okoye saw no one for that year except a virgin, teenaged male dwarf who cooked and attended to him and Oduh, whom he saw only twice. Okoye meditated day and night to atone for his sins and to receive grace and wisdom. He spoke to his attendant only when absolutely necessary.

By the third moon, Okoye had given up smoking and drinking and had adjusted to loneliness. He had learned how to talk to himself to fill the void. By the sixth moon, he had learned how to not talk to himself, but to let himself be talked to by the spirits. By this stage, he had become in command of his wishes. Whatever he wished would manifest. He could wish for sunshine or rain and it manifested.

Okoye had many visions and revelations, but what amazed him most was the accuracy of his predictions. With just a little information, he could predict events with almost ninety percent accuracy. He had come to realize that one of the reasons an Nri King need not go out of his compound was that with a little information, an Eze Nri could fairly accurately tell what was happening now and predict what would happen in the future. Most of that, of course, was through reasoning, but sometimes it was something more. Sometimes he knew things without knowing how he knew them. By his ninth moon in seclusion, Okoye had attained Amam-ife (wisdom).

Nri-Agu Village, Okoye's own village, was very happy to give him as much land as he wanted. So, before going into seclusion, Okoye had selected an uninhabited forest for himself. It was one of the best forests in Nri land, nearly ten times the size of his village's public square with a stream and a small pond that could qualify as a lake. No one could ask for anything more. Nri-Agu Village (Forest Village), as the name implied, had many untamed forests. So Okoye could have had more land if he had wanted it.

Construction on his new home started shortly after the land was appointed. The part of the forest with the lake was reserved for his retreat. A small hut with a kitchen and a manhole was built there. Big trees were cut down and the logs laid all over the holy forest so that visitors could sit on them to reflect. Another section of the forest was cleared for use as a public square. The square was as long as Igwe Nwadike's except that it was about five hundred footsteps from the rest of the compound.

Large logs were used to build Ogwe-style benches around the public square so that a person sitting behind another was one step higher and everyone could witness the event. Each side of the square had up to twelve elevations, unlike Igwe Nwadike's public square, which had many trees in the center. Okoye's square was open with few trees. It was an ideal place for a big wrestling match.

The public temple was next to Okoye's living quarters with only a mud wall separating them. The quarters were as big as Igwe Nwadike's and had the same design—a large hall with a big room behind the King's sitting place. Only the room had walls and a door. The rest of the hall was open with dwarf walls for people to sit on during a major event. The hall had a thatched roof supported on the sides by ten-foot iroko logs and twenty-foot logs at the center. The carved stone seats were in the first half of the hall. The second half, the tail half, had carved wooden stools for non-priests.

The stone throne (Mkpume-Onyilenyi) was raised higher than all the other seats and was located in the center of the first half of the hall. The throne had been retrieved from Igwe Nwadike's compound and a mud replica had been erected at Igwe Nwadike's compound as a replacement. At one time young Nze priests physically rolled the stone. Thanks to a new way of working, two bulls had dragged the stone to its new location. The stone was placed on planks that had been joined with a rope.

Okoye's living quarters were similar to Igwe Nwadike's. Okoye's personal quarters and obu were separate from the rest of the family, as were his official living quarters. Most of the logs used for construction were mahogany. The logs used for the sitting stools were ebony. The obu's walls were built of pottery-quality clay. Each Nri village had contributed labor and money for the construction. Woodworkers had been hired from around Igbo land and were paid according to the market rate.

The rolling of the stone throne to its new location marked the end of the eleven month construction period. It was a big event. Nze men from Adagbe Village, Igwe Nwadike's village, rolled the stone to their neighboring village where the next group took over at the village border as spectators cheered them on. The village in possession would keep the stone overnight, guarded constantly by Nze men. The next morning, Nze men would roll the stone to the border of the next neighboring village and hand it over with a big celebration. In this way, each of the twelve villages could touch the stone before it reached its final destination.

Although Adagbe Village was next to Nri-Agu Village, the starting place, the stone had to go around all of the villages before coming back to Nri-Agu. The rolling of the stone symbolized the rights and responsibilities of each village. Each shared the responsibility of rolling the stone and had the right to keep it for one night. They also had the right to not hand it over if they had any reservations about the new King. This had never happened before this coronation, and it did not happen this time. The process was only symbolic.

🌿 🌿 🌿

It had been exactly one year since Okoye had gone into seclusion. He sat on his stone throne facing the big hall in Okwu offor Nri, the temple of justice. All the Ozo and Nze men at Nri stood outside or in the big hall. Earlier everyone had gone to the Abananwara Holy Forest to receive Okoye. Since it was over an hour's walk to his village, Okoye had ridden back on horseback. The cheering villagers lined the path as the Ozo and Nze priests escorted Okoye to his new home.

Now Isi Ozo, Odu, stood in front of Okoye as if he were waiting for a sign from the ancient ancestors to tell him what to do next. Actually, he was waiting for all of the priests to take their positions. Then history could be made yet again with the formal installation of the Eze Nri.

Carrying a black wooden tray which held the crown of Eze Nri, Odu's deputy stood behind him. The crown was a red hat with eight eagle feathers sticking out around it. Once Odu satisfied himself that he had everyone's attention, he would motion to Obuekie, the leader of a group of special guests. The group sat at the right forefront of the temple and nearly separate from everyone else. They were the only people wearing white clothing. This special group was the Adama Council—the King Makers of Nri. Unlike the others in the temple who mingled and chatted informally, the Adama sat erectly and stoically, like holy beings who were in a state of perpetual adoration. In some ways they were the ultimate expression of the Nri moral conscience—The Nri of Nri.

They were neither Ozo nor Nze Priests, but simply Adama Priests. All of them wore three feathers except for Isi Adama, their leader, who wore five. He had sometimes been mistakenly called Eze Adama (Adama King) to indicate their separate and distinct position at Nri. But everyone knew that Nri had only one King—Eze Nri. The Adama Priests were rarely seen in public functions together and wore white only at the formal installation of the Eze Nri.

The Adama were like invisible hands in the Nri leadership. They automatically assumed leadership during the period between an ascended Eze Nri and the installation of the new king. They kept the paraphernalia of office and handed it over at the installation. The Adama Priests were "the peacemakers of the peacemakers," for they were the final custodians of Nri moral and spiritual leadership.

The Nwa Nri (descendants of Nri) went to Igbo and Uwa lands to make peace, but the Nwa Adama (descendants of Adama) made peace at Nri. The Nwa Nri prescribed and interpreted taboos at Igbo and Uwa lands, but the Nwa Adama prescribed and interpreted taboos at Nri. The Nri installed leaderships at Igbo and Uwa lands, but the Adama installed the Nri kings. At Nri, the saying went that "all humans bow to Eze Nri, but Eze Nri must bow to Nwa Adama" (his chief priest and spiritual counselor). In reality, Eze Nri did not bow to any human though a wise Eze Nri listened very closely to his Nwa Adama.

The Adama were a clan within the Nri clan and dwelt at the center of Adagbe village, though they were not members of the village. They were an independent institution at Nri. They had crowned every king though they could not become Eze Nri or assume any leadership position at Nri.

The origin of the Adama tradition was very vague and the subject of much speculation. The official Adama account was that they were the original Nri people who, after the explosive growth of the Nri kingdom and the immigration of much stronger groups, had retired to being councilors and peace brokers at Nri. But the average Nri believed that the Adama were the descendants of Adama, the cousin and best friend of Nri, whom Nri chose as the executor of his will and custodian of all of his children. The descendants of Adama had been playing that role for the Nri people ever since.

Another version said that the Adamas were descendants of Nri's first son and the most favored to lead Nri land after his death. But during the leadership crisis following the death of Nri, Adama decided to make peace and bring his brothers together at the expense of giving up what most thought was rightfully his—the Nri leadership. If this version was correct, then Adama had proved that true leadership does not really have to be visible. There was much other speculation about their origin, but everyone agreed that the Adamas were the final authority in spiritual matters and at the crowning of Eze Nri.

Now, at the installation of Okoye Nweri, Odu motioned to Obuekie, the Isi Adama, to come to where Okoye was seated. Two of Obuekie's priests joined him. One carried the Nne Offor Nri and the other held the Alor Nri (official paraphernalia of the Nri Kingship). Odu took the wooden tray from his assistant and held it for Obuekie. With both hands, Obuekie took the Crown of Leadership from the tray and placed it on Okoye's head as everyone looked on.

The only sound in the hall was the wailing of the bullhorn. The skillful blower had entertained the audience by telling them who he was and what was to come. Obuekie then placed bronze anklets on each of Okoye's ankles and carnelian beads on the right side of his chest. Then Obuekie dipped his fingers into a pot of holy oil made from akwu-ojukwu, a special brand of palm fruits, and rubbed the oil around Okoye's head at the edge of the red hat. As he rubbed, he said, "May your wisdom glow like that of well-ripened palm oil. And may it glow for all Nri and Igbo and Uwa people."

Stepping back four steps, Obuekie said, "Lead your people well in order that peace, truth, wisdom, justice, good health, and wealth may prevail in our land."

"Igwee!," "Igwee!!," "Igwee!!!," the crowd hailed. Everyone stood and continued to hail praises to Okoye as he rose and placed his new crown back on the wooden tray which now rested on the floor. Then Okoye moved to the center of the hall.

Ikenna, the teenage dwarf from the Adama lineage who had been with Okoye during his seclusion, walked to the center of the hall. Smiling shyly, he joined Okoye. The two mimicked a wrestling match and Ikenna fell to the ground immediately. Mgbafor, Okoye's first wife, came forward and did the same. She, too, fell. A young Ozo priest stepped forward and wrestled with Okoye, falling to the ground like the others. An Adama priest did the same and submitted to the new King as well.

"Does anyone else want to try me?" Okoye asked as he alternated his attention between the four people on the ground and the rest of the crowd.

"Not me!" someone yelled from the crowd, falling to the ground.

"Me neither!" someone else shouted and fell to the ground.

Everyone else dropped to the floor, including Ezu and all the Adama priests, leaving Okoye standing alone. Now Okoye was the greatest and no one in Nri land could challenge him.

The final part of the ceremony was probably the most symbolic. A grave had been dug just outside the temple. While everyone looked on, Okoye was led into the grave. After he removed his clothing, his two sisters washed his entire body and rubbed white holy chalk all over him. Then he put his clothing back on and came up out of the grave. A banana stem was placed in the grave to symbolize replacement of his body. When Okoye returned to his throne, he put his crown on again. While everyone else came back to the hall, young Nze priests covered the grave with sand.

Now Obuekie addressed Okoye as a spirit. "You are now Igwe (sky being). No one will address you as Okoye. As a spirit, you will show us how to make peace and speak the truth. You must show us how to be impartial in our judgments. You are the symbol of what is expected of a perfect human being. Please do not fail our people."

Obuekie recited a long list of taboos that Igwe Nweri must abide by. He was not to shake hands with humans. He could not see certain things, including dead bodies and masquerades. He must not leave his compound unaccompanied. When he did leave, he must be accompanied by Ozo men who would sound a loud bell to announce his presence. He must not speak directly to non-priests outside of his household. The list was long, but Okoye knew most of the taboos already.

At the end of this ceremony, a new one began—the funeral rites. After full rites were performed for him, Okoye was mourned for seven Igbo weeks (twenty-eight days, one Igbo month).

TWENTY-SIX

The Stranger

Three years had passed since Okoye's coronation. He had done relatively well. All the tension of not having a leader had evaporated like an early morning dew with the rising of the brand new sun. The Nri people now went about their business knowing that someone thought about their welfare day and night. On a hot and humid afternoon during the ninth moon, a stranger sat alone in the big temple of justice.

One could tell that he was not in a hurry, for he appeared very comfortable. He had been waiting for at least three hours, and from his relaxed manner, one could tell that he could wait the whole day if necessary. He had been told by the palace officials that Igwe was in a meeting that could last a long time, perhaps the entire day, but the stranger told them that he would be willing to wait as long as it took to see the King. He was even prepared to sleep in the big hall if that was necessary. He knew people at Nri where he could pass the night, but he did not trust them anymore. To him, everyone was dishonest. *They portray themselves as peace-loving holy people, but underneath they have hearts as ugly as everyone else. They are as dubious as dubious can be,* he had managed to convinced himself. He finished the last pinch of tobacco snuff in his left hand, and then rubbed the palm against his right hand to wash both hands clean. He drifted back into his thoughts. He did not hear the teenage dwarf come into the hall.

"Igwe can see you now," the dwarf said. He turned and headed into Igwe Nweri's living quarters. The stranger followed.

As they entered Igwe's private reception room, the stranger removed his hat.

"Igwe!" he hailed the lone figure seated in the reception area.

"Igwe is not here. You can sit down. Igwe will see you in a moment," said the man, pointing to the carved black stool next to his.

"Ndewoo! (Hello)," said the stranger as he sat next to him.

"Nnoo" (welcome)," the man replied and extended his hand to the stranger. "My name is Ozo Nwankwo Akoku. I am Igwe's interpreter. You may not speak directly to Igwe."

"My name is Okozo Akaluka. I am from the Mbaofia in Ikwine family," the stranger said. "You can call me Osondu, Osondu-agwu-ike. That is my salutation name. What is your salutation name?" he asked Ozo Akoku.

"You can call me Echidime," Ozo Akoku said.

"I like that name; it is a good name," said Osondu.

"Same with yours. Yours is a very good name too."

In Igbo land, people's salutation names or nicknames, which they chose as adults, summed up their personal philosophies about life. They showed how life had affected them or what was important to them. Their regular first and last names were just names. At best, they reflected their parents' philosophy or thinking. But the salutation name was what an individual consciously chose as an adult. They could always change it if their thinking changed, though that rarely happened. So when Igbo men or women told another that they liked their salutation name, they didn't mean that they liked the sound of it, but that they liked their philosophy. They stood where the other stood. In this case, Osondu's name meant that a person couldn't get tired when he was running for his life. Echidime meant that tomorrow was pregnant because one never knew what it might bring.

"I have been to your place a long time ago," Echidime told Osondu.

"Who do you know at my place? What village?" Osondu asked him. Just as Osondu was finishing his question, the bell started to ring. The young dwarf was still ringing the bell when he came out of the hallway leading to Igwe's personal quarters. An Ozo man came after him followed by Oduh. Okoye backed into the room and was a quarter of the way into the big room before he turned around. At that point everyone stood up.

"Igwe! Igwe!!" Igwe!!!" they continued to hail until he sat down.

Two other men in their twenties came out last. Osondu had wanted to sit down, but since Echidime was still standing, he decided to play it safe. Echidime started to speak, but Okoye interrupted him.

"Tell our guest that Igbo titled men do not need to take off their red hats in the presence of the Eze Nri."

Echidime repeated this statement to Osondu, but his red hat was already back on his head before Echidime could finish his sentence.

"Our visitor's name is Okozo Akaluka. He is from Mbaofia in Ikwine family," Echidime said.

"Ask him what we can do for him," Okoye said. Osondu started to respond, but was interrupted by Echidime who repeated the question directly to him.

"He would like to make a complaint," Echidime said after getting an answer from Osondu.

"Against whom?" Okoye asked.

"His name is Okeke Ubaka, Ezu Nri," Osondu said. There was silence and tension in the big room. The air seemed to stop circulating.

"Ask him to continue," Okoye told Echidime, breaking the silence. By the time Osondu had finished telling the story about what had transpired among him, Ezu Nri, and another man, Ezu's business associate, Oduh knew that there was more trouble here than he had previously thought.

Ezu was one of the wealthiest men in Nri. Most Nri businessmen traded one or two types of merchandise, but Ezu traded any item that would make money. And elephant tusk was one of them. Osondu had been trading calm wood for many years but had decided to move up to the elephant tusk trade. It was more lucrative, but required more capital. Ezu was one of the big names in the elephant tusk trade, and a Nri man.

So, naturally, Osondu approached him, thinking that as a Nri man Ezu would give him all the information and cooperation that he needed. Instead, Ezu referred him to one of his major suppliers, Udukwe. Osondu did not care as long as he was in the prestigious business and was making money. Udukwe told Osondu where he could buy and how much he, Udukwe, would be willing to buy from him. He also told Osondu that he would buy as much as he could supply him. Udukwe even offered to give him some money up front. Unknown to Osondu, there was a secret group of elephant tusk traders in Igbo land. Even though Ezu was not a part of the cult, he knew about them and bought tusks from them. Udukwe was a member of this cult.

The cult had perfected their tactics to frustrate newcomers to the business and drive them out. Osondu seemed very bright, so Udukwe had decided to use the most effective method to frustrate newcomers. He told Osondu that he was willing to buy any quantity Osondu could supply him.

"I have to test the market first before committing a lot of money," Osondu had said. Udukwe agreed with him. The first transaction went well, and Osondu made more money than he had anticipated. He was so happy that he bought gifts and sent them to Ezu.

The third time he decided to commit all his money plus the money that Udukwe had paid him up front. He never delivered the tusks. He lost everything to Uwa men who raided their trading party. But Udukwe was willing to forgive Osondu the advance because Ezu had referred him.

Osondu blamed the whole thing on bad luck. How else could he explain his misfortune? But when he went to his mother's birthplace to borrow money from his cousin, his eyes were opened. As soon as he started telling his cousin what had happened, his cousin's friend, who was visiting, finished the story.

"This happened to me a long time ago, and it has happened to a lot of people I know," the man told him. Osondu would also learn that Udukwe himself had been an Uwa operator before he had become very rich. In fact, most of the members of the elephant tusk cult used to be members of the Uwa men raiders when they were young. Osondu investigated and found out that this was not only true, but that Udukwe was actively sponsoring Uwa men, buying their stolen goods, and paying almost nothing for them.

Osondu went to Ezu for help, thinking that Ezu was naive about the people he was doing business with. Ezu's attitude suggested the opposite. He seemed indifferent to the whole thing. Osondu had to conclude that Ezu was part of the scheme.

"He would have been outraged if he was not a part of it," Osondu ended his story.

Outraged! That was the word to describe Okoye after he listened to the stranger produce the names of victims and his evidence. He tried to conceal it, but Okoye was not a man who hid his feelings.

Oduh spoke first. "I hope you know the heaviness of your accusations," he said, partly to fill the void before Okoye responded and partly just to be optimistic.

Okoye knew the truth. He could see through the stranger and he knew he was telling the truth. He could also tell that the stranger was not particularly holy himself. But that was not an excuse for what Ezu may have done.

"Tell our visitor to come back in three weeks so that we can investigate his complaint," Okoye told Echidime. Oduh thought he knew what was coming, but he did not know how far this was going to go.

TWENTY-SEVEN

Ijego at Nri

The first hour of the evening time was approaching when Osondu ate his lunch of okra soup and pounded yam. It tasted good.

"It has been a long day. A long day of waiting and waiting," he said.

"Yes, it has been," agreed the woman sitting opposite him who had cooked the food. Osondu had made the same observation three times, and his host had agreed three times.

"You have done me right, town girl. You have done me right, my people," Osondu said, leaning on the backrest of the rattan chair. He was grateful for more than the food. He was grateful for Ijego's encouragement for him to take his case directly to the King. The older of two young boys who were sitting nearby took the cue. He got up from the dwarf wall where they sat and walked towards Osondu. Picking up the brownish red calabash bowl filled with water he held it for Osondu, who dipped both hands into the bowl and started washing.

"You people have done me right," he said as he washed his hands.

"I only wish you could spend the night," said Ijego. "This time of the day is very tricky. You may think that you have daylight but when darkness comes, it descends fast."

"I will do just fine," said Osondu, drying his hands with a small piece of cloth. He picked up the half-filled calabash wine cup and drank what was left. It was fresh and honey sweet.

"After what happened today, believe me, you do not want to be seen with me until this thing is cleared up."

He rested the wine cup on the carved wooden cup rest.

"I just started a fight with the most powerful man in Nri. I am now like a leper. I will be snubbed by his loyalists. I took a risk by coming back here. I should have gone straight home after speaking to Igwe. But I had to let you know how it went."

Ijego adjusted herself twice on the mud clay daybed.

"Ezu is not the most powerful man in Nri. He may like to think so, but he is not. Igwe is the most powerful man here."

She picked up the big calabash palm wine jug. As she reached to refill his empty cup, Osondu covered it with his right palm.

"I am full. I can almost feel it in my throat."

Ijego giggled.

"You have done me right, town girl. I will be eternally grateful."

"I just hope that everything else will work out well for you." She let the palm wine jug rest on the red mud floor.

"I think it will, little sister. Igwe was so angry after my story that he found it difficult to speak. I think that something will happen. I think that he will do something."

"I told you that he is a very good man. Igwe did a lot of business with that group, but he was never a part of them. He is straight and talks straight."

"Yes, he does," agreed Osondu. "I did not expect him to show his anger in my presence, but he could not hide it."

"Ezu has a reputation around here, so he knows that you are telling the truth." She whispered. "If you insist on leaving today, then you must be going. The day has aged. If left to me, I would rather have you spend the night and leave very early."

Osondu got up and grabbed his brown goatskin bag.

"I have no choice. I will never forgive myself if I bring trouble to you. You have done well here. I do not want to spoil it for you. I will let you know of any progress."

He bent down to step outside.

"I insist on escorting you a little way," said Ijego, stepping outside as well.

Osondu stood up straight outside of the obu, surveying the compound. It was expensive-looking and very well and cleanly kept. It had two Mkpuke (wives' quarters). The path from the main gate to both the obu and the Mkpuke was paved with shiny gray gravel. The decoration of the open space had a feminine touch. Banana and pear trees were deliberately planted to complement the gravel path. Other parts of the open space were clearly laid out to provide shade.

Osondu shook his head. "You have made well here, town girl."

Ijego smiled. For several moments, she gazed at the long shadow on the ground made by the setting sun.

"You know what's funny? Too often I forget, but I met Igwe at the time I was asking questions about coming to Nri. That was twenty-six years ago. Then he was young and very childish. You are talking about a long day. How about a very long life? It has been a very long life!"

🌿 🌿 🌿

When Ijego studied the shadows on the pebbles of the yard's compound she could see the success that Osondu was talking about. She had built all of this from scratch. But she also saw lots of hard work, mixed with sorrow, and injected with much faith, faith in her chi and herself. Maybe it was more a pride in herself, but it was a positive kind of pride. It was the kind of pride that made one not sell oneself short, the kind of pride that made one demand more from oneself.

When she had migrated to Nri twenty-six years ago, Ijego was taken in by Ichie Idika, although it was really more his wife, Orjiugo, who took Ijego in, because Ijego saw very little of Ichie Idika. Ichie Idika and Orjiugo became her guardians. Ijego was still young and beautiful at the age of thirty. Her very dark skin looked as fresh as cocoyam leaf in the rainy season. Her presence at Ichie Idika's compound was a magnetic force for suitors who came in all shapes and grades. But Ijego refused them all. At that point in her life, she had tasted freedom and developed a suspicion of men though it was no longer the hatred or fear she had had at Ezikwe. She suspected that if she were taken in as a wife, her fate would be sealed. She would be forever taking directions and always seen as property. She did not want to be owned. Ijego wanted to be the one to own. She wanted to own a man. Hadn't she owned Uwakwe at some point? Hadn't she given directions and Uwakwe had obeyed them? But Nri men were different. She could never find one as humble and submissive as Uwakwe. They were all arrogant and full of themselves, ever running their mouths like overfed parrots. You could never control a man who ran his mouth faster than you could think.

But Nri women were even worse. Chineke! (God!) How they talked about Nri women who were unfortunate enough to have been born outside of Nri and so lucky to have been married to the almighty Nri men. Chineke! (God!) How they expected you to genuflect at every opportunity and reveal without reservation the thankfulness in your heart for having been so blessed.

Yes, it was suspicion and pride that made her remain a single woman—suspicion that she would not fit nicely into the stereotype of being a man's property. And not just property but, according to the Nri women's standard, lower grade property because she was not an indigenous citizen. Her pride was that she had what Nri women would never have: independence. Thanks to hidden rules. Almighty hidden rules!

Hidden rules! They were like miracles sent directly from the sky. They gave you options you never imagined you would have. It took a clever genius like Ichie Idika to see them and the perfect collaboration with his wife, Orjiugo, to make them a reality. There was a law in Nri culture that made it possible for a woman to marry another woman! There was, however, absolutely nothing physical in the relationship. The prerequisite was that the woman in question be married but barren, and her husband died without another wife who had children from him. The idea was that the barren woman would marry a younger wife in the name of her deceased husband. The young wife would meet with a male of her liking in their lineage family and have children in the name of the dead man and his living wife.

After eight years of trying to persuade Ijego, it must have dawned on Ichie Idika and Orjiugo that Ijego knew what she wanted—to live the rest of her life as a single, independent woman.

Ijego had successfully used the excuse that she was barren to refuse every suitor who approached her guardians.

It was an Nkwo market day in the seventh moon. The planting season was coming to an end. Ijego had again done most of the planting for her guardians. What energy! She had taken a cold bath and dressed elegantly as always for the market shopping. But she was temporarily delayed by an escalating drizzle. She sat on her bamboo bed in her sleeping room and waited for the rain to stop.

"Ugbana! Ugbana! Are you there?"

Ijego got up and peeped through the sleeping room door to the hut's sitting area before answering, "Nne mmadu."

Even before she looked she knew who it was. Only Orjiugo called her Ugbana after the elegant flamingo bird with long legs and a long neck that was forever pruning her immaculate body. Ijego responded by calling her 'someone's mother.' As Ijego entered the open sitting area, her first instinct told her that Orjiugo had remembered more items that she needed from the market. She often did. But this time, it was not so. Orjiugo sat on the mud daybed covered with raffia mat and invited Ijego to sit next to her.

"There is something I've been wanting to talk to you about," started Orjiugo. "Since it is raining, we might as well use this opportunity." The rain seemed to have taken a cue and poured harder. Ijego said nothing.

"Your singing was good. I heard you a moment ago. You have a very good voice, better than anyone I know around here."

Ijego simply smiled. Orjiugo complimented her singing all of the time, and Ijego welcomed it with lots of thank yous. But this time, she knew that Orjiugo did not come in from the rain just to compliment her singing. This must be a serious matter.

"It will be very possible for you to sing with the Nri-Agu women if the right things are done. You can even participate in whatever they are doing."

Ijego was listening.

"It is not good for a grown-up woman to live in isolation. I have seen how you glow whenever you sing. You will glow even more when you sing for the women of Nri-Agu in public."

Now Ijego was really listening.

Orjiugo told her how she had spoken to Ichie Idika, and he had agreed to let Ijego take over his late brother's lands and livestock if the right things were done.

"A full marriage ceremony will be performed in his name. After that, you can socialize fully with the Nri-Agu women. You can have children in his name. If you cannot have a child there are other things we can do."

At first Ijego could not speak. She became frozen, her mind blocked by too much information coming in at once. She could not breathe. She made a muffled sound that betrayed her frozen state of mind.

"You should think it over. I know you need some time," Orjiugo said before leaving.

The rain had stopped. *Was it true that Nri men could cause rain and then stop it at the right time? Had Ichie Idika caused the rain?* Ijego wondered.

She recovered more quickly than she had expected. On her way to Nkwo market, she was strangely excited. She had taken the loneliest path to the market. The whole proposal was as strange as strange could be. She could be married to a dead man and then inherit his property. As if that were not odd enough, she could then marry a young wife for herself, in his name, of course. The young bride would then bear children. What would the children call Ijego? Mother? Grandmother? Very strange!

Now, eighteen years later, her life looked as normal as normal could be. Ijego had become happier and much more fulfilled. At the age of fifty-two, she had a twenty-nine-year-old wife who had borne her two sons, twelve and nine years old, and a six-year-old daughter who some people swore looked like Ijego. Yes, Ijego had sung for the Nri-Agu women and her singing gave her exposure to other opportunities. But what gave her access to the richest families in Nri was her dried fish trade. Right after she inherited the land and name of Ichie Idika's late brother, Ijego became invisible. It was like absorbing all the energy of a dead man and adding it to her own. She restarted her fish business for the first time since leaving her first dead husband's village. Ijego knew dried fish. She could close her eyes and tell, just by the smell, the species and the part of the world where it came from.

When she restarted her fish business, she did it the old way by selling at the marketplace. But she soon discovered that those Nri women who had money and bought her grade of fish preferred that it be brought to their homes. She made her wealth by taking her fish from door to door, rubbing shoulders and gossiping with the who's who of Nri women. There she learned more about Nri politics than those who had educated her in them. It was not long before she was invited to join the affluent Iyom women's sect. Soon after she joined the Odozi-Obodo sect, she became their lead soloist. She did not disappoint those who thought she had the best voice in Nri. Because of her unique and privileged position, she was instantly recruited by the women's wing of the Ogbadu Eze (the eyes and ears of Eze Nri). So when Osondu, her birthplace acquaintance came to her looking for help, she knew exactly where to send him and even coached him on what to say and how to say it.

TWENTY-EIGHT

The Family Affairs

One day after Osondu brought his complaint against Ezu, Okoye sat in his obu with Enenebe, his junior wife. Okoye pondered Enenbe's complaint for a few moments. He did not know what to say. The matter seemed trivial, and he did not understand why two grown women should be making a fuss out of it.

"I do not want to get involved in it. It is a non-issue," he had said with a wave of his hand, which now rested on the back of his rattan chair. He was thinking about Osondu's complaint and was hoping to mention it to Enenebe. Time alone with her during the day was hard to come by these days.

"But you are already involved," said Enenebe. "If someone is telling lies about your wife, you cannot say you are not involved."

"Not when that other someone happens to be my wife too."

"You should at least ask her and let her deny it."

"And if she insists she was telling the truth, then what?"

"Then I will have a chance to deny it and say that I was not telling Nri women that I am Eze Nwanya (Queen). She is the ordained Eze Nwanya because she is your first wife. But I cannot push the Nri women away if they come to me all the time. If they come to me for advice more than they go to her, I cannot help it. I cannot become someone else so that Nri women will not come to me. That they come to me does not mean that I am competing to be Eze Nwanya."

Okoye wanted to ask her why she could not go to Mgbafor and talk with her and work things out. There was something in her voice that told Okoye the next stage would be crying. He detested that stage. He was not

267

in the mood to pet someone, at least not in the obu reception area where anyone could walk in.

"All right, I will ask her. I think it is all about perception. I will talk to her, but you two should be setting examples for Nri women."

"I am setting an example for Nri women. I am asking my husband to solve a problem between his two wives. I am not the one talking about it outside the house. She should have come to you first,"

"All right, I will talk to her," said Okoye, wanting to talk about Osondu and Ezu.

"And there is one other thing," said Enenebe. Okoye turned, looking at her as if to say "What now?"

"I think she is turning her children against us, me and my children. I can see it in Obuka's attitude. He has not entered my quarters for one moon now. He used to come and play with Unoma and Nnenna, but a few days ago—I think it was last Oye market—Unoma complained to me that Obuka was avoiding them. I know that Mgbafor has been saying something to them. His brother, Nwora, is different. He is carefree and acts his mind, just like his father."

Now Okoye was interested. It was one thing for two adults to involve themselves in trivial issues, but it was quite another to involve the children too.

"How do you know this? How do you know there is not a problem between the kids," asked Okoye.

"Because I asked Obuka already. He said that there was no problem between them. When I asked him why he does not come to my Mkpuke any more or play with Unoma and Nnenna, he said nothing."

Enenebe started sobbing now. "It is not good for the children. It is not good for them at all," she said wiping her face with her waist cloth. "When I was a young girl, I promised myself I would never share a husband with another woman. Now I see what I have done to myself."

"And you think that I planned to have two wives?"

"I am not saying that you did. I am just reflecting aloud, that's all," said Enenebe.

Okoye sighed as he recalled the events that had led to the second marriage. Maybe if Enenebe had not swayed her hips as she danced with her peers that day and smiled at him, maybe Okoye would not have noticed her. Maybe if Mgbafor was not playing hard-to-get wife, maybe Okoye would not have been so vulnerable to Enenebe's charm. But no! It had to be done. With Enenebe he felt like a married man because her loyalty was assured, and he knew what she was thinking and what she wanted at all times. She was everything a man needed in a woman. She was just like his grandmother. She did everything right and to his taste. She was the perfect woman. Every woman, every woman's smile, height, footsteps, voice, and dress was measured by hers. There was nothing more to add or subtract. Enenebe was the stick by which every woman was measured. It had to be done.

Okoye had first laid eyes on Enenebe, then known as Afulenu, at an Ozo ordainment ceremony at Nri Ejiofor, her village of birth. She was the lead dancer of her peers' Ijiputu dance, named after the legendry trade city of Ijiputu. She smiled the whole time she danced. Okoye thought she was smiling at him. But Enenebe didn't actually notice Okoye until nine days after that ceremony when they bumped into each other at the Nkwo market by accident, or, maybe, by destiny. Okoye recognized her immediately and complimented her dancing before even introducing himself. He would later learn that she was the second daughter of Ozo Ikunabo of Nri Ejiofor, an Oganiru priest. Okoye had known her father through Ezu but had never done any business with him or been to their house. Okoye asked Enenebe when the group was going to dance again and told her he would like to come and watch. But it was not her beauty, or her dancing, or that smile that locked Okoye's fate, but the way she put him at ease.

The marriage with Mgbafor had been arranged. She was a perfect cook and a good homemaker. But trying to get information from her was like trying to get a fish out of the mouth of an Nri Lake crocodile. At first Okoye thought she was just shy. Maybe if they got married in earnest and became intimate, she would loosen up and information would flow naturally between them. She had loosened up a little, but sharing her thoughts and everything else was a problem. Okoye laid everything out on the floor, and Mgbafor seemed to love that. But she just could not reciprocate. Maybe it was about rivalry or about control. Okoye could only speculate. But Okoye knew exactly what he wanted. And Enenebe had it.

That morning, after they had spoken for over an hour at Nkwo market, Okoye knew that Enenebe was the woman that Chineke had created just for him. Okoye had asked her if they could see each other again, and Enenebe said something that had caught Okoye completely off guard. But then, if Okoye was a woman, that was exactly how he would have said it.

"You can always come to our house. My father and mother have no problem with that. But I hope that you are not looking for a woman to sleep with. You will be disappointed." Okoye had smiled not knowing how to respond.

"I have to say this because I do not want to confuse you. My grandmother made me promise I would get married as a virgin. She is now resting with Chineke so she sees everything I do."

They had just met, and yet she had laid it all on the ground. Okoye was impressed. Enenebe was the female version of Okoye Nweri. Before they got married two months later, Okoye knew more about Enenebe than he knew about Mgbafor in the six years they had been married.

Now Okoye sat in his obu with a sobbing Enenebe. He stood up to pace around as he frequently did when confronted by women's issues.

"Maybe if you had not been swaying your hips and smiling at me, we would not have this problem," Okoye said, trying to get Enenebe to lighten up. It worked, because Enenebe smiled and shook her head.

"I don't know what you saw that day. But I was dancing like everyone else. You saw what you wanted to see, and now you have to live with it for the rest of your life." She was smiling. Okoye wanted to answer but heard someone coming.

It was Obuka, Okoye's thirteen-year-old first son, who had developed a routine of late. He would come by in the morning hours, mostly when Okoye was with someone. He would salute his father good morning and then vanish for the rest of the day. Okoye would not see him again unless he asked for him. If Okoye happened to be alone when he came, Obuka would stay around a little longer, but disappear at the first opportunity. He spent more time with his mother in her quarters where he slept. But he had also learned to go to his mother's birthplace at Nri Okpala Village for days in a row. He looked like a small version of Okoye, his father, but he acted like his mother. When he was alone with Okoye, Okoye did the talking while Obuka sat quietly like his mother, responding only with "Yes" or "No" to a question and "Really?" for a comment.

"Our father, Igwe!" he saluted as Okoye sat down on his chair.

"Eyee! Nna-bu-Ike!" Okoye acknowledged and saluted him back. Obuka was the reincarnation of Okoye's grandfather. Okoye called him the salutation name of his grandfather Nna-bu-Ike (Father is strength). There was a moment of hesitation, as if Obuka were deciding whether to stay or leave.

"I have not seen you for two days," said Okoye.

"That was because I went to Nri Okpala," replied Obuka. It was a perfect excuse and had worked miracles in the past. Mgbafor's father, Obuka's maternal grandfather, would not take it kindly if he heard that Okoye had objected to Obuka's visits. "That is another reason why I have come. Nna-Ochie, Grandfather, asked for my help with rebuilding the goat house today, so I will be going back this afternoon. I just wanted to let you know in advance in case you were looking for me."

Okoye said nothing in reply. Obuka turned to leave.

"Nna-bu-Ikeooo!" Enenebe saluted Obuka. The salute was drawn out, making it obvious that she was reminding Obuka that he had neglected to salute her.

"Enenebe!" Obuka turned back and saluted. "Sorry. I forgot." Then he turned to leave for good.

"Come back here!" barked Okoye. Obuka turned, walked back two steps, and stopped in front of his father. "Sit down!" commanded Okoye, waving to a stool at the left of Enenebe.

Obuka sat so that Enenebe was sitting between them. Okoye sat erectly, looking right at Obuka.

"Do you know this person?" he asked Obuka, pointing at Enenebe. Obuka smiled but said nothing, obviously confused. "I asked you a question. Do you know this woman sitting here?"

"Yes, Our Father," replied Obuka with a suppressed smile on his lips.

"Who is she?" There was a sternness in Okoye's tone and face that suggested to Obuka that whatever was coming was serious business.

"She is Unoma's mother," Obuka replied.

"Is that all?"

"She is Nnenna's mother too."

"Is that all?"

"She is Emenike's mother too."

"Is that all?"

Now very confused, Obuka said nothing, searching his father's face for any clue to his questions.

"Whose wife is she?" asked Okoye.

"She is your wife," Obuka said with a suppressed smile and some relief.

"Good! And what does that make you to her?"

"Her son too."

"Really?" said Okoye. "Are you sure of that?"

"Eyee!" answered Obuka in the affirmative, now relaxed.

"Has she been treating you like her son then?"

"I think so. Yes."

"I am happy to hear that. Now have you been treating her like your mother?"

Obuka made a half nod.

"I said have you been treating her like you treat your own blood mother?" There was no answer this time. Instead, Obuka stared at the floor and made an invisible mark with his right big toe.

"I will tell you what we are going to do," Okoye said, exhaling like an Isi-Ozo who had just decided on a perfect verdict after listening to a case. "Every morning when you wake up, before you come to salute me, you will go to her quarters and salute her first. Then you will ask her if there is any chore you can help her with for the day. You will do that every day before you see me, because I will ask you about it. Do you understand that?"

Obuka nodded.

"I said, do you understand that?"

"Eyee, Our Father."

"Also, if you are going to Nri Okpala, you should let her know as well, just as you would tell your blood mother and me, so that she will know where you are at all times. Do you understand this?"

"Eyee, Our Father."

"You should never involve yourself in the affairs of two adult women. It is very bad behavior," Okoye counseled with a long hiss. "Do you know what they did to children like you who were disrespectful to the adults in the old days?"

Obuka shook his head, now staring at his father.

"In the old days, if a child behaved the way you are behaving, his father would send him to live as a servant with a family friend in a very far Igbo land. He would give that family specific instructions not to be kind to him. That is exactly what I will do to you if you continue to disrespect adults. You will live there for three years. When you come back, you will be a good boy and appreciate your family. Now you can go!" said Okoye with the wave of a hand.

"Not yet," said Enenebe. Obuka, who was getting up, quickly sat down. "That is not enough," she added, now smiling. "I would like you to be close to your sisters, Unoma and Nnenna. I would like you to be a big brother to Emenike. Take him to the village once in awhile and show him around. If your blood mother is not at home and you are hungry, I would like you to come to my hut and ask for food as you used to. That is how it is done. You are the first child of your father, so all your siblings look up to you. You will set an example for them. You should be able to lead your father's family in the future when he is no more.

"Also, as the first son of your father, you should be closer to him than to anyone else. You should let him know where you are at all times. You should try to sit in on all the meetings so that you will know what is going on in the city and so you can learn different rituals. No one will ask you to leave because you are the first son. When your father gets old and he cannot remember certain things, you are the one to remind him. When your father is no more, older men will come to you asking you to recall some events. That is how it is done."

Okoye had always had good control of his life and that was why he was successful in business. But for the past four years since he had started his one-year isolation prior to his ordainment, he had lost most of that control. The events in his family made this clear. For one thing, there was too much to do—meetings to attend, rituals and spiritual devotions to be kept, and it seemed as if every Ozo priest in Nri wanted a piece of his time. Okoye now had little time for his family. But his family, especially Obuka, understood that the Eze Nri could not punish or judge someone.

He could refer the children and youth to the chief priest to punish them, but the Holy One could not whip his own children. Obuka understood that and Ezu understood that too.

TWENTY-NINE

Trouble in Nriland

Okoye decided to investigate the complaint before meeting with Ezu. That was the difference between him and his predecessor, Igwe Nwadike. Igwe Nwadike would have invited Ezu to meet with him and to persuade him to make peace between himself and Osondu. Then Ezu probably would have given Osondu a big contract and loaned him some fees for the contract. Ezu would have leaned on Udukwe and had him offer some of the money. At the end of the day, Osondu would have been happy because he would have negotiated his way into the inner circle of the big ivory business. Ezu would have been happy too. He would have saved face and played the fatherly role of helping a fellow Igbo man get on his feet after an unfortunate event. This would have been another feather in his cap that he could brag about. Udukwe would have been happy too. He would have avoided exposure. In their line of business, exposure was a no-no. If he was not exposed, whatever money he may have paid would have been recovered from another victim in a matter of weeks. All three men would have been better off themselves, but the underlying problem would have been much worse. That was diplomacy for you. To Igwe Nwadike, there were certain details a peacemaker didn't need to know. A peacemaker must look at the big picture. He must ask himself, "Is peace achieved between the parties?"

Okoye, the perfect outsider, was different. He wanted to know the details. He liked to solve problems from root causes. He liked to get to the bottom of things. He sent his best investigators. What they found broke Okoye's heart. Maybe there were certain details one should not know after all. The man who had duped Osondu was far deeper into crime than he had imagined. It was reported that Udukwe himself had not only been a member of the Uwa men when he was younger, but was one of their leaders. He started his business only after he was older and had raised a lot of money. But, even in his old age and with his wealth, he continued to sponsor young men who raided and sometimes killed innocent traders. He continued to deal in stolen goods. Udukwe was so notorious in his part of the world that there was no way Ezu could have been dealing with him for such a long time and not known him well.

It took only six days for Okoye to gather all of this information. The briefing concluded that either Ezu knew Udukwe's background and continued to deal with him, or he willingly shut his eyes and ears so he would not see or hear what was right in his face. But perhaps the most disturbing part of the report was that some other members of the Nri traders, mainly Oganiru or at least one or more individuals from Nri, also dealt with this man though infrequently. This other person, or persons, was very discreet and could not be easily identified. This was disturbing not just because the others dealt with this man, but because they seemed to know about his background. They must have known he was bad and that was why they didn't want to be seen with him.

By the time Okoye finally met with Ezu, he knew the whole truth or at least most of it. But he was still hoping for a miracle. He was hoping to hear Ezu deny the whole thing and claim that someone had been impersonating him or some other explanation. Anything was possible. Okoye had himself been involved in trade for twenty-one years and was in close contact with Ezu, but he had never heard about this man Udukwe. So it was entirely possible that Ezu may not have known.

Right after his contract with Igwe Nwadike had ended, Okoye had gone to Ezu to cash in on his promise. Ezu honored it and gave Okoye his first contract after less than two years of business apprenticeship. The contract was a thirty-five day round-trip journey if everything went well. The investment was big. Okoye returned after only twenty-two days and brought back the best quality tobacco leaf Nri people had ever seen. It was the proof he needed to show Ezu what he could do. After that first trip, other contracts came. After another two years of small contracts with Ezu, many offers came from other merchants. They were bigger contracts and the terms were better. When he accepted one of them, his relationship with Ezu temporarily suffered. Ezu felt betrayed because he thought that five years was the standard loyalty time for a newcomer when given a first contract.

Okoye mended things with his business master two years later when some big Nri names, including Ezu, sponsored a major trade expedition. Okoye was the most favored to lead the expedition. Ezu invited him and had the pleasure of announcing the offer, his way of giving his blessings and forgiving Okoye's past betrayal. After that expedition, Okoye made a lot of money and earned many commissions. He thought that he had earned the respect of the Oganiru men, but he had not. He made a lot of money all right, but the Oganiru men had their way of making an outsider know that he did not belong. They called wealthy outsiders "money-missed-roads," meaning that those wealthy nonmembers had earned their wealth by accident. That, of course, included Okoye. But Ezu carved out a special name for Okoye. Behind Okoye's back and in his own circle, Ezu called him Ike-kete-Olie (Suffering Man, who eats by his Sweat). Okoye knew about this, but he loved the action anyway.

The elders said that if you want to know what someone is saying about you behind your back, listen to what they say about others as soon as they have left the room. Ezu had an unkind name for everyone, including his perfect partner, Ugocha Nwoye. He was credited with calling Igwe Nwadike "Abonoba's Chicken" the first time. He abused people without thinking, and Okoye and everyone knew it. Okoye knew Ezu better than most people in Nri simply because he had worked for him in the past. He knew how far Ezu would go to maximize his profits. He knew how far he would go to put others down so that he could feel good about himself. But nothing he knew about Ezu could have prepared him for the report he received. Okoye knew that somewhere within the Oganiru circle was the lowest end of Nri morality. But he had not believed it could go that low. So he was willing to give Ezu the benefit of the doubt when he invited him for a talk about Osondu.

Ezu had no idea why he had been invited so he was his usual loud and jovial self. His voice filled the big reception area and outside too. The only time he used a low voice was when he was having a business meeting.

Ezu could not walk into a room or even a big temple without everyone feeling his presence. The dwarf who had spent his lifetime denying that he was one radiated so much energy and charisma that everyone around him felt it. But all that energy went away as soon as Igwe got down to the real business.

"There is a reason I invited you," Okoye stated. "A man from Mbaofia in Ikwine family by the name of Osondu came looking for my help. He wanted me to help him settle a small dispute he is having with another man he did business with. That man's name is Udukwe. Do you know either or both of these men?"

"Yes. But what does this have to do with me?"

"This man, Osondu, mentioned your name. He said that you introduced him to Udukwe as one of your business partners."

"That is true. But I still don't see how it has anything to do with me."

At that point, Oduh felt compelled to step in. "I think Igwe means that when you introduce someone to one of your business partners, you are sort of testifying to your partner's character."

"That was not what I meant when I mentioned Udukwe's name to him. I did not mean to testify to his character," Ezu said.

"Are you saying that you cannot testify to the character of the person you do business with on a frequent basis?" asked Okoye.

For almost an hour Okoye asked all sorts of questions and gave numerous clues, but Ezu refused to accept any responsibility. Instead, he remained with his theme that Osondu had come to him for help. He could not deal directly with a newcomer into the business, so he referred him to the first name that came to mind. When Okoye asked if he had ever received any other complaints against Udukwe before sending Osondu to him, he said yes. But he denied that Udukwe was questionable and insisted that his rivals were trying to destroy him by propaganda.

"Are you therefore testifying to his character?" Okoye asked at that point.

"I am not. I deal with many people, and I cannot testify to the character of each one of them," Ezu said. After another hour of not getting anywhere with his old business mentor, Okoye decided to use a different approach. He brought the issue close to home.

"If you were in my position as Eze Nri, and I were in your position as Ezu Nri, and this man, Osondu, came to you with this complaint, what would you do for him?"

"I think that I would have known you too well to know that the man is lying," Ezu said.

"Okay, let me rephrase the question. If you were Eze Nri and this man came to you with this complaint about another Nri man whom you did not know that well, what then would you do to help him?"

"I would be busier with the big problems in Nri and Igbo land, and I would not have time for some individual's business transactions," Ezu replied almost sarcastically.

"Maybe my question is not clear yet. Let me say it from another direction then. If you were just an Ozo man, and you were going about your business in Igbo land, and this man approached you and said, 'Nri-is-Holy! Nri-is-Holy!! I was involved in business with someone and they duped me of my money! Please help me to recover my money!' What then would you say to him?"

Ezu had had it with this line of seemingly unwarranted interrogation. When he looked across the room, he did not see the long red cap with eight eagle feathers sticking out all around it that sat on Okoye's head. He did not see the Nne Offor Nri, mantle of perfect justice, that lay on the floor between Okoye's legs. All he saw was the young man, twenty-five-years-old, who had come to him one rainy morning looking for employment. Of course he remembered that morning very well! Okoye had had no sandals on his feet. Rain dripped from his clothing, and the only eagle feather on his worn-out red cap was bent.

"I would tell this man, the hypothetical Igbo man, to go back to wherever he took a bath and look for his piece of clothing there, because I don't have it," Ezu told the twenty-five-year-old. It was a sarcastic answer and was meant to be. But it was also honest, straight from the man's heart.

Oduh did not believe what he just heard! The only other person in the room besides the three adults was Ikenna, the teenage dwarf who started choking. Or maybe he was faking it. He left the room, but no one noticed. Okoye must have stared at Ezu for a full moment. Ezu had given him the most selfish answer an Igbo man could give another. And that answer came out of the mouth of Nri Lake itself, the embodiment of all giving. *What had gone wrong?* When he had been dealing with Ezu, he always boasted about helping these people and those people. He boasted about helping people even when he had cheated them ten times over. There were no pretenses this time. It was a straight and honest answer from Nri Lake that everyone had drunk from at one time or another. How had the Nri people gotten to this point? Okoye suddenly realized that this man sitting in front of him was a complete stranger. He realized that they had been calling the wrong man, Osondu, a stranger.

He turned to Oduh. "Tell our man that Eze Nri can no longer speak directly with him until this whole issue has been resolved to my satisfaction by the full Ozo council meeting. Remind him that Eze Nri does not speak directly to strangers."

Okoye stood up. As he left the room, he could hear the questions, but he did not care to hear the answers because he already knew them.

"Is that what you truly believe or are you trying to make everyone angry? Don't you feel something in your heart for that man who lost all his money?" asked Oduh. "Ibukwa Nwa Nri? (Are you at all of Nri lineage?). Don't you listen to your own heartbeat? Listen! Listen to the lower right side of your chest and you will hear it. You will feel it.

Ibukwa Nwa Nri? Ibukwa Nwa Nri?"

Oduh kept asking questions, but there were no answers. Any answer would have yielded some particle of hope for the diplomat as it always did for diplomats. But there was none. When the young dwarf came in to retrieve his bell, Ezu was leaving and the old man, Oduh was weeping. He wept like a young child who had just found out that he had been abandoned in the wilderness by his parents.

Over the three years that they had worked together, Okoye had come to love Oduh. He had come to understand why Oduh was diplomatic with people. Oduh did not like to hurt anyone's feelings. He treated everyone like his own child or brother or sister. It was said that Nri people fed their children with their own saliva when they had nothing else to share. Oduh symbolized that way of thinking, for he would have been willing to share his saliva with anyone if that would have helped. Okoye had come to respect Oduh as his father. He even referred to him as "Nna-anyi," (Our Father), in private moments.

So when he heard that Oduh was weeping because of what Ezu had done, he felt it personally. But Okoye also recalled what Uwa men did to Erike's family twenty eight years ago when they killed his uncle and other people from his village. *How could a Nri priest have information about those people and not share it?*

Okoye had no problem with referring the matter to the Ozo council of which Oduh was the head. The Eze Nri would offer his advice, but no judgments, since he was forbidden from punishing anyone. Besides, the Ozo men had a moral code that guided their conduct, so it was better tested there, Okoye concluded.

❦ ❦ ❦

Given the state of mind at Nri, one could assume that most Ozo men would not care about a business deal gone wrong. But a lot of them actually did care, and emotions were high. About one out of five Ozo men, mostly Ozo-Mkputu priests and older men like Oduh, wanted to use this as an opportunity to vent their anger on the Oganiru men who had turned Nri upside down. But a third of the Ozo men, mostly Oganiru, were prepared to protect Ezu at all costs. They were all traders who had benefited from dealing with him in one way or another. Ordinarily, the rest of the Ozo men would not care at all about Osondu or Ezu because the situation did not affect them personally. But, surprisingly, they did care, though for the wrong reasons. They cared because Uwa men were involved.

For centuries, Uwa men had terrorized Igbo people though, most of the time, Nri people were not directly affected. But any Nri man or woman who traveled often had had one or more close calls with Uwa men. Nri men had witnessed this pirate group stealing from, assaulting, raping, and even killing their Igbo victims. For the witnesses, seeing someone else being assaulted was almost as effective as being assaulted themselves. The memory stuck with them for a long time. And yet no one could do anything about it, especially the Nri people, who did not believe in violence.

Their only weapon, apart from putting a spell on someone, which they rarely did, was to ostracize a person or an entire community. But Uwa men had no faces or names. They wore masks most of the time, and no one could identify them as a village or a family. So they could not really be ostracized. They lived and operated like ghosts, appearing and disappearing as it suited them. They were truly men of the underworld. So they were like a big sharp pain on the middle of the back of the Igbo and Nri people. One could not see it or touch it, but it was still killing one. So to finally put a face and a name to some Uwa men was enough to motivate a lot of Ozo men who ordinarily would not have cared about Ezu's business dealings with some Igbo man.

Emotions ran wild among the Ozo men. Most of them just wanted to know the truth first. Non-Ozo priests were not left out, for rumors had spread quickly throughout all the villages, and everyone had a version and an opinion, depending on whom you asked.

🌿 🌿 🌿

Ezu always walked into a meeting or an occasion at the last moment. That was to make his appearance most dramatic. His loyalists usually stood up and chanted "Ezu! Ezu!!" until he sat down, and he usually stood a long time so he could make the most of the moment. He was what Nri people call a tall dwarf, meaning that he was taller than an average dwarf. But he was still a dwarf, and his huge head and neck were a large part of his height. He was "the brain" and the genius of the Ubaka brothers. When he moved, he moved like lightning. It was rare to see him walking or pacing like an ordinary person. He was almost always in a hurry. If dwarves had more life force than regular people, as Nri people believed, then Ezu was the perfect example of that.

The big hall was full when Ezu zoomed in. Osondu sat next to the main entrance with the other non-Nri guests who had been called to testify. Trouble started as soon as Ezu saw Osondu. They had seen each other simultaneously, and Osondu rose from his seat. "Ezuuu!" he yelled in greeting as he took off his red hat to show respect. Ezu looked at him with contempt, as one would look at someone with a contagious disease and moved on without a word.

"Since when have Ozo meetings turned into a performance that anyone could come watch?" he asked Oduh, who was sitting in the front.

"This is not just a meeting. It is an inquiry, and we have invited some people to help us find the truth," said Oduh.

"It is not our custom to invite non-Nri Ozo men to our meeting, and I demand those people leave immediately."

"They will help us to determine the facts," Oduh told him again.

"Then they should be interviewed outside the hall and, if possible, at a private site outside the compound."

"Well, we have made a decision to hear their stories in a general meeting, and everyone present must hear their stories," Oduh reaffirmed.

Their dialogue could be heard halfway down the hall, and the rest of the Ubaka brothers stood up and approached the two men. They had all come in earlier, and either did not recognize Osondu or didn't have any problem with his presence. But now they did because Ezu did. Their core allies from the Oganiru men stood up too. And now they all had a problem with the strangers. It was always their tactic to disrupt a meeting when it was not in their favor, except this time the disruption was not preplanned or rehearsed. What followed was chaos. As soon as Ezu found out that he could not get his way, he left the meeting in protest.

"Non-Ozo Nri men have never been invited to an Ozo Nri meeting and it will not start with me!" he shouted before walking out on the whole congregation. The rest of the Ubaka brothers left with him.

Everyone else stayed behind. The rest of Ezu's allies wanted an adjournment so they could seek a compromise, but this could not be done, so the meeting moved on without Ezu. Victims told horror stories about the elephant tusk cult and their activities in Igbo land. They told of the connection with Uwa men. They told of Udukwe's background as an Uwa man and his present ties with them. It was impossible not to believe them, for they had never met each other before and yet their stories were identical. The names of the criminals, the settings, and the basic plots were similar. The victims, most of them responsible men in their villages and families, wept like children as they recounted their horror stories.

At the end of their testimonies, they were all excused. As soon as they had left, the real meeting started. The question before the Ozo men was not the truth of their testimonies because the witnesses were all credible and believable. And they all supported the investigation report that there was a secret cult that drove new traders out of business by stealing their money, that the cult sponsored Uwa men, and that Udukwe, whom Ezu dealt with, was an active member of that gang.

The big question before the Ozo men was: Did Ezu, one of their own, know all of this and not tell Eze Nri and the Ozo men? Did he know all this and still continue to deal with them and benefit from their crimes? If he did not have first-hand information, did he deliberately ignore all the signs that might have provoked his suspicions? In other words, did he violate the Ozo's men's code by knowingly dealing with criminals? If he was not guilty of this, was he willfully negligent of his duties as an Ozo man by not investigating or reporting a potential crime and, therefore, violating a different Ozo men's code? Only Ezu or his business partner, Udukwe, could answer those questions and neither of them was present. Udukwe had also been invited, but no one was surprised that he did not show up.

Ezu and Udukwe had been invited but decided not to answer for themselves. That was in itself a high offense to the Ozo council so the majority concluded that both men were guilty of the offenses as charged until they could honor their invitations and prove otherwise. Thus, the following punishments were given to Ezu: he would lose his Ezu, Ozo, and Nze titles. He would be reduced to an ordinary man in Nri until he could prove his innocence. He could not take any title for five years and, even after five years, he must show believable remorse for his actions before regaining any titles. He was to refund Osondu all of his money and apologize to him for the pains he had caused him. He must stop dealing with criminals and cooperate with Ozo men in their investigations of Uwa men and the elephant tusk cult.

As for Udukwe, his village would be ostracized until they, in turn, ostracized him. No friends of the Nri people would go to their market to trade until they had come clean and told all they knew. Any community or individual that dealt with him would lose favor in Nri. Udukwe must come to Nri and cooperate with the Ozo council in their investigation before his real punishment would be determined.

The rest of the Ubaka brothers, four of them, had to pay a fine of one cow each for walking out of the Ozo meeting. They were temporarily suspended until they paid the fines. Agents were sent to officially deliver the verdict to Ezu and his brothers. Some were sent to terminate the bond on Udukwe among his kinsmen and business patrons. Ezu must accept the verdict within twelve days or appeal in good faith to Oduh in front of other Ozo priests. The rest of the Ubaka brothers must also accept their penalties within twelve days. It was a fair verdict, but, even as they were giving the verdict, they knew Ezu would not accept it. Everyone knew that Ezu was Okeke Ubaka and Okeke Ubaka was Ezu. It was as if the Ezu title was made for him when he was born.

Twelve days went by and there was no response from Ezu or his four brothers. In fact, no one had seen Ezu for ten days or knew where he had gone. This was an open challenge to all Nri people, a tense moment in Nri. Many meetings were held among different groups.

Ezu and his brothers did not respond because they had no response. To them, what had happened had finally confirmed what they had feared for many years: that the Nri people were together against the rich dwarves—they were out to put them in their place. If not, why hadn't their friends walked out from the meeting with them? The entire group of Oganiru had walked out of meetings many times. Usually they got a small fine and, sometimes, they went with no reprimand.

THIRTY

The Showdown

Twenty-eight days had passed since the judgments on the Ubaka brothers. Neither Ezu nor his brothers had officially responded. On the twenty-ninth day, a gathering of young Nze men appeared at Igwe Okoye Nweri's compound. By the first hour of the morning time, they filled the palace's public square. They ranged between the ages of twenty and forty and numbered over two thousand with more men still coming. They came from all of the twelve villages of the Nri clan. All were bare-chested. In fact, most of them wore no clothing except for their loin cloths. In Nri, no one came to the palace wearing only their loin cloth. But this was something no one had seen before. The men chanted war song after war song. A young man led the chants and others led the response.

"Nzogbu! Nzogbu!! (Stomp! Stomp!!)," shouted the lead singer.

"Enyi-mgba enyi! (Just like a big elephant!)," responded the crowd of young men.

"Nzogbu!! (Stomp!!)"

"Enyi-mgba enyi! (Just like a big elephant!)"

"Nzogbu! (Stomp!)"

"Enyi-mgba enyi! (Just like a big elephant!)"

"Nzogbu Nwoke! (Stomp on a man.)"

"Enyi-mgba enyi! (Just like a big elephant!)"

"Nzogbu Nwanya! (Stomp on a woman.)"

"Enyi-mgba enyi! (Just like a big elephant!)"

"Nzogbu!! (Stomp!!)"

"Enyi-mgba enyi! (Just like a big elephant!)"

"Nzogbu!!! (Stomp!!!)"

"Enyi-mgba enyi! (Just like a big elephant!)"

So the chanting went, and at the end of each chant, the lead singer would ask the crowd, "Where are we heading?"

"To the Adagbe village," they would respond.

"To whose house?"

"To Ubaka's compound."

"Who are you waiting for?"

"We are waiting for Igwe to tell us what to do."

Then the leader would select another song and lead the crowd through it as they motivated themselves and waited for Okoye. Their chanting could be heard in the distant villages. Some beat their chests as they sang. Many others clenched their fists and shoved them into the air. There was a lot of foot stomping as they sang their songs. They chanted war songs, but all they had were their clenched fist and their stomping feet. They had absolutely no metal or metal support, not even a stone or a stick!

They had been chanting for about an hour and could be heard in all Nri-Agu and in neighboring villages. By now, the majority of the participants had arrived. Once in awhile a couple of men would run in looking guilty for showing up late. The crowd was now close to three thousand. All were ordained Nze priests. Suddenly, the bell started ringing, and everyone turned in its direction. Okoye was finally coming to talk to them.

"Igwe! Igwe!! Igwe!!!" the young men hailed him. But the hailing quickly turned into a war a song again.

"Nzogbu Nzogbu!

"Enyi-mgba enyi!"

"Nzogbu!!"

"Enyi-mgba enyi!!"

"Nzogbu!!!"

"Enyi-mgba enyi!!!"

"Nzogbu Nzogbu!"

"Enyi-mgba enyi!"

"Nzogbu!!"

"Enyi-mgba enyi!!"

"Nzogbu!!!"

"Enyi-mgba enyi!!!"

Okoye was very pleased that the young men were in this mood. He would have liked to lead such a noble mission when he was young to restore order and dignity to Nri Land. But it must be put in a proper context, he thought. As soon as he raised his white ceremonial horsetail, the chanting was replaced by the hailing of "Igwe! Igwe!!" Then there was complete silence.

Okoye thanked them for responding to such a noble cause. "It is not mandatory for you to be here, but you have all come. You have come because of your own will to defend our laws. Some people have insulted all of us and what we believe in. By doing so, they have insulted our forefathers whose sacred ways we have sworn as Nze priests to uphold and defend. From your songs, I can see how angry you are, and all well meaning Nri men and women are as angry as you are, including me. As a young man, I would have been very happy to do what you are about to do in order to restore dignity to our Nri holy land. But we must not do what our forefathers would not do. We must never engage in violence in order to protect our customs. We are peaceful people and we cannot engage in violence."

"You must never insult the Ubaka family or mistreat any of them. What you have to do is to retrieve all the Ozo anklets in that family. By doing so, they will cease to be Ozo or Nze priests. If any of them raises a stick or stone against you, you must retreat immediately, and we will find other means of dealing with them. You must not raise a stick or stone against them. That is not the way of our forefathers . . . ," he was saying. Just then, two young men rushed in.

They belonged to the Ogbadu Eze (King's Forerunners). Both were Nze men and part of the group posted at Adagbe village to monitor the activities there.

"Igwe! Igwe!!" one of them called as they both approached Okoye. Okoye interrupted his speech to listen to the young men. One of them said something to him in a very low voice. Okoye thought for a moment about what he had heard. Then he leaned toward Oduh, who was standing at his left, and they exchanged words.

"We have a new development," Okoye said to the entire crowd in a loud voice. "It looks as if the whole of the Ubaka family has decided to leave Nri clan. I just received word that they are on their way out of Nri as we speak. But you must still go to Adagbe village and confirm that. If you see them still in the Nri family, you must retrieve the Ozo anklets, but if they are already out of our family, do not go after them. Let them be."

"Igwe! Igwe! Igwe!!!"

"Nzogbu Nzogbu!"

"Enyi-mgba enyi!"

"Nzogbu!!"

"Enyi-mgba enyi!!"

So off went the well-motivated young Nze priests. They had no idea what this action meant for the Nri clan or what lay ahead. Most of them would live to tell stories in their old age about the saddest day in Nri.

❈ ❈ ❈

Ezu was the first in line. He was riding a white horse and was fully dressed in his ceremonial attire as Ezu Nri. He wore a blue garment and a red hat with four white eagle feathers on it. He was in the best spiritual standing he could afford because he had circled his eyes with white holy chalk. He held his ceremonial bronze spear in his left hand as he led the way. The rest of his household, seven wives, thirty-seven children, and eleven grandchildren, trailed behind him. Most of his household members also rode on horseback. There were as many servants as members of the family, and they carried some of the household loads while donkeys carried the rest of it. Even the servants looked their best.

Omile, Ezu's younger brother and his right-hand man, followed Ezu and his family. Omile's entire family came next. The other three Ubaka brothers followed in the order of age (except for Chiaka), trailed by their families. Chiaka, their oldest brother, and his family were the last of the Ubaka brothers. This must have signified his reluctance to leave.

News of their migration had quickly spread all over Nri. As they passed through each village, the people lined up at the side of the road to witness something they had never been seen before—Nri people moving out for good.

For centuries, Nri had been a sanctuary for Ndibia-Ndibia (immigrants), most of them banished from their own families and some fleeing from political or social oppression. In that part of the world, Nri had always been the last stop for the oppressed. But their own community had never really been tried. For centuries, it existed on the understanding that people are basically good and would coexist in good faith and not challenge authority.

Children watched, not knowing exactly what it meant, as Ezu led his people through each village and out of Nri. Women cried and beat their breasts. Men simply looked on helplessly. What baffled everyone was not that the Ubaka brothers had decided to leave, but the number of families they took with them. Half of Adagbe village showed their loyalty by following the Ubaka brothers.

"Nzogbu Nzogbu!"

"Enyi-mgba enyi!"

"Nzogbu!"

"Enyi-mgba enyi!"

"Nzogbu!!"

"Enyi-mgba enyi!!!"

"Nzogbu Nzogbu!"

"Enyi-mgba enyi!"

By the time the young Nze men arrived at Adagbe village, all the Ubakas and their entire families were already gone. The Nze watched helplessly as ordinary villagers who were loyal to the Ubaka family packed their things and followed the Big Head's trail. The exodus had started in the morning and lasted well into late evening with an occasional break in the chain between one household and another. It was a sad, gloomy day in Nri land.

THIRTY-ONE

The Adept

Ichie Idika was at his obu minding his business. He had learned to do so since Igwe Nwadike had passed on a few years back.

Why waste your energy talking to people who never understand? Let them have it their way! He was not really minding his business after all, but one of his son's businesses. He had volunteered to prepare tobacco snuff for his youngest son. He had always loved preparing his own tobacco.

"It just tastes better. At least you know what it is made of," he argued. But as he got older, the business became more than a matter of taste to him. It became his primary chance to get good exercise in addition to his late evening strolls. There was something about this activity that got his blood pumping hard. One didn't get that kind of exercise just by walking.

Ichie rolled out the big black marble stone from underneath his daybed and centered the stone on an old piece of cloth lying in the middle of the room. He had carved out the stone forty years earlier. It was about an arm's length by half an arm's length and the weight of a four-year-old child. He always told himself that when he could no longer roll out that stone, he would be as good as dead. Now he was 102 years old and still rolling out the stone. Next he reached under the daybed and took out the stone's arm which he placed on top of the stone. The arm weighed about the weight of a one-year-old baby and was about the size of three planting yam seeds put together. The tobacco leaves would be placed between the arm and the main stone and the pressure of the arm, when rolled over the leaves, would crush them. Ichie wiped both surfaces with his hands.

It was said that when elephants fought, it was the forest that would bear the loss. In this case, it was the tobacco leaves that suffered for when the showdown between the two marble stones was over, the tobacco leaf would be turned into a perfect powder. Nri people and Igbo people loved this powder. It was their primary source of caffeine next to kolanuts, except that kolanuts were eaten mostly on special occasions. But one could sniff tobacco whenever one felt like it. When a proper dose was taken, it stimulated the nerves. Thoughts flowed naturally and one looked better as well. Not only did Nri people love tobacco, their horses loved it even more. If one's horse was given tobacco on a regular basis, the owner was automatically the best friend of his horse. And if you let the animal have some tobacco after a good feeding, the horse's power was doubled. He would happily carry one farther and faster.

Ichie sat on the bare floor with the stone between his legs and laid some tobacco leaves on the main stone. He took one of the leaves and put it close to his nose. *Good tobacco,* he said to himself. Then he began to roll the arm across the leaves. He was only a couple of moments into his exercise when he heard his main gate squeak open. There was nothing unusual about that, except that no one came through for several quick-moments. He was beginning to wonder if it was some child or an animal, when a black he-goat came through followed by a man who was almost on his knees as he bent down to get through the gate. He was carrying a full basket of yams on his head. It was Erike! Ichie and Erike had not seen each other for over a year. Erike had been to Ichie's house only three times in twenty-eight years.

"This must be a good day!" Ichie said.

"It must be, Our Father," Erike added.

"Did I hear you say Our Father? What have I done to deserve that title, the Father of a Giant?"

Erike began laughing. "I missed you very much and I brought you a he-goat to prove it." Erike tied the goat to an Ogbu tree before he crawled into the hut. Once inside, he was able to stand up straight. Ichie stood up also and the two men shook hands.

"It is really good to see you, my friend," Ichie Idika said as he went into the inner room to fetch kolanut. Erike was not a good kolanut eater, nor did he like tobacco powder. He did not like caffeine, period. But, out of politeness, he managed to eat a small piece of kolanut. But he loved the fresh palm wine even though he did not drink very much because he belonged to the Nze Ikenga sect. He had two cups of wine as the two men chatted about different topics, from family to light politics and old times. Finally, Ichie Idika had to ask the question. Although the two men had genuine affection and respect for each other, it was not the kind of affection that causes two people to chat with each other just for the sake of enjoyment of one another's company.

"So what brought you to my place?" Ichie asked.

"Our Father, I cannot lie to you. I came for a reason. I have many questions and I need some answers."

"Go ahead. I may be able to help you."

"This is not really a life and death situation. It is just a child not being certain about some things."

"Sure, sure," Ichie agreed as he continued to grind the tobacco leaves.

"First was the conflict between our people and the Ubaka brothers. I have thought about it many times, and I cannot seem to find an answer. We said that we believe in nonviolence, yet we were ready to use force to retrieve the Ozo anklets from the Ubaka brothers. Isn't there a conflict in that behavior?"

Ichie was quiet for a moment before he shook his head in disbelief. "You mean to tell me that you have been losing sleep about that and that you have had to actually bring me a goat to buy an answer?"

Erike had thought that Ichie Idika would have liked to answer such a question and was embarrassed that he had asked a silly question after all. "No, it was not really my main question," he lied. "That was just one of them."

"That was the most intelligent question anyone has asked me for many years now. Not even my own children ask me such questions. The problem with our people is that we do not ask questions anymore, so we do not get answers. In the old days, our people used to get together in small groups, just as friends. They would pose questions that had nothing to do with their immediate needs. They asked deep questions and tried to answer them just for fun. But today our people think about their immediate needs only. You would be surprised how many of our people cannot see beyond the next thirteen moons. And they wonder why they are beginning to die so young. How can you live to be old if you are not planning beyond the next year?"

"That is true," Erike agreed.

"To answer your question, yes, our people believe in nonviolence. But first, what the youngsters did was not violent. It may have been an exercise in the use of force, but it was not violence. It could have led to violence, but it was not violence."

"What is the difference then?"

"Violence must have the intent to physically harm someone. They had no intention of harming anyone. They merely wanted to retrieve the property of our people that someone kept without our people's consent. That in itself was not violence, but it could have easily led to violence."

"Isn't it wrong because it had the potential of being violent?"

"Not really, and I will tell you why, my friend. First you have to believe that not all violence is wrong."

"Tell me more. Some violence can be good?"

"Some violence is certainly not wrong. It may not be good, but at the same time it is not wrong. What was wrong was our policy of nonviolence. You see, we live in a physical world, and we are bound to be physical sometimes to make a point. That physical force may lead to violence, but most of the time there is nothing we can do about it. We can use physical force to defend ourselves, for instance. If another human being or even an animal threatens your life, you have to defend yourself. It would be foolish not to. As a matter of fact, if they know that you are going to defend yourself, and you have more force than they do, most of the time they will not even try."

"That is true, very true."

"But, on the other hand, if they know that you have this policy of nonviolence with no exceptions, they will try to see how far they can get."

"That is very true."

"This brings me to the core problem we have at Nri. We cannot manage our own people because they know we have weaknesses in our system. There is absolutely nothing wrong in having a group of young men fully trained to fight and defend our people. Whenever I bring it up, our people tell me that we are peacemakers and that it will be a bad example to Igbo people to raise an army. What is the sense in making peace today when you are not around tomorrow to make more peace. My philosophy about it is that a peacemaker should have a white eagle feather in his right hand and a big stick in his left hand. Our people already have white eagle feathers on their heads but there is no big stick."

"This is not a conflict; it is a balance. We have just declared a war on Uwa men, and we have nothing to fight them with. Do you know that those men could march in tomorrow and kill everyone, including our own King? A good peacemaker should himself be the strongest, not only spiritually, but also intellectually and physically. We try to make peace among the Igbo people, and every Igbo family could march in and defeat our people any time they choose to. They have not done that only out of respect for what we stand for. But, right now, we stand for nothing. The most respected among us are dealing with thieves."

"But it does not end there. We are not providing a good example for the Igbo people. Do you know that some crazy Uwa people could march into Igbo land and make us all their slaves? So we are not only making ourselves weak, but also the Igbo people who look up to us."

"It looks like I must come here more often."

"Only on one condition—that you bring me a big cow each time you come," Ichie Idika joked.

"You are truly the Father of a Giant. And you deserve whatever your son can afford."

"I thought you said you have many questions?"

"Yes, I do, as a matter of fact, but I will ask a couple more and then save the rest for next time."

"That will be fine with me."

"Igwe Nwadike, may his heart rest well, used to say that the only thing a human being owes to another is fairness. But I never heard him define fairness. How do we know what fairness is?"

"That is an incomplete statement. He was giving us the short version, thinking that everyone in Nri already knew the complete sentence. He did not coin the phrase, but our elders did. That is exactly our problem in Nri.

We give our children the short version of a thought, and we think that they already know the rest, but they will grow up misinterpreting it. Our people believe in nonviolence, but I can assure you that is not the original idea. If we ask questions, we will find out that something is missing from that thought. Our elders used to say: 'The only thing a human being owes another is fairness. But don't ask me what is fairness because it is as large and complex as all Igbo and all Uwa land put together, and I have not been to all Uwa land so I cannot tell you.'"

"So you see how the short version can be misinterpreted by someone who does not know the whole statement. I am glad that you asked this particular question because I think it is part of, if not, our core problem. The first part of the phrase, 'The only thing a human being owes another is fairness,' tells us that we are not free because we owe this debt, right? But the second part tells us that we don't know the description of this debt. So how can you pay when you don't know how much you owe? You have to keep exploring all Uwa land and all Igbo land so that you can understand and describe them. You have to know and understand your neighbors completely before you can be fair to them. So when we tell our children or immigrants the first part, they think it is that simple and stop exploring. You see how it can cause problems?

"I can see that. I can see that clearly. Which brings me to my last question, for my head is already full. What would a perfect earth look like? I think that I already know your answer based on your last one, but I already had the question in mind so I might as well ask it."

"You are right, I have already answered it. You have to understand all your neighbors and their natures before you can know what a perfect earth would be like. When I say your neighbors, I don't mean just your human neighbors. I mean all animals and plants and the wind and the stars and so on. You have to understand their nature and composition first. But I can give you a hint. On a perfect earth, a victim would try his accused and be able to deliver a perfect judgment. The accused would be able to try himself and give a perfect judgment. He would not cheat himself or the victim."

Erike scratched his head

"What I am trying to say to you, my friend, is this. In an ideal earth, there will be no victims because there will be no offender. Everyone will understand each other perfectly well."

Erike could hardly contain his own laughter. "That is absolutely impossible. How could that be? Is it possible? Isn't it impossible?"

Ichie Idika simply shrugged.

"I think I should go home now! I have to go now!"

THIRTY-TWO

Ugocha Nwoye

One year had passed since Ezu had led the Ubaka brothers and their followers out of Nri. It was common knowledge at Nri that, after four day's journey, they had settled in a rich virgin forest. They called themselves Umu Adagbe after their original village in Nri. But that was the only information that most people at Nri agreed on. The rest of the story had different versions, and each version had different sub-versions. The most outrageous one was that Ezu had declared himself Eze Nri and that he was training some Uwa men to attack Nri land. Another popular story was that Ezu and his followers had become so rich that all the wealth in Nri could not match theirs. But other versions were not so kind. The most malicious one was that Ezu and all the other Ubaka brothers were dead except for their last born. They had all been killed by "Nri Menri," the collective spirit of departed Nri kings. So, after a full year, Ugocha Nwoye decided it was appropriate to visit with his good friend to see what had really become of him.

Ugocha Nwoye and his men crossed a creek and were climbing a small hill that would lead them into Umu-Adagbe when they heard voices and saw movements in the forest. Then a figure emerged from the forest. He was big and tall, bald, and naked except for the waist cloth that reached his knees and was open on both sides. His body, including his bald head, was covered with white chalk. In his right hand, he held a long shiny spear that was even taller than he was. There was nothing ceremonial about his spear or the look on his face. He looked angry and approached them without uttering a sound.

"Nshi! Wa Nshi!"

Ugocha Nwoye looked to the other side of the trail and saw many creatures who looked the same as the one in front of him. One of them came out of the bush and approached Ugocha Nwoye. He was not as tall as the first man.

"Yes! Nwa Nri, that's us. Do you know Ezu? Ezu?"

"Kao! Kao!!" Ugocha Nwoye could not understand this response, but the man's hand gesture seemed to be telling the others to wait, so they stayed put. All of the creatures stood up and came out of the bush. Ugocha Nwoye looked again at the giant they had first seen. The man was only a few footsteps away and looked even more angry at the mention of Ezu.

"Gaduooo!"

"Gadu!" yelled the one who had spoken to them.

"Haa! Haa!!" They heard from a distance. Then there was a familiar movement in the bush. Whatever or whoever it was was riding a horse and coming very fast. In a matter of quick-moments, the rider appeared on a black horse, and he, too, held a spear in his hand.

"Wa Nshi. What do you want here?" He spoke in commercial Igbo.

"We come to see Ezu," replied Ugocha Nwoye.

"Haa! Ezu. Do you come in peace?"

"We come in peace. We have no spears like you people!" Ugocha Nwoye said with hand gestures to be dramatic.

This must have seemed funny because the man showed his teeth. Then he said something to his men.

"Five of them will escort you to his place. Remember, Ezu wants no trouble! We live trouble. Plenty trouble!"

"Haa!" agreed another. "Plenty trouble!"

"Haa! Plenty trouble!" shouted the rest.

"We live trouble!" shouted the big man, raising his spear.

"Haa! Plenty trouble!" responded the rest.

"We live trouble!"

"Haa! Plenty trouble!

The men continued chanting as they left for Ezu's place. The group passed through two more security posts before they finally reached the large compound which their escorts said was Ezu's place.

"It is like going to see Chineke, God Himself," someone said. But the greatest surprise was that until they saw Ezu himself, they did not see a familiar face, not even a scarified face. The men who had met the travelers had marks on their faces and seemed to understand some Igbo, but they did not speak it. Ugocha Nwoye had doubts that he and his party had come to the right place, but they could only assume it was Umu-Adagbe. They must have waited an hour before "Ezu" came out, except that it was not really Ezu, but his younger brother Omile. Then Ugocha Nwoye learned that Ezu was no longer Ezu, but had made himself Eze Umu-Adagbe, and Omile had been ordained Ezu of Umu-Adagbe.

It would be another long journey to get to the real Ezu's place. The men also learned that Umu Adagbe had six villages. One village was called Ubaka, and the other five villages were each named after one of the Ubaka brothers. Each of the Ubaka brothers was Isi-Ozo (head) of his village, and Ezu was the overall leader, Eze. Ugocha Nwoye decided to address Ezu with the title he was known for. Even though he was no longer Ezu at Nri, Ugocha decided to still accord him that honor. That would be fair, he decided. But when Ezu came out and everyone else was hailing him as "Igwe! Igwe! !" accompanied with at least three different bells that were ringing left and right, and at least one bullhorn trumpet wailing, it became almost impossible not to call him Igweee.

"Igweee!" Ugocha Nwoye hailed, partly to tease and partly to not appear hostile to their host. Ezu was more than happy to see him and did not hide it.

"Ozo Dimma! (Ozo, the Goodman!)," Ezu called him.

"Igweeeee!!" Ugocha Nwoye called again with both hands raised in surrender. This time it was meant as a tease because it was loud and stretched out.

"So you heard," Ezu said.

"I had to come and see for myself," Ugocha Nwoye said as he reached out to embrace his old pal. But Ezu extended his white horsetail.

"Igwe of Adagbe does not shake hands or embrace anyone anymore. You do understand, right?"

"Completely! Totally, Lineage-Boy."

"So nice to see you. So nice," Ezu said.

"We have heard so many tales with so many variations. And I said that I just had to come and see for myself."

"You did well, my friend. You did well. But I must confess that I expected you a long time ago. It has been more than a year, and you did not care to ask if your friend was dead or alive."

"Believe me, I knew that Ezu was alive and well."

Ezu gave out his signature loud, confident laugh.

"You know, after your people left, everyone wanted to lie low for awhile and see which way the wind was going to blow. Everyone was watching me, you know. It was terrible. I had to be quiet for awhile. Surely you understand."

"I understand. I completely understand. How is the wise man doing these days?"

Ugocha Nwoye did not want to respond, especially in front of his servants.

"What a nice place you have carved out for yourself."

"It is okay. How is the wise man of Nri doing?"

"Must we get into that now? Everyone is good."

The two men understood each other, and Ezu invited him to the inner reception area.

"I don't have to ask how you are doing. I have seen for myself. It is amazing," Ugocha Nwoye said as the two men settled down.

"You have seen nothing. We lived in darkness at Nri. This place is total freedom. You have your own little kingdom, and you run it exactly the way you like."

"Who are those Uwa men you have working for you?"

"They are warriors from the Bantu tribe. Actually they sold this land to me. They provide me with security, and I make them very rich and very wise. They live for war and they are good at it. For them, to die on a battlefield is priceless."

"I have heard about Bantu warriors, but I have never seen one until now," said Ugocha Nwoye as he looked at the other two men in the room. They looked healthy and wicked with their skull heads and loin cloths. Though they could kill with their bare hands, each had a pair of bronze swords at their left side and held a long bronze spear in their right hand. He wondered if these men could hear their conversation, and Ezu seemed to read his mind.

"They are my personal guards and can understand commercial Igbo, but not the real Nri dialect. The Bantu are painfully honest people, but don't ever cross them. They neither forgive nor forget."

"That is good to know," Ugocha Nwoye said and decided to change the topic. "How is your family? I have not seen much of them."

"I have a bigger family now, and so we have a different arrangement. I took three more wives. All are Bantu women. It was like a bond between me and the Bantu tribe. So I decided to build a full compound for each of my wives. Each one lives with her children. I live completely on my own in my own world. It is a Bantu warrior system."

"Well, whatever works for you. Everyone is doing well at Nri."

"How is 'Ike-kete-Olie' doing these days?"

"That is our King you are insulting."

"But that is what he is. That is what he is. You know, I brought that man out of a half fallen and leaking hut and gave him a good haircut. I gave him a bath and washed his hands and invited him to dine with the rich and famous. What did he do? He turned around and stabbed me on my ikenga (right) palm."

Ugocha Nwoye could not stop laughing. He was slightly offended when Ezu called his King derogatory names, but he quickly remembered that he was talking to Ezu. After a year, he had almost forgotten that Ezu was well known for his loud mouth. Nri people had big hearts, but their mouths were as big as their hearts. Ezu seemed to have one and not the other. First he had called Okoye the wise man and then Ike-kete-Olie, one who became rich by using his muscles instead of his brain or one who became rich the hard way. Ugocha Nwoye was no longer offended once he remembered the old days. Ezu had always loved to host parties for rich people only, and he was always the life of every party. He liked to talk about poor people and how sorry he felt for them. He once said that poverty was an infectious illness and poor people must be avoided at all costs. But the story he told over and over again was about some pauper who came one morning and asked if he could marry one of his own daughters.

With Ezu one could hardly separate fact from fiction. He always said that the man, whose name he would never mention, had came to his house one morning with three of his clansmen. After many long statements and proverbs, he hinted that he was interested in marrying Ezu's second daughter. Ezu did not say yes or no; instead he asked his second wife, the mother of the daughter in question, to prepare very good food for their early morning visitors. After their guests ate, he gave them an exotic drink named konya. They had finished eating and drinking when Ezu spoke.

"You said that you want to marry the daughter of Ezu Nri?" he said.

The young man answered in the affirmative and instantly sat erect.

"Then I have another question for you, my son. Have you ever had this type of food or drink before?"

The young man shook his head and complimented the food again as his clansmen watched.

"Then what do you expect to feed my daughter when she comes to your house?"

There was complete silence in the big reception area. Ezu broke the silence that he himself had created.

"Well, I hope you enjoyed the food and drink because that is all you are going to get."

There was always a big outburst of laughter after each telling of the story. In some later versions, Ezu included that he gave the young man a big basket full of yams and a hen for all his trouble.

"Maybe he would become a good yam farmer or a famous chicken raiser with that," he would say. In some other versions, the chicken was actually a she-goat.

A half hour after his horsetail handshake with his old friend, Ugocha Nwoye had yet to be served a kolanut. All he had in abundance were name-callings and long tales. He decided to relax and let himself be entertained.

"I wanted to teach 'Ike-Fuo-Uzo,' (power-missed-road) a lesson after we settled here," Ezu said at one point. "Power-missed-road" meant that the authority of leadership had missed its intended destination and had accidentally gone to the wrong man.

"I wanted to take a handful of Bantu warriors and go back to Nri and teach the wise man a lesson, but I did not want to insult the motherland. Nri is still our holy land, and I did not want to insult it."

"You really thought about that?" asked Ugocha Nwoye scratching his head. This was one of the rumors that had circulated at Nri at one point.

"Of course I did. But I will tell you the real truth, Nwa Nnaa. It was my destiny to come to this place. I saw a vision many years ago. In that vision, I was told that I would lead some Nri people, not all, to a new land. And from that land would blossom a new civilization. I would lead them to one that was more practical than what we have at Nri. At first I laughed the idea off as a joke. I thought that it was some bad dream, never to come true. But when this happened, everything fell into place."

Ugocha Nwoye learned forward. "A new civilization," he said.

It was not a question. It was one of those "tell me more," statements. At last, here was something he could take home to Nri to share.

❦ ❦ ❦

Their second day was as entertaining as the first. Ezu had promised a tour of his new found empire that would soon grow into a great civilization. He made good on his promise. Ezu and Ugocha Nwoye had talked for three hours the day before with Ezu doing most of the talking and asking all of the questions. Ugocha Nwoye and his men had been taken to a very large compound which they learned was just for visitors. There had been several guests' quarters he was told. One by one, the rest of the Ubaka brothers came to visit him, but Ugocha and his group were still able to go to bed early enough to leave for sightseeing at dawn the second day.

First was a tour of Ezu's compound, which was like a whole village itself. His wives' compounds surrounded Ezu's. There was a big temple and a public square built after the Nri model, but they were far bigger and more expensive looking. The major roads were paved with stones, and there were more forests than farmland. The building architecture was far more spacious than that in Nri. In fact, everything about the place was made to impress. Ezu and Ugocha Nwoye rode side by side on horseback and talked the whole time. Ezu shared his plans for the place. Ugocha Nwoye noticed that farming was not in Ezu's plans for his civilization. Instead he talked about building the largest trading center the Igbo people and their Uwa neighbors had ever seen. Making peace and spirituality were also not in his plan.

After a three-hour tour of the six villages, Ugocha Nwoye was ready to go back to their quarters. But Ezu had other things in mind. At first, Ugocha thought they were returning to Ezu's compound, but when they started climbing a small hill, he knew they were heading to new territory, for he could recall no such hill on their tour.

"Is this also part of your place?" he asked Ezu.

"Not really, but I want to show you something."

Ugocha did not want to press his friend, assuming this was meant to be a surprise. When they reached the top of the hill, there was no other place to go, for what lay before them was a cliff. Ezu, who was leading the way, stopped first. He told his bodyguards, and Ugocha Nwoye's men, to wait for them. Then he took Ugocha Nwoye some forty footsteps to the left where they could talk privately. Now they were facing the cliff. What lay beyond was nothing but thick uninhabited forest.

"You see this land?" Ezu asked as he pointed to the territory beginning at the foot of the cliff and extending to what seemed like infinity. "You can have that land if you want to leave Nri. It would be nice to have someone like you close by."

"Who owns it?" Ugocha Nwoye asked. Not that he really wanted to know, but he asked in order to gain time, because he did not want to offend his host by rejecting his offer immediately.

"The Bantu people claim they own it, but they don't really use it for anything. I just need to say the word, and they will give it to you. You can pay them whatever you want."

"I could never leave Nri, the Motherland. You know that."

"I used to say that. But if you think about it, Nri is becoming overcrowded and half of the so-called Motherland is made of immigrants. It is also becoming very unstable. Only people who have foresight can position themselves properly before the obvious happens. You could play with that land and build your own kingdom just the way you want it. It would not prevent you from going back to Nri whenever you felt like it."

"I will think about it and get back to you," Ugocha Nwoye said, in order to delay his refusal. He was quite sure that he could never leave

Nri. Then it occurred to him that Ezu had been feeling lonely and needed company. He was right. Despite all the space and what seemed like a big empire in the making, Ezu was in fact missing the Nri community. The rest of the Ubaka brothers were no match for Ezu. He had their complete loyalty, but they could not give him something he craved, to be with his equals. Ezu liked to be challenged. Back at Nri, there were at least another fifty men who had the same will and ambitions he had, and those were men he had frequently invited to parties. He loved hanging around those people. They knew what he did and sometimes could outsmart him, but he loved the challenges they posed because it kept him sharp. But in his little kingdom, whatever he said went unchallenged. Most of the time he liked this, but, sometimes, he felt something was missing.

"I hope you think quickly about it, because it could go to someone else. Someone else from the motherland who came here before you asked me about it. I will not mention names. But I told him that I would inquire and see who owns it."

"It is a good piece of land. I will get back to you," said Ugocha Nwoye.

Ezu was not a fool. He knew that Ugocha Nwoye was not interested in his offer of free land. His lack of enthusiasm was written all over him. He would not have been interested himself if he had not had the problem at Nri. So, that evening, on the second day of their six-day visit, Ezu sent two men to Nri ahead of Ugocha Nwoye's return.

❦ ❦ ❦

After a year of finger pointing and reflection since Ezu and his people had left, things were beginning to get back to normal at Nri. The people had finally come to terms with Ezu and the Ubaka brothers being out of the picture. There were even talks about who would become the next Ezu Nri. But these temporarily stalled because Okoye wanted a higher spiritual standard for major positions like Ezu. And he also wanted less lavish spending on those positions. He even wanted whoever would be the next Ezu, and other positions, to go through some of the rigorous rituals that the Eze Nri went through. For instance, he wanted a six-month isolation and self-discovery period for each of the positions. That, of course, automatically eliminated most of the Oganiru cowry-bags who could not miss running their businesses for even a single week. So potential candidates were hesitant. Okoye was losing no sleep over it. Actually he was beginning to feel confident that changes could be made to recover the vision and reputation of the Nri people.

When Ugocha Nwoye arrived back at Nri, the Ozo council was waiting for him. He could not deny that he had visited the self-exiled former Ezu Nri with whom all Ozo men were forbidden to have contact. He could not deny it because the Ozo council had a lot of details about his visit. Many voices were raised and chests beaten at the council, but their decision boiled down to a big fine. Ugocha Nwoye gladly paid.

But Ezu was not done with his good friend yet. Ugocha Nwoye was one of the few people Ezu respected and genuinely liked, and he had something that Ezu would kill to have. It was not his money which he had plenty of, but his physical charisma. Ugocha was boyishly handsome, well built and tall with a smile and manners that could melt even an angry heart. Ugocha Nwoye had no enemies in or outside of Nri. He did not have a big ego and was always willing to apologize when he was wrong or forgive when he was offended. One could send him to a big nation to mingle and present a good image. But he was also a member of the Oganiru men and Ezu's closest friend. Ezu reasoned that if he could get Ugocha Nwoye to relocate, then Ugocha Nwoye would become an instant magnet for others to defect. So, since his first attempt to motivate his good friend had failed, he decided to try something else.

Barely two months after Ugocha Nwoye's visit, two men mysteriously appeared to see the Igwe Okoye Nweri. They were ready to testify and prove that Ugocha Nwoye had done business in the past with a man who dealt with Uwa men. Okoye referred them to the Ozo council. That was enough motivation for Ugocha Nwoye. He had not been the first to visit Ezu at his new home, and he certainly had not been the last. There were many others. Why was he the only person to be caught and punished? He knew of at least two others, apart from Ezu and himself, who had dealt with the same man and even more frequently. Why was he the only one mysteriously discovered after more than two years of not dealing with Udukwe. There was only one conclusion. Okoye wanted to destroy him or run him out as he had Ezu. And he was ready to dig up dirt from Ugo-cha Nwoye's past to do it. Maybe he was "power-missed-road," after all. Maybe his good friend Ezu was right all along.

Once again, anxiety mounted at Nri as Ugocha Nwoye's trial started. The Ozo men were evenly divided, and, at first, were slightly more in fa-vor of Ugocha Nwoye, until Ezu heard that his target was getting off the hook. Ezu then unleashed whatever loyalists he had left at Adagbe Village in Nri. The Ozo men of Adagbe Village argued that double standards were being used. How could one of their own be given the maximum penalty, and Ugocha Nwoye be about to be set free for the same offense? Maybe there were hidden rules in Nri they didn't know about. No one had an answer for their accusation. In the end, Ugocha Nwoye received the maximum penalty for his offenses. He paid a heavy fine and lost his Ozo and Nze priesthood titles. Unlike Ezu, Ugocha Nwoye accepted his fate. He paid all his fines and peacefully surrendered his anklet to the Ozo council and other properties of Ozo men he had. He seemed to take his misfortune gracefully, drawing a lot of sympathy. Maybe that was why the crisis that followed was much deeper than that of Ezu and the other Ubaka brothers. Also, when Ugocha Nwoye accepted his friend's offer to move, the decision was not quick, but gradual. He took his time, and ev-eryone knew what was happening but could do nothing about it. He was not seeking revenge. Ugocha simply wanted a change of atmosphere. He certainly could not have predicted the impact it would have at Nri, or he would have given it a second thought.

THIRTY-THREE

Journey Man

After Ugocha Nwoye moved out of Nri for good, what followed was nearly chaos. Less than two years later, twenty more Ozo men, all from the Oganiru group followed suit. Suddenly it had become fashionable to leave the Motherland. What had been unimaginable three years before, now had become a trend among the cowry-bags of Oganiru. Many others were adventurers looking for a new place to locate, or they had found one and were simply waiting for the right moment to move. But the trend was limited to Oganiru men and their followers. It was as though someone had pulled a mat out from under the authority of the Nri kingdom. The morale of those who were left behind was the lowest it had ever been, and it kept plunging. It was not uncommon to overhear a woman in the market asking another, "Guess who is moving out to Uwa land now?"

In two years, Igwe Okoye Nweri had had three partial strokes, but Okoye Rope was not about to give up without a fight. The fight was not with Ezu or anyone who had left or was planning to leave. In fact, he was not about to fight Nri people, Igbo people, or Uwa men. He just wanted some answers from the ones who had chosen him—the ancestral spirits—so he sent for Oduh, who had become a very old man in less than three years.

Okoye's favorite snack was dried fish and his favorite fish was catfish. Oduh was one of the very few people outside of Okoye's immediate household from whom Okoye could accept edible items and actually eat them. This had more to do with spiritual policy than with trust. So, this morning, Oduh brought him a small basket of dried fish. Oduh's only wife had personally prepared it. Okoye thanked him as always and sang praises to his wife as always. He and Oduh and whoever was around usually ate half or even the whole thing before their meeting was over. But this day, the two men were alone.

"Sometimes, I wish . . . I wish I were dead," Okoye said as he ate a piece of fish. He was looking outside and away from Oduh. He was almost talking to himself.

"Don't say that," Oduh intervened.

"How could all this be happening under my watch?"

"You have done nothing wrong. We have done nothing wrong. We are not the ones supporting Uwa men by purchasing stolen goods from them. Don't make it your fault."

"I know all that, but I still cannot understand why it had to happen under my care. Sometimes I think that it is happening because I was not an Ozo priest before assuming the Eze Nri position. You know that there has never been one before me who was not."

"That could be, but then, you did not have much say in those things. Maybe all of the capable Ozo men were so corrupt they were not chosen. I once told you that our ancestors had seen something very good in you. You must never compromise who you are in order to suit anyone. The spirits who see above and beyond any of us chose you. So we all look up to you for guidance. If anyone does not like the direction you are leading us, they can find their own way as some are doing. But you do have the anointing to lead us."

Okoye hissed. "Your reasoning is right. But you cannot help feeling a big loss in your heart."

"That is right. It is like a bad marriage. All your senses tell you that it has to end, but your heart cannot help feeling a deep loss. Our people say that the snake has long gone and the movements we see in the bush are only the plants in its trail."

"I will be going on a retreat in four days," Okoye said. He knew that what Oduh had said was all true, but he was not the one living the nightmare. Okoye was the one deeply feeling the pain. He must find some answers.

"I was thinking of that myself. Would you like me to join you?"

"This will be a very personal journey for me."

"How long will you be gone?"

"I will start with twelve days. It may be longer, but a lot depends on how soon I can get what I am looking for," Okoye replied.

As usual the two men chatted about how things should be handled while Okoye was gone. Oduh usually spent most of his time at the palace while Okoye was absent so he could respond to emergencies.

❧ ❧ ❧

Poor Ikenna, Okoye's personal assistant. Only four years ago he had been looking up to Ezu as his ultimate role model. But a lot had happened since then. He had first set eyes on Ezu when he was only seven years old. That was seven years ago when Ezu's mother had died. After her burial there was a seven week feast which was really a show of wealth. For twenty-eight days after the burial, Ezu cooked and fed everyone who set foot in his big compound. The food and wine were varied and the best of their kind. Several groups entertained each day. Ikenna even saw some masquerades he had never seen during the Year-Counting Ceremony. He must have gone to Ezu's house every one of the twenty-eight days. On one of those visits, he saw Ezu in his prime for the first time.

Ezu was addressing the crowd. Ikenna did not really remember what Ezu was saying, but his sense of humor stood out. He seemed to entertain the crowd with whatever he said. He spoke with an unquestionable confidence, and one could feel the connection he made with his audience. Ikenna could see in people's eyes how they respected and adored this man. Ikenna was himself a dwarf, and he, too, lived in Adagbe Village. After seeing Ezu work his audience, Ikenna concluded that when he grew up, he would be like this man. From that day forward, he did not miss any activities at Ezu's compound, and there were many. The more he encountered Ezu, the more he liked the man. His mother had once caught him staring like a goat at Ezu. She grabbed him by the ear and took him home.

"It is an act of disrespect to stare at an adult, especially Ezu himself, in that manner," his mother warned him.

But only three years after his first encounter with Ezu, Ikenna's dream of being like Ezu was destroyed. Igwe Nwadike had died and a new man had been selected. It was after the selection had been made Ikenna had heard the successor's name for the very first time. Ikenna was just returning home with his senior brother Emenike. They had been sweeping the village square all morning, and, afterwards, they had gone around collecting fines from the parents of those who came late or missed the chore without a good reason. Most of the time the brothers and their peers kept all of the money, but, once in a while, they took a little of it to buy treats for the participants and shared the rest with everyone, depending on their needs, at the end of the year. Sometimes they used most of the money to organize a new masquerade. This particular day they did the whole circle.

First, they swept the public square, then they collected fines, and then they bought small treats for the participants. They bought treats especially when the turnout was low and the fines collected were high. The rumor that treats were shared would always guarantee a huge turnout the next time around, which would be one week (four days) later. This time, they voted to buy igbah, (pressed bean cake). Every decision they made was by vote, although sometimes bullies intimidated the little ones to vote one way or another. But Ikenna always enjoyed the team spirit of his peers. Igbah happened to be his favorite treat, and he had plenty of fun eating his share. Life was good.

Life was good for Ikenna until he and Emenike came home that early afternoon. His father and two men were waiting for him. He knew both of the men, but one he knew particularly well. Both were from Adagbe Village. He knew Ideka Okoye well because he was a friend of his father. Akabuko, the other man, he knew just by his Nze name. The two boys wanted to sneak into their mother's hut, but Ikenna was not so lucky. His father called to him, which was very unusual. His father favored his senior brother and usually gave any directions through him. On this afternoon, his senior brother walked on while Ikenna went to answer his father's call. As he entered his father's obu, Ikenna greeted him first by calling him by his Nze title name. Then he accorded the same respect to their two visitors who smiled and called Ikenna by his father's title name. A boy had to answer his father's nickname or titled name until he was mature enough to get his own.

"Do you know this man?" his father asked as he pointed to one of their visitors.

"But he called us by name," Akabuko said. "I am very surprised that he knew my name. Children these days don't usually know the names of their distant village members. But your children are different. They know everyone's name."

"That is because his boys do not miss the village square sweeping exercise," Ideka Okoye said. "When they go around collecting fines they learn every family's name. Do you know that when one of my boys was sick and did not go to the sweeping exercise, they came to my compound to collect fines? I was not at home, and my wife pleaded with them that the boy was truly sick. They argued that the boy should have been in bed if he was so sick; instead he was outside playing. Do you know that while other children were still debating what they should take from our house as a fine, Ikenna was already busy loosening the biggest goat in my compound? My wife quickly paid the money to save the goat. Those children are tough."

Both Ikenna's father and Akabuko began laughing.

"When I got home, my wife was still angry about how disrespectful they were, especially Ikenna. But I told my son that whenever Ikenna fails to come to the sweeping exercise, you must be the one to take a big goat from his father's house. Do you know what my son told me? He told me that Ikenna and his brother did not miss the exercise even if they were sick. He told me that they would rather show up and not do anything than not show up at all. Your boys are well raised, especially Ikenna," Ideka Okoye concluded.

Ikenna's father cleared his throat. He was genuinely flattered by his friend's compliments. Ikenna was an exceptional child.

"Do you know who our new King will be?" his father asked Ikenna.

"Okoye Nweri," Ikenna replied, "but his nickname is Ochiagha and some people call him Okoye Udo. I have never seen him, but I have heard a lot about him. He is from Nri-Agu Village."

The three men exchanged looks and started laughing. They were impressed that the boy knew so much. Actually Ikenna knew more about Okoye and would have continued, but was cut off by their laughter. He thought he must have said something wrong, so he stopped.

"You must never call him Okoye Udo," his father said to him. "He does not like it. It is a name his peers used to call him when he was your age, but he has outgrown it."

"That is very funny, Okoye Udo," Idika Okoye said as he repeated the name and started laughing again.

"They know more than you think. You must be careful what you say in their presence," Akabuko added.

His father was still trying to figure out how to break the bad news when Ikenna asked the question, "So are we going to see him?"

"That is why these men are here. As descendents of Adama, we bear the task to provide a personal servant to the new King, and our elders have selected you."

Ikenna knew a lot for his age, but he did not know exactly what this meant. He knew he must be special to have been chosen out of many, but he did not know the level of responsibility involved. The details were left to his mother to tell him. She had been crying secretly for the five days since she had gotten the news.

Nominating a personal assistant to Eze Nri was the exclusive responsibility of the Adama Clan high priests. Each priest must secretly nominate an intelligent, honest, and conscientious young man whose family was in good standing. He must be a dwarf between the ages of eight and twelve years old. There were many dwarf families in Adama. If more than one candidate was nominated, as was most often the case, all Adama priests had to decide by vote which one to select. The Igwe's personal servant and high priest were the only staff not selected by the Igwe himself. Also, the personal servant was the only attendant selected prior to Igwe's one-year isolation before he was even installed as Eze Nri. The servant was the only person who would see Igwe on a daily basis during the isolation period.

After his selection and acceptance, Ikenna took an oath promising to treat any information obtained during his service to Igwe as confidential and not to be shared with anyone, especially his own biological family. He also pledged his ultimate loyalty to the Igwe. He swore to die if that was what it would take to protect his master. After taking the oath, he left his family and became the Igwe's adopted son. But he was more than a son. He was the only person with unlimited access to Igwe. Even Igwe's biological children and his wives would sometimes have to seek Ikenna's permission before they could see Igwe. The position of personal servant was very privileged, and it was not uncommon for powerful men and women in Nri to seek favors from him. But there were responsibilities almost as tedious as those the King carried. Ikenna's involved a lot of physical errands, but he was equal to that task. It was the emotional ones that he was not prepared for. Being that close to another causes one to feel what the other feels—sadness, loneliness, and happiness. The past four years had been rocky for Igwe Okoye Nweri, and they had also taken a toll on Ikenna.

Ikenna was a hard worker and so was Okoye. They were both perfectionists, so they were meant for each other and had bonded during the one-year isolation period. During that time, Ikenna matured spiritually, even more than most adults. He had found a new hero in Okoye, but he still thought about Ezu sometimes and respected him as well. So, when his former hero and his new hero fell out, the young soul was devastated. After Okoye explained to him what had happened, it did not take Ikenna long to recover. But he was still disappointed in Ezu. A lot had happened after the initial problem, and it had been an emotional up-and-down for the now fourteen-year-old.

🐦 🐦 🐦

As soon as Ikenna stepped into the small hut, he knew that something was wrong because although Okoye was still breathing, he was in the same position he had been in the day before. He was on his back, his left leg straight, but his right leg folded and leaning on his left leg. His head was tilted to the left, his mouth wide open, and his eyes shut. His left arm was straight at his side and his right hand was crossed on his lower chest.

It was the eighth day of Igwe Nweri's retreat, and Ikenna was the only one who had seen him since the morning of the day before when he had found him lying in this position. Ikenna had brought some clean clothing, refilled the jar with fresh water, and left Okoye some garden egg leaves and pulp. That was the only thing he would eat during his retreat. Three things were unusual. He had never seen Igwe Nweri still sleeping at that time of the morning. He was usually meditating or chanting. Second, Okoye was one of those people who slept like a dog. The smallest noise woke him up. When Ikenna entered in the morning, he usually tapped gently on the wooden door before opening it. If the tap did not wake Okoye, the squeaky noise of the door would. Also, Okoye was a careful man, and Ikenna had never caught him with his mouth open as he slept. Yet now his mouth was wide open, and even his private area was slightly exposed. Ikenna was tempted to wake him up so that he could at least close his mouth, but he decided against doing that. *Give him an hour, he will change position and probably close his mouth*, he had thought.

"Nna-anyi! (Our Father), Nna-anyi," Ikenna called several times while he shaking Okoye's body to wake him up. The only effect was that his breathing stopped momentarily and then was less heavy. He was not snoring, but Ikenna could hear him breathe. But when he tried to wake Okoye up, his breathing was no longer audible though Ikenna could see his stomach rising and falling. His body was quite warm, but that was the only sign of life in him. Ikenna repositioned Okoye's body, straightening his arms and legs and neck. *The stroke must have happened again.* He must get some help fast!

Ikenna was heading to the chief priest's quarters when he heard a voice coming from Igwe's quarters. So he went there instead.

Ichie Idika had made it his business to stay out of politics after Igwe Nwadike, his good friend, had moved on. For three years, he had done that well. But later events made him change his mind. First was Ezu, of all people, leaving and then Ezu's core allies following his trail. Ichie Idika saw a new beginning where others saw doom.

The kid is finally beginning to shake some termites off the wooden beacon of the house, he had thought to himself. But the kid had also had several strokes and mild heart attacks in a short period of time. Ichie Idika did what any patriotic and wise man would do. He ate his words and came out of hiding. He decided to make himself available, if for no other reason than to show the kid that he had Ichie's moral support. Ichie Idika was now 106 years old but still as strong as an eighty-year-old. He started hanging out at the palace at every opportunity he could get, and Okoye had already learned a few things from the wise, old man.

Ikenna did not know what to do when he saw the three men inside Igwe's quarters. He decided to tell the chief priest privately. So he called him outside and told him what he'd seen. But Ichie Idika and Oduh were good observers, and they knew something was wrong. It was written all over the boy's face and body. And they knew that whatever had happened likely had to do with the boy's master. With Ikenna leading the way, the chief priest was already heading towards the holy forest. Oduh and Ichie Idika followed closely behind.

"It is the Otunaka Aru (stroke) again, but this one is more serious," the chief priest announced after examining Okoye.

"Then we must call Ikuku, the herbal doctor, right away," Oduh suggested.

"Let me go and send someone," said the chief priest. "Meanwhile, you can get fresh ogilisi leaves and gently touch them to his arms and legs and, once in awhile, to his face. Ikuku had suggested that the last time he had a stroke. I will send someone right away."

Ikenna went to fetch the ogilisi leaves, and the chief priest sent for the herbal doctor.

Now Ichie had his chance to examine the kid who was lying in front of him on a bamboo bed. He opened Okoye's right eye and studied it. He put the back of his palm on Okoye's heart and studied it. He touched Okoye's neck and both hands and legs. He held each part for some time and studied it.

"This is not a stroke. In fact, it is not an illness," he said. "His spirit has simply left his body for some reason." He said it with so much assurance and confidence that Oduh did not argue with him.

"So what can we do now?"

"Not very much. In the old days, when our people were very spiritual, they could be in this state for days. It usually does not exceed the fourth day. It is the highest form of meditation, but it is very, very risky. It is usually induced by going for many days without food."

"Does it mean that we do nothing?"

"We can monitor his body, but his spirit is still strongly connected to his body. So it looks good right now. If we try to wake him up, his spirit might lose connection with his body, and it may never come back or it may come back in fragments. If he does not come around by tomorrow, we can try to feed him some liquid just to help his body. His spirit is in a very far place." Just then Ikenna came in with a bundle of ogilisi leaves.

Ichie was one of those people who did not say something with such confidence unless he was absolutely sure of it, but something kept asking Oduh, *What if this man is wrong?*

Just as they were beginning to worry, on the morning of the fourth day, Okoye sneezed loudly. Then he started smiling even before he opened his eyes.

"Ikenga!" he called as he tried to get up, but his body was weak even though his spirit was as strong as ever.

"Don't try to get up," Oduh said and rushed to his side. "Just lie still for awhile."

"Welcome journey man, welcome journey man," Ichie Idika said as he reached for his tobacco container.

Two days later, Okoye sat in his private reception area with the two old men, each old enough to be his father. They were the only ones in the room.

"Thank you for honoring my invitation," Okoye started. "I feel obligated to share with you what happened to me and what I saw for myself during my isolation period."

Ikenna was in the next room, listening too.

THIRTY-FOUR

Nri Future

"I did not eat for seven days. I drank only water. I fooled even Ikenna who brought me food. I emptied the plates in the toilet pit. I needed answers from the spirit, and I was willing to die unless I got some answers. On the eighth day, I must have meditated for half a day without stopping. I invoked the names of Igwe Nwadike and all the Igwe before him. I was overpowered by a tickling sensation all over my body. I did not even know how I got to the bed because I had been on the floor. This sensation became so powerful that my body could no longer stand it. Then I saw a ball of light. It was like looking directly at the sun on a bright, sunny day. At first I could see nothing but the brightness of this light. After what seemed several moments, I noticed that what looked like a ball of light was actually a figure. It took more time for me to recognize the figure as Nri-Menri Nwadike. Dazzling light radiated from his body. Then I realized that I was having a vision."

"What do you want of me?" He asked.

"You know what I want," I said. "I have lots of questions and I need some answers."

"Follow me then," he said, as he turned and led the way through what appeared to be a long hallway in a big temple. We entered what seemed like a large temple that had no visible walls. There I saw a semicircle of light. As my eyes got used to the hall, the semicircle became balls of light. And then the balls of light became figures that looked like Nri-Menri Nwadike. All were dressed in our traditional Igbo robes. Their faces were scarified like Nri-Menri Nwadike's. They sat on what

319

seemed to be stones, but even the stones radiated light of their own. Each figure had what looked like an Nri log of justice, lying in front of them. These objects glowed with a different kind of bright light—a red light. Before Nri-Menri Nwadike spoke again, I already knew who the figures were.

"This is the Nri-Menri council," Nri-Menri Nwadike announced to me. He was standing by my left side, and we were now in the center of the semicircle. Nri-Menri Nwadike moved a few steps from me before he spoke again.

"This is Okoye Udo," he said as he pointed at me. For a moment, I wanted to be angry. I wanted to yell at him, "That is not my name. I am Okoye Nweri! Igwe Okoye Nweri." But, instead, what overpowered me was amusement. I was amused that even these beings called me Okoye Udo. It occurred to me that I would never shake off that nickname. *Maybe it is a good name after all*, I thought.

"'He is the son of Nweri Nweke, the son of Nweke Anaedo, the son of Anaedo Nwana, the son of Nwana Okoye, the son of Okoye Edozie, the son of Edozie Alike, the son of Alike Udala, the son of Udala Ndibe, the son of Ndibe Nwankwo, the son of Nwankwo Ijedimma, the son of Ijedimma Iguedo, the son of Iguedo Nri, the son of Nri Eri. He is the current holder of Nne Offor Nri, and he has a question for the council.'"

"'You may ask your question, my son,' the figure in the middle of the semicircle said."

"Over the years, I had developed a mental picture of what ancient men would look like—old men with gray hair—confident-looking men who did not smile and had just enough time to get things done. Men who have no time for pounded yam. These men were not far off from that image. They were not mean, but they were serious looking. Though he did not introduce himself, somehow I knew instantly that the figure at center was Nri himself. For a split moment, I felt guilty for disturbing their peace. But then it occurred to me that they were the ones who had disturbed my peace. I had been a perfectly happy man minding my own business, smoking my tobacco, and drinking Konya when I felt like it. I had been a perfectly happy man going to Nkwo market and to scarification ceremonies when I felt like it. And then they came pushing down my walls and killing my livestock and making me and my entire family sick. Yes, I was a peaceful man until they disturbed my peace!"

"'Yes, I have lots of questions. But the one I am dying to have answered is why did you select me to lead Nri people and then pull the mat from under my feet?'"

"The one sitting at Nri's right hand spoke. He did not introduce himself, but I knew intuitively that he was Nri-Menri Ejiofor."

"'You have very little hand in what is happening at Nri. The Nri people were given knowledge to serve and educate all Igbo and all Uwa people, but they are using it for selfish ends. They made their choices long before you were born. You are just helping to make the consequences of their choices manifest themselves sooner. You are a perfect candidate for that job. We knew your temperament before we picked you. Nri-Menri Nwadike was the last intervention we sent, but the ears of the people were closed. So just be yourself and let things happen naturally.'"

"I had many more questions, but he had already answered all of them. I had really just wanted to know that what was happening was not my fault. And I had just learned that I had done nothing wrong. I wanted to know what I could do to help, and I had just learned that there was very little I could do to alter the course our people are taking. The counsel had answered all of my questions. So my next and last question was simply from curiosity."

"'So what will happen to our people? What will the future look like?' I asked."

"'Nri people will be scattered all over the earth. They will be scattered throughout Igbo and Uwa land. They will serve Igbo people and Uwa people, but they will be serving while bound in ropes. They will continue to serve while bound until they learn how to serve willingly. They are agents of peace, and until that is the priority of every Nri man and woman, they will continue to serve in ropes. They can only realize the glories reserved for them and them alone through their bondage.'"

"At this point, I had nothing more to say. I wanted to thank them and leave, but Big Father, Nri said, 'Since you want to know what the future will look like, Nri-Menri Nwadike, your host, will take you to the future and show you around.'"

"I thanked them very generously for relieving me of this burden."

༤ ༤ ༤

"I found myself standing in the middle of Nkwo market at Nri, but it looked nothing like the Nkwo market of our day. The market was nearly empty and the scanty commodities were all of a lower quality. The spirit of both buyers and sellers was very low. I did not hear the buzz of activity that is the signature of our Nkwo market. What I saw was another village market in Igbo land."

"'You said that this is the future?' I asked Igwe Nwadike. We were both in the flesh, posing as ordinary Igbo shoppers in the market. We wore no scarifications."

"'Yes, this is exactly six generations into the future from your time,' Igwe Nwadike assured me."

"So what happened to all of our people? Where did they go? Was there a war? A flood? A plague? What happened to the Nri people?"

"'Mass migration. Mass migration to the Igbo mainland and some Uwa lands.'"

"*Mass migration*, I repeated to myself."

"'Yes, mass migration,' he repeated. 'Most of the best and the brightest left to live among the Igbo and Uwa people. It is not about the Nri people you know. It is about the Igbo and the Uwa people. Nri people are good only as long as they give to Igbo and Uwa people.'"

"How did this happen?"

"'Ezu set a precedent when he left Nri. The rest of the migration was gradual and by mutual consent. People just got tired of being Nri people. That got old and they wanted something fresh.'"

"'Something fresh?' I repeated. 'But this still does not explain the low standard that I am looking at here.'"

"Half of the women wore only one layer of clothing, which is taboo in Nri, that I know. They had either half-done Uli marks or none at all. Most of them had no necklace or other form of jewelry. In all of the market, I did not see a single full-face scarification among the men. Instead I saw a pattern-less half-face scarification that looked nothing like the rays of the sun. I even saw an Ozo man wearing an Ozo anklet who was selling chickens in the marketplace and eating a bean cake in front of everyone.

Everything about these people indicated that they did not think before acting, people who were content with half measures. They seemed to be in hurry, yet I saw no destination or purpose. They seemed to be afraid of something, and yet I saw no Igah masquerade running after them with a whip. I looked in their eyes and I did not see the bold, penetrating eyes that Nri people are known for. Instead, I saw eyes that were half hidden and very frightened."

"As we roamed Nkwo market, I noticed that Nri-Menri Nwadike had not responded to my last comment, so I decided to phrase it as a question. 'Why has the standard of conduct been lowered this much compared to our time?'"

"'Most of the best and the brightest left to live among the Igbo and Uwa people. But even in your generation, the standards were much lower than in the generations before.'"

"'But this is no standard at all,' I said.'"

"'That is what you think. The generations before your time thought exactly the same of your generation. The point is that Nri people developed to a certain level and could not go any higher. Instead they kept going further and further down. Their peak was meant to be much higher, but when all fails, people have to lower their expectations. So, instead of watching Nri decline to nothing, they moved to the Igbo mainland and some Uwa lands. Maybe this movement will wear on those people and inspire something different and new. Remember, this is not about Nri people. It is about Igbo and Uwa people. Nri people are only good as long as they serve Igbo and Uwa people. They are doing that on a new level now,' he said."

"All the standards I could use to identify Nri people seemed to be gone except for one. And I had a feeling that they were not going to lose that anytime soon. It was their big hearts. As my mother once said, when you are surrounded by the enemy or when the future seems bleak, you can always count on your big heart to open doors for you. So maybe these strange people still had a chance. As we were walking along the palm wine section of the Nkwo market, a particular man called us and offered drinks. At first, I thought he was trying to sell us wine, but it turned out he wasn't."

"'You can have as much drink as you want,' he said after we'd each had a cup."

"'What is your name?' I finally asked him."

"'My full name is Okoye Ukommadu. But you can call me Udo-Di-noke (peace is at the boundary). That is my Nze name.'"

"'My name is Okoye Rope,' I said as we shook hands."

"'That is a funny name. Is that your real name?'"

"'That is what my people decided to call me. You can call me that,' I said. 'My master calls me that too.' I pointed to Nri-Menri Nwadike who was talking to another man and drinking wine from his cup."

"'Where did you people come from?'"

"'We are actually Nri people, but we come from the past, six centuries ago.'"

"He must have concluded that I was crazy, for he suppressed a smile."

"'A funny man with a funny name and a funny story,' he finally said. "'What are you people shopping for today?'"

"I knew that my answer would disappoint him, but I was not in a mood to lie to him, especially when my master was only a few feet from me."

"'We are conducting a market observation, just to see how your generation is faring,' I said."

"My newfound friend stared at me. He seemed confused about what to say next to his uncooperative guest. At that moment, I decided to see what my master was up to. Nri-Menri Nwadike was on his third cup of palm wine and in deep conversation with a customer. He seemed to be having quite a good time himself. I wondered how often he comes to this place. I started smiling. Turning to my new friend, I said, 'I don't know about my master, but I have a particular interest in fabrics, jewelry, elephant tusks, and carriage animals like horses and donkeys.'"

"'You speak perfect Igbo, but you must have come from another generation,' he joked. 'The things you are asking for are traded in the morning, and you cannot get good quality at Nri. I have heard about horses and donkeys, but I have never seen one in my lifetime.'"

"'So where can I get good quality fabric and jewelry?'"

"'Afor Ubulu market. It is very far, about two and a half day's journey. You people can pass the night at my house. You can leave in the morning.'"

"'Let me talk to my master first,' I said. But my master was on his fourth cup of palm wine, so I asked. 'Who is the Eze Nri?'"

"'Well, it depends on the village you come from. Currently, we have three to choose from.'"

"'Three to choose from?'"

"'Yeah, two of them claimed that they had revelations to become Eze Nri. So they became Eze Nri at the same time. Because of that, the Nri people are divided and each village chooses which one they want to follow. The third one claimed that Eze Nri was always a rotating position and that it was his village's turn to produce one. So his village made him Eze Nri.'"

"'That is a lot of Eze Nri for a small community. So which one do the Igbo people recognize?' As soon as I asked the question, I knew the answer."

"'Igbo people recognize the one they want to recognize. It depends on each Igbo family to decide which one they want. You people must be some of those Uwa people who speak perfect Igbo.'"

"I would have liked to spend a night at this man's house and heard more about the Nri people of his generation. I would have liked to know what they believe in and what they think of their future. I had a lot of questions, but Nri-Menri Nwadike tapped me on the shoulder and told me that my time was up and that some people were worried about my health, so we left."

THIRTY-FIVE

The Man of Peace

It had been Ijego's fifth visit to Ezu's country in three years. The last time they saw each other was ten moons before. But as soon as Ijego saw Ezu, she knew instantly that something had happened to him. Ezu looked haggard and depressed—much slower in speech and movement though his voice still filled the room. But it had a heaviness that suggested resignation. As they chatted, Ijego could not help noticing that Ezu was actually thinking about what he was saying and that he sometimes pondered before speaking. Before this, Ezu just opened his mouth without really thinking about what he was saying. Now Ezu looked at least twenty years older than he was. He seemed at least seventy, like some of the old men with unshaven gray beards. He did not call Ijego Dike Nwanya, (Warrior Woman) or Akataka Nwanya (Tough Woman) or other teasing names as he had in the past. Ezu had many names for Ijego and, each time they met, he usually saluted her with at least three of them. All of them meant "a tough woman." This usually put Ijego on the defensive and made her a little sensitive, especially when other people were around. This suited Ezu just fine because he wanted to be in control all of the time. But this afternoon when Ijego was escorted into the big reception, Ezu was all by himself, which was very unusual. And, for the very first time, he called her Ada Nri, Daughter of Nri.

After they saluted each other and chatted for awhile about family and health, Ijego had to ask, "What happened to you?"

"What do you mean?" asked Ezu, not understanding the question.

"What happened to your personal guards?" Ijego asked, looking around for the big, mean-looking guards who used to stand like statues of the Ngene deity.

"I don't need them anymore. A man of peace does not need that many bodyguards. I still have one person at the entrance and that should be enough."

Ijego smiled, not quite sure what to say. This could be a big bluff, and she did not want to be fooled. But thinking about it, she had not seen the guards at the border when she crossed the creek. Those guards usually asked many questions and escorted her to Ezu's place.

"It is good of you to come," said Ezu, breaking the silence as a little boy brought in a wooden bowl of kolanuts.

"Something has happened here. What is it?" asked Ijego. She had never been offered kolanuts that quickly at Ezu's place, if they were offered at all. And there would have been many visitors, some in the reception area and many waiting outside.

"Many things have happened since you last came about a year and half ago, maybe two years ago."

"It has not been up to eight moons, has it?" asked Ijego.

"It has been at least one year, to my recollection," said Ezu as he washed his hands in the finely-decorated terracotta bowl that the young man held for him. "Many things have happened, and I will tell you, but first we will each have some kolanut."

They talked about family while they ate, which was again very unusual because Ezu was never interested in Ijego's family. Before, they would have talked about politics, starting with Ezu asking about Ike-kete-Olie or Ike-fuo-Uzo. This day he even remembered Ijego's daughter's name. She had come with Ijego during her last visit. As they chatted, Ijego learned that one of Ezu's daughters had gotten married seven moons before. She noticed that Ezu did not seem very happy about it.

"It appears that it did not have your blessings," Ijego remarked.

"Eyee vunu (of course) it had all my blessings, because I arranged it myself. That is why it was painful when the young man died less than two moons after they were married, leaving her pregnant. His father was a very good friend of mine, and the marriage was supposed to create a lasting bond between his clan and my people. But the young man was murdered only seven weeks after they were married."

"Murdered? By whom?" Ijego asked, drawing her stool closer.

"Nwa Nri, it is a very long, heartbreaking story, and I will not put you through it. You do not deserve it. No one deserves it," Ezu said looking at the young lad who was still standing close to the entrance. The lad took the cue and left.

The Bantu tribe and the Kwazu clan were mortal enemies until Ezu came along and brought them together. Ezu was not necessarily being a peacemaker because he had commercial interests at the bottom of his heart. He could not do business with the Kwazu people because he lived among the Bantu people who had given him land and security. He did not want to offend his Bantu hosts by doing business with their enemy. So he had to bring them together so he could exploit both groups at the same time. Ezu, who wanted to build the biggest commercial city Nri people had ever seen, reasoned that his success depended on the cooperation and patronage of his immediate neighbors.

No one living at the time knew exactly what had started the enmity between the Bantu and Kwazu people who spoke the same language and shared the same river that served as their boundary. Information about their origins was as elusive as that of their conflicts. Bantu people believed that the founders of their two clans were two brothers, Kwazu Magbu and Bantu Magbu. Both spoke the Magbu language and belonged to the larger Magbu tribe. But a Kwazu man would sigh at this story because his people believed it to be a distortion of history. The Kwazu were more sophisticated and religious than the Bantu. They believed that Bantu warriors came down the river many generations ago and forced their Kwazu ancestors to move to the eastern part of the great Magbu River, leaving the west to the Bantu. The two clans had been fighting ever since.

Ezu did not really care about what each side claimed. He believed that only Chineke knew what his descendants would be claiming after his death.

Back in Nri, Ozo-Mkputu priests had made peace and established credibility for the Nri people. The rest of the Nri people, including the Oganiru priests, harvested the fruits of that credibility by converting it into wealth. Now, living on his own among the Bantu people, the most distrustful people on the face of the earth, Ezu must have realized that he needed to cultivate some sort of credibility to sound believable. That was another reason he was playing with peacemaking as if it were a toy. And that was also another reason why his approach did not work because to him making peace was something to play with. He had no passion for peace. Obviously, his way was not working but, at least, he could do business with the Kwazu people.

Ezu had already taken three Bantu women as wives and had given one of his daughters to a Bantu loyalist. Why not give another daughter to the Kwazu people and tie that bond as well? That way Ezu would be the bridge that connected the citizens of both sides of the Magbu River. While the rest of the Bantu people seemed to reluctantly swallow the dish Ezu was cooking, the Bantu's Duwantu village did not. They lived next to the river and, therefore, were closest to the Kwazu people. The Bantu had killed so many Kwazu people and done them so much wrong that the Bantu trembled at the thought of eating at a table with a Kwazu person. And yet Ezu often talked about the day that Bantu and Kwazu people would sit and share the same bowl of food and the same cup of wine. In spite of Ezu's talk, the Bantu had laid ambush and killed the young man that Ezu was already calling his son.

Three market weeks after one of the biggest marriage feasts the Bantu people had ever seen, Ezu invited Ikanou, his new son-in-law, for a visit. Ikanou was the son of a Kwazu leader. They spent a week together touring Ezu's empire and discussing the future of the two families. Before Ikanou and his wife left on the morning of the fifth day, the groom had learned a few trading secrets from his crafty father-in-law. Ikanou and three Kwazu servants were kidnapped that morning in front of his pregnant wife as they were entering a canoe to cross the Magbu River. His body was later found floating on the Bantu side of the river. The Kwazu people refused to accept his badly mutilated body.

"I had to take his body to them myself and beg before they accepted and buried it," said Ezu as he fought tears. "If it were this one incident, one could mourn his death for seven weeks and then move ahead. But violence is everyday life here. Human beings are killed like chickens. Sometimes people just disappear and are never seen again. Sometimes you will see a corpse on the side of the road with its head or some other body part missing. When no one can identify the body, it is buried in a shallow grave. Sometimes vultures eat half of the body before it is buried. What are considered the highest abominations in Nri are committed here many times in a single day. Bantu people kill and mutilate their own people. At first, I tried to overlook this, saying that they play by different rules. But when I saw the mutilated body of this young man, I was shaken. It occurred to me that human life is sacred no matter what food they eat or the language they speak. The same rules apply to all of us, Umu-Nri or Umu-Igbo or Umu-Uwa."

"How is she taking it—I mean our daughter. How is she?" asked Ijego wiping tears from her eyes, obviously shaken herself.

"She recovered more quickly than I expected. At first, she fell very ill, but she is doing well. As you know, she is pregnant and is due in two moons. I promised my friend, her father-in-law, that she would return to them with the baby as soon as it is born and she has rested."

The woman-side of Ijego, the woman warrior, gave in. She was already sobbing—for the young man she could only imagine, for Ezu's daughter, and for the haggard-looking Ezu. But Ijego was also sobbing for what she considered to be her sins against Ezu. She could bear it no longer. She had always secretly blamed herself for causing the problem between Ezu and Okoye Nweri. She could have made peace between Osondu and Ezu if she wanted to, but she didn't. Instead she directed Osondu to the highest authority in the land knowing full well that Ezu would be embarrassed. But that was all she wanted—to bring embarrassment to Ezu. Instead things got out of hand, and she had contributed to the downfall of her sanctuary, her adopted home. *Could she ever atone enough for her actions?*

Ezu was embarrassed by her prolonged sobbing which was now becoming more vocal. He contemplated getting up to console her, but Ijego rose up herself and went to him instead and knelt in front of him, burying her tear-soaked face in his lap. Ezu could smell her female body and thoughts of their brief, but intense, love affair twenty years before overcame him.

Back then, Ezu was at his prime with lots of energy, and Ijego was just another trophy in his collection of concubines and lovers around Nri and the major trade cities in Igbo land. Ezu had demanded more from Ijego. He wanted marriage. There was something interesting and even romantic about how Ijego spoke the Igbo language with her birthplace dialect. Ezu loved that. But Ijego wanted her independence. Ezu would have been all right with that if Ijego had been faithful and loyal in their love affairs. Ijego was neither because the man did not pay dowry on her head. She had used Ezu when she needed exposure, but after she had that, Ijego discovered young Nri men, mostly immigrants who needed guidance and who did not think that she spoke Igbo language with a phony dialect. When it came to his women, Ezu could be as jealous and emotional as a teenager. He went on a mission of destruction, but Ijego was completely shielded by her godfather, Ichie Idika. But seeds of resentment had been sown between them. So when Ijego saw an opportunity to embarrass Ezu, she seized it. That was all she wanted to do, to embarrass him. But everything got out of hand.

"I have done you wrong and I seek your forgiveness," Ijego said in a muffled voice with her head still buried in Ezu's lap. Ezu did not understand. Was she working for the Bantu? The Kwazu? This could not be. Of course Ezu knew that Ijego belonged to the Ogbadu Eze sect (the eyes and ears of Eze Nri).

"I do not understand," said Ezu. It was an honest statement showing that he was a changed man. Before he would have pretended that he knew her sins and then that he wanted her to confess in her own words. With her face completely hidden in Ezu's lap, Ijego told her story—confessing how she had directed Osondu to Igwe Okoye Nweri.

"If I had not pointed him to Nne-Obu-Nri, Osondu would not have been brave enough to go on his own and all this would not have happened. I did not know it would go this far. I did not mean for this to happen. You must believe me. You must forgive me," she said.

Ezu laughed before speaking. "Ada-Nri (Daughter of Nri) you have done nothing wrong. I knew what you just told me before we left Nri. I knew that Osondu came to you and that you directed him to Igwe. I heard about it from many sources. It is not a secret. But you did nothing wrong."

For the first time since she buried her head in his lap, Ijego looked up into Ezu's face. "You mean you knew all along since I have been coming here and you said nothing?"

She had discovered another side of Ezu she did not know, a more complicated side. Ezu did not reply, but sat in reflection. Ijego wiped her face with her waist cloth and went back to her seat, two foot steps away from Ezu. There was a long silence. When Ezu spoke again, he was almost speaking to himself.

"I should be apologizing to everyone and not just you. What I did was wrong. A lot of what I did in my life was wrong. Our people said that if a woman marries two husbands, she will know which one is better than the other. My dwelling among the Bantu people has opened my eyes about what we had at Nri. But I believe in Akalaka (Destiny), and it is my Akalaka that brought me here among the Bantu people, and we are going to make some good come out of it."

Ezu laughed loudly as he got up from his seat. "I have learned more about our forefathers since I came to live here than I learned my entire life before that."

Ijego said nothing because Ezu went into his inner room before he finished the sentence. When he came back, he had a jar of wine and two finely decorated wine cups. Ijego refused when he offered her one of the cups, saying that she wanted to eat first. Ezu rang a little bronze bell, and the young dwarf who had brought them kolanut appeared. Ezu told him to arrange for food for Ada-Nri. When he left, Ezu drank from his cup.

"Yes, I was saying that I have learned so much about Ndi-ichie (our forefathers) since I came here."

Ijego must have sensed a very long discussion or maybe it was the hope that food was coming that made her change her mind about the wine.

"What have you learned?" she asked as she picked up the other cup from the side stool and held it for Ezu who filled it with konya.

"What have I learned?" asked Ezu, drinking from his cup. "A lot. I have learned about why the Nri made peace. I have always wondered their real reason for making peace—the real reason behind the sammelele udo (Peace Mantra). They wanted to be the leaders in their environment. They wanted to be somewhat in charge of their surroundings and there were only two ways they could do that. One way was to be willing to kill or subdue any opposition. That way, everyone else would be afraid to go against them. Another way was to make peace and bring people together. Those are the two ways that guarantee one is in charge. One either becomes the most selfish or the most selfless. The Nri chose the latter."

Ezu told Ijego how Bantu young men had invited him to a meeting less than two moons after they had killed his son-in-law. They told Ezu that the lands their fathers sold him were actually leased lands and that they were ready to take them back. Ezu asked them if they had consulted with their parents before coming, and they said that they did not need to. Ezu realized that it was an open challenge when one of them said that he, Ezu, had deceived their parents, and they were willing to correct that wrong.

"I know most of them personally, and I know their weaknesses. They had worked for me at one time or another. I know that they don't have that much sense, so their parents must have sent them. I told them that I would get back to them. My first instinct was to call all of them to a meeting and surround them with hired thugs from up the river and kill all of them. But then I realized that if I did that, I would have to exterminate all of the Bantu clan because they do not forget or forgive."

Ezu thought about what he had just said and shook his head. "Can you believe that I actually considered it for one full izu (week). Oduh once asked me if I am a descendant of Nri. I didn't understand his question then, but now I do. I have never killed a human being in my life. I have never heard that a descendant of Nri has killed a human being. Why should I be the first? I had the resources to do it, but I do not have the heart to kill and destroy human beings. I want to be the best at what I do, but I do not want to be the best at killing people. You have to be the best to beat the Bantu people in what they do best."

"I was not a fool when I came here. I knew that when I opened their eyes, they would challenge me in order to assert their independence. I thought that when that happened I could hire thugs to deal with them. But now I realize that you would have to kill all of them if you ever start a war with the Bantu people. That is not in my blood. To be a very good warrior you have to actually enjoy killing people. Having the might is not enough."

"Our ancestors were brave, industrious, and very intelligent people like me. They wanted to dominate their environment as I do, but they did not want to kill and destroy in order to do this, so they made peace."

All the time, Ezu was speaking like someone in a trance. Maybe the konya had something to do with it. "The Nri motivation for making peace is not so simple. It was not all about dominating in their environment. I believe that their religion has a lot to do with their soft hearts and peacemaking. But being in control has something to do with it too. I know because I can feel their hearts in my heart. I want to be a part of my environment all of the time. That is in my blood. But there is one thing I still don't understand about Nri people and, therefore, about me. That is, did their religion make their hearts soft or did they found a religion that suited their soft hearts?"

Just then, a pair of young girls came in with two wooden trays of food. Their entrance must have awakened Ezu from his trance.

"Ada-Nri, we have to eat. Do not listen to me any more. I am an old man and you know that they say old people talk about strange things."

THIRTY-SIX

Signs of Peace

It was now seventeen moons since Okoye saw the vision of Nri's future. It was the sixth moon of the year in Nri land, the season of cocoyam planting and the first yam pruning and the second hour of the morning, the last moments before the sun emerged from the far east. The air was cold, but Okoye did not feel it as he stood in the middle of his yam farm between the four ridges of yam plants. The plants were as high as his waist and lay about two steps apart. He could hardly see the heads of Obuka, his first son, and Nwadike, his adopted son, who were working about two hundred steps away. Ikenna, his personal assistant who was now like his own son, worked two rows ahead of him laying down two bamboo poles on the ridges.

Okoye surveyed the entire farm. It was about three hundred footsteps long and wide. At their current speed, it would take about three days to finish. He made two holes in the ridge in front of him with a long, narrow hole digger. Then he picked up one of the bamboo poles lying on the ridge and stuck it into one of the holes. With his right foot he filled the hole with mud sand. After doing the same with the second bamboo pole, he bent both poles so they touched and crossed over at the middle of the ridge. Using an Ekwele tie made of a palm frond, he tied the poles together. Then he picked up one of the two yam plants that crawled down from the middle of the ridge to the floor like a tiny green snake. He twisted the coiled plant up the closest bamboo pole from right to left until it stuck as if it had always belonged there. He picked up the second plant and was about to coil it when he heard a familiar voice behind him.

"Igwe! Well done work!" It was Erike.

"Nwune-Di-namba!" Okoye greeted him back. "This must be a blessed day."

"It must be since I will have the pleasure of participating in the holy fun," joked Erike.

"It is holy fun, indeed. I have ignored it for too long. Can you see how long the plants are? Doesn't that tell you something?"

"It has Igwe Nweri, the lazy man, written all over it," Erike said, picking up the metal hole digger.

"I was lucky that the sun has not been very hot. The plants would have been cooked by the hot crust," said Okoye as he coiled the second plant around the other bamboo pole.

Erike made two holes on the next ridge. "It has been good weather for the yam."

"If I am lucky, the sun will be mild for another week until we are done with this." Okoye picked up a bamboo pole.

"But, if not, that will teach you to use the volunteers that fill all the villages to do the work of Eze Nri."

Okoye laughed. "Then I will be really good for nothing if I do that. How are Nwamma and your family?"

"Everyone is well. I have seen Eze Nwanya, the Queen. She told me where to find you."

There was a moment of silence as Okoye surveyed the yam plants for any sign of yellow leaves so he could prune them. There were none. He moved on to the next plants. Ikenna, now seven rows ahead, was laying the bamboo poles and ekwele ties as fast as he could. It was like a race between him and Okoye with Okoye playing catch-up and Ikenna doing all he could to keep as much distance between them as he could. He had gone back to where he had been working after saying hello to Erike who was now a regular face at the palace. Ikenna had doubled the space between himself and Okoye as the two adults chatted. But he could not be fooled. It would be just a matter of time before they caught up with him since they were sharing the work. But the current distance between Ikenna and the two men worked best for Erike. He must use the space to make his case before they closed the gap.

"I saw Ijego yesterday. She sends greetings," Erike stated.

"Dike Nwanya (the Warrior Woman). How is she doing?"

"Not very well. That is one of the reasons I came."

"What is the matter? Is she ill or in some trouble?"

"Maybe in trouble with her conscience."

"She did something wrong?"

"She seems to think so."

"What happened?"

"I will tell you from the beginning," Erike said, supporting himself with the hole digger. Okoye sensed that this was a serious matter and stood still to listen. Ikenna was not still. He saw them not moving and this was good news for him. He knew he must go as fast as he could to widen the distance between them. Then they would never catch up with him.

"She came to my house yesterday morning just after the cock crowed. I thought someone had died. She seemed very distressed. She said that she had a confession to make. I thought she was going to confess about something she did to me. Instead, she said that she had a hand in what happened between you and Okeke Ubaka (Ezu) and his brothers. To be frank, I thought that she had something serious to say, perhaps a big secret. Instead she said that she was the one who had directed Osondu to come directly to you with his complaint. I asked her if Osondu had told you the truth. She said 'Yes.'"

"I failed to see what she had done wrong. But by this time, she was weeping like a baby. If I hadn't known her so well, I would have thought she was either hiding something or lying about it. She had committed an offense against the Ozo council though, but she was not bothered by that . . . ."

"What offense?" Okoye asked, breaking his silence.

"She told me that she has been visiting with Okeke Ubaka at his new place. She has been trying to persuade him to apologize to you and seek reconciliation. She blames everything that happened on herself. She thinks that she may have acted out of her dislike of Okeke Ubaka."

"There is nothing to it," said Okoye, picking up a bamboo pole again. "I still don't understand why she does not come here as often as she did to Igwe Nwadike's palace when he was around."

"Well, the story gets more interesting because that is not the only reason she came to see me." Erike could barely see Ikenna's head in the distance.

"She said that Okeke Ubaka has finally agreed to come to apologize to you."

As soon as Erike finished his sentence, Okoye turned and went back to work. The Eze Nri must never show his anger or speak when he is angry. Okoye was not angry at anyone in particular. He was just angry. Period. For the next five ridges of pruning, both men worked in silence. The Eze Nri must always engage in an activity to keep his mind occupied and empty at the first sign of anger. Suddenly they were working faster and faster, catching up with Ikenna. Then there was another greeting to Igwe, a familiar voice, the voice of Oduh. Oduh saluted Okoye. Okoye saluted without looking at him. Oduh exchanged pleasantries with Erike.

"Is something the matter with Igwe?" Oduh asked after a few moments had passed in silence.

"He will tell you what he told me," Okoye said, pointing at Erike. "Go ahead. Tell him."

"What is it?" Oduh Erike asked.

Before answering, Erike pondered, not knowing where to start.

Oduh laughed as soon as Erike finished his story. Okoye could not hide his surprise. It was not a laughing matter.

"You know, I had a dream two nights ago which I now think might have been a vision after hearing this story. In the dream, I was at Nkwo market bargaining for tobacco leaves when there was a big uproar at the market entrance. Everyone in the whole market was running. I thought something terrible had happened. They were all running, and no one would stop to tell me what was going on. Instead of running away like all the others, I walked to the market entrance. Then I saw Okeke Ubaka walking barefoot. He looked distressed and haggard. Trailing behind him were all his brothers and his families. He did not seem to recognize me. Instead, he asked me to direct him to Nne Obu Nri (the palace). He said that he had been looking but could not find it. I embraced him and asked him to follow me. Then I woke up. The more I thought about it, the more joy it brought me, just the thought of his coming back here. This could be a good sign of things to come," Oduh concluded.

Oduh was glowing and Okoye saw it. His old eyes glittered and his wrinkled face had come alive.

"I cannot meet with him. I don't think it is proper. I don't know what he has been doing or who he has been dealing with or how tainted he is. He can apologize to you on my behalf. You can accept for me. If he wants something more than that, then a full cleansing must be done for him and his family. I have nothing else against him. I leave everything up to you."

THIRTY-SEVEN

Nri at Home – In Diaspora

The congregation had gathered. The Nri Temple of Justice was full. Kolanuts had been blessed and eaten. Very fine Ufie music played outside the temple. The Eze Nri, Okoye Nweri, sat on Mkpume-Onyilenyi (his stone throne) facing the congregation. On his left facing him sat about forty-six men. Unlike all of the other men in the temple, these men had no red caps including the man who was once Ezu Nri. All forty-six men had been members of the Oganiru. All of them had migrated out of Nri to found their own little kingdoms or empires. Sitting behind them were the Nze priests. And at their right were the Ozo priests. It was midday, but the sun had just disappeared behind a thick cloud as if it were hiding its face from the Nri people. The temperature was just right, not too hot or too cold. It was a perfect afternoon for an important ceremony. The program was simple. Okoye was going to make a short formal reconciliatory speech. It was going to be brief because everything had been said the day before in a closed-door meeting between the Nri-Bu-Nuno (Nri at Home) led by Oduh and the Nri-Bu-Namba (Nri abroad) led by the man formerly known as Ezu with Igwe Okoye Nweri presiding.

After the short speech, Oduh was going to call each of the forty-six men by name and lead them to Okoye. Okoye would then formally pronounce them Isi-Ozo of whatever the name of their newly found empire was. Some of the names were quite creative and others revealed ambitious minds. Some were newly-founded kingdoms with names like Nri- Ukwu (Nri-Big) or Nri-Nine (Nri-All) or Nri-Ofuu (New-Nri). Their empires would then be automatically annexed to the Nri clan. After the formal installation, there would be Nlikor, eating and drinking together of former adversaries, the last phase of every peace-making process according to Nri traditions.

The Ufie music suddenly stopped. It was now time for the next item on the agenda, the soul of the gathering. All eyes turned to the King, Okoye. Oduh leaned down and said something to him. Okoye nodded a couple of times. Then Oduh faced the congregation.

"Our brother wants to say something to Igwe," he said with a raised voice while making a hand gesture towards Ezu.

As Ezu got up, everyone held his breath. Ezu bent down and took off his sandals. This was a sign that whatever he was going to say was automatically under oath. He walked to the space between the congregation and Okoye and turned to the crowd. "I want to formally apologize to Our Father, Igwe." He knelt down facing Okoye.

"I have rebelled against you, therefore, rebelling against our ancestors and everything they stood for. Because of my foolishness, I have caused irreversible damage to the Motherland. Ever since I left the Nri heartland, I have engaged in soul-searching. For a very long time, my heart was hardened. I could not see anything wrong in my ways. My views were clouded and my reasoning distorted. It took a long time, but I did find salvation. I have peace within me now. All burdens have been lifted. I am like a newborn, a new leaf. I have a lot of energy now. When I lived a life of selfishness and foolishness, I lived it with all the energy in me. Now I am a man on a new mission, and I will pursue it too with all the energy left in me."

There was a pause. Ezu wiped his face with his clothes. The silence in the temple was greater than had ever happened before.

"I will take the message of peace and fair play to all Uwa lands that I can reach, especially those around me. I call you Our Father because you are the Chosen One, the incarnation of all our holy ancestors in the flesh. I ask you to forgive my past imperfections and to forgive my brethren whom I bring before you. I know that you do not need these kinds of public apologies. But I speak so that my brethren may hear and be touched by my testimony. I owe them that much because I have deceived them in the past."

His voice filled the temple as he spoke. His listeners felt some unease, but his powerful voice and sincere words kept them listening. Now he suddenly stopped, creating a vacuum, empty air that stood still. Okoye was more touched than the others. It was embarrassing to look at his business mentor prostrated before him. Ezu had taken off his sandals, so Okoye believed everything that came out of his mouth. Suddenly he recalled what Big Father had said when Okoye had his vision. "Nri people made their choices a long time before you were born. You have very little hand in what is happening. You are just helping to make their choices manifest sooner."

Okoye wondered about Ezu's hand in what had happened. Was he, too, like Okoye, playing his part so that choices made a long time ego would manifest themselves? Was Ijego, too, an actor? Erike? Ichie Idika? Oduh? The others? Were they all victims, victims of destiny, a destiny decided a long time ego?

Okoye was moved, but his position forbade him from showing his emotions. He was Eze Nri, holder of Nne Offor Nri, incarnation of all the holy ancestors in the flesh, manifester of the ideal. He was the perfect spirit, never to be ruled by emotions. But he must do something, say something appropriate on this unique occasion. Since Ezu did not stand up after his statement, Okoye rose from his throne. He walked down to where Ezu was still prostrated, took him by both hands, and lifted him up to a standing position.

As Ezu stood, Okoye was tempted to embrace his brother, but remembered. *Eze Nri, a spirit, could not embrace people. He would just shake his hand. That would do it. No! No! That too was forbidden! Eze Nri could not shake hands with humans. Damn rules! Damn roles! Nonsense rules!* With two hands, Okoye grabbed his brother by his right hand and shook it. *No! Wait, not dramatic enough!* He bent down and embraced his dwarf brother like a child. There were watery eyes, but nothing that the congregation could see. *Damn rules! Stupid rules!*

"Anger against one's sibling ends on the flesh. It does not get down to the bone marrow. On behalf of Agbala, I forgive and absolve you of any mistakes you and all our brethren you bring may have made. I have looked into the future, and I know that a lot of challenges await us. That is another reason why we must pull together. All Nri people and all Igbo people must put their strength together. All Nri-Bu-Nuno and Nri-Bu-

Namba must pull together. I have seen the future, and I know that all Nri people and Igbo people will be well eventually. We have big tasks and challenges ahead of us, but we will eventually be fine."

"Igwe!" yelled Oduh and started to clap. Erike joined him. Ijego, sitting between Mgbafor and Enenebe with the Nze priests, joined them. The congregation started clapping. The bullhorn blew.

"Paapapupapuuupu! (Well said!)"

"Paapu paaupapuuutu! (Nothing more left to say!)"

"Pupuu papupuuupuuupu! (The sun is shining: It is a new day.)"

"Pupuu mputulululu lupapupupupupupuuu! (A brand new day, new life, new hope, but the same mission.)"

Okoye took this as a cue from his spiritual counselor. He walked back to his seat as the Ufie music began playing. It was very fine music, very inviting. But Eze Nri, the mirror of all that is holy, must never dance. The chief priest was still speaking through his bullhorn as Okoye sat down and looked at his flock. Those who knew the bullhorn's language fondly call it "Voice of the ages" or "Ancient Voices." This time the bullhorn was not speaking to Okoye, but to everyone who could hear it.

Paaapapupapupu! Paaapapupapupu! (Eyes clear! Eyes clear!), it says.

Umu-Nri Eyes clear!

Remember . . . whatever killed the mother hen has not left the neighborhood; so its young chicks must be ever watchful.

Eyes clear!

Is our survival not tied to our mission!?
Is our respect not tied to our mission!?
Will the mission not keep us focused and ground our feet on the earth!?

Eyes Clear!

If the mother hen abandons its familiar tone, Kwom! Kwom! Kwom!,
how else can it call its chicks together? How can her chicks recognize her?

*If the lizard of the homestead does not behave like one, will it not be
confused for the lizard of the wild— and eaten?*
*If an adult does not behave like one, will children not confuse him for
a playmate—and throw sand at him?*

Umu-Igbo Eyes clear!

He who is running for his life must never get tired.
*He who is surrounded by the enemy cannot afford to close his eyes or
lose his focus.*
*When a pestle misses its targeted mortar, does it not ends up on the
ground?*
*When a fish becomes confused in the river, does it not ends up in the
soup pot?*

Eyes clear!

Does the death that kills a dog not first stop it from smelling its food?
*Does the fly without an adviser not usually follow the corpse into its
grave?*
*If the ear does not listen to a wise counsel and the head is cut off, does
the same ear not fall with it?*

Eyes Clear!

A bird does not shit in its own nest.
He whose house is on fire does not chase after a rat.
*And remember . . . anger against a sibling ends on the flesh, it does not
get down to the bone.*

Umu-Igbo Eyes clear!

THIRTY-EIGHT

New Nri

Eight years later. . .

The position of Eze Nri was a very lonely one because the holder had to maintain his distance so that he could remain an impartial presider over human affairs. After all, he was a spirit dwelling among imperfect humans. Because of this loneliness, every Eze Nri had developed some unique hobby to fill that void. Igwe Nwadike sang and told stories to children. He loved playing his une (Nri local guitar). But he loved philosophy more. He loved just sitting on an ogwe (stair bench) at the holy forest thinking about the nature of things and relationships that are not readily apparent to a casual observer. He was a natural philosopher.

Okoye was not a natural-born philosopher and was not gifted with a voice for singing and had never played any instrument in his life. And, although he told stories of his travels to people close to him, he did not use them to make his points or philosophize about them as Igwe Nwadike would have. He simply told about his experiences, perhaps something funny and unique. He did not make connections and read hidden meanings as Igwe Nwadike would have. Telling stories was simply not his hobby. His hobby was shooting at a dot on a tree with a bow and arrow. He had received the bow and arrows from an Igbo warrior after settling a dispute between one village and another. The warrior who led the peace delegation from his village had voluntarily donated his bow and arrows to Okoye as a pledge that he had laid down his arms for good. Okoye, who had never shot an arrow in his life, had hung it in his personal obu as a trophy. Sometimes when he was alone he would walk to where it hung and stare at it. He wondered what he would do if someone aimed that object at him. Should he jump into the bush or get on his knees and beg for his life, or maybe run as fast as he could, swerving from side to side, hoping the shooter would miss? Okoye had not decided on the proper course of action for that hypothetical situation. These were some of the few occasions when Okoye was glad he was Eze Nri and away from the reach of some crazy people. This frightening object of human destruction hung on the wall of his obu as a display of one of his accomplishments until Erike, a veteran hunter, showed him how to hold it and shoot at the dots. Okoye learned well because Erike had never beaten him in a shooting match.

At age fifty-two, Okoye enjoyed shooting his bow and arrow as spectators watched in amazement at his accuracy.

"Now here is a good use for a menacing object," he seemed to be saying to his audience.

Another of Okoye's hobbies was interpreting dreams. He was very good at shooting dots with his bow and arrow, but he had gained a far better reputation for his interpretation of dreams. He had started this hobby after his near death experience about ten years before. So when Erike had the same dream five days in a row, he naturally told Okoye about it.

🐦 🐦 🐦

There were shouts when the young man in Erike's dream stumbled. There was jubilation that turned into outright celebration whenever the ukpa basket fell from his head. Those who walked close to him on the dry, baking-hot, sandy desert spat on him when he seemed to be doing well. When he held his ground they rewarded him with whippings and called him all sorts of ugly names. They said nasty things about his mother. They called him a bastard and implied he had no father. "Tell us who your father is. Tell us his name. Have you ever asked your mother who your true father is?"

Tears rolled from his eyes. Sweat flowed like water and soaked his entire garment. Once in awhile, especially when the basket fell off his head, he would retrieve a stick that resembled an Offor club (Nri Club of Justice) from his waist. He would point it at the blazing sun as he moved his mouth and murmured something. He would then pound the club on the bare ground like a mad man and babble some gibberish that no one understood. Erike had a feeling that not even the young man understood those words. But whatever it was seemed to be working for him, because after some heavy pounding and babbling, he gained some strength. He would move on through the path that appeared to lead nowhere with a mob of abusers trailing behind him.

Five nights in a row, Erike had the same dream. The path was always different. The environment and scenery were always different. But the young, light-skinned face was always the same. He looked like an Uwa man with light, sun-tanned skin and long dark-stretched hair. But he had the Nri facial scarification. He was between twenty-five and forty years of age and strongly built with a broad chest and muscular arms. Even when tears rolled from his eyes he seemed to be smiling, showing a big dimple. The smile always made Erike feel uneasy, maybe guilty. The mob was as numerous as the desert sand. They were men and women, young and old, dark-and light-skinned, Umu-Igbo and Umu-Uwa. In one of his dreams, the young man was climbing a long and steep mountain in a barren wilderness. In another he was crossing a river. But in the other three, he was crossing hot, dry deserts; each a different desert.

After Erike had first narrated his dreams, Okoye had pondered for several moments before asking, "Does he have a name?"

"No one called him by his real name. They just called him bad names."

"Do you know what is in the basket that he carried?"

"They look like rocks . . . small rocks. But they must be precious rocks for they glitter. The basket is long and very deep. It must be very heavy for it takes many people to put it on his head when it falls down."

Okoye pondered again. "And you said that you have never seen that face before?"

"Now it looks familiar. It seems as though I have known him for ages. But I am quite sure that I have not seen him before the first dream."

"Does he say anything you can hear?"

"As I said before, the only time he said something was when he was hitting the club on the ground. He hits with this piece of stick that looks like an Offor club, but I am sure it is not.

"Well. Don't be too sure about that. Dreams are tricky . . . ."

"It could be."

"If you have had that dream five times, then you will surely have it again. Next time ask him his name. Ask if you can help him. It looks like who or whatever it might be is testing your sympathy. This is not just a dream. You are having a vision of some sort."

That night, Erike had his sixth and last dream about the young man. He wanted to get close to him and ask questions. He wanted to offer his help, but he was too afraid of his captors. The men that surrounded and escorted the young man had whips. They looked mean and strong. There was fire in their eyes.

❦ ❦ ❦

It had been ten days since Erike first told Okoye about his unusual dreams and nine days after he had his sixth and last dream about the young man. It was Eke market morning. Okoye knelt on his left knee and stretched his left arm to hold his bow. He took a deep gulp of air and exhaled. This Eke market morning, the sun was rising, but he did not feel the warmth. He had temporarily forgotten about his surroundings, including Erike, his only spectator. All of his attention was on the eye of the circle, the big red dot that was in the middle of the seven layers of circles. The circles were attached to a piece of plank which hung on the wall in his shooting area. The shooting area was about twenty footsteps in each direction and was bordered with high, thick mud walls. Behind Okoye and Erike were okwe benches that could comfortably seat fifteen spectators. But this morning there were no spectators.

With his right hand, Okoye positioned his arrow on the anchor between his left fingers. There was another long breathing in and out. He pulled back the string with his thumb and index finger, drawing it a little over half way and held it there. This was like a meditation for him. All he could see was that red dot the size of a thumb print. But in his present state, that red dot was as big as the whole world. It was his world at the moment. His right wrist was straight and in line with his arm, so there was no torque as he released the string and the base of the arrow. It was effortless, and the arrow glided into the dot ten foot steps away. It was like the coming home of an eagle into its nest. This made it his fifth perfect shot in a row.

"What shall I say? Another perfect one!" complimented Erike as Okoye began to come out of his meditative state.

"You can say that. I make my best shots without a lot of eyes watching."

"If only I could learn to hold the bow as straight as you do and then release it with two fingers instead of using all of them. But one cannot learn to be left handed at an old age."

Okoye chuckled and rose from his kneeling position. "When you have as much free time as I have and can practice as often as I do, then it would not matter how you hold the bow or release the string. Besides, today is a particularly good day. I have never made five perfect shots one after another. I must be feasting with the spirits today."

"Then it must be a good day to interpret a mysterious dream too. I had that dream again last night," said Erike as he positioned his arrow to shoot. He felt comfortable standing, so he stood with both legs apart to maintain his balance. He also felt comfortable talking about his dream while aiming the arrow. With all five fingers, he pulled the string to a full draw. When he released it, the arrow landed between the two innermost circles.

"That is a good one," complimented Okoye.

"Yes. My best is your worst of the morning."

"You would do much better if you were not talking all the time while shooting. To me, shooting is more like meditation. When I shoot, I hear or see nothing else. I think of nothing else."

"I agree. That is how it should be. But I learned to shoot in the wild. In the wild, you cannot afford to give all your attention to your target because you may be a target for something else. The elders said that the hunter who is aiming for the antelope does not know that the mosquito is aiming for his neck."

"Or maybe a lion is aiming for his throat," Okoye joked.

"I know about that one," said Erike.

"Maybe that is how it should be after all. Maybe that is fairer. You had the same dream again?"

"Finally—the night before last. And it was as clear as the previous ones. I agree with you; it is a vision of some sort. Dreams are usually not this clear. It was as if I knew what I was doing all the time."

"What happened this time?" asked Okoye walking towards the ogwe.

✵ ✵ ✵

It took twelve days before he had seen the young man's face in his dream again. But this time he looked a bit older, at least thirty. His body was the shade of cast bronze and as shiny. His dark hair was longer and reached below his shoulders. He was not Igbo, but he wore Nri facial scarification. His scarification was natural and deep as if he was born with it. The scarification emitted dazzling lights like those of the sun. He had very big, bold eyes which also sparkled with light. Erike found it hard to look at his face and could only steal glances now and then. The man also wore what looked like an Ozo anklet on both ankles. But his was bronze and seemed to be natural because it was attached to his skin. Erike was standing next to him. Erike had a whip, too, like the others who stood around the young man. Somehow Erike knew that he had used the whip to fake his way and get close.

"What is your name" Erike asked.

There was no answer. Instead the man looked at Erike as if he were another betrayer, another traitor.

"I said, what is your name? Don't you hear Igbo?" He was met with silence.

"I want to help you. Do you want some water? You surely would like some food. I have some roast yam and roast ukwa and some water. You can have some . . . ."

"What do you care about my name? What do you care about me?" He spoke for the first time. He did not speak commercial Igbo. He spoke a perfect Nri-Igbo dialect, better than Erike's. It must have taken a lot of his energy because he stumbled a few times after speaking.

"He is speaking! He is speaking!!" Someone yelled from the crowd. "I swear I heard him speak! He is not dumb after all and he is not deaf either."

"Who said he cannot speak," said one of his captors, who was holding a whip. "Who said he is deaf or dumb. He is just a smart head. He thinks he is better than all of us, that's all."

"Yes! We say to him prove it," said another of his captors. "Prove yourself wiser than all of us put together," said another with a stroke of the whip.

350

"Yes! Prove it, smart mouth! Prove it, smart buttocks!" said another as he whipped at his back with a long, black whip.

"Prove it! Prove it!! Prove it!!!" thundered the crowd of Umu-Igbo na Umu-Uwa who trailed behind the captive.

"Add more stones to his basket. Make him prove it. More loads to his basket," said one of his captors.

"More load! More load!! More load!!!" chanted the mob.

Erike woke up with a headache and a fast beating heart, but he felt proud of himself. He did not get a name as Okoye had suggested, but at least he had offered to help. That must be a good sign.

When he went back to sleep about an hour later, he saw the man sitting on a stone near a creek. Erike, too, was sitting on a stone next to him. The rest of the people were either sitting on the bare ground or standing. Every one seemed exhausted. The creek was in a valley, and there were mountains on both sides.

"What is your name, Sir?" Erike asked.

"I have many names, Son. But you can call me Shonwu."

"Shonwu," Erike repeated. "It is a unique name. What does it mean? What does it say? Is it your Ozo title name?"

"A name is just a name. It is just a label. It is what is in the heart that matters."

"You speak a perfect Nri dialect, and you have scarification, but your name sounds different. Where do you come from? Who are your people? What language do they speak?"

"That is not important. What is important is where we are all going. When we get there, we will speak one language, one dialect, one voice, one faith, one nation, one name. . . ."

"Tell me more, Sir. Tell me more about this place where we are going."

"It is the most beautiful place you can imagine. It is our real home, but it is very far and, as you can see, the road is very rough and difficult. There is no hunger or thirst there, no war or conflict because all is one and the interest of one is the interest of all. There is no pride or envy there. At that place you can say: 'Come! Water come!' Water will come in a fine cup on a tray and hang in the air in front of you. You can say: 'Come roast yam!' or

'Come roast ukwa!' and it will come served on a beautiful bowl and tray. You can wish for anything and it will come to you. Do you like fine music?"

Erike nodded.

"Then fine music will come to you whenever you say the word. If you like children, you can say: 'Children come! Six boys and six girls!' Beautiful children—well-mannered will come to you."

Erike, who loved children, laughed at this new idea. "Where would all this be coming from?"

"Does it matter where it comes from? What matters is that you get your wish just by speaking the word. But I can tell you this—most beings wish for nothing else because they have eternal happiness, eternal bliss, listening to the continuous, sweet humming of the most holy beings and they ask for nothing else . . . ."

"What is this place called? Does it have a name?"

"New Nri. You can call it New Nri. It is the Holy City—our real home and it belongs to everyone. I can get there in no time at all, but I cannot enter the gate by myself. I must wait for all to arrive before we can enter the Holy City together. We must get into that city as a team, for that is the rule. I tell our people to walk faster, and they call me smart head. Some walk very slowly. Others just sit and complain about their load being too heavy. And yet others walk in the opposite direction—backwards. I tell them that we may never make it to the holy city and they gang up on me. That was when I gave them the challenge. The challenge was meant to motivate them, but they took offense. I told them that I could carry all their loads and make more progress than the progress they were making at their current pace. They called me smart ass and vowed to make it as difficult as possible so they could prove me wrong. They called me slave boy and whipped me. They said, 'You are no good. You think you know too much. That is why your own friends sold you out for cowry money. You heard them call me a bastard. I was only trying to help. I do not mean harm to anyone.'"

There were tears in Erike's eyes. "How could they do that to an innocent man? How could they be that cruel to you? That is not right! Wicked Umu Uwa!" shouted Erike. "There must be something I can do to help."

"Yes. There is something you can do. But first, you have to go and exercise your arms and legs for the long journey ahead. You must exercise your neck for your share of the load is heavy. Then you must learn how to talk and chant what will seem like foreign tongues just like me for that will be your source of strength."

Erike woke from his sleep. There were many tears on his face and much sweat on his bed.

⚕ ⚕ ⚕

Okoye took an unusually long time to ponder Erike's latest encounter with the young man. He shook his head before speaking.

"The young man you saw in your vision is Anyanwu (The Light). You have just accepted to share in his burden and become his perfect servant, following in his footsteps. What you saw will not happen in our lifetime but in many generations in the future. Since it took you eleven days to accept, I am thinking it will take about eleven generations in the future. You will bear some heavy burdens for a lot of people in the far future. It does not look good because some people whom you will try to help will persecute you . . . ."

"Will the responsibility be more than that of Eze Nri?" asked Erike leaning back on the okwe.

"It is much more than that of Eze Nri—ten times more because I see a lot of un-scarified faces in that congregation and many Uwa people in it too. And, as I said, this will not happen in our lifetime, but many generations after our own . . . ."

"Then you may be talking about someone else, perhaps someone many generations from my descendants."

"I say many incarnations of you. It will take many incarnations before you accept the challenge. Just as you first saw the dream six times, you will first incarnate six times in a row but will not accept your fate. Then, since it took eleven days for you to see the vision again, it will take eleven generations before you will incarnate again and accept it and fulfill your destiny."

There was silence as both men pondered what Okoye had said.

Okoye laughed. "Those who hold the people hostage and tell them to stand still and take it easy or encourage them to move in the opposite direction will trust you because you will initially come as one of them, a criminal. Then you will betray them all and do the right thing, and they will not make it easy on you. I really pity you because I cannot even imagine the suffering you will go through. I was sent to spread Nri people across the world, but you will come to find them and bring them together. You will find them wherever they are hiding all over the world while digging for gold or setting traps for cowry. You will remind them who they are and of their agreement with Chineke and with Anyanwa and Agbala to bring peace to the earth and make Aja-Ana (Earth Goddess) proud. That Holy Land that he talked about is the image of the true Nri that our ancestors sought to manifest. That place is not for Igbo alone. It is a land for all people because the interest of one will become the interest of all.

"I was sent to destroy the Holy City we had, but you will come to build a new one—a bigger and more ideal one. The Holy City was destroyed so that the people will build a new one—a better one."

"The Holy City was destroyed so that a lasting one may be built with precious stones," said Erike. It was a statement that sounded like a question. But it sounded like an answer, too.

🌿 🌿 🌿

As Okoye and Erike exited the shooting ground, Erike trailed behind and admired his friend, the king. He heard how Okoye had spoken with so much confidence and understanding. Erike thought back to how far Okoye had come since they first met at their Nze ordination thirty something years ago.

"You have done very well as Eze Nri. You speak with much wisdom and understanding. Besides, you have not run away from Nri," Erike said.

Okoye stopped, facing his friend. "Run away? How do you mean?"

"You may have forgotten, but I remember it very well. The evening before our Nze ordination—the evening that you took away my innocence about Nri and introduced me to the ugly Nri politics, you said other things that I cannot forget. You said that Igwe Nwadike was a very boring man and that you will run away from Nri if you had to undergo another retreat with him or live like him…"

Okoye giggled. "I have said a lot of things that I don't remember. I fall short in many things, but I have never fallen short with my mouth. But do you know something?"

"What?" asked Erike.

"I am thinking about it. Would that not make a very good story in Igbo lands?—The Eze Nri who ran away from office—disappeared overnight. I can bet you that Nri people will be nicer to the next Eze Nri after that. They would probably watch him day and night too!"

Erike laughed, Okoye laughed.

"The only problem is that Nri people are everywhere this days," said Okoye. "In the old days, people used to joke that they will take a leave from Nri and go to some Igbo or Uwa land for a while and escape Nri politics. But these days where can you go to in Igbo land or Uwa land and not see scarified faces staring back at you? Where can Okoye run to?—that is the big question. Nowhere, my man. You take whatever life gives you and live with it, making it your own. I learned that many years ago."

"You are right. It is very true," said Erike. "I used to think that I have missed out by leaving my birth village. But now, even if I have a chance, I cannot change anything about the life I have lived. When I think of what I have learned and gained spiritually—the people that I have met and dealt with—things that I have done. No! I would not have my life another way. It started out very tragic with a life lost and two families broken up, but what I have is good and genuine."

Okoye did not know what to say. He folded his arms across his chest and listened to his friend who opened up to him. He had always admired that quality in Erike's friendship with him.

"I would have been a very good hunter at Umu-Uwakwe, probably the best in all of Amoko family, but the world is much more than being a good hunter."

Okoye was touched by Erike's sincere and emotional gratitude to the life he had led. "As Eze Nri, I wanted to be like Igwe Nwadike," confessed Okoye. "He had a lot of charm with the people. I was afraid of falling short of being like him. But once I learned that is not what accomplishments are, being like someone else, I started living. Achievement is making the best efforts with what life has given you, and in good faith. After I became Eze Nri, I always blamed myself for going into trade—maybe if I hadn't gone into trade I would have been a better Eze Nri. But now I don't know what type of Eze Nri I would have been without my seeing the world first. I am glad that I did all that first."

Both men looked at each other. Neither man had ever thanked each other for being a friend—at least not verbally. But in that look everything was said. Erike was a loner before they meet—he was thankful for Okoye's friendship. Okoye had many friends but none like Erike. As they headed towards Okoye's quarters, they exchanged another look. Some things are better understood than said.

"Haven't we met before—in another life?" asked Okoye.

"Of course we have…" said Erike. "…in ancient times."

"That's what I thought."

Author's Ending Notes

This is more than an Igbo story or an African story. This is a human story, for there is something inherent in a human being that propels him to reach for the ideal—to manifest God—the ultimate goodness. That desire is what creates civility in a human being and in a community. But there is also something that whispers in the ear: "Just survive, you fool! Survive at all costs, you damn fool! Did you create the imperfect world? Why fix it then? God created it, let Him come down from his hiding place to fix it!"

Nri civilization did not build a large empire like other famous civilizations that we know about. They did not build great pyramids like the Egyptians or the Mayans. They did not build large marble temples like the Greeks or the Romans. But they did have what those civilizations had: a desire to be ideal human beings and to inspire the rest of the world around them. One could argue that technology does not make a civilization, but discipline of the mind does. Technology is just the product of a disciplined mind (if that is what was important to the mind at the time). Two very important people in history proved this idea. Einstein was a great scientific genius, more so than any scientist in history. But when we compare him with Jesus Christ, the man, we can see that Jesus, who was an ordinary carpenter, was a far more civilized figure than any human who ever walked on earth because of the fairness he preached and lived.

The Nri set out to create a holy ground where all human beings, dwarves and giants, males and females, light-skinned and dark-skinned, young and old, could walk without fear of harassment, molestation, or intimidation. For to them, all human beings are not only equal but sacred.

Today, descendants of Nri are called Umu-Nri (Children of Nri) comprising four towns which were founded by four sons of Nri. These towns are Agukwu, Enugwu-Agidi, Enugwu-Ukwu, and Nawfia. The towns make up the former Umu-Nri Local Government Area (district or county) and stretch about twenty square miles in Anambra State in southeastern Nigeria. In fact, each of the four towns, just like other towns in Igbo land today, has its own traditional King or Chief. Also, each town has the Ozo and Nze brotherhoods, but they are no longer priestly or political positions. They are simply a social club of the elite and, at best, operate as a lobby or pressure group in the mainstream politics.

Without getting into politics, I must mention here that the town of Agukwu (aka Nri) has been playing major roles in representing Umu-Nri traditions. She currently has an Eze Nri, Igwe Obidiegwu Onyesoh. Enugwu-Ukwu, through Igwe Osita Agwuna (Igwe Enugwu-Ukwu and Eze Umu-Nri and a former human rights activist) has played major roles in representing Umu-Nri in Nigeria as well. But the four towns mentioned above were the four towns broken out from the original Nri Kingdom and still occupy their original locations. Today they are working together, trying to maintain the ancient traditions.

But these four towns are only a small segment of Umu-Nri. Larger groups of Umu-Nri left Nri mainland over many generations; some founded new communities in Igbo and Non-Igbo areas. And others who moved out simply lived among existing Igbo and non-Igbo towns as spiritual counselors who, over the years, assimilated into those communities. Most Igbo communities today claim some form of relationship with Nri. In fact, it is quite difficult for an Igbo person to say to another, "I am of more Nri lineage than you are," because there was a huge immigration into Nri by Igbo people at its peak. At its decline, there was high migration of Nri people into the Igbo mainland. Today, one can correctly argue that Nri is Igbo and Igbo is Nri, not only because of this cross migration, but because those who founded Nri culture were themselves Igbo people. In turn, Nri gave Igbo its culture and spirituality through the priests. Although some non-Igbo communities in Nigeria will not readily admit it, the movement of Nri priests can easily be traced to most of southern and middle Nigeria.

But the movement of Umu-Nri did not end in Nigeria. Between the seventeenth and nineteenth centuries, many Nri and Igbo people were taken as slaves to different parts of the world. Descendants of Umu-Nri slaves can be found in the United States, the United Kingdom, Brazil, Jamaica, and Haiti. A very large number of Igbo and Umu-Nri are in the state of Georgia in the United States. There is a place in Georgia today called Igbo (or Ibo) Landing where many Igbo slaves were brought to the United States. There is a legend about Igbo Landing; one version states that some Igbo chiefs who were brought to the United States as captives, walked on water back to Africa immediately after their ship landed. It is said that other Igbo slaves who came with them tried to do the same but drowned in the swamp. A more realistic version would be that they all drowned themselves rather than live as slaves. Those who died are still remembered in a yearly ceremony in the state of Georgia.

Also, at the turn of the twentieth century, many more Igbo people migrated from Africa, some to gain higher education and others as immigrant workers to various countries. Today, Nri communities can be found in many parts of the world. The Nri live and work like everyone else. They are bus drivers, nurses, lawyers, educators, stockbrokers, and, yes, even clergy. Just like me (until a few years ago), they had little or no idea of the difference their ancestors made to the world. As I did my research and writing, I could not help but wonder if they would wear their hats differently in whatever trade they found themselves if they knew what their ancestors had done. If they knew their true heritage, would they carry themselves differently? If they knew the true moral beliefs of their ancestors, would it make them better Christians or Buddhists or Muslims? One can only wonder.

READER'S COMPANION

"The Nri set out to create a holy ground where all human beings, dwarves and giants, males and females, light-skinned and dark-skinned, young and old, could walk without fear of harassment, molestation, or intimidation. For to them, all human beings are not only equal, but sacred."
-- *Chikodi Añunobi, author of NRI WARRIORS OF PEACE*

NRI WARRIORS OF PEACE chronicles a people whose civilization and immutable spirit have endured and thrived for more than a millennium. This story is a tale of mysticism and commonplace pursuits, of treachery and honor, of actions and their consequences. Though set long ago in a place far removed from most readers' lives, we can still learn many powerful lessons from the Nri people.

The following topic questions and background information are provided to help inspire your group discussion:

1. The Nri Civilization of the 11th century was based on deeply held spiritual beliefs and philosophies. How did these beliefs and philosophies shape the political structure of the Nri community? What were some of the inherent weaknesses of their system of government? What were some of the strengths?

2. Okoye and Erike both had the qualities of a good King, although Erike seemed to possess a deeper wisdom and knowledge of Nri customs. Why do you think Okoye was chosen instead of Erike?

3. Nri civilization incorporated spiritual beliefs and practices into their political and economic systems. Compare and contrast the different interpretations of these beliefs and practices and how they were applied by the leaders of the various Nri sects.

4. Nri was built to pursue a humanitarian mission—outreach to other communities. Should a community or nation have such a mission, or should it be left to private individuals (like Ichie Idika) and organizations (like Ozo Mkputu priests)?

5. Nri was also built to be a diverse civilization, a place where anyone who shared its beliefs and values was welcome—foreign and natural born alike. What are some of the challenges an "open" society like Nri faces? How do the different factions of the Nri society view the burdens of overpopulation? How does this create conflict?

6. The character Ijego was an independent woman who was in control of her life and destiny. Compared to Enenebe, Okoye's favorite wife, who do you think best represents the ideal woman of today?

7. Nri culture used parables as a means of preserving and sharing the wisdom of their forefathers, and as object lessons. Re-read the story of Abonoba's chicken on pg 110. It is recalled several times throughout the book. What is the moral of this story? Does it apply to you, or people you know?

8. As part of the cleansing ritual performed by Akalaka at Umuaku (p. 81-82), he repeats the absolution: "What you do not know will not know you." What do you think this means? Why do you think it brought comfort to the people of Umuaku village?

9. "The only debt a being owes another is fairness. What is fairness?" This phrase is a universal question in the book, intended to be a "philosophical clue to finding peace". As with all ideals, the phrase means different things to different people. Examine the concept of fairness. How does it differ from person to person?

10. It can be said that we are not very far removed from the Ancient culture described in this story. Indeed, we share many of the same traits, and are faced with similar challenges and choices in our day to day existence. How does Nri civilization compare to today's societies? How is it different? How could the tenets and practices of Nri civilization be applied in today's world? Would they work?

FOR FURTHER DISCUSSION:

Traditions & Beliefs of the Nri Civilization

The Mission of the Nri People

"It is their first duty to accept anybody who walks into the Nri community seeking to have a new life. It does not matter if their former communities rejected them or if they willingly left their communities as long as those immigrants respect Nri laws. He said that the second duty Nri people owe to their environment is to actively spread the message of peace, tolerance, fair play, and non-violence as Agbala (God -- The Perfect Spirit) and Aja-Ana (Earth Goddess, Mother Earth) had shown them. He reminded them that the third duty of the Nri community to their environment is to prescribe and interpret moral laws according to Aja-Ana (the Earth Goddess) and to cleanse whoever had offended Aja-Ana....the fourth duty Nri owe to the earth is to continue to explore what it means to be a perfect human being and, therefore, a perfect society and then make those discoveries a reality in the world." P. 118-119

Belief in the Sun

"Nri people believed that the sun was the dwelling place of Anyanwu (The God of Light) and Agbala (The Holy Spirit). They believed Agbala to be the collective spirit of all holy beings (human and nonhuman). The Holy Spirit was the perfect agent of Chi-Ukwu or Chineke (the big God or the Creator God). The Holy Spirit chose its human and nonhuman agents only by their merit. It knew no politics. It transcended religion and culture and, of course, gender. It worked with the humble and the truthful. They believed Anyanwu, the Light, to be the symbol of human perfection that all must seek. Anyanwu was perfection and Agbala was entrusted to lead us there. Since both Anyanwu and Agbala dwelt in the sun, they worshipped the sun." P. 210

Leadership

"It had been said that Nri people did not think with their heads but with their hearts. And nowhere was that saying revealed more than in the way they described leadership. The male quarters, which was also the leadership center of the family, was referred to as the heart (obu or obi) of the compound. To Nri people, one used one's head to survive and one's heart to live a life of purpose and of service and fulfillment. The rest of the body did not serve the heart. Rather, the heart served the rest of the body with life-saving blood. It was the heart that recycled and cleansed any polluted blood and made it usable again. The heart understood how much blood was needed and where and when to send it. To Nri people, a leader must be ruled by the heart....To the Nri, a leader who could not feel with his heart was not worthy of leadership." P. 106

The Year Counting Ceremony

"Igu Aro (the year-counting and –keeping ceremony) was one of the ties that bound Eze Nri [the king] and Igbo families and solidified his influence over their communities. Based on the official years recordings of Ezi Nri and his officials, Igbo people observed special days and communal events. In return, they sent representatives to pay tribute during the year-counting ceremony to show their loyalty and to receive blessings on behalf of their people. It was one of the rare services that Ezi Nri personally performed rather than one of his Ozo or Nze emissaries. It was one, if not the only, regular event at which he could speak directly to all Igbo people. He took this time to reflect on the end of the year or the century, as the case may be, and to count blessings from the past, to reaffirm the Igbo mission and philosophy, and to share his new vision or any spiritual messages he had received." P. 143

Scarification

"In a standard Nri scarification, the artist would carve the first line to run from the center of the forehead down to the center of the chin. They would then carve a second line to run across the face, from the right cheek to the left. The second line met the first at the center of the nose, making it a perfect cross. The second cross was drawn with one line running from the left side of the forehead down to the right side of the chin and another line running the opposite direction. This sequence and pattern was repeated until the pattern looked like the rays of the sun. Altogether it took sixteen straight lines, eight crosses, for a full-face scarification that mirrored the rays of the sun. It was their way of honoring the sun that they worshipped. But it was more than that. It was the face of service and another way of losing one's facial personality." P. 203-204

Nicknames

"In Igbo land, people's salutation names or nicknames, which they chose as adults, summed up their personal philosophies about life. They showed how life had affected them or what was important to them. Their regular first and last names were just names. At best, they reflected their parents' philosophy or thinking. But the salutation name was what an individual consciously chose as an adult. They could always change it if their thinking changed, though that rarely happened. So when Igbo men or women told another that they liked their salutation name, they didn't mean that they liked the sound of it, but that they liked their philosophy." P. 256

Death

"The burial, funeral, and mourning for the dead were very serious business in Nri and all of Igbo land, especially if the deceased was a well-established family man or woman. The funeral rites and official mourning for the dead lasted up to seven market weeks, twenty-eight days. Then family members and close relatives would try to ease themselves back into their regular routines." P. 12

Additional Discussion Questions:

Akalogheli offered alliance and promised great strength and wealth to Nri and Nri land. Nri refused, rejecting "metal and metal support" as too high a price and an abomination against the Nri way of life. Knowing what we know now about the downfall of Nri and slavery in Igbo Land generations later, was Akalogheli right? Could Nri have prevented slavery? Could he have prevented the eventual rise of the Uwa men (wilderness robbers)?

Nri was a community with a calling, a mission—that of inclusion and outreach. Ezu and his supporters believed that looking outward caused the community to neglect its own problems. Do you agree?

Nri culture obviously failed in some ways. What were the strengths and weaknesses of Nri ideals? What changes could have been made to avoid the failures?

Igwe Nwadike said, "As human beings, we are as guilty and uncivilized as the parties fighting each other if we do not attempt to break up a fight." This issue of civic and moral duty is often debated today. Do you agree with Igwe Nwadike? Are we, as human beings, duty bound to intervene?

To achieve peace, Igwe Nwadike sometimes chose to overlook small infractions and focused on the larger conflicts in order to maintain stability. On the other hand, Okoye felt he needed to expose every wrong no matter what the cost. Whose strategy is better? Is it possible to achieve stability and justice without sacrificing one for the other?

Igwe Nwadike said, "Truthfulness is the foundation of a good person and therefore, the foundation of a good community." A wonderful ideal, but is it practical? Did it work for Nri people? Would it work for your community?

NRI LEADERSHIP HIERARCHY

(according to the book)

Ceremonial Ranks: Lifetime Appointments

Eze Nri:	Nri King (Supreme Leader of Nri. No one will challenge him).
Ezu Nri:	External Affairs Minister (Ezu means Nri Lake).
Obah Nri:	Internal Affairs Minister (Obah means Crocodile—Governor of the sacred Nri Lake).
Ide Nri:	Cultural Affairs and Intelligence Minister (Ide means Pillar).
Eze Nwanya:	Queen (The King's Wife or King's First Wife—Supreme Leader of Nri women).
Ozo:	All Ozo priests are visiting ambassadors of peace to different Igbo towns and villages.
Odozi Obodo:	Wives of high-ranking Ozo priests led by the Queen (fictional to the book).

Administrative Positions: Ozo Priesthood:

Ozo Priests:	They are like senators or lords and have a lifetime position which can be inherited or acquired. They make major administrative laws and enforce them through Nra (fines) or Mmachi (excommunication) when fines are not paid.
Isi-Ozo Nri:	Head Ozo Council of all Nri. Also Justice Minister (not a lifetime position).
Isi-Ozo (Village):	Head of Ozo Council of a particular village. Also Supreme Judge for Village affairs (not a lifetime position).
Ozo Mkputu priests:	A particular sub-sect among Ozo priests. Very spiritual Ozo priests who advocate goodwill and service (fictional to the book). More of a political power block.
Ozo Oganiru:	A particular sub-sect among Ozo priests (fictional to the book). More of a political power block.
Ozo Mkpaa:	An extinct sub sect among Ozo priests who preached and practiced total spirituality (fictional to the book).

Nze Priesthood:

Nze Priests:	They are like guardian priests and protectors of law and order. They make some laws and help to enforce all laws. They are like the hands and feet of Ozo Priests.
Isi-Nze Nri:	Head Nze Council of all Nri (not a lifetime position).
Isi-Nze (Village):	Head of Nze Council of a particular village (not a lifetime position).
Nze Ikenga:	A particular sub-sect among Nze priests. Very spiritual Nze priests who serve and initiate Ozo Mgbu priests (fictional to the book).

Iyom Priestesshood:

Iyom Priestesses:	Highly spiritual women, mostly wives of Ozo priests, but any married woman could join based on her own accomplishments. They made laws that govern women's behavior and character. They advocate for women's issues.
Isi-Iyom Nri:	Head Iyom Council of Nri (not a lifetime position).
Isi-Iyom (Village):	Head of Iyom Council of a particular village.

Ndi Inyom:

Ndi Inyom:	All married women in Nri. Makes laws and settles disputes among married women.
Isi-Inyom Nri:	Head of Inyom Council of Nri (not a lifetime position).
Isi-Inyom (Village):	Head of Inyom Council of a particular village.

Nri (Igbo) Gods and Cosmology

Sky Gods (Heavenly Beings):

Chi-Ukwu:	Big-God, Supreme God (same as Creator God).
Chi neke:	Creator God (created all things; same as Supreme God).
Anyanwu:	God of Light or God the Light (Model of Perfection).
Agbala:	Perfect and Holy Spirit (embodiment of all holy beings in one). Charged with service and vocation. Giver of insight and wisdom.
Eke:	God\Governor of the eastern sky (Heaven). Also the patron of Eke Markets and days.
Oye:	God\Governor of the western sky (Heaven). Also the patron of Oye Markets and days.
Afo:	God\Governor of the northern sky (Heaven). Also the patron of Afo Markets and days.
Nkwo:	God\Governor of the southern sky (Heaven). Also the patron of Nkwo Markets and days.
Nri Menri:	Council of all ascended Eze Nri (Nri Kings).
Eze Nri:	Nri King, also called Igwe (Heavenly One. Ambassador of God on earth).

Earthly Gods (Deities):

Aja-Ana:	Earth Goddess\Governess (Deliverer of Perfect Justice. The Seeker of Peace and Harmony).
Ikenga:	God of Strength. Appealed to for strength.
Agwu:	God of Human Psychology (Regulator of Human Psychology). Appealed to for individual focus.
Ifiejioku:	God of Yam or Agriculture. Regulates Agriculture.
Aro:	God of Year. God of Time. God of All Seasons.
Chi:	God in a person (human beings are seen as Gods as well and considered sacred).

NRI TIME AND SPACE

Nri Time:

Century:	Fictional to book. But it is possible that Nri used generations to count a century.
Year (Aro):	Thirteen lunar moons equal a year.
Month (Onwa):	One lunar moon cycle: twenty-eight days; seven market weeks.
Week (Izu):	Four market day cycle: starts with Eke and ends with Nkwo.
Days (Ubosi):	Four quarters of the day: Ututu (morning hours), Efifie (afternoon hours), Mgbede (evening hours), Anyasi (night hours).
Hours:	Twelve hour cycle in a full day: (1) Onu-Ututu (early morning), (2) Ututu (morning), (3) Ngwucha-Ututu (late morning), (4) Onu-Efifie (early noon), (5) Etiti-Efifie (mid-afternoon), (6) Ngwucha-Efifie (late noon), (7) Onu-Mgbede (early evening), (8) Mgbede (evening), (9) Ngwucha-Mgbede (late evening), (10) Anyasi (night), (11) Etiti-Ndeeli (mid-night), (12) Ngwucha-Anyasi (late night).

Nri Space:

Igwe :	Sky or Heaven
Ana:	Earth
Ime-Ana:	Underworld–Home of bad spirits or transitional human spirits.
Eke:	East
Oye:	West
Afo:	North
Nkwo:	South

Some Igbo Words And Meanings

(As used in the story)

A

Acham-akwu	Enlightenment
Ada	Senior or first daughter
Ada-anyi-Nwanya	Our-Seniors-Sister
Adama Council	A league of high priests and spiritual counselors at Nri
Afor	North, God of the northern sky, a market day, a market place
Agbada	Prestigious robe
Agbala	God—The Perfect Spirit, Giver of Wisdom
Agu	Wilderness
Aja-Ana	Earth Goddess, Mother Earth
Ajo	Evil, bad
Ajo-ofia	Evil forest
Akah	1. Dwarf, 2. Tourmaline neck beads
Akalogheli	Mischievous trickster spirit—encourages greed and violence
Aku	Wealth
Aku-fulu-uzo	Opportunistic wealthy person—undeserved wealth
Alo Nri	Nri King's ceremonial spear, staff of office
Alu	Abomination, sin, taboo
Alu mee	Abomination (sin, taboo) has been committed
Amam-ife	Wisdom
Anyanwu	God of Light, God—The Light
Apali	Wild rope
Avuana	Rattlesnake

C

Chineke	Creator God (Same as Chi-Ukwu)
Chi-Ukwu	Big God (Same as Chineke)

D

Dalu	Thank you
Di-Azu	Husband of Fish, Great Fisherman
Dike	Warrior

E

Ebe	Public square
Echi-dime	Tomorrow is pregnant—a mystery
Efufu	Boils
Eke	East, God of the eastern sky, a market day, a market place
Ekwele	String
Ekwensu	Evil one, devil
Eze	King, Kingship
Eze-Nwanya	Queen
Ezi-Ndu	Good health or good life
Ezi-Okwu	Truth

G

Gbacha-Gbacha	Agile
Gbata-oso	Emergency, SOS

I

Igah	Nri police masquerade
Igba	Bean cake
Igu-Aro	Year counting and keeping
Igwe	Sky or Heaven or Heavenly One
Ike-Ekpe	Will or last advice before death
Ike-fulu-uzo	Opportunist—Accidental leadership—unmerited leadership
Ike-kete-olie	Suffering man, manual laborer
Ikenga	God of strength
Ikenga arm	Right arm
Ikpe-Kwu-Oto	Justice
Ikpo	Daybed
Isa-asisa	Trancelike public confession
Isee	Amen
Isi	Head

K

Kpakpando	Star
Kwenu!	Affirm-with-me!

M

Mbia-Mbia	Immigrant
Mkpokota	Consolidation
Mkpuke	Family inner huts
Mkpume-Onyilenyi	Nri sacred stone throne
Mmonwu	Masquerade (wearing a costume to pose as a spirit)

N

Nchi	Beaver—grass cutter
Nchu-Agwo	Snake repellent, incense
Ndewoo	Hello
Ndibia-Ndibia	Immigration
Ndi-Ichie	Forebearers—ancient ancestors
Ndi-Igbo	Igbo folks
Ngene	One of Nri deities
Nkwo	South, God of the southern sky, a market day, a market place
Nna	Father
Nna-anyi	Our Father
Nnabata	Welcoming or acceptance
Nna-ochie	Grandfather or symbolic maternal uncle
Nne	Mother
Nnoo	Welcome
Nri [Nn'rih]	1. A clan of the Igbo tribe, 2. Founder of the Nri Clan, 3. Manifestation (of the ideal) or Transformation (into the ideal), 4. Ideal community
Nri-Bu-Namba	Nri people in diaspora
Nri-Bu-Nuno	Nri people living at Nriland
Nwa-anyi	Our Child
Nwam	My Child
Nwekota	Acquisition
Nze	Shepherd\Guardian, priesthood
Nzofuta	Liberation, to save
Nzu	White chalk (Holy white chalk, used to sprinkle over a person or object as sign of blessing)

O

Obu (Obi)	Heart, the family worship\reception area, male hut
Obejili	Sword-like machete often used in fighting
Ochaa-gbute	Mediocre, low- standard
Ochara-gbute	
Ochiagha	War leader
Ochioha	Leader of All
Odachi	Death or misfortune
Odugboo	Ancient heritage
Ofia	Bush or forest
Offor Nri	Nri staff of justice
Oganiru	Forward-moving or progressive
Ogbadu	Forerunner, spy
Ogbu tree	Life tree, planted for the living spirit
Ogbuadana	Big-headed machete used in cutting woods
Ogene	Metal Gong
Ogilisi tree	Life tree, planted for the departed spirit, grave maker
Ogini	A mouse-like animal with spotted shiny skin used as pets
Ogwe	Stair of benches spectators sit on to witness public events
Okwu	Temple or shrine
Okwulu	Okra
Onugbu	Bitter leaf used for soup
Onye-Ndumodu	Counselor, adviser
Onye-Nze	An Nze priest
Onye-Ozo	An Ozo Priest
Osu	Outcast
Otonsi	Nri priestly ceremonial spear or staff
Otunaka-aru	Stroke
Otti	Fruit bugs
Oye	West, God of the western sky, a market day, a market place
Ozo	Nri Savior Priesthood

U

Udala	An Igbo apple
Udo	Peace
Ufie	A musical orchestra

Ugbana	Flamingo bird
Ugwu	Hill or mountain
Ukpa	Rectangle basket for hauling big loads
Ukpaka	Dried spicy vegetable
Ukwa	Breadfruit
Uli	Body decorative dye
Umu-Igbo	Igbo folks
Umu-nna	Communal family or extended lineage family
Umu-Nkwu	Disciples, attendants
Umu-Uwa	Non-Igbo people
Umu-Nri	Descendants of Nri
Une	Nri local guitar

ACKNOWLEDGMENTS

I thank the Holy Spirit for giving me the project and guiding me through it.

❦ ❦ ❦

I would also like to thank the following professionals who helped with the book project:

Jennifer McCord of Jennifer McCord Associates LLC, book project manager; Sarah DeMoney of Jennifer McCord Associates LLC, assistant book project manager; Gloria Campbell of Sundial Press LLC, substantive and copyeditor; Larry Campbell of Sundial Press LLC, proofreader; Paul Blumenthal, cover artwork; Tami Taylor of Tami Taylor Graphics, book interior design & cover layout; Marti Kanna of New Leaf Editorial Services, initial editorial work; Guirong Zhou, map artwork; Molly Gerhard and Roberta Trahan, proofing; Catherine Wirth and Peter Burtch, Northwestern University, Illinois, for making very important and rare research material (Holy Grails of Africa) available to me; Okey Ndibe, journalist, author and academic for his advice.

❦ ❦ ❦

I would like to thank all my family and extended families for their support, especially:

Mrs. Theresa N. Onwubuya, my aunt, for her unwavering motherly support during all stages of my life; my wife, Josephine I. Añunobi, and our two daughters, Oluchi and Ugochi, for their support; my late parents, Nze Samuel Ozoemene Añunobi and Augustina Egonekwu Añunobi, for living a good life and giving us a positive example; my brothers and sisters, Eddy Añunobi, Anthony Añunobi, the late Mrs. Jane Akpofe, Eucharia Añunobi, Mrs. Helen Nkwonta, Nonso (Oscar) Añunobi, Ms Anna Akubue, Ms Monica Añunobi, Mrs. Victoria Orji, and Ifeacho Añunobi.

❦ ❦ ❦

I would also like to thank Mr. and Mrs. Anthony A. Onyia and family, the Onwubuya (Mrs. T. N. Onwubuya) family, the Mrs. Benedit E. Nwosu and family, Mrs. Agbomma Otuo and family, the Ifeadigo family, and all of the Añunobi family.

BIOGRAPHY

Chikodi Añunobi is a descendant of Nri from Enugwu-Ukwu Nri in Anambra State, Southeastern Nigeria. Growing up, he learned a little about his heritage from oral history and from observing rituals but didn't learn about Nri history in school. The limited writing done about Nri was for university level students only and was not available to ordinary people. Ironically, it was in the United States, during his undergraduate studies at the University of Washington, that he started to learn more about Nri culture. An eye-opening experience for Añunobi, he decided to write a historical novel about Nri that would be both educational and inspirational.

Chikodi Añunobi works as a Software QA Engineer in Redmond, Washington, USA, and is a graduate of the University of Washington at Bothell, Washington. He lives with his wife and two daughters in Bellevue. Chikodi can be contacted by email at ChikodiAnunobi@yahoo.com

❦ ❦ ❦